Book Tw...

KARMA

Jamie Kincaid

All rights reserved. All characters appearing in this work are fictitious. Any resemblance to real persons, living or dead is purely coincidental.

No part of this publication may be reproduced, distributed, or transmitted in any form or by any means, including photocopying, recording, or other electronic or mechanical methods, either now known or unknown, without the written permission of the publisher, except in the case of brief quotations embodied in critical reviews and certain other noncommercial uses permitted by copyright law. For permission requests, write to the publisher, "Attention: Permissions Coordinator", at the address below.

Grey Wolfe Publishing, LLC
PO Box 1088
Birmingham, Michigan 48009
www.GreyWolfePublishing.com

© 2015 Jamie Kincaid
Published by Grey Wolfe Publishing, LLC
www.GreyWolfePublishing.com
All Rights Reserved

ISBN: 978-1628281101
Library of Congress Control Number: 2015955112

Karma
Book Two Of The Kismet Series

Jamie Kincaid

Dedication

"Life is short, time is fleeting and spares no one and includes everyone..."

You can't go on or live without time but time can and will go on without you. So be sure to capture the moments that fill your time with happiness and even sadness, even these emotions will embrace and sustain you and make you stronger over time.

Time takes from us but also gives to us, allowing us opportunities that can only be seen and felt by the heart, we just need to open our eyes to it.

To my husband, David, thank you for always believing in me, you pushed me to try and now I can fly... and showing me how to believe in myself... thank you... belief, prayer, strength, love are there always.

To my beautiful children, Jacob, Joe and Julia... I thank God every day for blessing me with you... to be a part of your life, to see your smiles, laughter, orneriness, to see you stumble and to see you succeed... there is no greater love than the love that a mom has for her children and my love for all three of you goes beyond measure. Believe in yourself and reach for the stars... and remember that I believe in you and that no matter where you roam, I will be here... your home... keep God in your life and in your heart. My love is endless and goes to the moon and back...♡

And to my Shiner... my shadow and my mister, my baby, you are the best dog in the world and you are always there for me, so very lucky to have your endless wags and wet kisses, mommy loves you... thank you for your soul and seeing life through your eyes... Goldens rule...♡

Thank you, God... for without You in my life, this would not be possible.

Prologue

Spencer is a quaint, little town nestled deep in the hills of West Virginia, a town that lives for its football team and hails the boys who play the game as heroes, especially Liam Larson. It had been almost a year since Liam had stepped foot on the grassy turf he used to call home every Friday night, but that didn't matter to the folks of Spencer. He was and would always be their "it" boy, the boy they believed in, the boy who could do no wrong and have it all just for his asking.

But he didn't want it all. What he did want was me, and after some restraint and hesitation on my part, I became a believer in that boy too. We were connected at the hip and could hardly go a day without hearing each other's voice. We were deeply in love and nothing was going to change, that, of course, was before Johnny Bryant and April 11th. Both had determined that our love and fate should be tested, but little did they know how deep our love actually ran and that no amount of outside influence could encumber our fate. The old saying that what goes around comes around seems to be rearing its ugly head to us. Liam and Johnny have fought the fight, but have they won the war? I'm ready to move forward with Liam and leave my past behind, but unfortunately, that is not the case for Liam or Johnny. Their past consequences seem to be haunting them and denying them the chance to carry on. The question remains whether this is truly over for all three of us. There are still ghosts in the attic haunting us, and until they are gone none of us will be able to have the life we desire.

It had been over four weeks since Liam had come back to me. It was strange. I never thought that we would be at a crossroads so early in our relationship. April 11th had changed both of us, and we both knew that neither one of us could ever be the same two people we were when we first met, but to me, that was a good thing, not that the accident had been a blessing, but I had come out of it much stronger mentally. The girl with the awkward presence and shy behavior that Liam had met last year was gone. She had been replaced with a young woman who had found a resiliency that would in time turn out to be her greatest strength.

The next few weeks seemed like old times, as though the accident hadn't happened, but we both knew that wasn't the case. For all the good times we had been having lately, there was a portentous cloud hanging over us, reminding us that the accident was all too real.

I knew Liam was making great strides from what had happened that fateful night. Some people didn't understand why I didn't have many issues regarding the accident since I was unconscious for most of the time. Liam and I did talk about it but only to a degree. There were still parts of me that felt he was holding back, keeping things inside instead of allowing me to help. He had to live with it day in and day out from the very beginning. He remembered everything, unlike me who can't remember anything past the truck spinning out of control. My only memory beyond that is waking up in the hospital with Liam by my side. Everything else is a dark shroud, unwilling to unveil its secrets. But for Liam, it's like watching a bad movie over and over again, scene by scene. He was in and out of semi-consciousness but always aware of what had happened: the screaming from me, the awful feeling of not being able to reach me, the pandemonium from the crowd, the broken glass that blanketed us, and the blood that poured from our bodies. There's also the little detail that it was Johnny Bryant who came to my rescue.

This was why it was so hard for Liam. He could endure anything. Hell, for only being eighteen he had endured a lot in the short time God had placed him on this earth, but the accident could have been the breaking point for him. I almost lost Liam that night, not from his injuries that he sustained but from the mental torment he carried. All this could have been avoided, he thought, if he only looked past the idiocy that the number eleven represented and realized that this number had been in our lives for a reason.

He blamed himself, and nothing could change his mind: not Grandpa, his friends, myself or even Johnny. Yes, not even Johnny Bryant, the one person who took partial blame for the almost demise of us all. It all started over me. Most girls would have loved the fact that there were two guys fawning for their attention, and yes, I will admit it would have been nice if the circumstances were different. But I loved Liam, and because of that, Johnny felt compelled to manipulate the situation until Liam had no other choice than to race him. In the beginning, they raced for me but in the end, for their self-worth and posterity. The irony is that in proving themselves to each other, they almost destroyed themselves in the process. As I said, I don't remember much about those two months when I was hovering in the darkness between here and there. My only accounts are the before and after. That's where Liam's issues differ from mine. I'm begging to remember anything that will shed light on what I lost while I was on the brink of dying, and Liam is begging to forget everything that led up to, during, and after the accident. He's carrying much more than guilt and regret; he's carrying demons that he can't move past.

He once told me he was afraid of hurting me again and that he let me down by breaking his promise to me that nothing would ever happen to me. He has always seen himself as my protector and maybe that was part of his problem. Sometimes we put too much pressure on ourselves, and when we can't keep our promises something breaks down inside of us. Maybe it would have been different if Johnny wasn't the one to pull me from the wreckage. Maybe Liam could have handled the situation better if it was someone that didn't care about me the way Johnny did. Liam can never take credit for what Johnny did for me, and Liam knows that for as long as we walk on this earth everyone that was witness to that night knows that too. That's what eats him up inside. He would do anything for me, but he couldn't help me that night, the one time I needed him more than anything, he was unable to be there for me.

Was it fate that Johnny helped me instead of Liam? It doesn't make sense if that's the case. My fate, my destiny is with Liam. Liam was only inches from me whereas Johnny, who was nowhere near me, was the first to me. Why though? There were dozens of other people there. Half the school had shown up for that illicit race, but not one of them made it to me except for the one person that needed to stay the farthest away. It was an act that Johnny said anyone would have done. Anyone? Then why didn't anyone else come to my aid before Johnny?

The answer is still unknown, but I do know that sometimes when fate intervenes, your karma can be changed. I think Liam realizes that too. He couldn't take back that night or prevent Johnny being there for me, and in the end, this is what almost took him away from me, and maybe it still will. He felt compelled to stay away from me. His self-worth was damaged. His control of our relationship was somehow altered due to the fact that it was Johnny who was my savior and not him. Liam was living in his own personal hell, and the more I tried to be there for him the worse it became. I became a demon in Liam's eyes too. Only because I was a constant reminder of what Johnny did for me. I had been touched by the enemy, saved by none other than the demon himself. I knew Johnny had even tried to be there for Liam, but it didn't matter. Maybe it was a façade for Liam to make Johnny believe things were better between them, but in the back of my mind, I felt different. Were they still playing their game? Did Liam feel that the race was still going on, even if it was only in theory now? Did he think the accident was only a deterrent until the race could be finished? Did Liam feel that Johnny was still there behind us, clawing his way to the front to take control and win the race?

Only time would tell. I do know that Liam and I are trying to make the best out of our situation. I love him with all of my heart, and I know that he loves me more than anything and maybe even more than before. The test of time will be the conduit that will allow us to know what the future holds for us. Will the number eleven still be as prevalent as it had been during this past year? And if it is, what will it mean now? Will the ominous feelings that I was succumbed to in the past be there as well, making me wonder when and if the next tragedy is to happen? But more importantly, is this over for Liam and me? Can we endure whatever comes our way, come hell or high water? Will our past still dictate our actions?

Liam is my life, and I would literally die without him. With all the misgivings and demons he carries, I carry my own too. I guess only time will tell, but I do know we were placed on this earth to be together, soul mates to the very end.

Chapter One
Summer's Secret

    Summertime. I love everything that has to do with this warm and tranquil season: the never ending hot, hazy days that lead into serene, cool starlit nights, the warm breezes that enlighten your senses, the sound of crickets at dusk, lightening bugs, and the most important memory for me is that summer is when Liam returned to me. And the month that means the most to me is August, especially this August.

    A week ago I saw myself alone; my entire world seemed desolate and remote. I was scared if I'm honest with myself. I thought I had lost Liam; he had convinced me with his sequestered behavior towards me that our lives were better off if we were apart from one another. I was at a loss as I faced this crossroad in my life. To say I was confused and hurt would be an understatement. I was beyond consoling and was relinquishing to the reality that what I thought was real was nothing more than a mere illusion that had left an irreplaceable impression in my heart and my memory forever.

But thankfully, Liam had come to his senses and with that had realized the truth. He knew we weren't better off without each other. Neither one of us could live without the other, every single breath we took, we took together, where his left off mine began, and without the other we realized we were both living a miserable half-life. It was in this month of August that he had once told me he had seen me for the first time, and it was also in this month on the 11th that he realized that our lives were destined to be together. Neither one of us knew it at the time, but the number eleven held so much significance in our lives. We still didn't understand its presence, but at least we were learning to live with it and not question its existence. It had manifested from being a mere digit of our everyday lives to the catalyst that brought us together and almost tore us apart.

"What are you thinking about?" Liam asked as he brushed the hair from my eyes. I was lying with my head on his lap, and he was leaning up against the one oak tree that resided by his house, his guitar by his side.

"Nothing really."

"Are you sure? You look like you're off in your own little world."

"I am. But I'm not alone; you're with me." I turned over to face him. "I've been so scared these past few weeks, Liam, more scared than I think I wanted to admit. I thought we were over. I honestly believed that I was never going to see you again."

Liam pulled me closer to him as he positioned me on his lap, my legs cradling the side of his. "I'm so sorry I put you through that, Jenny. I never meant to hurt you that way. Do you forgive me?" He asked as his grasp on me became tighter.

"There was nothing to forgive," I said kindly. "I thought I understood what being scared was, but nothing compared to the thought that you might not be in my life, Liam. I want to forget about these past few months and just concentrate on us and our future. I sometimes question why the number eleven is so much a part of our lives. It doesn't make sense. Why us, Liam? Nobody else seems to have the same issues that we do."

Liam just stared intently at me. He knew I was just rambling on, releasing some of the frustration that I had been holding onto. We kissed. The touch was sweet and tender, but the emotions behind it were close to obsessive. We seemed to continually be trying to make up for the lost time that summer had brought us.

"I don't understand it myself, Jenny, nor do I think I ever will. You were always more accepting to it than I <u>was</u> but I will say that while I was doing my soul searching this summer I came to the conclusion that it's a part of us and may always be. We have something very special, and we have a second chance with each other. You thought you had lost me, but it doesn't even compare to how I felt while you were in the hospital. You shouldn't even be here. I never thought I would be holding you <u>again like</u> I am right now. Everyone thought it was only a matter of time before you slipped away. Everybody thought that but me. I knew you were still in there and when you opened your eyes on that fateful June 11th, I knew we were going to have our chance again. I don't know why the eleven seems to make itself appear <u>before</u> us so often or why it's such an integral part of us, but it is, and I'm willing to accept it. Jenny, I know we are responsible for our destiny. For what happens to us, we have that control, and if this number isn't going to go away then we need to embrace it for what it is and let its influence always be in our favor. Maybe it's an affirmation of our love for one another. I do love you, Jenny King. All I can say is I can't believe how I've acted this summer. I feel like such an ass."

"Would you stop it? You said it yourself, we're together now and that's all that matters." I kissed him again, our hold even tighter than before. I had noticed that his touch on me was stronger than I had ever remembered it to be. It was as if he needed to always make sure I was real to him, that our touch was not just in his imagination.

"What is it?" I asked him. The expression in his eyes had changed.

"I feel like I need to keep apologizing to you. I can't forgive myself for how I treated you and left you all alone this summer. I was so selfish, and you needed me. I am so sorry, Jenny. I was in a dark place, and I sometimes feel I'm still there. I just can't seem to get out of it. I don't want to ever lose you again." His words were emphatic. The somberness of his voice almost frightened me, as though he was letting me in on something that was much deeper than him just missing me.

"You're never going to lose me. You have me forever. I know things were bad for you, that's why I was so scared. But look at me, we're together now and nothing is ever going to change that." I held his face in my hands; his eyes sparkled as he stared back at me.

"I know, Jenny, it's just that sometimes I..." his voice trailed off, and I could tell there was more he wasn't telling me.

"What, Liam?"

"Jenny, please stay with me. You belong here. You know it just as much as me, and as far as your parents are concerned, they want you to be happy. They want us to be happy."

One of my only problems with Liam was my inability to say no to him. I couldn't resist him, and no matter how hard I tried to argue the point, he was right: I belonged there, and I too was tired of leaving him at night. Most nights never ended for us until the sun came up anyway, and I knew my parents would agree to this. It was just the little girl inside of me who seemed to argue the point. Leaving my parents meant accepting that I was ready to be on my own, to be a grown up, and carry the responsibilities that went along with it. There were so many times in my life where their presence had always comforted me, but as I gazed into Liam's eyes I realized he gave me that same feeling of reassurance that I still longed for and needed. He had always made me feel safe and loved, and those feelings had only grown since we had been together. My life was with him now. "Okay," I said.

"You mean you'll move in with me, here at the house?" The giddiness in his voice could only be compared to a child's joy on Christmas morning.

"Yes, I'll move in if you're sure that's what you really want?" He didn't answer me back, but his long and impassioned kiss that knocked me to the ground told me this was exactly what he wanted.

I was somewhat surprised at my parents' reaction to moving in with Liam. Of course, there were some tears, but they were first-hand witnesses to the hell Liam and I had suffered over the last several months and they were more than happy to see us start the next phase of our lives together. They said we deserved it. I was relieved and also a little taken aback. I thought there would be more of a struggle to convince them, but it was as if they were expecting it.

It took over a week for me to sort through my things and decide what I wanted to take with me and what I was willing to leave behind. This was still and would always be my home, and I couldn't bear to see my room completely vacant. I needed to keep some of my belongings in my room just to remind me that this was still my home. It was harder for me than I realized, even sorting through my stuffed animals was almost too much for me to take. With Liam's presence by my side, I was able to end this chapter in my life and begin my next. I turned and stood in front of my house as Liam helped my dad with the last of my boxes.

"Are you ready, babe?" Liam asked as he put his arm around me.

"Uh-huh," I said. Mom hugged me tightly along with Dad; it was as if I was never going to see them again.

"Don't be a stranger," Dad said as his voice weakened.

"I love you, Dad."

"I love you too, hon."

"It's not like you're moving halfway around the world. We want you and Liam to come home as often and whenever you want. This is still your home."

"I know Mom. I love you."

"I love you too, honey."

My parents embraced Liam as Dad whispered in his ear. "Take care of my girl. She means the world to me."

"Don't worry, Mr. King. I always will."

With those final words, Liam helped me into my seat and we drove away.

"Are you okay?" Liam asked me as he squeezed my hand.

"Yeah, I'm fine. It was just harder than I thought it would be. I just realized that this will be the very first time in many years that my parents won't have a child living in the house with them."

"They're going to be fine, Jenny. You know this is what they wanted for us as much as we did."

"I know, I guess I'm just thinking that I deserted them. That's all."

Liam gently kissed the top of the head as we headed to his house, our home as he referred to it now. It only took a couple of trips to unload my boxes and put them away in Liam's bedroom. During the past week while Liam worked at Joe's shop, Grandpa had helped me unload my belongings and find a suitable place for each item, especially my pictures. They went right next to their pictures on the fireplace mantle. It was his way of telling me I belonged here. That evening, Liam and I settled into each other's arms as we sat in front of a warm fire that crackled before us. Grandpa had conveniently made himself absent. The evening couldn't have been more perfect.

"So, how does it feel to finally call this place home, babe?"

"It feels nice. But to be honest, you and Grandpa have always made me feel so welcome here that I've considered this home for a long time now."

"I'm glad to hear you say that because that's exactly how I've wanted you to feel. I'm just glad that I don't have to see you leave me anymore. I hated it when I had to take you back to your house. This seems so natural and right that I think we should have done it a long time ago."

"A long time ago? When, during our senior year? My parents may have been open with us moving in now, but I can guarantee you that they wouldn't have been so supportive back then."

"I guess, but it's just that the moment I saw you I was in love with you. I've been counting the days until this moment. I've wanted this for so long, the only thing I want more is to marry you. The accident made me realize how fragile our lives are, and I don't want either one of us to waste another second. I want to marry you, and I want to do it soon."

"You're hopeless, Liam."

"I know, for you."

"I want that too."

"Come here, then." Liam carried me upstairs and held me close to him as he led me to his room.

"Where are we going?"

"Our room. It's time to celebrate one milestone met and another one to go." I smiled as he carried me inside.

We fell asleep in each other's arms that night, the day's events and our tireless lovemaking draining us both. I was in a deep and contented sleep when I heard what I thought were the sounds of Liam's voice screaming for me. I thought I was dreaming and continued to sleep as I tried to figure out why I could only hear Liam in my dream and not see him. I searched for him in the darkness, my eyes darting in the black veil that swept over me. I couldn't see anything but his voice was as clear as a bell.

"Liam, where are you?" I screamed but to no avail. He didn't answer me. Again, I screamed for him, "Liam, where are you? I can't see you!" Again, I waited for his voice to respond to me, but I heard nothing. And then in the far distance, his frantic voice beckoned for me again.

"Jenny, don't leave me. I'm right here baby, reach for me," he pleaded.

The sound of his voice scared me as I searched for him. I was desperate and only when I felt his touch squeezing me tightly did I realize this wasn't a dream at all. The pain shot through me like a cannon as Liam's grasp on me continued to tighten around my body. I could hardly breathe as I opened my eyes, I found myself fighting Liam off of me as his unconscious self fought to keep me in his confides.

"Liam, stop it. You're hurting me! Please wake up!"

Liam was drenched in sweat. He kept calling for me in a frantic tone. His voice was raspy as his screams grew louder. I fought to wake him up, pushing his body away from me as I yelled his name aloud.

"Liam, it's me, Jenny! Wake up! I'm right here!"
I thought I was fighting a losing battle, and only when I was ready to give in did Liam finally open his eyes to find mine shrouded in tears.

"Jenny, what happened?" he asked, disoriented.

"Oh my God, Liam, you had me scared to death. You wouldn't wake up, and you were holding me so tightly that I couldn't even breathe. You kept repeating my name and saying that you wouldn't leave me, just to reach out for you. What were you dreaming?"

Liam became eerily quiet as he sat up in bed. His crystal-blue eyes focused on his bedroom door.

"Liam? What's wrong? What were you dreaming about?"

He finally turned his head in my direction, only to give me a look that sent a chill up my spine.

"Jenny, I'm sorry you had to see me like this. I thought everything would be okay once you were here. I guess I was wrong."

"What are you talking about? What do you mean; everything would be okay, once I got here?" Liam sighed heavily. I could tell he was holding something in, that there was something he needed to tell me but was finding it hard to say. "Please, Liam, you have to tell me. You can't keep me in the dark like this, especially after what I just witnessed."

"You're right. It's just that I didn't think I would have to tell you. I thought they would go away."

"They? Liam, dammit, please tell me! I don't want any secrets between us!"

"Jenny, ever since the accident you know I had a hard time dealing with things. One of the reasons I stayed away from you was because I was afraid of the person I was turning into, or more importantly the person I was leaving behind. I thought my behavior had changed after the accident, and I wasn't going to be the man I needed to be for you, but with your help I realized I was wrong. But even still, I've been carrying these feelings that I can't seem to let go."

"What kind of feelings, Liam?"

"I still harbor this resentment that I couldn't help free you in the accident."

"Liam, are you kidding me? You were hurt too. It's never bothered me that you didn't free me, as you so put it. You were always there for me, and if you must know, you were the one who brought me out of my coma. I heard your voice, and that's why I woke up. To me, that's much more important."

"Thank you, Jenny, but it still bothers me. I can't get the image out of my head of Johnny pulling you from the truck as I lay helpless watching him do it. You don't know how it eats me up inside and because of that I can't let go of it. And that's where the dreams come in, or in my opinion, nightmares."

"You mean this isn't your first one?"

"No, as a matter of fact, I've had so many I couldn't tell you what number this one was."

"How often are you having them, Liam?"

"Almost every night."

"What?" I was astonished by his admission, especially since we had been inseparable the past few weeks and this was the first I knew about them.

"That's why I've wanted you here. In my nightmares, I'm always reaching for you, and just when I think I have you, I lose you. I always wake up with this God-awful feeling that you're gone, and not once do I ever reach you. You always disappear from my sight. That's why I thought having you next to me, always knowing you're here with me, would bring an end to these nightmares. But I guess that's not the case."

Liam's face was pale as the sweat trickled down. I could see the impact the nightmares were having on him, not just emotionally but physically too.

"I didn't mean to keep this a secret from you, Jenny, I just really thought they would be gone by now. That's all I want is for them to go away. Sometimes I lay here in bed, and I'm so tired that all I want to do is fall asleep, but I become afraid. I know what waits for me once my eyes close, and I hate it. I've always been a strong person, never afraid of anything, but I'm afraid of these nightmares. I can't control them. I try to focus on something positive before falling asleep, hoping that will somehow lead my subconscious in another direction, but no matter what I do or try, I still have the same nightmare. It's scaring me to the point that I'm hardly getting any sleep. I never meant to keep it a secret from you. That has never been my intention. My sleep deprivation though has been affecting me more than I thought. I'm more tired and my focus is off. Grandpa has noticed it and so have Parker and Joe. That's why I brought it up with you about moving in with me. You know I've always wanted you here but especially lately. I just thought having you here would change things for me. I honestly didn't think I was going to have one of those God-awful dreams with you by my side."

"I can't believe you've been having them almost every night and you haven't told me. Does Grandpa know about them?"

"Sometimes I think he does, I know he's been worried about me, especially since the accident. He's always checking on me and asking me how I'm doing. If he does know, he hasn't told me."

Our gaze met as Liam spoke; his beautiful crystal-blue eyes looked paler than usual. I've only been truly scared a few times in my eighteen years, and each time they have concerned Liam. The first time was when Liam and his grandpa were in the accident last Christmas. The second was the accident that Liam and I were in. The third was this summer when I thought Liam and I were through. I now could add a fourth time: his nightmares. I prayed to God that these were only a phase and that with time they would pass, but in the back of my mind I didn't really believe it. I was afraid the nightmares held more precedence than I or Liam were willing to give them. I had to have hope though that with my help the nightmares would leave him and he would never be plagued with them again.

"It's going to be okay, Liam. I just know it. They're not real, and I'm going to be here for you if and when you have the next one, babe," I said as I snuggled my body into his.

"I know you are, Jenny, you're here with me right now and that's how it's always going to be. I know I'll never lose you." Liam squeezed me tightly as we both settled into each other's embrace, both of us yearning for the sleep that seemed to deprive us.

"Good night, Jenny, I love you."

"Goodnight, Liam, I love you too...and Liam?"

"Yes, Jenny?"

"Sweet dreams."

Liam paused before answering me. "Thanks, babe. I hope so. I really, really hope so."

Chapter Two
The Letter

    The next day was my first official day as a farm hand. It was late summer, and Grandpa liked to get a head start on tilling the ground before cold weather showed its icy face. It was something that was totally foreign to me. Even though Spencer was considered a small town in all accounts, I was still the city girl when it came to Liam and me. He was the country boy through and through, and getting my hands dirty and working with the earth that the good Lord had given us was something that was going to be a day to day learning process. Luckily, Liam and Grandpa were excellent teachers, and I tried to be a quick learner.

    By the end of my first week, I had grown accustomed to riding a full-size tractor, cleaning the horse stalls, and having my usually soft and supple hands turn into calloused, blistered appendages that daily needed bandaging. I questioned at times what I had gotten myself into. My love was blind at times, not to say I needed pampering. I was used to work and I had helped my parents with their business since I was able to walk, but working in a grocery store is far different from working on a farm.

I tried not to complain. I actually loved the work, mostly because I was near Liam. I was seeing a whole new side of him. I marveled as I watched him and his grandpa work on their farm and the respect they gave one another. It was another reason why I loved Liam so much. He was the real deal. There was nothing fake about him. What you saw was what you got: an allegiance of inner strength and love that exuded from him for the people he cared about. I had often questioned why he never wanted to play college football, but after seeing him work on the farm and the satisfaction that he received from it, I knew for sure he had made the right decision. He wasn't the college type at all. He was more mature than most people who were ten years older than him, and he knew what he wanted out of life and went for it with a vengeance, including me. By week's end on the farm, I had never taken more hot baths in my life. My entire body ached, and muscles I didn't know existed became stiff and sore. The good part about each day was Liam was always there to rub me down and smooth out the kinks that came from being a farm girl.

"Mmm, you can do this all night, babe," I said as Liam's strong hands rubbed lotion on my back.

"Your wish is my command, my dear. Are you feeling better? I didn't expect this to happen to you."

"I'm fine. I'm getting used to the hard labor that comes with working on the farm," I said, laughing. I rolled over, exposing my bare chest to him. He never stopped rubbing me. I had forgotten about every single ache in my body as I wrapped my arms around Liam's neck and pulled him closer to me. "You know if you decide not to go into business with Joe, I think you have a pretty good career as a masseuse. You definitely have the hands for it," I whispered to him.

"Yeah, I guess, but there's a problem with your theory."

"And what is that?"

"These hands are for you only," he said as he whispered sensually in my ear. "I don't think I would have much of a career."

"This is true." This time my lips closed in on Liam's. He didn't have a chance as I seduced him. It was my favorite way to end our day.

I awoke the next morning to find a cup of coffee, a stack of misshapen pancakes, and a lavender rose waiting by my bedside. Liam's side of the bed was empty, and as I rubbed my eyes and inhaled the smell of the coffee I could hear his voice outside the bedroom window. From what I could hear, he was on his phone talking to Joe. I quickly devoured the breakfast that Liam had lovingly made for me, got dressed, and proceeded downstairs. I made it halfway when Liam walked in the front door.

"Hello, gorgeous! What are you doing up?" he said as he planted a long and endearing kiss on my lips.

"It's almost eleven o'clock. I should have been up hours ago. Why didn't you wake me?"

"I wanted you to sleep in. You've been working so hard since you've moved here; I wanted you to have a break. I never intended for you to become our hired help. Besides, you looked so sweet while you were sleeping, I didn't have the heart to wake you. Did you enjoy your breakfast?"

"Yes, I did. Thank you. So, what's the plan for today?"

"Well you, my dear, can do whatever you want. The house is yours. Grandpa went to Calhoun County for the day, and I'm going to Joe's to help him work on some motorcycles. I haven't been there in over a week, and I guess he's really behind."

"You mean I'm going to be all alone in this big house by myself and you're not going to be here to keep me company?" I said with a playful pout to my voice.

"Mmm... don't do that to me, Jenny, I won't be able to leave you."

"That's my plan."

"I would stay in a heartbeat if I could, but Joe really needs my help. Do you understand?"

"Yeah, I do. And it might be fun having the house to myself. I could do some exploring, that is if you don't mind."

"I don't mind one bit. The house is yours. I need to get a shower, I told Joe I would be at the shop in a half an hour." Liam kissed me tenderly before heading up the stairs. He looked back as he came to the landing and gave me his famous wink.

I walked in to find the usually neat and orderly kitchen in disarray. There was spilled coffee on the floor, a broken egg shell on the counter, and numerous pots and pans with pancake batter dripping from them. "Hmm...looks like my adventure starts here," I said as I began to clean up the morning dishes. I was putting the last piece of china away when Liam walked up behind me. He quietly put his soft lips on my neck. His touch sent a shiver down my spine.

"Did I startle you?" he asked.

"Not at all. I knew you were behind me. I could smell you before you even entered the room. It's very intoxicating. Don't you think you should have waited for your shower until after you were done at Joe's? I'm sure you'll need one then."

"Don't worry, I definitely plan on showering when I get home... with you. I won't be home till late, probably after ten o'clock. Wait up for me, okay?"

"Definitely." I poured him a cup of coffee to go and watched him leave. When his black truck was completely out of view, I turned to go inside with faithful Blue by my side. After finishing the breakfast dishes and talking to my mom for over an hour, I found myself alone. I listened to the silence of the house as Blue snored softly next to me. The house was huge, and for the first time ever, I realized the vastness the home carried. I walked slowly through the rooms, each one providing me with a vivid memory of Liam and me. I could see the dining room as it was covered in rose petals and the teddy bear that graced the center of it. The living room provided me with ample memories: the Christmas tree, the first time Liam brought me to his house, the endless times we nestled into each other's arms as we did nothing but listen to our heartbeats become synchronized to each other's.

I looked at the fireplace mantle and the family pictures that adorned it. I became stuck on the one of his mom. She was so beautiful, and I felt so sorry for her. Her life ended so abruptly that she never had the chance to see her son grow into the man he had become. She never got to witness his high school football career or any other of his accomplishments, and Liam never got to enjoy having her there for him either. They both were shortchanged.

I touched her face, and a chill instantly ran through my fingertips. I was drawn to her and felt like I had known her all of my life. An inner calmness came over me as I walked away from her picture. I made my way through the vast hallway until I came to the stairs that led to the second floor. I stared at them as I could see Liam carrying me up each one of them in his arms: my hopeless romantic. If he had his way, my feet would never touch the ground. I walked softly and slowly up the staircase. With each step I took, a creak echoed behind me as it reverberated through the house. At the top, I turned to my right and stared down the narrow hallway that led to the two bedrooms, hall closet, and the one bathroom. I began to take my first step when a voice inside me told me to turn around. I did slowly and found myself facing the back of the hallway. There wasn't much to it. It covered about eleven feet of length and where the right of the hallway had four doors, this way only had one. Peculiar, I thought. For as many times that I had been here and knew that this room existed, not once did my curiosity compel me to enter it. I walked cautiously to it; a foreboding feeling consumed me as my hand embraced the ornately beveled doorknob.

My heart pounded as the knob turned effortlessly. I secretly had hoped it would be locked, so I could simply walk away and not worry about what secrets lie behind it. But that was not the case. The door opened and welcomed my presence. Once inside, I marveled at the small room with the old-fashioned, yellow rose wallpaper. In the center of the room, an old, faded area rug graced the wood floor, and the ceiling to floor windows were dressed with a tattered, cream colored sheer that hung limply in front of them. There was nothing else in the room except cardboard boxes stacked neatly in the far left corner. The room felt unusually cold for a late summer day. Goosebumps prickled on me as I made myself comfortable in the room. Even though I was completely alone, I felt as if I wasn't.

The wooden floor creaked beneath me as I made my way to the boxes. I stared at them with curiosity. They looked like they hadn't been touched in years; dust and debris had settled on top of them, covering what little writing there was to be seen. I unfolded the flap of the top box, sending a cloud of dust into the air. I felt somewhat ashamed as I opened it, feeling as though I was invading the privacy of Grandpa and possibly Liam. I discovered that the contents contained nothing more than some old canning jars and cookbooks. I set the box down and opened the next. This box contained much of the same: more cookbooks, canning jars, and magazines dating from the 1940's. I sighed. There seemed to be nothing here, but memories boxed away for another day. I began to place the brown boxes back in their rightful spot when out of the corner of my eye I noticed a piece of paper protruding from one of the untampered boxes.

My head told me just to leave it, but my inner voice urged me to investigate. Besides, Liam did say the house was mine to explore, and that was exactly what I was doing. I sat myself on the area rug. Blue appeared from the doorway and made himself comfortable next to me, snuggling into my leg as he began to snore immediately. His muffled breathing brought a chuckle to me. I proceeded to unfold the paper and found that it was a letter written to Grandpa Mack. The date on it was June 11th, 1997. It was torn on one corner as though it had been ripped from a binder with rushed enthusiasm. I knew I shouldn't be reading it, but the beautiful handwriting beckoned for me to do so, compelling me, even though I was sure I was invading Grandpa's privacy. I couldn't leave the room without knowing the contents the letter held. I found myself looking around to see if anyone was there, there of course, wasn't, only Blue, and he wasn't about to chastise me for my impending actions. So I began.

Dear Dad,

It's about ten minutes until midnight and once again I find myself unable to sleep. There has been so much on my mind lately that sleep has been absent from me for some time. As I lay here, there's so much that I want to say to you that I really don't know where to begin. I've always been able to come to you and Mom, and now I find it hard. Maybe that is why I have resorted to writing you instead of talking to you face to face. I'm ashamed, Dad. I'm ashamed that I have let my life get so out of hand, and I'm ashamed that I haven't taken better control of it. You and Mom raised a strong, independent girl, and in the past few months that girl has been lost. I can't seem to find her, and I've become weak in the process. You have always been my rock and inspiration in good times and in bad, and without you both I know I would not carry the resiliency that you bestowed upon me. You have helped me immensely with Liam, my little angel, who you know I love more than life itself. He is the only reason that I am still here today. And he is the reason I am writing this letter to you.

    I am scared, Dad, more scared than I have ever been in my entire life. I sit here in my bed and pray to God that my bedroom door will remain closed. I wish you could hold me in your strong and protective arms as you did when I was a little girl when I was afraid of the monsters under my bed. You always were able to get rid of them and comfort me until I fell fast asleep. I wish you were able to do that now, but the monster that scares me now can't be vanquished by your sweet voice.

    Allen has changed, Dad. I look back on my life, and I wonder what went wrong, what I did that could have triggered his anger. He has always been a sweet, kind and loving man, a man to look up to and one to admire, a man I fell desperately in love with, but the past year has been hard for Allen and me; you know that as well as anyone. I have done my best to be there for Allen and to rectify our situation, but it has gotten out of control and thus, so has Allen's drinking. This is where my fear stems from, Dad. Allen's drinking has become worse, and the more he drinks, the more violent he becomes. I used to look forward to his return every night from work, but now that joy has been replaced with a foreboding dread. I worry about how he will make it home, and I worry about what will happen once he arrives. I try to remain positive and remember the good times that Allen and I have shared, especially once we had Liam. He was our missing piece that completed us, and I thought nothing could ever change our utopian world once our little boy entered it. It's hard for me to understand how a caring man can change 180 degrees and instantly turn into a monster.

    I know you and Mom have asked me on numerous occasions if Allen has ever hurt me. I've never been able to face you and tell you this because I didn't want to see the hurt in your eyes, but he has hurt me, but on the inside. He has never harmed me physically, not yet at least. But that's what I'm afraid of. Allen's behavior has increasingly gotten worse over the past few days, and I'm afraid it's *only a matter of time before he takes his anger out on me physically. I honestly don't think he would touch a hair on Liam's precious little head, but I would be devastated beyond words if Liam was to ever see his father lay a hand on me. It would be horrible for Liam to witness, and I know it would affect the rest of his life. I couldn't bear the thought of that. He loves Allen so very much. You know our troubles, Dad, and you also know I have done everything in my power to make things right, but our relationship seems to be beyond repair, and I have come to accept that. Maybe some things aren't meant to be fixed.*

I saw myself growing old with Allen. He was my knight in shining armor but not anymore. I yearn for the man I fell in love with, but he's gone and replaced by a stranger that now occupies my bed. I guess this letter is my plea for help, my last bit of hope before it's too late. Dad, I promise you that I will never let anything happen to Liam, but I can't make that same promise for myself. I fear my life is in jeopardy. I feel my prayers are futile, but I continue to ask for God's hand to pass over us and relieve us from this hell we are enduring. I'm afraid for Liam. He is my ray of sunshine, my everything, and if anything should ever happen to me I want to know that you will promise to take care of him for me and take him away from this place that was once our happy home. I don't want him growing up with Allen's influence. I know this is horrible for you to read, but I can't let Allen's addictions and problems rub off on Liam. I love Liam too much for him to bear the burden his father carries. Liam deserves better than that. Liam is an extraordinary boy. I know God placed him on this earth for a reason, and I will be damned if Allen interferes with Liam's fate.

My time is short. I can feel it. I am trying to fill my last days on this earth with happiness and joy for Liam's sake. I want his days to be filled with memories that will remind him of the good times, and I hope that if I am taken from him that you will continue on with those memories. Please talk often to him about me, share your stories of me with him. I don't ever want him to forget me. My proudest role is being his mama. I love him dearly, and I will continue to with my last dying breath and beyond. He will never be without me. Please, Daddy, help me. You and Mom are my only hope. I am so scared for Liam. He deserves to be happy and find the love that I know exists.

I'm sure this letter is coming as a shock to you and may be hard for you to read, but I implore to you to take my words to heart and to listen to what I have said. I have never been more serious in all of my life. I must end this now, Liam is calling me. His sweet voice is so soothing to my ears; I know I will miss it when I am gone. My only gratification is knowing that one day we will all be together again, and the hurt and pain will be forever gone. Until then, please teach Liam life's lessons the way you taught me. To be kind to one another, to help one another, and not to take things for granted, especially if he finds his one true love. Take him fishing and play ball with him. Say prayers with him and sing to him. His favorite song is "You are my Sunshine." I know that is why he's calling for me now. It is the only song that puts him to sleep. Teach him to be a gentleman, to open the door for a girl and to always treat her with the utmost respect. The way you are Dad, I can't think of a better teacher for Liam than you. Thank you, Dad; I know I can leave this earth knowing Liam will be taken care of. I love him with all of my heart and soul and always will. Please tell him that I will never leave him, and if he needs me, I'm only a prayer away. I will always be in his heart. I love you, Dad; please tell Mom I love her too. This isn't goodbye; this is until we see each other again.

Your girl,

Jessica

I found myself wiping tears from my eyes. I stared intently at the letter and could hear Liam as he told the story of how his father killed her; I could honestly feel her fear. She had been scared, and from what I could tell, her fear was for Liam and not herself. She was willing to face her own death as long as her son was protected. I was still staring at the letter when my thoughts were interrupted by the familiar hum of Liam's truck pulling into the driveway. I quickly folded the letter back into its original design and placed it back in the cardboard box. I stacked the other boxes back on top and quickly left the room as I had entered it. Liam was in the kitchen before I even walked down the stairs.

"There you are beautiful, I was looking for you. Where were you?" His hands had found my waist.

"Upstairs. You're home early."

"I know. We had to stop. Joe needed a part he didn't have for one of the bikes, so I decided to come home to you. So what were you doing upstairs?"

"Oh, nothing really. I was just looking around, you know, exploring." I didn't want to tell him about the letter, for one reason: I didn't know if he knew about it.

"Exploring? Did you find anything interesting?"

"Wouldn't you like to know?" I said, teasing him.

Liam didn't answer me back. Instead he kissed me. It was a long and tender kiss. "I missed you today. I couldn't wait to get back to you."

"I missed you too. Did you have a good day?"

Liam grabbed a bottle of water from the fridge and motioned me to the kitchen table to sit down.

"I did, Jenny. It was a great day."

I could tell by his mile-wide grin that he was telling the truth. He began telling me about his day with Joe and how he and Joe were able to take a motorcycle that had come into the shop as a complete pile of junk and practically make it over into a one of a kind, custom bike. He was beaming as he spoke, and I could tell that he was truly in his element. He could hardly contain himself. I could also see more than ever that he was destined to become partners with Joe. I could hear it in his voice. I always thought football was Liam's niche, but now I could see that Liam's real love (of course besides me) was working on anything with wheels. He absolutely loved it and could lose himself for hours at a time without realizing it.

"And I haven't even told you the best part yet."

"What?"

"I sold a truck!"

"What do you mean you sold a truck?"

"Well, about a month ago, Joe let me have a go at restoring an old truck that was sitting on his lot. I've been working on it in my spare time. Joe got a call on it yesterday, and when I went in today, Drew Metz was there with his dad to pick it up."

"You mean Drew bought it from you?"

"Yes, he did, for $1,100."

"Oh my God, that is wonderful, babe. I'm so proud of you!"

"This is only the beginning for us. From here on out the world is ours for the taking. Can you believe it, the first truck I get to restore and I sell it for $1,100."

"I know, and, of course, it's $1,100. What other number would it be?"

"It's a good thing, Jenny. It's a good thing. That number is our good luck charm; it's only going to bring us the best." Liam swung me in his arms. He was covered in grease, but I didn't care. The smell of petrol oil was exciting, and I could have gotten lost in its scent. He still was the most infectious person I knew. One glance from his eyes and one turn of his crooked smile was enough to take me over the edge. My heart would begin palpitating, and my breath became labored and erratic. As I always thought, if you had to go, there wasn't a better way to go than to have Liam Larson's lips touching yours.

"You know Grandpa Mack will be back soon. You said you would have the horses in before he returned." I glanced to the field, where four Tennessee Walkers grazed on late summer grass.

"Yeah, I know. But we've got plenty of time." His crooked grin increased to a full-fledged ear-to-ear smile. He kept me close to him as he carefully bit my lower lip, being sure that he didn't let go.

"Come on, let's go upstairs," he whispered in my ear.

I giggled softly as Liam carried me to our room. We made love for hours, our eyes glued to each other as we explored each other's bodies.

"I'm never going to get tired of this, Jenny. You've answered my prayers by coming into my life. I don't want any of this to ever change."

"It won't, Liam," I said as I snuggled closer to him, his protective arms holding me close to his side.

"Hungry?" I asked, as I heard his stomach grumbling.

"Definitely, how did you know?"

"Because you're always hungry after we're together, and besides, I can hear your stomach."

"I guess that's a dead giveaway, but I could say the same about you, you seem to work up a bigger appetite than me usually." He was right about that. I hungered not only to be one with him but also for the food I craved after he had touched me. Liam pulled his jeans on while I laid back on the bed and watched him. It was like my own personal show that he put on just for me. His body was in incredible condition, and even though he wasn't playing football anymore, he seemed to have been given a gift from the Gods. All the definitions in his arms and torso were even more defined and chiseled than before.

"I feel like I should be giving you some money."

"Huh? What are you talking about?" Liam looked aimlessly for his t-shirt that somehow had gotten lost on the floor.

"I mean I feel like I'm watching my own private Chippendale's show. How many girls can say that they get to watch Liam Larson get dressed in such a provocative manner? Really, I should be jailed for some of the things I'm thinking about you right now," I said as I maneuvered myself over to him, grabbing the belt loops of his jeans. I brought his beautiful body back to me, kissing every inch of his torso. His deep sigh told me he was pleased, and I knew we were destined to stay in bed for a little longer. Our desires for each other restrained both of us from leaving his room, only when we heard the familiar hum and rattle of Grandpa's '67 Chevy pull up to the house did we begin to move.

"Liam, Grandpa's here!"

"I know," he said, unfazed.

"Come on, get up! Get up! He can't find me in your room like this!" I said anxiously.

"Why not? You do live here now, and I'm sure he suspects that we mess around once in a while. He would be a fool not to, Jenny," Liam said with his crooked grin broadening. I still had to remember that this was my house too; I just felt weird lying naked in Liam's bed when I knew his grandpa was so close. It was something I was going to have to get used to and stop worrying about. But still, I gave Liam the look that told him I still wanted to get dressed and go downstairs before Grandpa realized where we were.

"Don't worry, babe. It'll be fine. Grandpa's a man of routine. We have plenty of time. He's going to park his truck, call for Blue, and then make his way to the barn. He'll spend at least fifteen minutes or so there before he even considers coming into the house. He'll then proceed into the kitchen where he will make himself a cup of coffee; he'll then look over the mail while he makes his way into the living room to sit for a while. It'll be at least another half hour before he even thinks about you and me. We could even mess around a little more and he'd be none the wiser," he said with an intense gaze. "Although you might not be able to scream as loud as you normally do," he said, laughing.

"Screaming! I do not scream. I may sigh heavily, but I definitely do not scream."

Liam just stared at me. He knew better, and honestly, I did too. When he touched me, he sent a euphoria through me that was too hard for me to conceal.

"Well, no matter, I'm not taking any chances on your theory. We better get dressed. Our luck, he'll change his routine today. And for the record, I'm not the only vocal one during our little romps." I desperately tried to get out of bed only to have Liam pull me back under the covers.

"Liam! Your grandpa!" He planted several kisses on my stomach as he held me tight.

"Just a little more foreplay before we have to end this." I gave him the look that meant now was not the time.

"You're right. Let's go, gorgeous."

Liam made his way downstairs first, followed by me a few minutes later. I met Grandpa Mack outside just when he had brought in the last horse: a beautiful chestnut colored Tennessee Walker with a white patch on her nose, who was affectionately known as Sugar Dumplin'.

"Jenny, hon', how are you?"

"Hi, Grandpa I'm fine. Did you have a nice trip?"

"I did, but it's good to finally be home. How was your day? Did you get to enjoy some down time, or did Liam have you working in the barn again?" he asked with a chuckle.

"No, he gave me the day off. I enjoyed my day very much, thank you. I actually did some exploring, if you must know. Your house is amazing."

"That's good, dear, but remember this is your home too. No need to call it just mine or Liam's for that matter. This is your place as much as it is ours." Grandpa put his firm but gentle hand on my shoulder and lovingly squeezed it.

"Thanks, Grandpa, I know; I'm just not used to saying that." The thought occurred to me to bring up the letter, but Liam was beside me. I didn't dare mention it to Grandpa until I could speak to him alone. It would have to wait.

"Well, guys, I'm going to call it a night. I'm dead tired and my back is killing me. I'm going to go take a good hot bath and then get some shut eye. I'll see you two in the morning." Grandpa tipped his hat and disappeared inside the house.

"Ready to go inside too?" Liam asked.

"Yes, I'm actually tired."

"It must have been because of me," he said with a wink.

"You know it, babe."

"I think I'm going to sleep hard, Jenny this really was a great day. Nothing could spoil it."

"You really do enjoy working at Joe's, don't you?"

"I do. It's better than I ever imagined. I don't regret my decision at all not to play college football, not that I could anyway with my bum leg, but even if that wasn't the case, it wouldn't matter. I know this was meant for me."

In that instant, I knew Liam was destined to become partners with Joe.

"Come on, babe, let's go to bed." Liam lifted me in his arms and carried me upstairs. It had been an eventful day for both of us. We were both looking forward to a peaceful night's sleep.

Chapter Three
Johnny

Life was going good, too good if I was being totally honest. Liam and I were in a great place, and we finally seemed to have turned the corner that the past few months had given us. I had been living with him for almost a full month, and out of those thirty days, Liam had only had one nightmare, the first night I moved in. Life on the farm was going well too. I had become a pro at working on the farm and could handle the tractor as well as Liam, a feat that even my parents were amazed to learn.

I still tried to help out at the store as much as possible. Dad's health had been declining and with school starting, he had lost a lot of his help. I first noticed Dad's health problems after my return from the hospital. I've often wondered if my accident had contributed to it. I do know, from what Mom and many others have informed me, that my parents almost didn't make it either when I was in the hospital. The accident had affected so many others besides just me and Liam, and in time, I would find out even Johnny.

It was Wednesday evening, and I had the house to myself again. Grandpa was away at a horse auction and Liam was at Joe's. I had been on the phone for almost two hours with Mom trying to decide if she should expand her hobby of baking into a full-fledged business or just help Dad with the store. The only issue with the store was it was almost too much for just her and Dad, and even though I was more than willing to help, it wasn't enough. Ashley wasn't an option. Her career was blossoming, and we didn't see her returning to West Virginia anytime soon. She loved California way too much.

Mom and Dad had just returned from Charleston when she had called me. Dad had seen a cardiologist; he had been having chest pains for the past week without telling Mom. She was livid when she found out. They both knew they had come to a crossroads in their life. Ashley and I are out of the house now, and the store was becoming too much for them to handle by themselves. They knew they had a decision to make. According to Dr. David Thompson, the cardiologist, Dad's heart was working overtime. If he didn't slow down and start taking it a little easier, his heart could give out on him at any time. This was scary for me to hear. I always thought of my dad as a hard-working man who was invincible, and this tidbit of news made me realize how human he really was.

I didn't want anything to happen to him. I knew how it felt to be vulnerable and the way Liam and my parents must have felt when I was on the brink of death. I tried to give Mom some advice and told her not worry about becoming a baker. They didn't need the money, and it would just be more unwanted stress that they didn't need at this point in their lives. They had always talked about retiring at some point and moving to the Carolinas, and it seemed that time had finally arrived. She took my advice with a grain of salt. She knew I was right but wasn't ready to accept it. They had lived in Spencer all of their lives, born and raised here. Selling the business and moving away was something she didn't know if she was ready to do, but Dr. Thompson had given them the same advice. It was something my parents needed to seriously think about.

When I hung up the phone, I felt very sad, melancholy to be exact, the same way my mom must be feeling. This past year had been a whirlwind for all of us. Who would have thought this time last year that I would be living with the love of my life, that my life would have almost ended, and that Johnny would have been a part of my life? It made my head spin just thinking about it. It was at this moment that Liam entered the room just when I needed him.

"Hey beautiful, how's my favorite girl?" I had become accustomed to him coming home from Joe's shop or anywhere for that matter and asking me that. He would proceed to suffocate me with one of his long and endearing kisses, always reminding me just how much I meant to him.

"Better, now that you're home."

"Why? What's wrong?" I was quiet. "Jenny, you seem upset."

"Oh nothing really, it's just that Mom told me that Dad's having some health issues. He's been having chest pains for about a week now. They just got back from Charleston. He had to see a cardiologist."

"I'm sorry, Jenny. Do you want to go see him?"

"I do, but not now. Right now I just want you to hold me."

"Your wish is my command, my love," Liam said as he picked me up into his arms and carried me to the sofa.

"I love you, Liam. Thank you."

"For what?"

"For this. I didn't really feel like talking about what Mom told me, and you seem to know that. What I needed was just to be comforted, and you knew that too, instinctively. You're always here for me, no matter what."

"I will always be here for you, I love you." Liam kissed me tenderly, our lips barely touching.

"So, what did you and Joe do today?"

Liam gave me a pensive look.

"What?" I asked.

"Jenny, I think I'm going to tell Joe yes tomorrow."

"You mean you've decided?"

"Yes. There's no reason for me to keep thinking about it. It's what I want. Are you okay with this?"

I was. I had given up hope a long time ago that Liam would consider college. How could I not be okay with him pursuing his dream?

"Yeah, I think it's great. You know I'm actually very proud of you."

"Why's that?"

"Because, you know what you want. Most kids our age are still trying to figure life out. You seem to have a handle on it already."

"I think I owe you credit for that, and honestly, I don't have it figured out. I do know what I want. I want you, and whatever comes after that is just an added bonus. This business wouldn't mean a damn thing to me if you weren't in my life. I'm doing this for you, for us. Besides, if I had things figured out, I don't think I would still be having those nightmares."

"But you haven't had a nightmare in over a month now. Don't you think you're done with them?"

"I hope so. But you know, there was a period this summer where I went a couple of weeks without having them too. I thought I had gotten rid of them then, but one night, for no reason at all, they came back. I don't know if that's going to happen again, but I do know that every night when we go to bed, I wonder if I'm going to be able to sleep through the night. I keep thinking the nightmares are Johnny's way of telling me he's still here, that he's not giving up."

"Are you serious? And for that matter, does it really even matter? I love you. Johnny doesn't have any control over us. Never has and never will."

Liam's stare intensified as if he was looking right through me and into my soul.

"Marry me, Jenny," he whispered.

"What?"

"Marry me."

"Of course, Liam. That's what we're going to do."

"I mean now. I don't want to wait any longer. Having you here has been the best thing in my life. I want to make it official. Please baby, marry me. We could leave tonight."

"Where are we going to go?"

"I don't care. We can call the justice of the peace, or better yet, let's go to Vegas. We can drive all night, just you and me babe.

We'll do it in some cute little white chapel with an Elvis impersonator. Please, baby." Liam begged me as he drew me near him. His lips touching mine as he spoke.

My heart ached to say yes. The spontaneity of the moment was so romantic, and I couldn't think of a better way to begin our life as husband and wife, but my head was telling me to think clearly. I wanted to marry Liam, but I wanted to do it the right way with our families there to witness our love for one another. Especially now that I knew my dad's health was at risk, I wanted him to walk me down the aisle.

"You know I want this more than anything, maybe even more than you do, and the thought of running off together is very tempting. But babe, I want our families to be with us. I couldn't stand it if something was to happen to my dad or even your grandpa and neither one of them witnessed our wedding. Don't you agree?" I asked, as my fingers outlined Liam's sensual, soft lips.

He sighed heavily. "Yes, I agree, I just can't wait, that's all. I want this more than I've ever wanted anything."

"Isn't having me here with you enough until we can make it official? It's not like I'm going anywhere."

"I guess. It's just those nightmares, I wake up afraid that you're gone. I guess my logic stems from just making sure you're mine, that there's no way in hell Johnny can come after you."

"He won't, Liam. I am yours today, tomorrow, and always, whether we're married now or a year from now. Johnny isn't going to interfere with us. But there is something I need to ask you."

"What is it?"

"This summer, you and Johnny both told me that you had made up with each other. The way you talk about him now makes me think you didn't." Liam didn't answer me. In fact, he looked away from me, but even with no words coming from his mouth, his silence was speaking volumes to me. "Liam?"

"Jenny, what if I told you that I lied to you about Johnny and me?"

"What do you mean lied to me?"

"Well, I can't really speak for Johnny, but as far as me, you know I was in a really dark place after our accident. I was willing to do anything to escape it. I didn't see any relief for me, especially when it concerned Johnny. I wanted to make things right. I did a lot of soul searching and praying. I just wanted you back, Jenny. You know how I feel about the accident, that it was my fault. And especially then, I was willing to try and do anything if it meant I could have you back. One night when I was in your hospital room, I laid there watching you. You were still in the coma, but you looked so peaceful, just like an angel. I should have been in my own room, but I never stayed there. I wanted to be next to you, so finally after my relentlessness, the nurses brought in a cot for me so I could get some sleep, not that I really got any sleep. It was hard for me to do anything but watch you; I was so afraid that if I walked away or closed my eyes you would slip away from me. I spent a lot of my time just praying for you to get better, and of course, I did a lot of thinking.

"I kept thinking about what happened leading up to the accident. How you used to tell me about the number eleven and how it scared you. I know I listened to you, Jenny, but I never took it quite as seriously as you did. I don't want you to think I was just trying to pacify you, but I really didn't think there was anything for us to worry about. But then we had the accident.

So many people had so many thoughts and theories about our accident and why it happened. I even had some people tell me it was my fault for not walking away from Johnny's threats and just trying to be the better person. Instead, I had to be the tough guy showing off, and look where it got us. So, to make things right, I thought maybe I should really try and forgive Johnny and get past our differences and try to rekindle the friendship we once had. The very next day, he came to see me. It seemed like old times. He apologized for his behavior, and I did too. Things were going well between us, and then one night that all changed.

    I was lying in the cot next to your hospital window; I was almost asleep when I heard footsteps. To be honest, I remember thinking for a moment it was your footsteps. When I opened my eyes, it was Johnny who was entering your room. He walked over to your bed and sat down next to you. I watched him as he spoke to you. His voice was low, and I couldn't really hear what he was saying to you, but it didn't matter. I could tell. He was holding your hand the way I do, the way someone does when they love that person. I knew right then and there that it wasn't over for Johnny. His feelings for you were as strong as ever. I felt my anger building as I watched him. I wanted to get up and punch the living daylights out of him, but instead I just laid there watching him caress your hand. After what seemed like hours, he finally stood up, gently brought your hand to his lips, and kissed it. He then turned and faced me. I closed my eyes immediately and pretended to be asleep. I clenched my fists as he approached me. I wanted to open my eyes and let him know that I knew he was here. He bent down next to me. I must say I wasn't prepared for what he said."

    "What was it, Liam?"

    "He told me he loved you, Jenny. He told me that he always had and always will. He admitted that our little truce was nothing more than an act for him and he didn't mean a word of it and he was doing it for your sake. He didn't want you to hurt anymore, and he knew that his actions towards you were causing you pain. I knew then that I could never be friends with him again. I don't know if he knew that I was awake or not, but the way he spoke to me made me think he did know."

    "What happened then?"

"Nothing, Jenny. I just pretended to be asleep. I honestly don't think I had the energy to do anything. You know I will fight for you until my last dying breath, but I just didn't know what to do at that exact moment. My world seemed so messed up anyway. I had no idea if you were going to make it, and I didn't want to waste my time on Johnny. I just wanted to concentrate on you, and that's exactly what I did."

"So, everything that you said to me and what Johnny said to me about the two of you isn't true at all?"

"No, it isn't. I'm sorry, Jenny. I know I've told you that I would never keep anything from you again, or lie to you, and this really wasn't a blatant lie, but after we got back together, I just didn't think it was important. We were moving on, and Johnny seemed to be out of the picture, but every time I have these horrible nightmares, he's right back again."

I looked at Liam's face. His expression seemed calm, and his eyes were conveying to me the honesty that he seemed at times to be without. I knew I should be mad at Liam, but I wasn't. I understood. This wasn't some sort of trivial lie over a misunderstanding or a missed phone call; this was much bigger than that. I don't remember much from the accident, but I do know that Liam went through hell over it, and if this was how he was able to cope with everything, then it was enough for me.

"I'm not mad, Liam."

"You're not?"

"No. Maybe I should be, but your reason for keeping it from me is understandable. I don't blame you for it; I might have done the same thing. But, honestly I don't think you have to worry about Johnny. If I don't care for him, does it really matter if he does? It's not going to change my feelings for you."

"I know that, Jenny, but you don't know what it's like to know that there's someone out there who feels almost the same way that I do. It's driving me crazy, and it's not helping to have him show up in my sleep. I'm trying so hard to let go of my guilt, and it's not fair that Johnny has to be pushing me backwards for every step I take forward."

"Listen, Liam, I know this is hard for you, but it really doesn't matter. I meant it when I said he means nothing to me. I love you and I'm going to marry you. I know as long as we have each other we can make it. We've made it this far. If we can weather this past storm we've been in, we can weather anything. And your nightmares are nothing more than dreams that have taken control of your unconscious state."

"So then you'll marry me, Jenny?"

"Yes, just like I told you the last time. But I want us to do it the right way. I want to walk down the aisle in my dad's arms wearing the white dress and blue Converse tennis shoes that I've told you about. I want my mom and sister to be there and your grandpa and our friends. I love you and I want the world to witness us becoming one." My lips were on Liam's now. The two of us could hardly control our urge as I spoke.

"Baby, I'd die without you. We'll do it the right way then. But I want us to set the date. I don't want to waste any more time not knowing when you will become Mrs. Liam Larson." This time Liam didn't allow me to speak; his lips molded into mine as he kissed me, forcing me back on the couch as his body hovered over mine.

That night it happened again. "No, Jenny, don't leave me! I'm right here, baby, just reach out your hand and grab mine! No! You can't take her, you bastard! Leave her alone!" Liam's primal screams were igniting the entire room. I shook him furiously to wake him, but it was done with a futile attempt. He seemed to be in a deep sleep that had him chained in his unconscious world, there was nothing I could do to bring him back to me.

"Liam, baby, please wake up, you're scaring me!" I was crying at this point as I wrestled with him. He fought back, his arms flailing in the air as I tried to calm him down.

"Jenny, it's okay, let me help," Grandpa said as he ran into our room.

"Oh, Grandpa, I don't know what to do. Liam won't wake up for me." Liam's screams were louder at this point as Grandpa and I both wrangled with him. I tried to keep his arms down while Grandpa slapped his face, hoping the sting would penetrate deep down inside Liam's unconsciousness and bring him back to our world. After minutes of desperation that seemed more like hours, Liam slowly began to open his eyes. His entire body was drenched in sweat as his bewildered eyes began to focus in on me and Grandpa. He seemed confused as his eyes batted back and forth from us. The look on my face must have said it all. Liam knew instantly why Grandpa and I were both leaning over him.

"It's happened again, hasn't it?" His crystal-blue eyes were hazed by impending tears that he fought to withhold.

"Yes, it was really bad this time. You had me scared. I couldn't wake you up."

"What are you doing here, Grandpa?" Liam asked as his eyes shifted to him.

"You woke me up with your screaming. I could have heard it in the barn, it was that loud. I heard Jenny yelling for you to wake up, so I came in here to help her. You were in a bad state of mind, son. This is the worst I've seen you."

Liam slowly lifted himself into a sitting position while Grandpa went to the bathroom to get him a glass of water.

"Liam, what happened this time? I swear I didn't think you were going to wake up for me. I was so scared," I said as I allowed my tears to fall. Liam's arms surrounded me as I fell onto his chest. He was completely soaked from his ordeal. His skin was clammy and cold, and beads of sweat dangled from his chiseled chin.

I sank into him as I tried to regain my composure.

"I don't know, Jenny, all I remember is trying to save you. It was the same scene I always dream. You're lying only inches away from me, but I can't reach you. Then when I think I have you, Johnny appears and picks you up. But this time he spoke to me, he told me that he's your savior and that I'll never see you again. I try to pull you to me, but as soon as I touch you, Johnny disappears with you in his arms, laughing this God-awful sinister laugh the entire time. I guess I wanted to get you back. It was so real, I really felt like you were gone this time. I don't think I wanted to wake up knowing you might not be here when I did."

Grandpa appeared in the door, holding the glass of tap water in his hands. The water was moving back and forth as Grandpa's shaking hands tried to hold it. He was sincerely worried about his grandson.

"Here, Liam, take a drink of this. It'll calm you down."

Liam politely took a huge gulp of the water before placing the glass next to the bedside table.

"Thanks, Grandpa, I'm fine now."

"Are you sure, son? You don't look it. As a matter of fact, you look like you've been to hell and back."

"I think I have, Grandpa, but I'm okay now. It was just another bad dream, that's all."

Neither Grandpa nor I believed him. Grandpa's body shifted as his gaze turned to me, and my stomach knotted as the pensive look on Grandpa grew. "Liam, I think it's finally time you spoke to somebody."

"You mean a shrink? Grandpa, there's no way in hell I'm talking to anybody about this stuff. I can handle it by myself. I'm fine."

Grandpa didn't respond, he just gave me a very worrisome stare. I knew he was hoping I would intercede and back him up.

"Liam, maybe..." but that's as much as I got out.

"Jenny, not you too. I can't believe you guys. I don't need any help. These are just some stupid damn nightmares. Everybody has them. Come on, Jenny, I thought you were on my side."

"I am on your side, but you don't know how bad it was. I honestly didn't think you were going to wake up. I've never seen anything like it. This was so much more than just a nightmare. And look at you; you're a complete mess. Dreams don't do that to people. You're completely covered in sweat, baby. I just want to help you and so does Grandpa."

Liam got out of bed and stormed off in a huff, slamming the bathroom door so hard that it made the glass of water shake. Grandpa and I looked at one another.

"I don't know what to do," I said to him.

"You're going to have to help him. I know this boy, and I should have known better than to ask that of him. Hell, I wouldn't go to a shrink either, but I can't stand to see him suffer the way he does with these nightmares. I don't know what's going to happen, but you're going to have to be the one to pull him out of this. He loves you. I've only seen a love like this one other time in my life, and it was the love I carry for my own wife, God rest her soul. He's talked to me so much about you, hell I knew about you before you even met me. I knew you were the one, and getting to know you over this past year validated my opinion. He's suffering in a bad way, Jenny, and I don't know what's going to happen, but you have to be there for him or we're both going to lose him." Grandpa became silent for a moment. I looked behind me to see if Liam was there. He wasn't. The bathroom door was still closed shut. "Jenny, do you know about Liam's drinking?"

I was completely caught off guard by his statement.

"His drinking? I don't know what you mean. I know Liam has a beer now and again, but that's it."

"So you haven't noticed the increase in his drinking?"

I racked my brain trying to recall any time that I could remember Liam having anything more than a couple of beers with me. The entire time I had known Liam I don't think I had ever even seen him drunk. "No, Grandpa, I haven't. Are you sure you know what you're talking about?"

"Very sure. I didn't say anything because of the accident. I thought it was Liam's way of trying to get over what happened, but when these damn nightmares began, I noticed a little bit of a change in his behavior. It was subtle to begin with, and I didn't put much stock into it, but one day I drove Liam's truck into town because mine had a flat tire. I was in shock at the amount of empty beer cans in his cab. Later that day I confronted him about it, and he denied there was anything wrong. He said I had just happened to come upon some stuff from a gathering at Joe's. The cans belonged to everybody who had been there, so I shrugged it off. But then one night about a month ago, maybe right before you moved in with us, Liam hadn't made it home yet. I thought he was with you until I heard a truck pull into our driveway. Of course I thought it was Liam, but it was Parker. Liam was drunk, and to be honest, Parker had been drinking a little too much himself. I made both of them go inside and sleep it off.

The next day I confronted both of them. Liam again said there was nothing to it. He wouldn't talk about it anymore and stomped off to the barn. He didn't talk to me for the rest of the day. That's when I asked Parker. I'm not saying it's happening all the time. To be honest, I haven't seen him pick up a beer since you've been here. Maybe it was just a phase as he tried to work things out this summer. I can't really blame him. It was harder than hell for him to get past that accident and the blame and that whole damn thing with Johnny liking you. He didn't know what to do, but I'm just asking you to watch out for him. I don't want anything to happen to him, Jenny." The thought occurred to me to mention the letter I had found, but just when I began to speak Grandpa's eyes swung to the hallway behind me as Liam emerged from the bathroom. "You okay, son?" Grandpa asked earnestly.

Liam just nodded his head as he walked to my side. "I'm fine, Grandpa, sorry about this. I guess I'm still dealing with some shit."

I hugged Liam tightly. "It's going to be okay," I whispered into his ear.

"I know, babe."

"Well guys, I'm going back to bed. I'll see you two in the morning." Grandpa squeezed Liam's shoulder firmly as he gave me a quick wink.

"Are you sure you're okay?"

"Yeah, I'm sorry you had to see that, Jenny."

"You know I'm here for you."

"I know. I think I know what can help me, though."

"What's that?"

"I want to take you some place."

"Brush Creek Road?"

"No, this is a new place: a place I've wanted to take you for a while but didn't know when the best time would be. I think the time has finally come."

I had no idea where Liam meant.

"I have to talk to Joe in the morning, but I'm free on Friday. We can go then." He hugged me tightly as we got back in bed. "This is going to be great, babe. I think I should have taken you there a long time ago."

"You have me completely in the dark. Why can't you tell me before Friday?"

"You'll just have to wait and see, but believe me, it will be worth the wait."

Chapter Four
Serenity Hill

The alarm went off early on Friday morning. I thought since Liam had taken the day off we could enjoy ourselves and take our time for the drive he had planned for us, but to my dismay, he had other thoughts.

"Why is the alarm going off at six o'clock in the morning?" I slammed it off, knocking it onto the hardwood floor.

"I want to get an early start, babe. We have a little bit of a drive ahead of us."

I moaned in disgust as I rolled over, burying myself in the covers. I could feel Liam's tender touch on me as he used his ulterior methods to get me up.

"It doesn't matter how much you try and coax me with your kisses, I'm not getting out of bed until eight."

"Are you sure about that?" Liam asked, as his hands made their way under the covers.

"Very sure." My stomach began feeling all weird inside as Liam's hands made their way down my side. His touch was sensual, and I instantly found myself turning to face him.

"We can get out of bed at eight if you want, but I'm not going to let you sleep," he said with his crooked grin. I smiled back as I lifted the blankets over his head, this time burying us both beneath them. He was right, well almost. We didn't get out of bed until eight-thirty. We gave ourselves an extra half-hour for cuddling.

By the time we had left, it was past ten.

"So, are you going to tell me where you are taking me?"

"No. Like I said, I want to surprise you."

The day was perfect for the drive. It was gorgeous for the end of summer. I should have been enjoying the drive and the beautiful view, but my thoughts kept returning to the other night and what Grandpa had told me. I scoped Liam's cab. There was nothing unusual in it to make me think he had been drinking. In fact, the only thing that one would think if they saw Liam's truck was that he liked working on it. The truck was in pristine condition. He had revamped the entire body after the accident. Grandpa had offered to help him buy a new one, but Liam didn't want too; he wanted this one. It was his first truck, and he loved it. The truck looked completely new, even carried the new car smell. I dismissed the thoughts for now and concentrated on our day ahead. We drove for another hour when Liam pulled off the road. We were in the middle of nowhere, nothing around except open pastures and hills for miles.

"This can't be where you meant?"

"No, but we're close. I need to do something before we continue." He leaned ever so gently into me and put one arm behind my back.

"Liam, really, this is why you pulled over?"

He let out a wicked laugh. "You wish, my darlin'. Actually I pulled over to do this to you." He pressed his free arm around me, pulling me to him. His hand came over my face as my eyes closed automatically. "There," he said as I felt the feel of fabric on my face. My hands went up instantly to remove it. "No, you can't take it off." He said eagerly.

"But why? Why are you blindfolding me?"

"Because we're almost there and I want this to be a surprise. I've already told you that."

He pressed his sweet, soft lips against mine as he whispered to me. "We're so close, babe, just humor me with this. I promise you'll know soon." His words turned into a long and lingering kiss. "Mmm, I kind of like having you blindfolded," he said with that same wicked laugh.

"I'm sure you do, but could we please leave now, so I can find out what this is all about. I'm dying with curiosity."

He gave me one final kiss and drove off. He kept his right hand securely in mine for reassurance as we continued our drive. Not fifteen minutes later, we pulled off again. We seemed to be on a dirt road that was irregular and bumpy. Liam drove slowly, his hand squeezing mine tighter as we progressed, and then in an instant he stopped. He was silent.

"Well, are we here?"

"Yeah, we're here," he said sweetly.

"Can I take this off now?" I began to remove it only to have Liam's hands intercept mine and pull them away from the blindfold.

"What is it, Liam?"

"Nothing, it's just that you're so beautiful. I'm enjoying looking at you, that's all. Here, let me do it." His hands were rough and rugged, but when he touched me, he did it tenderly, barely touching me at all as he removed the bandana. When I opened my eyes, my first view was of his magnetic blue eyes staring into mine. "There," he said, "even more beautiful."

"You're making me blush, you know."

"Why, because I think you're beautiful? You are. You're the most beautiful person I've ever seen."

"I love you, Liam."

"I love you too. Are you ready?"

I looked around to see where we were. My mouth opened in awe. It was absolutely one of the most beautiful places I had ever seen, almost prettier than Brush Creek Road. I could tell we were at the top of a ridge, and the view of the peaks of hills before me was adorned with trees, and at the far right side of me I could hear the sound of running water as it trickled down its path.

"Oh my God, Liam, it's breathtaking. Where are we?"

"It's a place my Grandpa and I call Serenity Hill. I've been coming here since I was little. My parents used to bring me here to go fishing, and after they died Grandpa would bring me here. When I just want to get away or need some time alone, I always find myself here. I found myself here a lot this summer."

"I can see why. It feels like we're at the doorstep to heaven. I don't think I've ever been so close to the sky before in my entire life. I feel like I could reach out and touch the clouds."

"Come on, I want to show you why I brought you here." Liam took my hand in his as he led me out of the cab of his truck. The place was gorgeous, the grass was green and the flowers were abundant. The air was sweet and the light wind that blew around us, enticed my senses. He smiled sweetly at me as I followed close behind him, my hand securely placed in his.

About fifty feet in front of us stood a large oak tree that looked to be as old as the hills themselves. As we approached it, I noticed a small granite marker right beneath the one gigantic branch that jutted from the tree. I marveled at its beauty as we approached. It seemed to welcome us as the leaves danced in the wind. Liam's gait slowed as we approached the tree. The marker was more evident now, and I could see the writing on it. I thought it might signify that this property belonged to Liam's family for wanderers who happened to tread upon their land, but as I began to make out the reading, I knew I was wrong. Liam stopped walking, for the first time in weeks I noticed that his limp was more pronounced, maybe it was because of the rocky terrain the hill provided. Liam took both of my hands in his and pulled me to him, blocking my view of the granite marker.

"Jenny, I want you to know that I love you, and my heart has been pounding out of my chest today. I've wanted to bring you here since the day I met you. You are so important to me, and you mean the world to me."

"You're scaring me, Liam. What's this all about?"

Liam let out a huge sigh before continuing. "Besides my Grandpa, there has really been only one other person that I have ever wanted you to meet, and it breaks my heart that you haven't been able to, but this summer I realized that her actual presence wasn't really necessary for you to meet her. She's always been with me, if only in spirit, so I knew I could bring you here and you would understand." Liam moved to the side as the granite marker came into my view once again. "Jenny, this is my mom, Jessica." He carefully bent down on his knees, bringing me with him. "Mom, this is Jenny."

I didn't know what to say. A flood of emotions came over me as I stared at the granite stone. I knew it sounded silly, but I felt nervous, the same way I did when I met Grandpa for the first time. She wasn't here in body, but in spirit she was, and my heart accelerated as I stared at the stone as though I was really meeting her. The stone was simple and small, and the inscription was sweet and to the point.

Jessica Larson
An Angel to All, A Mom to One
Loved & Missed
October 12, 1967 – July 11, 1997
Until We Meet Again

I rubbed the writing as I read it; it was as if I was touching his mom instead. A welcome hug that was long overdue between the two of us. My body shivered as my fingers outlined the letters that made out her name. "I don't know what to say, Liam, but it means so much to me that you brought me here."

"I've wanted to do this for so long, Jenny, but I didn't know how you would feel about it. I mean I thought you would be happy, but in the beginning when I first met you, I was afraid to bring you here. Don't ask me why, I just was, but after our accident and almost losing you, I came here a lot. I would talk to her, and I know she heard me. I could feel her, like she was standing right next to me. Maybe it's this place or just the fact I'm reminded of her when I come here. Whatever the reason, it was here that I had decided I needed to bring you. When I think I can't get through something, all I have to do is spend some time here and things begin to make sense. My clouded judgment is gone and I know what's right." Liam stopped talking as he stared at me.

"What is it, Jenny?"

"I don't know. I just think what you said was so touching. I can understand why this place is so important to you, and I'm happy that you love me enough to want to share it with me."

"Are you kidding? I want to share the world with you. I wanted to share my mom with you a long time ago. Believe me, this day was a long time coming for me."

We sat down by Jessica's grave as Liam continued to tell me stories of his childhood. He was young when his parents brought him here, but he remembered them. His eyes danced as he spoke of the times they fished together, how his mom detested the mere sight of a worm much less handling one, and the pure joy Liam received in watching her wince as she tried to put the wriggly creature on her hook, only giving up when Liam would do it for her.

I was enjoying listening to his stories of his life before me that included a time when he had two parents to love him and two that he could love. We stayed under the oak tree most of that afternoon, neither of us in a hurry to leave. I couldn't get over how beautiful it was here, and my mind kept thinking of Liam as he contemplated his life during our little hiatus this summer. I could see why he would come here. The place brought a feeling of contentment and that this was what life was about, not the worries that seemed to invade us normally. I swear Serenity Hill carried some sort of magical power with it because it seemed like all the troubles and heartache that Liam and I had endured over the past few months had vanished. It was like it used to be before Johnny had entered the picture. Time had stopped for us while we were there. We enjoyed everything that the hill brought with it, and as the day ended and the evening sky shown its twilight shades, we felt like the two luckiest people in the world.

"I'm so glad you brought me here, Liam, it means more than I can say."

"I hope so. Like I said, I've been here a lot these past few months, especially after the accident and especially when my nightmares began."

"Have you told me everything, Liam?"

"You mean about the nightmares?"

"Yes, and I guess anything else. I mean, I'm still trying to fill in the pieces when I was in the hospital. All I have to go on is what you and everyone else tells me. I just want to make sure that you're not keeping anything from me because you know you can tell me anything. I don't want us to hold anything back from each other. We've been through too much for that to happen. I want to be here for you, Liam."

"You are here for me." Liam paused as he played with a blade of grass; a habit he had developed when he was deep in thought.

"What, Liam?"

"I think I should tell you about my nightmares."

"You mean there's more to them than what you've already told me?"

"Yeah," he said solemnly. "A lot more. Tell me, do you remember anything about the accident? Aside from the race itself, can you recall anything about that night?"

"Not really. I've tried to on numerous occasions. Believe me, there are so many unanswered questions, but every time I rack my brain over it I come up empty. My mind is a fog. I remember being in the truck with you and approaching the home stretch, but after that I don't remember anything. I wish I did; it frustrates me when I try to recall that night. I get to where the deer appears and then my mind goes blank."

"You don't remember me yelling for you after the truck hit the deer?"

"No. My next memory is waking up in the hospital."

"So, when you were yelling for me to help you, that doesn't come through either?"

I shook my head again. "Why, Liam?"

"It's just that I remember everything." Liam paused for a brief moment. "I guess I should just tell you everything from the beginning. You know, since I was little I've had to grow a tough exterior and learn to hold my feelings inside and be strong. When most kids were outside playing or having stories read to them by their parents, I was learning how to live without them. Grandpa taught me how to deal with my problems and just move on, but it's different when you're being raised by a man. He felt it was best to keep your feelings inside, and for the most part, that's what I did, whether it was school or football, but then you entered my life. That changed everything, and then Johnny who I thought was my friend entered our lives, and everything really changed. And of course there was the accident." Liam's voice trailed off for another brief moment. "Jenny, you know when you're sleeping but you somehow realize it, and you know that you're dreaming?"

"Yeah."

"Like you can feel you're awake but you're not and know you can control what happens just by waking up?"

"Yeah, I think so, Liam."

"Well that's exactly how my nightmares are. Everything is fine, and then in an instant it's not. My mind goes straight to the accident, and I can see the fear and pain in your face. It's as clear as day to me. I reach for you, to comfort you, and I can't. Your face begins to fade from me as it grows smaller and smaller. Your screams don't diminish though; they become louder; they shoot right through me. I think I'm watching you die right in front of me. You tell me how scared you are and beg for me to help you. It just about kills me every time I think about it. I keep trying, but the more I reach for you the farther away you become, and then as your screams can't get any louder, I can hear your voice settling. I become aware that you are looking above you. I see this hand reach down for you, and the fear that overcame you seems to disappear as this hand embraces you. I can't understand who it is, and then I see his face, and it's Johnny. The anger inside of me begins to boil as Johnny just gives me this smile and look of triumph as he cradles your bloody body against his. I beg him to leave you alone, but he just laughs at me in this evil, sinister tone. I just wanted to take you away from him, Jenny."

"Liam you don't have to go on. I don't need to hear anymore."

"No, I want to go on. You should know everything and maybe you'll understand a little better why my nightmares are so bad. He keeps laughing at me and says to me, *I've got her now, Liam. You've done enough damage, just look at her you did this to her, not me. This is your fault. I would never hurt her. She'll never forgive you for this. If she dies you'll be to blame, everyone will know the truth. She's better off with me. This is the way it was meant to be. She wants me not you.* I couldn't believe what I was hearing, and this all goes on while we are being rescued. There are people all around us, the sounds of metal and glass crunching beneath their feet, but it's all a blur to me. All I can do is watch helplessly as Johnny takes you away from me, flaunting himself in front of everybody as if he was being heralded as the winner, you know like he had won the race by pulling you from the wreckage. I know that is why I am having trouble sleeping. Johnny's winning, and I can't handle it. In my dreams, he's won by winning your heart. I know it sounds ridiculous, but it's the way I feel. I have to let this go, or I'm not going to be any good to you. You deserve…no, we deserve to be able to have our lives back the way they used to be, the way we used to talk about our future being. I'm not going to let Johnny destroy that, not ever."

"Liam, we are going to have the future we want, and Johnny isn't going to be a part of it. You have never needed to worry about him, and I don't know why your subconscious seems to be playing tricks with you now, but they're not real, I am. I'm here with you now, tomorrow, and always. I'm not going anywhere. Maybe if you can just concentrate on that, your nightmares will go away. Mind over matter, babe."

"But that's just it. Sometimes I feel like you aren't here. That's why I wanted you to move in with me. I need to know you're real, to see you. It helps me to have you always close to me. I never want to lose you, and I know what you're saying, but it's really hard. I'm trying, but right now the nightmares are winning. Do you understand a little bit better where I'm coming from and why these nightmares are so hard for me to get rid of?"

"I do, and I know it's not easy for you, but it will get easier because I'm going to be here for you, and together we're going to make them go away."

Liam smiled his beautiful crooked smile as he pulled me to him. "You're the best thing that's ever happened to me, Jenny," he whispered as he kissed the top of my head.

We left that night as the evening sky turned into a beautiful, star-filled night. I had always felt close to Liam, and after today, I felt even closer. We seemed to be joined at the hip. Whatever he felt, I felt, and whatever I felt, he seemed to feel as well. We had a sense for each other that strengthened after our accident. Maybe it was always there between us, but for some unknown reason, we weren't aware of it. We were now, and that was all that mattered to me.

Chapter Five
The Demons Reveal Themselves

It was after nine when we pulled into Liam's driveway. Grandpa Mack's truck was nowhere to be seen, and except for a small light in the front window, the house looked vacant. Liam took my hand in his as we slid out of his truck. We made our way up the porch steps when my weight gave in, causing me to lose my balance. Liam grabbed my arm. The second step that led to the porch was broken.

"Watch your step. Sorry, I've been meaning to get that fixed."

"That's okay. When did this happen?"

"Last night actually. Grandpa fell into it. The steps are old to begin with, and I guess it finally gave way. Like I said, I'll fix it soon. I don't want you breaking your ankle." Liam smiled at me, as he held my arm and lifted me over the step. He led me inside to the living room where we sat quietly in each other's arms. I couldn't take my eyes off him.

"Jenny, what are you thinking about?"

"I want to thank you for taking me to see where your mom is buried. It really meant a lot to me."

"You don't have to thank me. I should have done it a long time ago. But you're welcome."

"I want to apologize to you too. I'm so sorry I've been berating you about the nightmares. It wasn't fair, especially now that I know what you've been going through with them. Now I understand why you didn't want to tell me about them. I know it must have been hard for you."

"I didn't take it as you were berating me. I've always wanted you to know about them; I just didn't know how to tell you. I didn't know how you would react when you found out that Johnny was the source of them. I guess it still worries me that you might have feelings for him."

"That's ridiculous. My feelings for Johnny have always been on a platonic level. Never, ever have I felt about him the way I feel about you."

"I guess, but it's different from my perspective. I have to deal with someone who does feel the same way about you that I do. I know he's in love with you. And no matter what I've said or he has said to make things sound differently, I know he's not giving up on you."

"But does it really matter, Liam? I'm not influenced by his feelings. Don't you think if I was going to be I would have by now? He's felt this way for some time."

"Yeah, I know. That's what worries me, Jen. It's going on a year since he met you, and his feelings seem to be as strong if not stronger than ever. I know we have a solid relationship, but things happen, and he's trying to find a weak spot in our relationship."

"But there isn't one, Liam."

"Don't you realize what he's doing, Jen?" Obviously I didn't, I thought to myself. "He's trying to wear you down."

"That's absurd, Liam."

"Is it? Don't take him for granted, Jen. Remember that I've known him a lot longer than you have. I know how he operates. He believes that if he can at least win you over with his friendship, he'll have an in with you, and with that he'll slowly weasel his way to your heart. It will all seem innocent enough but he'll still be playing his game with you. You'll start feeling sorry for him. It will be exactly how he wants it to work. He's a player, and you're his deck of cards."

"I can't believe you, Liam. Do you think that I'm that vulnerable that I would even remotely allow Johnny to do that to me? Come on; give me at least a little credit. I'm a big girl. I think I can handle myself and Johnny too."

"I know you are, but look at it so far. Don't you think I've called it? You yourself told me that the two of you made a truce and are now friends. That's exactly what he wanted. It's just his way. He wants you, and he's going about it the best way he knows how, with his debonair charm and kindness. If he couldn't get you the old-fashioned way, he's going to try to get you this way. You won't even know you've been hit if he has his way with you."

"My God Liam, you're actually talking crazy. I've never heard such nonsense in all my life. So, are you saying I should have seen this when he came to see me this summer? Is it that out of the ordinary to forgive someone and to thank someone for saving their life? What was I supposed to do? I did owe him a debt of gratitude. Whether you want to believe it or not, he did help in saving me that night."

"I know he did, Jenny," Liam said as his head lowered.

I should have never said that. Johnny's actions were the root of all of Liam's guilt. "I'm sorry. I didn't mean for it to come out like that. I just meant…"

"I know what you meant babe, and you're right. He did save you. Thank God for that because now I still have you. But I think Johnny's going to use that to his advantage, no matter how pathetic it sounds. I think he believes he's got one up on me because of that. And maybe he does, but…"

"There's no buts, Liam. He saved me. That's it. I'm not in love with him because of that; I'm just thankful to him. There's a big difference between those two words. My love lies with you and you alone," I said, kissing Liam gently on his lips. "You're still my savior. It was you that pulled me out of the coma. Your love, your prayers and your constant belief that I would wake up is what truly saved me."

"Jenny, if I could only hang on to that and believe it."

"Why can't you?"

"It's not that simple. I can't explain it."

"Liam?"

"Yeah?"

"Did you really tell me everything today about your nightmares?"

"Yes and no."
"What did you leave out?"

"I have told you why I'm having them and what happens in them but only to a point. I guess what I left out was the part that I have a hard time remembering myself. Once Johnny takes you away from me, I keep feeling I'm going to see more, but instead I'm left in total darkness. I can hear your voice and Johnny's, but I can't see either one of you. It's almost worse than the actual nightmare itself. It's like the missing piece of the puzzle. I sometimes try to will myself to stay asleep in hopes that I will find out more. It's pretty ironic considering I don't want to fall asleep most nights. All I know, and you know this too since you've witnessed it, is that I'm in a cold sweat and left with this awful, empty feeling inside of me. I can't describe it. It's almost like any happiness or hope I ever had has evaporated from my being. It's the worst feeling ever. That's what I meant when I said even though I'm asleep I could tell the nightmares are going on, because the same feeling I'm experiencing when I'm asleep is the same way I'm feeling when I wake up. That's why I always want you near me, and then I know it's only a bad dream. In my nightmare you're gone forever." Liam paused as he tightened his hold on me.

"What are you staring at?"

"I look at you sometimes, and I can't believe you're here. And I don't mean that literally. I mean that you're mine. I'm just amazed by you. You possess this inner strength that awes me. I've seen a side of you over these past few months that I've never seen before. You have an inner resilience that just permeates. You know most girls would keel over and give up with what you have endured, but not you. You take what's dealt you and ask for more."

"Does that surprise you, Liam?"

"I guess. Not that I didn't think you had a backbone before all this crap, it's just you're not intimidated by anything. I love that about you. I know that's why when I'm feeling discouraged I think of you and I want to try harder."

"You're pretty resilient yourself, you know?"

"I don't know, Jen. I used to think I was, but not anymore. I want to be that guy who wasn't afraid of anything: not football, not racing, and not losing you."

"First off, you're not ever going to lose me, and secondly, you are strong. You've always been strong. You're the same person I met last October, only now, for some reason, you can't find that strength because it's being hidden by these illusions of weakness. It's still in you, in your heart and mind. You just have to find it again. You just need to let go of all that crap, like you so eloquently put it, and you'll realize your self-confidence and inner strength is still there. And I guarantee that when you do your nightmares will end too."

"I don't know if I believe what you're saying, but I do know that my world would be lost without you in it."

Liam began to stare at me again. He didn't have to speak. I knew exactly what he was thinking as he shifted his body closer to me, pulling himself over me as his lips found mine. Gradually and delicately, he kissed me as he effortlessly undressed me. He loved me that night, the only way Liam knew how, with his mind, body, and soul.

Hours later, I lay there quietly with Liam's arms securely around my body. He was fast asleep, and I found myself completely content as I listened to his slumber, snuggling closer to him as I prepared for what I hoped would be a well-deserved and good night's sleep.

"No! No! Please don't leave me, not again. I'm right here! Reach for me Jenny, please reach for me! Don't leave me, I'm sorry baby, I'm so sorry!"

Liam kept screaming over and over again.

"Liam, wake up! I'm right here, babe. Liam, it's okay!" Not again, I thought. His body was drenched in sweat and shaking so uncontrollably that I couldn't calm him down.

"Liam, please baby wake up!"

"Please Liam, for me!"

"Don't go, Jenny please, baby, I'm sorry. Jenny where are you? No! Not you! Please don't take her!"

Liam's screams were louder with each breath he took.

"Liam, please wake up. It's only a dream, it's not real, I'm right here!" I kept repeating as if our lives depended on it. His face grimaced and his mouth was clenched as he fought me off. It was the same struggle as last time. My screams to awaken him were futile as he remained a prisoner to his nightmare. I didn't understand why he wouldn't wake up for me, and then I remembered what he had told me. Maybe Liam was in the part of his nightmare where he is in total darkness, my voice only a ghost to him as Johnny carries me off. Maybe he was trying to find me, the way I searched for Liam when I was in total darkness. I found my voice subsiding as I watched him, his actions almost foreign to me as he seemed to fight this battle alone. I whispered to him, *"it's okay, Liam. I'm here. You just have to find me. Listen to my voice. Follow it, babe. I'm right here waiting for you."* With those words I immediately noticed a change in Liam's body. The stiff, rigid man who fought off his unconscious intruder was now relaxing. His jaw that was clenched tightly slowly relaxing too, allowing his chiseled face to once again calm down.

"Jenny," he whispered as his eyes opened to meet mine.

"I'm right here, Liam."

He brought me to him, my head lying on his chest as his racing heartbeat slowed down.

"It's alright, Liam. I never left you."

"I know, Jenny. I know, but in my dream I saw you leave me again. Johnny took you from my grasp. I had you, I could feel your touch, and then you were gone, like always, in his arms as he laughed at me."

"Were you looking for me again? Was it dark?"

"I was looking for you everywhere, and it was very dark. But I heard you crying out for me. I wanted to find you."

"Is that why you didn't wake up for me?"

"Yes. I needed to find you. I know it sounds strange saying that with you lying here next to me, but it's like these nightmares are trying to tell me something. I'm not going to have closure until I can find you." Liam's grasp tightened around me.

I knew what I was about to say would be wrong, but I felt compelled to say it, even if I knew Liam's answer already. "Liam, would you talk to somebody about your nightmares for me?"

"You mean a shrink? Jenny, you know my answer. Why would you ask that already knowing I don't want to?"

"Liam, we need to see someone. I'll be with you all the way. I'm not going to let you go through this alone, but please do it for me."

"I don't know, Jenny. I don't think I'm ready for that. I know that having you here is helping me."

"What if we went to somebody we knew?"

"You know of a shrink?"

"No, but I do know of someone who seems to know a lot about dreams and things like that."

"You don't mean Johnny's mom, do you?" I just looked at him. "Hell no! It's one thing to ask me to see a shrink, but it's even worse for you to ask me to see my worst enemy's mom and ask for advice! Why in the world would you even consider her, knowing how I feel about Johnny? It took a lot for me to open up to you. There's no way in hell I want her to know anything about me!" Liam was livid that I suggested this; I knew I had struck a nerve.

"I'm sorry, Liam. I just thought she might be the answer. I know she would be discreet."

"You don't think Johnny would find out? My God, Jenny, that's his mom. Believe me, he would find out, and that would be the worst thing ever for me. And furthermore, why would I want to tell her that her son is the reason I'm having these freakin' nightmares?"

"I guess I wasn't thinking clearly about it. I guess I was just thinking more along the lines of her giving some advice. She really did help me last year with the whole number eleven thing. She's quite brilliant when it comes to that stuff, whether you want to think so or not. But I won't bring it up again; it was stupid for me to even consider her, especially after what you've told me. I'm sorry."

Liam sighed. "It's okay. I didn't mean to yell at you, but you do understand that I could never go to her."

"Yeah, I do."

I didn't press it anymore. I knew the nightmares took a toll on Liam, and sleep was something he needed. But as the nights wore on, so did the nightmares, and what used to be sporadic was turning into regular occurrences. Each night, like clockwork, Liam would have another nightmare, and each night, like clockwork, I would struggle to wake him up and help him through them. It had become a routine for us, but one that I was more than willing to continue. Our hope, as it had always been, was that by me being there the nightmares would finally depart from Liam's unconsciousness.

Every free moment I had, I researched nightmares, trying to learn anything that could help Liam. My days and nights were a blur, and I became so consumed with my research that I had only spoken to my parents a handful of times. Dad's health was continuing to be an issue. He had been ordered by Dr. Thompson to take some time off, so my parents were planning a trip to Myrtle Beach. Mom said it would only be for a few days, but I had a sense that they were using their time to look for a place to live. I volunteered to help run the store while they were gone, but Dad said that wouldn't be necessary. They had hired a new manager who would be in charge in their absence. I felt somewhat betrayed that they hadn't come to me, but I could hear the worry in their voice as they asked about Liam. I knew Grandpa had told them what was going on, and they wanted us to have the time we needed without worries of the store.

By the end of September, the majestic hilltops of West Virginia began to display their kaleidoscope hues on every tree. Liam was slowly improving. His nightmares seemed to be waning, and I felt more comfortable leaving him for longer periods of time. He began spending more time with Joe again which in turn gave me more free time. So, even though I wasn't needed at the store, I found myself spending my free time there. Dad's new manager was great but didn't know a thing about running a wholesale grocery business.

Billy Cottrell was an older gentleman about my dad's age with a receding hair line and a belly as a big as three watermelons. He always wore a crisp white shirt with a checkered bow tie and suspenders to match. He was a kind man who liked to smoke a cigar and talk at the same time. A talent I found fascinating as I waited patiently for the cigar to fall during our conversations. It turned out that he went to school with Dad and was in need of some money. He actually had come to Dad for a loan when Dad gave him a job instead.

We hadn't had a manager in the store for years; Dad took on that role saying he didn't need to hire someone to do the work he could do himself. Billy had told me the position was only temporary and that my parents were making some changes with the store and once the changes were made his services would no longer be needed. I took that to mean that my parents were already in the process of closing the business. I was sad. The store had been a part of my life since I was born; I felt another chapter closing in my life, but knowing the future of this did help me in my own future. I still wanted to go to college, and now more than ever I thought it was time. I thought of Kendra and sat down and dialed her number.

"Hello?"

"Kendra, it's Jenny."

"Dawg! How are you? I thought you had forgotten about me."

"I'm sorry. I've just been really busy. It's been kind of crazy here."

"Is everything okay? I mean anything you need to tell me?"

Kendra still knew me too well.

"It's nothing really. Besides I don't want to talk about it over the phone. How is college life?"

"It's good. A lot more work, but a lot more fun too." Kendra said with a giggle.

"Sounds like college life is agreeing with you. How are you and Tony?"

"Umm… we're okay, I guess."

"That doesn't sound too convincing."

There was a long pause of silence before Kendra answered me. "Tony and I aren't seeing each other, Jenny."

"What? When did this happen?"

"A few weeks ago."

"I'm sorry, Kendra. If I had known, I would have called you sooner. What happened? I thought everything was going good between you two?"

"It was, or at least I thought it was, but it's hard when you're not going to the same school. We just drifted apart. To be honest, I could see it coming before we left for school. He was acting a little different then, and I guess I just didn't want to believe it. I thought we could work it out, you know? But it's okay. It was a mutual decision between the two of us, and we're still friends, good friends actually."

"Well that's good to hear, but I'm still sorry."

"How are you and Liam? Have you guys set the date yet?"

"We're fine and no, no date. If it was up to Liam we'd be eloping to Vegas."

"Ahh, Jenny, he is still such the romantic. I'm glad to hear things are better between you guys. You two had a rough summer."

"Thanks, Kendra." I hesitated. "Things are real good."

"Jen, what's wrong? I can hear something in your voice. Are you and Liam having problems?"

"No, nothing like that. We're just still going through some stuff... you know, with the accident."

"Still? What?"

"I can't really get into it. It's complicated."

"This is about Johnny, isn't it?"

I didn't answer. I didn't have to.

"You know I see Johnny every once in a while. He's always asking about you."

"You see him? Where?"

"He's going to school here, Jenny. Every time I run into him the first thing out of his mouth is if I have spoken to you. I don't know what kind of effect you have on guys, but you sure must be doing something right, especially when it comes to Liam and Johnny. I've never seen two guys totally flipped over one girl before in all my life."

"Kendra, that's not fair. And Johnny is not flipped over me, as you put it. We went through a lot together with the accident. There's just a connection between us."

"If you say so but I still think he's holding onto something, and I wouldn't necessarily call it a connection."

I didn't reply, not wanting to give her the satisfaction that she could be right.

"Jenny, why don't you come over next weekend for a visit? I could show you around campus and we could spend some much needed girl time together."

"I don't know, Kendra."

"Come on. It would be fun. Besides it sounds like you could use a girl's weekend."

"Well…."

"I'm not going to take no for an answer."

"Well okay, you're right. It sounds like fun. I'll be there next Friday night."

"Great. I'll see you then. And Jen?"

"Yeah?"

"I expect to hear what's bothering you then."

"We'll see," I said before hanging up the phone.

It was perfect timing. Liam was walking in the door.

"Hey, babe," he said as he swooped me in his arms, spinning me around.

"Whoa, what's this all about?" My mind tried to focus on the objects spinning around me.

"I just finished at Joe's." He was smiling ear to ear.

"What, Liam?" I said as I regained my balance.

"Joe accepted my offer. We're partners."

"You're kidding? That's great, Liam! I'm so happy for you."

"You mean happy for us. This is for both of us, babe." Liam again picked me up and started swinging me around the room. He only stopped to kiss me. His kiss was so emphatic that I found myself arching backwards.

"This is amazing, Liam, I can't believe it. My man the entrepreneur, I like how that sounds."

"I do too. We should celebrate." Liam gave me a slight grin as he squeezed me tighter to him. "You wanna go upstairs?"

"Yeah, I think a celebration is definitely in order," I said as he carried me up the stairs.

We slept well that night. Nothing disturbed either one of us. Liam didn't have his nightmare, and I wasn't awakened by his screaming.

Chapter Six
The Weekend

For a while, life seemed back to normal for us. Liam was showering me daily with his affection and spoiling me rotten as well. He seemed to have his focus back. Every morning he was up at the crack of dawn to help Grandpa with the horses before leaving for Joe's. But before his daily departure he always came in to kiss me goodbye and hand me a cup of coffee, most times accompanied with a lavender rose. I loved his rituals and never grew tired of them. I knew I was going to miss him when I visited Kendra--even though it was only a weekend trip--it would be the first time we had been apart since this summer. My only hope was that while I was away that Liam remained nightmare free.

It was late Wednesday when Liam picked me up from the store. My parents were still away, and I was helping Billy with payroll. Liam had been at the shop working most of the day on a '67 Camaro while Joe delivered a couple of motorcycles to some guy who lived in Glenville.

"Hello there, beautiful. How's my girl?" Liam said effervescently.

"Your girl is just fine. How are you?"

"Great now that I've got you. Are you hungry? Do you want to get something to eat?"

"No, I'm good. I'd rather just go back to the house."

"As always, your wish is my command," he said, leaving my driveway. He seemed unusually preoccupied as we drove, but his demeanor led me to believe that there was nothing to worry about.

"So did you have a good day today?"

"I did. Grandpa and I went to the bank to sign for the loan."

"So it's official?"

"It should all be legal within a few days, which had me thinking. Why don't we do something extra special this weekend to celebrate? You know maybe go somewhere alone."

"Oh Liam, I'd loved to, but did you forget, I was seeing Kendra this weekend?"

"Ah yes, the Glenville trip." He seemed truly let down.

"I don't have to go. I can see her anytime. This is much more important. I'll call her and just cancel."

"No, don't do that. You should see her. I know you miss hanging out with her, and besides, we can celebrate when you come back."

"Are you sure?"

"Yes, I'm positive. Besides, it'll be good for you. I'll miss you, but it'll just be that much better when you get back. We can celebrate then."

"You're really the best, do you know that?"

"Yeah, I've been told that a time or two before."

"At least you're not modest," I said, laughing. "And I promise, when I get home on Sunday we'll celebrate."

"Of course we will."

Friday came before I knew it. I must have been looking forward to the trip more than I thought as I eagerly packed my overnight bag. There was so much I wanted to tell Kendra and so much I wanted to know about her since she had left. I felt that I couldn't get to Glenville fast enough. Liam helped me pack my car, and with one more kiss and embrace from him, I was on my way. The hour drive seemed to take forever. By the time I finally arrived, it was already dark, but in the distance I could still see the college. Mostly the dormitories were in view, but I knew exactly where to go. I drove up the steep hill to find a Kendra waiting for me.

"Hey dawg, it's so good to see you. I thought you would never get here."

"Oh my God, it's so good to see you too, Kendra," I said as we hugged each other.

"Well come on, let's get your stuff and head up to my room."

Kendra lived on the third floor in a room she had to herself.

"This is nice. I see not much has changed." I tried to make through the mountain of clothes that kept me from reaching her bed. There were books, cd's, and take out boxes strewn haphazardly everywhere except where they should be.

"Yeah, I know it's a little messy."

"A little?" I said sarcastically.

"Well I never claimed to be a neat freak. Just move some stuff out of the way and put your things down. It doesn't matter where."

I dropped my bags where I stood and fell on Kendra's bed. Within minutes we were laughing and talking as if no time had passed.

"I miss doing this with you, Kendra. So much has happened since you left; I forgot how much we used to talk."

"You mean stuff with Liam?"

"Yeah, I guess."

"Like what? Is everything alright? I could tell something was wrong when we talked. Does it still have to do with that number eleven?"

"I wish. Then it might be easier to fix, or at least it would be me and not Liam."

"What do you mean by that?"

"I just mean there's still some stuff going on with him. Nothing between us though, we're fine."

"Like what? Is he having problems with his leg?"

"No. His leg is fine. I mean, he has a limp, but it's hardly even noticeable." I paused, reflecting on my decision to tell Kendra about Liam's nightmares. I knew he didn't want anybody to know about them, but I really didn't think he would care if I told my very best friend. Besides I needed to talk to someone about them before I went crazy.

"Liam would kill me if he knew I was telling you. You have to give me your solemn word that you won't repeat it."

"Jenny, I promise. What the hell is this about?"

"Well, it does have to do with the accident, and you were right when you asked if it involved Johnny."

"I knew it!"

"Liam's been having some bad dreams, Kendra, really bad ones, nightmares actually."

"Nightmares? What are they about?"

"The accident. It all revolves around what happened that night. He keeps seeing the same scene over and over again. I'm lying there next to him in the truck and screaming for him, but he can't find me. He can see me, but for some reason he can't reach me. I keep drifting farther and farther away from him. I'm covered in blood, and all I can do is yell for Liam as I try to find him. And then just when he thinks he has me, where he can touch me, I'm pulled away from him again, but this time someone picks me up." I paused watching for Kendra's reaction to this.

"Johnny?"

"Yeah."

"Oh my God, Jenny, that is twisted."

"It's been horrible, Kendra, and until just recently, he's been experiencing them every night."

"What happened to change things?"

"I moved in with him. He was so shaken by the visions that he had to make sure I was real. In the beginning I just watched Liam as he struggled with them. My first night I watched him as he wrestled with them, screaming out for me as I tried to wake him up. He would wake drenched in sweat and shaking in a horrible, frenzied manner. He really thinks these nightmares are trying to send him some sort of message, maybe that it's not over with Johnny."

"I thought you guys worked things out with him?"

"I thought so too. But Liam said he did that for me. He didn't really mean it. He said he wanted to be the bigger person, and he thought by saying he was forgiving Johnny things would turn around for him, but it's been the complete opposite. Liam has been a mess, and we haven't even seen Johnny since this summer. It's like Johnny has this invisible power over him, and he can't get rid of it."

"Are you sure Liam isn't just blowing this out of proportion?"

"I don't think so. Kendra, these nightmares are horrible. They're not your average bad dreams. He positively believes there's something behind them, and honestly, I do too. I've witnessed him going through them, and maybe if he only had one or two of them I wouldn't put too much thought into them, but they've happened so often, and they're so real to Liam. He can't seem to shake them."

"Well, Jenny, I hope he's able to stop having them. You guys have been through enough without adding something else to your plate."

"I agree."

"Hey, enough of this. You didn't come here just to sit in my room. Why don't I show you around? We could go downtown if you want or I could show you the campus. Although I will say, it's better to do that during the day."

"Whatever you want. I'm up for anything."

"I think we should go downtown. Some of my friends are going to be at this one bar. I could introduce you to them. They're a riot."

"Great, sounds like fun."

It didn't take us long to get ready. I felt like I should call Liam and tell him I made it in, but I was sure he was keeping himself busy at Joe's shop. I made a mental note to call him when we returned from downtown. The town was extremely busy upon our arrival. For such a small town, I couldn't believe how many kids were there. The streets were jam packed. Kendra and I could hardly walk side by side without being bumped by other people.

"I can't believe the crowds. Is it always like this?"

"Not always. But it is Friday night. Everyone is done with their classes, so they're all itching to let loose for a while. There's not much to do here besides going to the bars."

In a little over a month that Kendra had been away, I had seen a change in her. She was still the Kendra I had grown up with, but I saw her in a new light. She exuded a confidence that I hadn't seen in her before. Maybe it was the independence she had gained from leaving home, maybe it was the freedom she now had from being single again, or maybe it was always there and I just never noticed it. Whatever it was, Kendra was beaming with it. We walked for another block before arriving at a bar known as *The Dock,* appropriately named because it was right next to a large creek. Or more appropriately for the four foot bed of water that ran under the bar that could easily be seen by the broken boards that made up the front deck.

"This is nice, Kendra," I said somewhat cynically. "Do you need to take out a life insurance policy before entering?"

"Very funny. The place may be on the dilapidated side, but it's got character. You'll see. Come on."

I carefully stepped over the broken boards as Liam's voice echoed in my head. *"Be careful, Jenny, watch your step."* I couldn't help but wonder if anyone had slipped through the boards and fallen into the water. It wouldn't be that hard to do, especially if the person had been drunk. I was perfectly sober and was finding it difficult. Kendra was right though, inside *The Dock* did have character and lots of it. It was your basic college bar but there was a good vibe to the place. It was all laid out in a dark, weathered wood. The chandeliers that hung low from the discolored tiled ceiling were actual beer bottles, and on each one of them hung an eclectic assortment of colored bras.

"Interesting." I said, peering at the amusing light fixtures.

Kendra laughed. "Do you like it? If the bartender likes you he might ask you to volunteer your bra for his collection, but most of the time the girls give them up willingly. It's kinda like a trophy room. They see it as an honor to have their bra dangling from the lights."

"Really?"

"Yeah, most girls want their personal undergarments hanging on them."

"Where's yours?"

"I haven't given one up…yet." Kendra said as a boisterous laugh came out of her. "Come on, I see my friends." I saw three girls motioning with their hands for us to join them. "Jenny, I'd like to introduce you to Savannah Hardman, Lydia Miller, and Melanie Jarvis. Guys, this is Jenny King."

"Hi."

"Hello, nice to meet you," Melanie said first. "It's nice to finally meet Kendra's friend from home."

"Yes, definitely." Savannah and Lydia said agreeing.

"Thank you."

"Jen, these are my girls, the ones who took me under their wing and showed me the ropes."

"Oh really?"

"If it weren't for them, I'd still be lost."

"So I take it you guys aren't freshmen?"

"No. We're all sophomores." Melanie answered.

"Kendra's in our Liberal Arts class, and we're only a couple of doors down from each other in the dorms. We hit it off instantly. Your friend is a hoot. We've been having a blast ever since she arrived. She's the first at the party and the last to leave. Sometimes we can't keep up with her."

"Really?" I commented with genuine surprise. I'd known Kendra my entire life and never knew her to be such the party girl. She was always known to have a good time, but I was getting the impression that she was letting her hair down just a little bit more since she arrived at Glenville.

"Jen, they're making me sound like I'm a party animal. I'm not that bad. But I will admit that I am enjoying the college life."
"It sounds like it."

"How 'bout we get some drinks girls? We waited for you two to arrive. A round of beers for everybody?"

"Sure," Savannah said. "You do drink beer don't you, Jenny?" she asked me politely.

"Of course. Whatever you guys are having I'll have too."

"Great, I'll be right back."

Lydia arrived a couple minutes later, carrying with her a pitcher of beer and five chilled mugs on an old wooden tray.

"So, Kendra tells us that you're engaged," Melanie asked as her inquisitive body leaned closer to me from across our table.

"Yes I am. His name is Liam."

"Kendra says he's gorgeous."

"Yeah, I think so."

All three of the girls were staring at my left hand. Savannah was the first to ask. "Is that your engagement ring?"

I found myself twirling it around my finger, preoccupied with it as I succumbed to the barrage of questions.

"Yes."

Savannah took my left hand in hers. "It's beautiful. I've never seen a heart-shaped diamond before." As the other two also grabbed my hand and twirled my ring with their fingers.

"It belonged to his mom."

"He's real a sweetheart," Kendra added. I was sure the girls were wondering what I was thinking being so young and engaged already when in their eyes all that I should be thinking about is having a good time. I didn't feel the need to tell them that Liam and I were soul mates, that our love ran much deeper than any of them would ever understand and that we didn't need to wait any longer when we knew what we both wanted were each other. "If there were ever two soul mates in this world it would have to be Jenny and Liam. They were made for one another," Kendra continued.

I smiled politely as Kendra spoke. She could tell I was feeling uncomfortable, so her contribution to the conversation came as a welcome relief.

The awkward silence at our table was apparent; all five of us nervously drank our beer as we waited for someone to continue the conversation. Kendra was doing her best to make me feel comfortable but more than anything I was wishing I was home with Liam instead of being in this bar. And as fate would have it, as if he knew I needed him, he called me.

"I'll be right back." I grabbed my cell and headed outside.

"Hello."

"Hey babe, how's my girl?"

"I'm good. I miss you." That was the understatement of the year. I had never felt more alone with a group of people than I did right then. Even with Kendra things didn't seem the same.

"I miss you too. Are you having fun?"

"Yeah," I lied.

"Are you sure?" Liam could tell.

"Yeah, really I am. Kendra and I are downtown right now at this bar called *The Dock*, having a beer with some of her girlfriends."

"You're at *The Dock?* Jenny, that's nothing more than a meat market. It's a pick-up joint."

"Liam, don't be silly. We're just having a few beers with some of her friends. That's all. And besides no one has even given me the time of the day. Don't worry so much. I can handle myself."

"I know you can, it's the guy who wants to pick you up that I'm concerned about. I've been there, Jen. I know what kind of place it is. Just be careful, okay? For me."

"Always, and if you ask me, you're sounding a little jealous. I like it. Maybe this is good for us."

"Not funny, Jen. And of course I'm jealous. I'll be the first to admit it. You're gorgeous and like I've always told you, I see how guys watch you. I can be there in less than an hour if you just say the word."

"That's not necessary. I'm fine. Kendra and I are having fun. We've been doing a lot of catching up."

"Well, I just wanted to make sure you arrived safely. You didn't have any problems getting there, did you?"

"No, none at all. What are you doing?"

"I'm still at Joe's. We're just finishing up. Parker and I are going over to his house and have a couple of beers."

"Alright. I'll see you Sunday. Love you."

"Love you more. Be careful and remember what I said."

"I will. See you soon."

It was cute to hear Liam. I knew he cared for me but it was always good to hear the jealousy in his voice.

"Is everything okay?" Kendra said, coming up from behind.

"Yeah. Liam was just checking that I made it here okay. I should have called him when I first arrived."

"Well, the girls are hooking up with some guys on the dance floor. I figured now would be as good a time as any to get out of here."

"We don't have to leave, Kendra. I mean if you're not ready we can still stay a while."

"Are you sure? I know it was a little uncomfortable for you earlier when they were playing twenty questions with you. I didn't think they were going to grill you so much."

"It's fine, really. I'd be asking questions if I were them. Anyway, I really didn't mind."

"I tell you what, let's go back in and have one more beer, and then we'll call it a night. We've got the whole weekend; we don't have to do everything tonight."

"Sounds good."

Kendra was right. Melanie, Savannah, and Lydia were on the dance floor swaying to the beat of some country crooner as their partners grinded their bodies. We ordered a couple more drinks while we enjoyed watching the blatant display of public ogling that was going on the dance floor.

"So, Kendra, it seems like you really like it here."

"Yeah, I like it a lot, Jen. Not just this part. I really enjoy my classes too. Although I will admit, I should go home soon. I haven't been back to Spencer since I left. Mom and Dad have been asking me to come home for the past couple of weeks. I figured I would wait until the Black Walnut Festival. It's only a couple of weeks away."

"I totally forgot about the festival. Do you realize that Liam and I are coming up to our one year anniversary since we met?"

"It's been a year already for you two? In some ways, it seems like you guys have been together for a lot longer."

"Yeah, I know what you mean. You know, I think with everything that's been going on, our anniversary was the last thing on either one of our minds. I can almost guarantee that Liam hasn't remembered it."

"You don't think? He's been pretty thoughtful. I wouldn't put it past him."

"I know. But he hasn't said anything, and with the nightmares preoccupying his thoughts, I can't imagine he's thought about it."

"I bet he has, Jenny. Are you ready to go?"

"Whenever you are."

We took a couple more sips of our beers, paid the waitress, and waved goodbye to Kendra's friends, who were now all involved in a line dance that stretched easily over thirty people long.

"Your friends are nice. I'm glad I met them."

We headed for the front door when we were almost knocked down by a group of guys stumbling in.

"Sorry, are you okay?"

"Fine. Thank you." I dusted myself off and proceeded to leave when I felt myself being intentionally turned around.

"Jenny, is that you?"

"Oh my God, Johnny!"

We both stood there like statues for the longest time staring at one another, until Johnny finally made the first move and warmly but hesitantly gave me a hug. "I can't believe it's you."

"I can't believe it's you either."

"What are you doing here, Jenny?"

"I came over to spend the weekend with Kendra."

"Hi, Johnny," Kendra said as she stood in the background.

"Hey," he said politely while his focus remained on me.

"Well, how are you? How are things going?"

"Good. Really good, Johnny." We still kept staring at one another as though we both had found a long lost friend. I honestly didn't think I would ever see Johnny again and now he was standing in front of me. We continued our staring contest, both of us still in shock.

"Well, I should go in. My friends are waiting for me. It's so good to see you, Jenny."

"It's good to see you too."

"Tell Liam hi for me, okay?"

"I will."

"Well see ya round, Jenny. Bye Kendra."

"Bye, Johnny."

Johnny walked inside the bar. That familiar yet anxious feeling came over me as I saw the door close behind him. The same feeling I felt on my porch when he came to see me this summer. He said goodbye to me that day too as if it would be the last time I would ever see his face. It didn't sit well with me then, and it didn't sit well with me again.

"Jenny, you okay?"

"Yeah, I'm fine. Let's go."

I was still in my own little world as we walked back to the dormitories. Kendra talked the entire time, but I didn't hear one word she said. All I could think about was running into Johnny. I wished to God that I could have spent more time with him tonight. To talk to him, to see what he's been up to, anything, I thought, as long as we could carry on a conversation together. I had realized in that brief but significant encounter just how important he was to me, not as a love interest but as the friend I missed. I didn't consider Johnny the enemy anymore. I wanted to be his friend, but I knew that would never be the case as long as Liam felt the way he did. And for that reason and that reason alone, I knew that I could never maintain a friendship with Johnny, ever. I had to keep this to myself. I didn't even feel like I could share this with Kendra. Maybe last year I could have, but not now. She had changed. No, this would have to be my little secret, maybe forever. To be friends with Johnny would only cause problems for Liam and me. It wouldn't be worth it, especially with what Liam was enduring.

We were already in Kendra's room before I realized it.

"So what do you think? Should I go, Jenny?"

"Huh?" I asked.

I hadn't a clue as to what she was talking about.

"To the dance with Garrett."

"Who's Garrett?"

"Garrett Fisher. I just told you about him. He's the guy in my Algebra class who asked me to Glenville's homecoming dance. Didn't you hear anything I just said to you? I've been telling you about him for the past twenty minutes."

"I'm sorry, Kendra. I must have spaced out there for a while. You should go with him. Sounds like a good time." I said trying to sound mollifying. It was a lame gesture. I didn't even believe it.

"You're still thinking about Johnny aren't you?"

"No, why would you ask that?"

"Because you've been in this funk ever since you saw him. Do you want to go back downtown?"

"Of course not." Secretly I did.

"It just was weird to run into him, that's all. I mean I never thought I would see him again. When we said goodbye over the summer, I thought that was it. So it was just strange to run into him."

"Well, he sure seemed happy to have run into you."

"He was? Do you really think so?"

"He was beaming from ear to ear. I could tell he didn't want to stop talking to you. If his buddies hadn't been calling him to go inside, I can guarantee the two of you would still be standing down there on that broken deck talking. I know he still has a thing for you. I don't care what he told you over the summer. I've seen the look he gives you, and it's the same one he's always given you. I'd be careful, Jen, unless you want the attention. It all makes sense now, why he's always asking about you."

"What is that supposed to mean, Kendra?"

"Just that if you don't watch your step, you're going to have Johnny back in your life. I don't think that's going to go over too well with Liam, especially after what you told me."

"I didn't do anything. It's not my fault we ran into each another. It wasn't like it was planned or anything. What do you want me to do? Become a hermit so I avoid confrontation altogether? I'm not starting anything. We just said hi. What's wrong with that?"

"You don't owe me an explanation, but I'm just telling you what I'm seeing. I told you that when I see Johnny the very first thing out of his mouth is you. And by the way he was acting tonight, he was ecstatic to have ran into you. I'm just saying, be careful. Whether you think it's platonic or not, I think Johnny has other ideas. And I don't think he really cares if you're engaged to Liam or not. Believe me, if he saw his chance, especially here where Liam isn't even near you, Johnny wouldn't even hesitate to jump on you, and I mean that literally!"

I listened to Kendra, but I didn't want to believe her. I didn't want her to be right. That part of my life was over. It had to be. I was engaged to Liam, and that's who I loved. Besides, with Liam's nightmares about Johnny, this could make them a little too real. I did realize that I wanted Johnny in my life too, but as a friend. Kendra was right, and I knew it; I always knew it. We could never carry on a friendship no matter how civil we were to one another. It would never be possible. Liam wouldn't allow it, and I couldn't do it behind Liam's back either.

Kendra and I spent the rest of the evening on her bed, and we talked until morning. She told me how she loved college life and what really happened between her and Tony: nothing more than they both had decided they wanted to date other people. Tony was at WVU, and with Kendra here, it was making it next to impossible for them to carry on their relationship. It had been a mutual decision between the two of them. I tried to listen with open and intentional ears. Of course she wanted to know more about me and my life since she had left. I did tell her how Liam was more than ready to elope to Vegas; all I had to do was say the word. She continued to remind me how much he loved me and didn't hesitate to tell me that I should keep my distance from Johnny, something I thought would be easy to do since this was the first time I saw him in months. He had begun a new life. Our brief encounter was nothing more than that, an encounter, but I was feeling guilty for thinking about Johnny so much. In fact, my entire visit consisted of me trying to seem enthused about Kendra's new college life while I kept looking over my shoulder in hopes of seeing Johnny one more time.

By Sunday afternoon, I was more than ready to go home. I packed my car and gathered some papers on the school, my other reason for visiting. But more importantly, I was eager to leave because I was missing Liam and knew by leaving I would stop thinking about Johnny, or at least I hoped. The entire visit seemed to consume me with thoughts of him. I now wished we had never run into one another. In all honesty, I couldn't leave Glenville fast enough. All I could think about was collapsing into Liam's arms.

"It was so good seeing you, girl." We hugged each other tightly.

"Definitely. I missed you."

"I'll see you when I come home, okay?"

"You better, Kendra. Don't be a stranger."

We waved goodbye. In my rearview mirror, I saw Kendra run towards the door. She was going to Melanie's room to get ready for a frat party. College life definitely agreed with her.

My mind was racing as I thought about Liam's warm body touching mine. He was all I needed, and the hour drive between us was almost too long. I wanted to forget all about this weekend.

The weather wasn't helping my feelings either. It was raining a slow drizzle, not enough for the full wiper use but enough that I needed to use them intermittently to clear the droplets that easily rested on my windshield. And no matter how I tried to concentrate on the road ahead and on Liam, my thoughts continued to go back to Johnny. I didn't understand why he was on my mind so much. It wasn't like we had spent any time together. It was two minutes, if that, just enough to remind me how important he still was to me. I had to move on though, but that was harder than I thought. Maybe I could invite him to our wedding, I thought. No, that would be the worst thing I could do. It would be better to just leave well enough alone.

As I continued my drive, I began to feel relieved at my decision to stop thinking about Johnny, but that was soon replaced with fear as I heard a loud pop resonating from my car. A sound so loud and foreign to me that I gripped the steering wheel tightly as I tried to figure out what the hell was happening. The popping sound turned into a deafening rumble noise as I felt the car veer towards the center of the road. With all my strength, I tried to keep my car under control as visions of the accident flashed through my head.

"Not again. Please dear God, help me through this. Not again, please, not again." I prayed as I forcibly manipulated my steering wheel. I could feel the weight of the car lean to one side as I slowly came to a relieving stop. The rain was steady now and to make matters worse, it was pitch black outside, and I was only inches off of the road in the middle of a huge curve. I was a target waiting to get hit. I walked around to the rear, everything looked fine, but as I made my way to the front, I noticed that the car was leaning to the right. I took my flashlight and shined the light down on my right, front tire. It was flatter than a pancake. "Great," I thought. Of all people to get a flat tire, it would have to be me. I didn't even know how to hammer a nail into a board, and now I was going to have to deal with a flat tire.

I looked around. There was nothing for what looked like miles; it was just me, an open road, and a flat tire. My car seemed to pick the most desolate of places to fail on me. I couldn't even see a barn nearby much less a house. The only visible signs of life were pieces of litter that cluttered the ground around me. I sighed heavily as I pondered my next move. There was no way in hell I would be able to fix this on my own, so I did what any girlfriend with a boyfriend who could fix cars would do. I called Liam. His cell rang and rang. By the fifth try, I had concluded that either his phone was dead or he wasn't near it. I was becoming angry at him for not being there for my beck and call. Didn't he think that I might need to talk to him while I was on the road? He told me to be careful; he should have his phone with him just for this reason. I realized how stupid I sounded to myself. Blaming Liam for not answering his phone wasn't going to help me. I tried Joe's, hoping he or Tony would answer, but my attempt was futile. It looked like I was stuck. I opened my trunk and looked at the extra tire. It was intimidating to me, almost mocking me as it too knew I couldn't do what was being asked of me. I wanted to scream but instead settled on crying. I stared at my phone trying to will it to ring. I left five messages for Liam and three at Joe's. Why in the hell wasn't somebody answering their damn phone? I could call Kendra, but she didn't even own a car.

I felt completely helpless as I continued my crying fit. At this point, I was just tired and wanted to get home. The pity party I was throwing myself wasn't indulging me at all. I had watched Liam a thousand times change a tire on his truck. I could do this. I knew I could; I just had to have confidence in myself, that's all. I would just go through the motions with him, visualizing the step by step procedures that he did. With a huge sigh and prayer, I reopened my trunk and proceeded to do the impossible.

For the next hour, I was able to accomplish nothing more than smashing my right thumb and covering my legs in wet mud after losing my balance as I tried to poise myself while reading the car manual. I was pathetic. I had begun to give up all hope when in the near distance I could hear the sound of a loud motor as it came closer to me. Within seconds the headlights were shining my way, giving light to my situation. The truck's driver had seen me and carefully slowed down and pulled over behind me. I prayed to God that whoever was behind the wheel was not a serial killer but a friendly person who only wanted to show his kindness and charity towards me. I had been told too many stories by my parents about girls who had turned into victims when it came to having a stranger give them a ride or help them in times of their distress. I waited patiently but hesitantly as the driver proceeded to get out of his truck, the bright lights blinding me from distinguishing who he was.

"Is everything okay?" he asked.

"No. I have a flat tire."

"Well, let me take a look at it," he said as he came closer. He was shielding his face with his hand as to keep the rain from hitting it. I backed up allowing myself space between the two of us, just in case his intentions were not admirable. I still couldn't see him clearly. The lights on his truck were glaring down on us, blinding my view of him. He bent down and assessed the damage to my car.

"Yeah, I would say you were right. Looks like you ran over a nail. Let me get my jack." He raised himself up from the crouching position.

We both walked back to my trunk. I tightened my grip on my flashlight, just in case I needed to use it as a weapon. Maybe I was being a little overly cautious, but it was raining and very dark, and I felt very vulnerable without Liam by my side.

"The tire's in…"

I didn't finish. My flashlight dropped from my hand as the stranger's face came into my view.

Chapter Seven
Five More Minutes

"Johnny?"

"Jenny?"

"I can't believe it's you. I was afraid you might be some deranged lunatic."

"Well, lucky for you, I'm not. What happened?"

"I don't know exactly. I was driving home when I heard a loud pop. The car veered towards the middle of the road, so I pulled over here. That's when I realized I had a flat tire."

"How long have you been here?"

"I'm not sure, a while, though."

"Why didn't you call Liam?"

"I have, but he isn't answering his phone. I've even called Joe's shop, but there doesn't seem to be anybody there either."

"What about your parents?"

"They're in Myrtle Beach. I don't think they could help me right now even if they wanted to."

"Well, it's a good thing I showed up. Sounds like you could have been here all night."

"Yeah, I guess. I'm really relieved to see you. I definitely didn't want to be stranded here."

Johnny stared at me while holding the jack in his hand. If he only knew how happy I was that he was there. He rose from his knelt position and gave me a long and heartfelt hug just like he had at *The Dock*. I could have held on to him forever at that moment. It seemed surreal that it would be him to come to my rescue. He seemed to do that a lot. No matter what the circumstance, Johnny always seemed to have my back and knew when I was in distress, a gift I wondered if he had received from his mom. In reality, I wanted to forget about the flat tire and just talk to him, to continue where we had left off on Friday night. I wanted to be near him and find out what his world was like now. So much had happened in our lives that had connected us. I didn't want to lose that connection. Now that I had him to myself, for at least a while, I wanted to take full advantage of it.

"Well, let me see if I can get you back on the road. I'm sure Liam will be wondering where you are."

I would have thought so too, especially after I left him five messages. I should have been home by now. It didn't help to mull over that though. In no time, Johnny would have my tire replaced, and I would be on my way. My only hope was that he would take his good sweet time. After twenty minutes or so, the rain began pouring in buckets. I could tell Johnny was working fervently in trying to change the tire despite the duress of the weather. He seemed frustrated.

"Jen, I think you're out of luck with this spare tire. It has a hole in it."

"You're kidding? Now what am I supposed to do?"

"Well, you can't stay here by yourself. Let me take you home. You can have Liam drive you out here tomorrow to pick up your car."

I hesitated, knowing what that meant, but there was no other choice, unless I wanted to stay there all night. I knew Liam wouldn't be happy with Johnny bringing me home either, even if it was out of the kindness of his heart. Liam would never see that. In his eyes, he would think that Johnny intentionally planned this. Only Liam would think something so absurd and ridiculous, but our past history with Johnny led him to think no other way.

"You're not answering me, Jenny."

"Huh? Oh, I'm sorry, Johnny. I was just thinking."

"Thinking about what? How Liam might react when he finds out that it's me bringing you home?"

I smiled apologetically at him. "Yeah, that's exactly what I'm thinking. I know it sounds ridiculous, but I know how Liam is going to react. He's not going to be happy with your generosity. If it was anybody else..."

"I get it, Jen. If it was anybody else but me. Right?"

I just nodded my head.

Johnny took a deep breath. I could tell his frustration was growing this time over me and not the hole in the spare. "Look, I'm not going to leave you here by yourself, so either you agree on letting me take you home or we both sit here until the sun comes up, but either way you're not getting rid of me. I'm here to help, and Liam is just going to have to see it that way. It's too dangerous. He's just going to have to understand. He's not going to get mad over this. I know he wouldn't want you here by yourself. It'll be fine."

If Johnny only knew what I knew, I thought to myself.

"Well, okay."

Liam couldn't get mad over this, I continued to think as I tried to justify it. *I mean, he wouldn't want me to stay here in the middle of nowhere, and since I couldn't reach him, I think he would be relieved knowing Johnny was here for me. Yeah, keep trying to convince yourself of that, Jenny.*

"Are we going or not?" Johnny asked.

"We're going, just let me grab my bags."

"Here, I'll help you."

Johnny threw my overnight bag in the back of his truck and hastily wiped down my seat. "Here," he said as he helped me in. "Sorry for the mess. I wasn't expecting any company with me tonight."

"No need to apologize. It's fine. Believe me, I've seen a lot worse."

The rain was relentless as it continued its deluge on us. Johnny ran to his side and hopped in. He instinctively started shaking his head back and forth vigorously as the pellets of water flew from his head and onto me.

"Oh, sorry, I didn't mean for that to happen."

"It's okay; it wasn't like I was dry to begin with."

We both started laughing as we realized how wet and ridiculous we looked. I grabbed the towel to dry myself off.

"Here, let me help you," he said softly.

He took the towel and began to dry my face, our hands touching as we both clutched it. The look he gave me made me turn away instantly. It was the same look Liam had given me a million times. Johnny let go of the towel as it fell into my lap, my hand still holding onto it.

"Let me turn on some heat before we both catch our death."

He pulled out of our makeshift parking spot, and we continued on our way to Spencer. The heat from his truck was finally billowing forth from the vents, and it felt good as it hit my body.

"Are you getting warmer?"

"Yes, thank you."

The silence was deafening as he drove. My heart beat out of my chest as I tried to focus on the outlines of scenery that we passed. Many times I had thought about Johnny and wanted to call him. He had turned from someone I completely despised and hated to a friend I couldn't get out of my mind. The tables had turned after the accident. The only thing was Liam; his feelings hadn't changed one bit. Well, maybe they had. Liam hated Johnny even more.

"So, where am I taking you when we get into Spencer?"

"Umm, Liam's."

"Oh, okay."

I remained quiet, only glancing over at Johnny occasionally.

"You know Jen, it's okay to talk to me. I'm not going to bite."

"I'm sorry, Johnny. I didn't mean to be so quiet, but you have to admit, after everything that has happened between us, the irony here is pretty funny."

"Irony?"

"For months you tried to ask me out or give me a ride, and I always refused you, and now here I am finally in your truck."

"Wow, I guess you're right. Maybe I should have sabotaged your car months ago if I knew that's what it would take to get you in here. This was too easy," Johnny said with a smile.

"Very funny."

I nervously played with my hands, a habit I developed since the accident, twisting my engagement ring around my finger over and over again.

"Have you and Liam picked a date?" Johnny glanced down at my left hand.

"A date?"

"Yes, to get married."

"No not yet." I consciously stopped twisting my ring.

"Liam wants to get married soon. He would elope tonight if I just said the word. But I can't do that to my family or to Grandpa Mack."

"Oh I see. Well that doesn't surprise me. I knew he was ready last year to marry you. How are things with him?"

"He's good. He's been busy with Joe at his shop. He just became partners with him."

"You're kidding? You know I heard a rumor about that. I knew he was spending a lot of time there. I never thought he was seriously interested in becoming partners with Joe, though."

"Well, it was kind of Joe's idea. He brought it up months ago, it was before the accident. I knew it was only a matter of time before Liam accepted his offer."

Johnny didn't respond to my last comment.

"So, how's your mom? Is her shop doing well?"

"The shop is going really well, it's keeping her busy. You wouldn't believe how many people come to her for advice."

"I think I can. She's really gifted at what she does; it doesn't surprise me at all that her shop is a success."

"She's got customers coming from all over. Asking her everything from will they ever be married to what number they should be playing in the lottery. It's a little insane if you want my honest opinion."

"Sounds like she's busy."

"Extremely. I try to help her on the nights I don't have class."

"Help her? Like, give readings and stuff?" I asked, intrigued.

"Hell no. I leave that nonsense to Mom. I'm considered the stock boy. I take care of the maintenance for her: carrying heavy boxes, moving furniture around, that kind of shit, the manual work."

"Oh I see. What about your dad? Does he help?"

"Not really. My parents are going through a bad time right now."

"I'm sorry to hear that."

"It's okay, you didn't know. It's actually been going on for a while. I think they might be getting a divorce. Dad hardly comes home anymore and when he does he makes himself absent from Mom."

"I don't know what to say except that I'm really sorry."

"There's nothing to say. Honestly, I think they would both be better off if they were to get a divorce. They haven't been happy for years, which is one of the reasons why Mom wanted to move back to Spencer. She was hoping that being back in her hometown would help, but I think it's only made things worse."

"I'm still sorry. I like your Mom a lot. I hope things work out for her and for you."

"Thanks. She likes you too. She still asks about you all the time. You should stop in and see her. She would love that. Between you and me, she still keeps track of your spiritual numbers, you know, your eleven."

"She does?"

"Yeah, especially after the accident. She was reading and doing all these chants and charts, she tried to send you positive energy as she puts it. She wanted your aura to be blessed."

"I'm flattered. And I will stop by and see her; it's just been really busy for me, that's all."

"Jen, you can tell me the truth."

"The truth?"

"I'm sure the reason why you haven't been to see my mom is because of Liam. I know he wouldn't be too thrilled if he knew you were patronizing my mom's shop."

I didn't say anything, but I didn't have to. Like his mom, Johnny had the innate ability to read me like a book. I don't know how but Johnny knew me.

We continued to make idle chit chat, but it didn't help. I still felt weird being in Johnny's truck. Even though it was all perfectly innocent, I felt like I was cheating on Liam. I nervously played with my ring again as Johnny hummed along to the radio.

"Jen, can I ask you something?"

"Sure."

"Are you happy?"

"Excuse me?"

"Are you happy?"

"Of course I'm happy. Why do you ask?"

"I don't mean in the literal sense. I'm talking about you and Liam. Remember our visit this summer, on your porch?"

"Yeah."

"Do you remember what I said to you?"

"I think. Well, a little bit of it. What part do you mean?"

"I told you that you would always hold a special place in my heart. I wrote that on your cast. Do you remember that?"

"Yes, I do remember."

"I meant that, meant it with all my heart." He paused. "I still think about you a lot. Maybe I shouldn't, but I do." His warm hand glided over to mine. My eyes went to them as they touched each other. I could not look at Johnny. I kept thinking about Liam telling me about Johnny confessing his feelings for me in the hospital. I could tell by Johnny's demeanor that Liam was right. This wasn't over for him. I didn't know what to do. I couldn't lead him on. I had to make sure Johnny knew that my feelings for him were only platonic.

"You know, it's just that we've been through so much with each other in such a short amount of time, and we really don't know one another. But it feels like I've known you my entire life. I feel connected to you, and I know it's probably something you don't want to hear, but it's true."

"Johnny..."

"I know what you're going to say: You're in love with Liam and I need to realize that and move on. I know, Jen. But you can't tell me that you don't feel something for me. Even a little bit? I mean, I can tell every time we're together, the few times those have been, that there's something between us."

"I do feel something between us, but it's totally different for me. My feelings for you stem from gratitude and appreciation. There is a love there, but it's not the same way you feel. I'm sorry." I lowered my head ashamed for saying that, knowing that wasn't what Johnny wanted to hear from me.

"There's no need for an apology, Jenny."

"You won't give up, will you?"

"I guess not. You know after I saw you this summer I had all intentions of leaving Spencer and never looking back. I didn't want to be near any place or anything that would remind me of you. I used to sit in my truck and just think about how things could have been for us if Liam wasn't in the picture. But then I realized I was just wasting my time. My friends tried to help me as much as possible. I even moved in with Jake. My mom would talk about you all the time, and I couldn't stand it anymore. I know that sounds mean, but I needed to clear my head of you and I couldn't do that if I was still living at home. I thought being with Jake would help, but it didn't. I lived with him for about a month before I found an apartment in Glenville. I signed up for some classes and made some new friends. I'm trying to move on. That was until this past Friday night when I saw you at *The Dock*. Jenny, all those feelings I thought I had gotten rid of, resurfaced. I can't begin to tell you how hard it was for me to walk away from you Friday night. I saw my opportunity to be with you and all I could do was let it slip by. I couldn't allow myself to go there. Not again. The past few months my entire existence has been focused on forgetting you, and all that flew out the window in one night. When you and Kendra left the bar I watched from the inside, I couldn't stand to see you disappear, so instead of staying with my friends like I should have done, I instead followed you."

"You did? I never saw you."

"I wouldn't let you. I stayed far enough back that you never would have seen me. I just wanted to see you, keep your image fresh in my head. I didn't realize how much I had missed you until then. I know you're engaged to Liam. Believe me, the entire world knows it. And I don't mean to be out of line by talking to you like this, but I think there was a reason that brought us together tonight. I think I was supposed to be here to help you."

"Johnny, that's crazy. It's just a coincidence that it was you."

"Is it? Shouldn't Liam have been the one to be here? You said you called him five times, you even called Joe's. No one was able to help you but me. I think I was meant to be the one. I'm not saying it's any more than that, I just mean I think we need to be in each other's lives. I think fate had something to do with it. I think someone or something realized that we needed to be a part of each other's lives and decided that tonight would be that night. Maybe your flat tire was just a ruse so I could be here for you. I wasn't even supposed to be coming into Spencer tonight. I had plans with some friends, but at the last minute I decided to change them. You can't tell me that's a coincidence."

"You're beginning to sound like your mom."

"Maybe I am. You can't live with someone like her for eighteen years of your life without having some stuff rub off on you. I know how Liam feels about me. I've known from the beginning. And I can't blame him, but I can't help how I feel. I know this summer when we tried to patch things up between the two of us, it wasn't real. We've been friends for most of our lives and I could tell he wasn't sincere, and to be quite honest, I think he could tell I wasn't either. I've come to grips that Liam and I are never going to be friends again. I've lost a friend in him and it's my fault. I've learned to accept that, but I can't accept not having you in my life. I tried, Jenny, and seeing you this weekend made me realize I can't do it."

"Johnny, you're asking something of me I can't do."

"I'm not asking anything of you that I don't think you can do. I just want us to be friends, Jenny. I want to be there for you, like tonight. I want to know that I can call you once in a while, even if it's just to shoot the breeze." Johnny pulled off the road without me realizing it. This time he placed both of his hands on mine.

"Jenny, please tell me you want this too."

"Johnny, you're right. You do mean a lot to me. Maybe more than I'm willing to admit. But having even just a platonic friendship with you would kill Liam. I don't think you realize how much anger he still harbors over you."

"I understand. But I want to be a part of your life even if we have to keep it a secret. If that's the only way I can see you, then I'm willing to do that. Hell, Jenny, I know what I'm asking from you, but in my eyes just having the chance to talk to you every once in a while would mean the world to me. I know it might not matter to you, but it sure as hell matters to me."

"Yes, it does matter, Johnny. You matter, you really do. But it doesn't change anything. You'll always mean something to me, but it can never be any more than just friends between us and I really don't even think that's even going to be possible. I love Liam."

"Just friends, Jenny." Johnny scoffed.

"Johnny, please don't do this."

"You're right. I'll stop. I'm sorry. We should just go. It's getting late anyway. I'm sure Liam is wondering where you are. But before we leave, please think about what I've said. Try to keep an open mind about it, who knows if we'll ever have this opportunity to be alone again. I want to be there for you; I'm not going away. I can't, especially after seeing you again, this weekend confirmed it for me." Johnny leaned in closer to me. I felt myself leaning in to him too, without realizing it. There was a dead silence surrounding us except for the torrential rain that continued to plummet down from the darkened skies as it hit his truck with a violent force. "I'm always going to be the bad guy; I've come to accept that. Liam and I lost something last spring and we'll never have the friendship we once did. It's a shame, we were good friends at one point, but that's over. It's the end of a chapter." He paused again as he stared at the stretch of road in front of us. "But I'm okay with that. You learn to deal with that kind of shit. I just want you to know that I'm here for you like I've always been. You can't tell me that there haven't been times when you wish you could talk to somebody. Let me be that somebody, Jenny."

"You know that's next to impossible, Johnny."

"I don't think so, or I wouldn't be saying it. You need someone to talk to besides Liam. I know you have your family and friends, but I know for a fact that's even changed."

He was even closer to me now; he had the instinctive ability to sneak up on me even with me staring him in the face.

"I miss you." The words poetically fell from his mouth.

"Johnny, we didn't even have a relationship for you to miss, and what we did have was filled with anger. How can you say you miss me when we didn't spend enough time together to form anything between us?"

"You're right, we didn't spend a lot of quality time together, but we did spend time together. I count every second I've been near you as time spent with you. Do you forget the times I worked at your dad's store or even at school? They may not have been the best of times, but I felt very fortunate to have them because you were a part of them."

"How can you say that? Except for maybe the beginning when we first met, I can't recall one time that I didn't loathe the very ground you walked on."

"I believe anger can be the highest form of flattery someone can give another person."

"You are not making a bit of sense. How can you interpret my anger as anything close to flattery? I despised you back then."

"Did you, Jenny? Really, truly, honestly, did you? Can't you be honest with yourself and me and at least admit that some of that anger you built up against me was your way of masking your true feelings? It's just you and me right now, nobody else. You don't have to say what you think is the right thing to say because you're afraid of what Liam might say if he heard you. There's nobody here but us; you can be honest with yourself and with me. I know I came on strong, but I felt something between us and it wasn't anger. And I know you felt it too, especially our kiss in your dad's office."

Johnny had stirred emotions in me that I didn't want to admit, but it wasn't my nature to feel something for someone else when I was completely in love with Liam. But sitting with him, I knew I harbored something much deeper.

"Everything you've said does mean something, but you know as well as I do that nothing can stem from this. There can never be a you-and-me in that regard. This would be easy if Liam wasn't in the picture, but he is, and no matter how I feel about you, I can't let it take over and ruin what I have with him. I just can't. I love Liam too much." I lowered my face into my hands as I tried to cover the tears.

"Jen, I'm sorry. I didn't mean to make you cry."

"It's okay. Don't be sorry. I'm sorry that things can't be different between us. I would love to have what you are offering me, but if Liam ever found out, I don't even want to think what he might do. His feelings towards you have only gotten worse."

"I hate seeing you upset like this. If you want me to stay out of your life, I guess I will, just say the word. But honestly, Jenny I don't think you do. I promise you, I won't interfere if you don't want me too, but I won't stop believing in us. I'm not taking back anything I've said. And furthermore, I will be here for you. And if you never take me up on that offer then I won't be offended or hurt. But if you do need me, Jenny please know that I'll be there for you in a heartbeat. All you have to do is say the word."

"Thank you, Johnny."

He cautiously leaned in even closer to me and gently kissed me on the lips. I didn't resist him. He was being the gentleman, knowing that going any further would cross boundaries he knew I wouldn't allow him to cross.

"You do have the best kisses, Jenny."

"Johnny."

"I know, I know. I'm just stating the obvious."

We had been sitting there for over an hour. I was surprised by how fast the time had gone by, but not nearly as surprised as my not having heard from Liam. I should have been back in Spencer hours ago. I blew it off, but I knew I was just making excuses. I put my head down as I played with my ring.

"Johnny, just for the record, I am happy. I love Liam with all of my heart. He's always been the one, and now more than ever, he needs me. But it does hurt me to know that because of our history, our future will be dictated by our past actions. Sometimes forgiveness isn't possible, and in Liam's case, I think that's true. And because of that and because of my love for him, I have to stand by him. You were the one I despised, loathed to be more adequate. But after the accident, what you did for me, it made me think differently about you. That scares me, Johnny. My feelings for you have to stay within me, for Liam's sake and possibly mine as well.

"Jenny, can you answer me one more question?"

"Sure." I was nervous.

"Do you think if the situation had been different, if maybe the stars had aligned more in my favor instead of Liam's, you would have given me a chance?"

I remained quiet, not knowing how in the hell to answer. "That's not a fair question. I mean how am I supposed to answer that?"

"With your heart."

"I can't give you an answer."

"Can't, Jenny? Or won't? Even though you say you can't answer me, I think I know your answer. Your hesitation gives more of an answer than you think."

Johnny put the truck back into drive and headed towards Spencer. Before I knew it, the skyline of the town crested before us. It was late, really late. I still hadn't heard from Liam. I was somewhat miffed, wondering why the guy who I had just defended with my love and loyalty didn't have the decency to call me to see where I was. At the red light, I stared blankly at the street. I was clouded with thoughts of Johnny and his impending presence in my life, our conversation going over and over in my head. Silence can be a blessing or an enemy. In my case, it was the latter. The less that was said between Johnny and I the more I thought about us and not Liam. Johnny's thoughts and persuasive words were causing me to second guess myself. Liam was my life. But since the accident, everything was an uphill battle, a struggle. The good times were wonderful but getting to them seemed more work than ever before. We were able to move on from the events that had forsaken our perfect world, or so I thought. The eleven we had decided was a good thing, showing us our path, a path that we were on together.

But why was Johnny on this path too? The eleven was apparent with him too, that's what bothered me. People do come into our life for a reason. I knew why Liam's was in mine, but why was Johnny? Our time was over, wasn't it? It would be so easy to go to Gertie and ask for help, but I couldn't. She was the devil's advocate. I felt like I was being pulled in opposite directions until my body gave in and fell apart. I looked over at Johnny. He was staring straight ahead, his right hand was down next to mine, as if it was waiting for me to place mine on top of his this time. His moves were always so bold and daring. He was always sure of himself, an attitude that some might describe as cocky and arrogant. I didn't dare move from my position; any sudden change would attract attention, and right now, I didn't want it. Johnny said we were brought together tonight for a reason. Couldn't it be as simple as an act of kindness? A friend helping a friend? Maybe if it was anybody else, but not us. It seemed everything that happened in all three of our lives happened for a reason bigger than we realized at the time. Was this one of those times too? I hadn't seen Johnny for months, and now I was in his truck as he professed to me that we were brought back together by unforeseen forces, an aligning of the stars if you will. I looked at the time, it was 12:11. Why eleven, why now and why with Johnny? That was my number with Liam, not Johnny. A knot had formed in the pit of my stomach. I ached for Liam; he was my refuge, and all was right when I was with him.

"Is anything wrong, Jenny?"

"No. I'm just tired. It's been a busy weekend. I'm ready to go home."

"You mean your home?"

"Yes, but that would be Liam's too. Please take me there."

"Listen, we've got about five more minutes, five more minutes that I have you all to myself, without the presence of Liam to distort your judgment. I've never wanted to make you feel guilt or doubt, but I've never been able to hide my feelings for you. I've tried, believe me. But something about you that when I'm near you makes my rational side forget itself and allows my heart to speak. I can't help but feel that there might be a small glimmer of hope for us. I think that's why it's never been hard for me to open up to you and maybe why I was so open with you tonight. We've shared more in this hour than just a flat tire."

"Johnny, I can't think about this anymore. I will always be grateful for what you did for me tonight and in the past, but right now I can't think about it. I need time."

"I see. I guess this is goodbye then."

We were in Liam's driveway; his house in view. He stopped his truck before reaching the house.

"What are you doing?"

"Before I let you go I want you to have this." He was scribbling something feverishly on a piece of paper.

"It's my cell number. I want you to memorize it, and if you ever, and I mean ever need to talk, I want you to think of me and call. I will always be here for you whether you want me to or not."

I took the paper and hastily put it in my purse, scrunching it up in the process.

"Johnny, I'm sorry."

"Never say you're sorry around me. I knew I wasn't going to win your heart tonight. But you'll never know how happy I was about having this time with you."

He leaned in to me.

"Johnny, please, you can't."

He paused as he redirected his lips to the side of my face and softly kissed my cheek. He then proceeded to drive until we were at the front of the house. Liam's truck was nowhere to be seen. He must still be at Joe's, I thought. And then at that very moment, I found myself becoming madder than hell as I realized he didn't even care that I had been gone so long. I should have been home hours ago, and he wasn't even there, pacing as he waited for my arrival. I felt my blood boiling as I allowed my anger to take over.

"Looks like Liam isn't here. Do you want me to wait here with you?"

"No, that won't be necessary, and honestly, I don't think that would be a good idea."

"Yeah, you're probably right."

I began to open my door when Johnny grabbed my hand. "Jenny, please don't count me out. I promise I'll keep my distance, but I need this...I need you." His warm hand squeezed mine in earnest.

I nodded my head as I left his truck.

The timing couldn't have been worse. In the distance, I saw Liam's headlights approaching the house.

"Well, looks like your knight in shining armor has finally arrived." Johnny handed me my bag.

"Your sarcasm isn't very subtle."

"It wasn't meant to be."

"Hey babe," I said as Liam made his way to me in a huff. The look on his face was awful. If looks could kill, Johnny would have died a thousand deaths in the few minutes Liam had stared at him.

"What's going on, Jen? Where's your car? And what's he doing here?"

"Didn't you get any of my messages? I had a flat tire coming home. Johnny happened to be driving by and pulled over to help me."

"Yeah, Liam, I didn't even know it was Jenny until I got out of my truck. Lucky for her that it was me driving by, there are a lot of crazies out there."

"Yeah, lucky for her." He stared at Johnny.

"Well, where's your car then?" He turned his focus back on to me.

"You're going to have to get it tomorrow, Liam. I tried to put the spare on for her, but there was a hole in it too. It wouldn't have been safe for her to drive it."

Liam returned his stern and stoic face to Johnny. He showed no emotion except for the tight grip he kept on my hand.

"I called you at least five times; you never answered."

"I'm sorry, Jen. I must've had it on silence."

"I guess this is it then. I better be going."

"Thanks, Johnny. I really appreciate it."

He gave me a smile. "Don't mention it, Jen. I'm glad I was driving by."

I watched as Johnny drove off, not even realizing that Liam had already gone inside. I walked in the house only to find him walking upstairs with my bag still in his hand. When I reached his room, he was sitting away from me in a chair facing the window.

"Is there something wrong, Liam?"

"No, why do you ask?"

"I don't know, maybe because you've hardly said two words to me since you arrived and you seem to be giving me the silent treatment right now while you aimlessly look out the window."

He didn't say a word, only adjusting his position in the chair, crossing his arms as he focused straight ahead.

"So, I am receiving the silent treatment. Is it because Johnny brought me home?" Liam remained quiet. "Dammit, Liam. I didn't do anything. Would you rather I had stayed there? Maybe slept in the car? As far as I see it, I should be upset with you. Why, of all times, would you have your phone on silence knowing full well I was driving home by myself? You should be thankful Johnny drove by when he did. It could have been some deranged lunatic who could have had his way with me. In my opinion, Johnny was a God send. Did you want me to refuse his help? Maybe wait for you? I'd still be waiting!" I screamed so hard my throat hurt. "AHH! You beat all, Liam! I don't get you. It wasn't like it was planned! For God's sake, get over yourself already!" Liam stood from his seated position and turned to face me. He still had the same stoic expression on his face that he had given Johnny. "What?" I said sarcastically.

"You don't get it do you, Jen?"

"Get what? I'm tryin' to get it, but you're making it really hard for me to understand. If anything you're acting very selfish in my opinion. I'm the one who needed your help and you weren't there, and now I'm being blamed for your inadequacies. It's not my fault or my problem. You should have been here like you said you were going to be, with your phone on! Thank God, Johnny was there to help me."

"That's just it, it was Johnny again. The glorious, almighty Johnny to your rescue."

"Are you kidding? You can't be serious? You do wish I would have refused his help don't you? That's what you're really saying, that's what this is all about, huh?!"

"I'm just sick and tired of Johnny. It's not enough that he's the reason for my nightmares, I have to be thankful that he's able to help you again when you're in trouble?! Dammit, Jenny! I can't take it anymore! I can't take him anymore!"

"What's there to take? You're acting crazy, Liam! All he did was offer me a ride home, which I took him up on since you weren't coming any time soon, to my rescue!" I blurted in his face.

"That's not fair, Jenny."

"It's just as fair as you being mad at me for allowing Johnny to bring me home. Why didn't you answer any of my phone calls?"

"I already told you, I had my phone on silence."

"Why, though? You still haven't answered me that. Why of all times would you have your phone on silence? Didn't you think I might need to call you, or just want to talk to you?"

Liam walked towards me; the expression on his face had softened, and his eyes seemed to be conveying to me a different message. I backed up as he accidentally tripped, catching himself on his bedpost. "Jenny, I'm sorry. I have no excuse for it. I was helping Joe, and I kept getting calls, and the interruptions were distracting. I turned my phone off just for that reason. I wasn't thinking about you or that you might be calling me."

"Liam, you're really not making any sense. You told me before I left this morning that you would be waiting here at the house. You knew I was going to be home tonight. Didn't you even wonder where I was when it started getting late? I mean I know we don't have to know where each other is twenty-four-seven, but knowing I was supposed to be home at certain time and I wasn't should at least make you worry a tiny bit. Besides, I thought we were going to celebrate your partnership with Joe?"

Liam leaned towards me, taking my hands into his. "Jen, I have no excuse. And I was here for the most part. Parker called and wanted to come over, and we ended up at Joe's."

"Your breath reeks of alcohol, Liam. I thought you were working at Joe's?"

"We did for a while, but we took a break and had a few beers."

"A few? You smell like you took a bath in the stuff." My thoughts went to Grandpa as he told me of his concern with Liam's drinking.

I pushed his face away from me in order to avoid the stench of his breath.

"Hey, don't do that. I'm trying to make up with you."

"I don't want to make up with you in this condition. You're drunk. You drove home like this?"

"I'm not drunk; having a few beers doesn't necessarily qualify someone as drunk. And I was perfectly fine to drive. As you can see, I'm here in one piece and so is my truck."

"You know, I don't know why you felt the need to have a party with your friends on the night I was coming home. I thought we were going to celebrate together? Apparently that was more important than me. Furthermore, you are in no condition to talk or discuss what happened tonight. I think I'm just going to go to bed, something you should also consider."

"Jen, don't, I just had a few beers."

"I've seen you after you have had a few beers, and you never act like this. Sleep it off and I'll talk to you tomorrow."

"Jenny, please listen to me, it just about killed me to drive up and see Johnny's Bronco in my driveway and you getting out of it. I didn't know how to react to that. With everything I'm going through, you should understand that. And I'm sorry I didn't return your phone calls, and I'm sorry my phone wasn't on. It was thoughtless of me. You're right, that was a dumbass move on my part. I missed you this weekend," he said in a sweeter tone, his eyes still trying to tell me that he didn't want to stay mad. Liam lightly kissed me on the lips. I missed his lips, but they reeked of alcohol.

"You have a funny way of showing you missed me."

"Please don't be mad at me," he whispered in my ear as his hair tickled the side of my face.

"I'm not just mad, Liam, I'm hurt. I don't understand. The last time we talked you gave me the impression that we were going to celebrate when I returned home. You couldn't wait to see me, and then I can't reach you when I needed you. I understand how it must have looked seeing me get out of Johnny's truck, and believe me, I contemplated about even having him bring me home, but you wouldn't answer my calls. All Johnny did was bring me home, to you. Don't you think if there was anything going on between us we would have gone someplace else? I wanted to come home, to be with you."

Liam looked sincerely at me; he had me close to him, and he clenched me around my waist. I knew that it was hard for him to see what happened. It was like living his nightmares instead of dreaming them. I closed in on him, hugging him tightly. "I love you, Liam. Please believe me."

"I do, Jenny. I'm sorry for not being there for you, again."

"Stop that. You're always here for me, and when you're not, I always find my way to you, even tonight."

"I missed you this weekend."

"I missed you too."

Chapter Eight
My Turn

It seemed so familiar to me, as though I had been there before. It was Liam's truck, overturned with shards of broken glass blanketing me and the smell of gasoline consuming my every breath. I felt the pressure and pain as I tried to manipulate my way out of my seat, only to find that I was confined by the dashboard that made me its prisoner. Everything happened in slow motion as I screamed for Liam. I could see the outline of figures running towards me as they yelled for Liam and me.

"It's okay, don't panic, help is on its way! She's not breathing; hurry up, the truck is going to explode! There's gasoline everywhere! You need to get them out. Someone help Liam. I'll get Jenny. I'm right here baby, don't leave me, Jenny! Please, I'm reaching for you, just grab my hand!" The voices were chaotic in nature but spoke to me in a harmonic and choreographed tone, as though they had practiced their lines for this moment. Their voices frightened me even more.

But then out of the confusion, there was a more distinct voice rising above the others. *"Jenny, you don't have to worry anymore. I'll take you away from all of this. You'll never hurt again, I promise. I'm here for you, I'm your protector, your guardian. I'm the one who loves you, who really wants you."*

This voice was different: familiar but different all the same. I looked frantically around to see who was talking to me, but there was so much commotion amidst the fog and haze of the accident that I couldn't make out anybody. But the voice seemed so recognizable to me and so very close.

"It's okay, Jenny. I'm right here. Don't be afraid."

His voice was calming and peaceful. There was no panic or fear behind it, assuring me everything would be alright. The anxiety and fear that had been encompassing me slowly dissipated as his soothing and unruffled voice calmed me down. I felt my eyes shift back and forth from the phantom voice to Liam's; my world teetering on the brink of oblivion as I tried in vain to stay focused and conscious. My regard returned to Liam. His crystal-blue eyes were darkened with fear as he desperately reached for me. The more he tried, the further I drifted from him. Fear returned as I felt myself slipping from his sight. An ominous almost forbidding feeling embraced me as I watched Liam's futile attempts continue to fail.

"Liam! Help me! Please!" I screamed.

His eyes were fading from my view. I was even farther away from him now. All the voices became distant figments of my imagination as I became encompassed in darkness. I felt the pain in my body subsiding as I relinquished my fear and gave in to its darkness as my body was lifted by this strong and unruffled presence. Liam finally has me, I thought as I relaxed in his arms. I felt safe. I faintly opened my eyes to meet his, but to my horror it wasn't Liam. Shock engulfed me as I looked into my beholder's eyes.

"Johnny? No, you're supposed to be Liam!"

"*No, Jenny it's supposed to be me, not Liam,*" Johnny said affably.

His smile was devious yet at the same time peculiarly welcoming as he carried me in his arms, cradling me as his grip tightened around my broken body, protecting me as we both drifted away from the carnage in which that I had laid. The mayhem and turmoil that the accident provided was becoming nothing more than a distant memory and so was Liam. I could no longer see or hear his voice. The literal pain my body had endured had vanished as Johnny held me securely in his nurturing care. I felt peace in Johnny's arms, as though what he had said to me was the truth. The truth? All along he had said he would never hurt me, that he wanted to take care of me, that I would always feel comforted when I was with him, and so I did. I relaxed even more in Johnny's embrace as he continued to carry me away in his arms. We walked farther and farther from the mess that my life had been experiencing before. He looked at me with his tender and touching eyes.

"*I told you I would always be here for you, Jenny. I've never lied to you, and I will never hurt you. You'll always be safe with me. It will never be like it was with Liam. It will only be better. He wasn't the one for you, I am.*" His smile broadened as his words trickled from his mouth.

I was succumbing to his cherishing behavior when I realized that this was wrong, something wasn't right about what was happening to me. I began to look for Liam. He was nowhere to be seen, gone in an instant, not only from my sight but from me. A feeling of emptiness enveloped me. My eyes began to widen as Johnny spoke. The nurturing feeling that Johnny was giving me was replaced with tension. I wanted him to release his hold on me, but the more I tried to wrangle from his grip the more constricted his grasp was on me.

"NO! It's Liam I want, not you! Why can't you just leave me alone?!" I screamed as I tried to free myself from his shackling hold. The calm and comforting smile that had graced his face was replaced by a repulsive and malevolent laugh. An undeniable evil hidden beneath his exterior was exposed when he became adamant of his will towards me.

"You're mine, Jenny! You'll always be mine and I'll never let you go! Stop dreaming and wake up to your reality! Wake up, Jenny! Wake up! I'm your dream, not Liam! Wake up!"

"Jenny, wake up you're having a bad dream, wake up! It's me, Liam, wake up!"

Liam was wrestling me as I tried to stave him off. I continued my rampage until I opened my blurry eyes to see him hovering over me, his actions echoing my same behavior with him during his nightmares.

"Liam, what's going on? What are you doing?"

"You were dreaming, Jenny you were screaming for me. Are you alright?"

"Yeah, I think so. I think I'm just really tired from my trip this weekend. I'm sorry I woke you." I was drenched in sweat. "What time is it?"

"4:11."

"Really?"

"Yeah, I know. Babe, you were scaring me. I thought I was the one with the bad dreams, not you? How long has this been going on?"

"It's the first time. I've never had a dream like this." I looked gravely at him.

"What, Jenny, what's wrong?"

"Liam, my dream, it was just like yours."

"What do you mean like mine?"

"It was the accident, everything like you described to me, the broken glass, the blood, the yelling and…"
"And what, Jenny?"

"Johnny, Liam. I saw you reaching for me, and I went to grab your hand and just when I did, Johnny carried me away. Oh my God, Liam, I'm so sorry. I felt so scared, I couldn't see you anymore." I began sobbing as I fell into Liam's arms. "I understand now what you've been trying to tell me. It was awful, Liam."

"It's okay, Jenny. But why? Why did you have the same dream?"

"I think I know why. This was your nightmare to a T, except mine seemed to continue where yours left off. It was as if someone, or more importantly something, was trying to fill in the missing pieces from your nightmare. Johnny talked to me in this sweet but sadistic tone. He told me that he was always the one for me. He carried me away from you. At first I thought he was being genuine, and then I realized he wasn't. I tried to get away from him, but the harder I tried the more he held onto me; his grip was so tight. I swear I can still feel it."

"Babe, I'm so sorry you had to go through that, but now do you understand what I've been going through and why last night bothered me so much. It wasn't that you came home with some guy; it was Johnny! Even though you say he's out of our lives, he isn't, and last night proved that for me."

I was haunted by Johnny's confession to me last night as he reminded me that he needed to be a part of my life whether Liam knew about it or not. "I know, Liam, but Johnny's actions last night were only honorable."

"Honorable, Jenny?"

"I'm just saying he was trying to do the right thing for a friend."

"You still don't get it. How can you say that after what just happened? Look at you; you're drenched in sweat, that wasn't an ordinary dream you had. How can you still defend Johnny after experiencing what I do almost on a regular basis?"

"I'm not defending Johnny, Liam. I just know that he was trying to help, that's all." The look of worry in Liam's eyes was instantly replaced with a look of shock as he tried to process my last statement.

"I can't believe you, Jenny. I can't believe what I'm hearing come out of your mouth."

"What? What are you talking about? Why are you suddenly mad? If we're going to hold on to being mad at each other, maybe I should still be mad at you for not having your cell on!"

Liam remained quiet as his blue eyes bore through mine. I wanted him to say something to me, anything to break the silence, but instead he rose from our bed and began to get dressed.

"What are you doing?"

He continued to dress himself, buttoning his shirt as he gazed ou the window. Only when he put on his boots did he find his voice. "I'm going to go out for a while. It's a little hot in here and I need to cool off."

Liam spoke to me as he would a stranger. There was no feeling behind his words and his eyes were solemn as he looked at me. I felt horrible. "I don't understand. Where are you going at this hour and why? You're going to walk out on me over this?"

"Obviously Johnny's presence in our lives or more importantly your life doesn't seem to bother you the way it does me. You've known from almost day one when I realized Johnny's intentions towards you were not decent that I didn't want anything more to do with him. I don't want him in our lives, but if you are going to lie there in our bed and defend him on whether his actions last night were honorable or not then I need to walk away from this conversation. I love you, but I can't stand to hear you talk about him. I've told you the hurt I've gone through and continue to go through because of him. I would think you would be on my side, especially after experiencing that God-awful dream.

And as far as not being able to reach me last night, I've already tried to apologize for that. I told you what happened. It was a mistake, but if you're going to chastise me for it, then I don't really have any more to say about it. You've always been my priority, always, and when I realized how late it had gotten last night, I immediately thought of you. You never really gave me a chance to tell you and as soon as I realized what time it was I checked my phone and saw your missed calls. I even called you to let you know I was on my way home, but you never answered. You can even ask Parker; he was right there with me when I called you. Maybe you should check your phone too. I'm not walking out on you, Jenny. I'm trying to be the bigger person and walk away from this infantile conversation over someone you know I detest. You shouldn't want to persecute me over any of this. Don't you think

I'm being persecuted enough with the hell I've had to endure since April 11th?"

Liam walked quietly away, closing the bedroom door behind him. It was eerily silent as his footsteps hit the floor, his uneven gait echoing as each boot hit the wooden planks, fading the further he walked until, before I knew it, they were gone. The only sound coming from the house was the screen door as it slammed shut. I pounded my fists into my pillows as I began wallowing in my tears. Grandpa's room was only a few feet away from ours; I tried to muffle my despair as my body fought to release it. I didn't want to have to explain to him why Liam left and why I was so upset. I didn't understand how one minute Liam could be consoling me and then the next we were arguing. We never argued and in the past few months that had changed. The accident had turned into a curse, bringing with it guilt and despair.

I glanced at the clock. It was 4:43 in the morning. Where in the world could Liam be going at such an hour? I knew I couldn't fall back asleep; my mind was too troubled. I had to go after him and try to clear this mess up, but where? I rose from bed and quietly got dressed. I tiptoed my way down the hallway past Grandpa's room, slowly descending down the stairs and grabbing Grandpa's keys to his truck. I hastily scribbled a note to Grandpa, and then I left.

I found myself driving through town and towards Brush Creek Road, my hope was he would be there waiting for me, but as I made the turn that led to our spot I found nothing more than a clearing that gave way to the morning sun as it crested above the hills. Any other time I would be in awe of the sight, but not this time. I continued on, thinking that possibly he was in my driveway. I was disappointed again. The driveway to my house was vacant; the only vehicles were of Dad's, the morning shipments being unloaded by Billy. I gave him a wave and continued on my journey. I was running out of options on where to look for Liam. I even drove by the high school in hopes that maybe, just maybe, I would find his Ford F-150 black truck in its usual parking spot from last year. Maybe he was on the football field reliving his glory days as he tried to muddle through the events that had unfolded over the last year to turn his life and mine into such a topsy-turvy ride. But the lot was vacant.

I sat there at a loss, not knowing where I should go or what I should do. I glared at my cell, hoping it would ring, but it remained silent. I checked for missed messages, there were none except for the one Liam had left after realizing how late it had gotten. I felt even worse; he had called. I called Liam numerous times only to hear his raspy but melodic voice tell me he was with me and to leave him a message. "Liam, it's Jenny. Could you please call me? I love you." I left the same message eleven times. I continued on my way driving aimlessly as I tried to figure out where Liam's truck had taken him. I had been looking for him for over two and a half hours with no luck. I was almost a mile out of town when I saw it; it was hard to miss the huge black exterior with chrome detail sitting at Joe's shop. I don't know why I never thought about checking there. I pulled in hesitantly and parked next to it. The shop seemed deserted except for the lights that shone down on the far stall. I heard the sound of clinking tools reverberating as they made impact. Upon entering, I found Liam as he worked on my car. He was kneeling down with his back towards me and Parker was next to him.

"Hello, Jenny." Parker's words made Liam turn around.

"Hello, Parker."

Liam gave Parker a look and immediately Parker rose from his knelt position and walked past me. I looked earnestly at Parker for any feedback on how Liam was. All Parker could do was give me a nod and half smile. The same smile I had received after Liam and Grandpa Mack's accident in reassurance that they would be okay. My heart dropped a little at Parker's gaze.

Liam remained turned from me as he continued to replace my tire. I began to make my way towards him as I took in the details of Joe's shop. There were four car lifts that made up most of the shop, with an attached garage behind the main building for detail and priming work. Oil and paint cans, as well as hundreds of tools and other car paraphernalia, filled the shop. In one corner, it looked like Joe was making a shrine to all the spring break beauties and the months they adorned. But it was the other corner that caught my attention more than the pin-up beauties and their poses. In the opposite corner, there were three oil barrels that were deluged with filthy rags, empty oil cans and innumerable beer cans and alcohol bottles as they overflowed from the barrels.

Again I was haunted by Grandpa's words as they resonated in my head. "This can't be," I thought to myself. "These obviously belong to Joe. Liam wouldn't have done so much drinking," I said to myself as I tried to justify the myriad of empty alcohol containers. My heart sank deeper as I felt I was being shown a side of Liam I had never seen before. I didn't want Grandpa's words to be true. This wasn't Liam's behavior, maybe his father but not Liam. One thing he despised about his father was his drinking. No, these empty beer cans belonged to Joe and possibly a few to Parker and maybe some patrons of the shop, but not Liam. I continued to say this to convince myself as I made my way to Liam's side. Liam had just finished putting my new tire on as I stood by him, I didn't speak, and neither did he. The echoing of his tools was the only communication between us. I stood idle, patiently waiting for him to make the first move, but my patience was in vain. He remained poised in his knelt position with his focus on my newly replaced tire.

"Hi," I said sincerely.

"Hi," he repeated with the same tone.

"I see you got my car."

"Yep."

"Did Parker go with you?"

"Yep."

Liam's vocabulary had been reduced to a one syllable word.

"Don't you have anything to say to me?"

"Nope, don't think so."

Oh, I take that back, five words, all one syllables.

"I guess I should go if you don't want to talk to me." I began to walk back to Grandpa's truck when I felt Liam's familiar touch on my shoulder.

"Why did you come after me, Jenny?"

"Because I love you and hated what happened. I never meant for you to feel like I had betrayed you or that I was defending Johnny. I didn't come here to argue anymore; I came here to make up with you. I guess I see what happened last night differently than you, and I don't mean that in a bad way. We have been through so much, and I'm just tired of it. I'm trying to see the good and that's all I saw in Johnny, an act of kindness. I know how you feel and I never meant to hurt you. I honestly was just taking him up on his offer to bring me home. You truly didn't want me to be stranded, did you?"

"I would have come after you, Jenny," he said coolly.

"I know that, Liam. But at the time I didn't, you weren't answering your phone."

"Don't you understand that Johnny looks at these missed opportunities by me as golden ones for him? I can guarantee you that he is reveling in the fact that he had you in his truck. I know it. I saw his face last night when he dropped you off. He was beaming, knowing he had you to himself for a little while. You're off limits, Jenny. Everyone knows that. I'm surprised he didn't cruise through town to show you off. The whole town knows our history; can't you see why this infuriates me so much? He always seems to be at the right place when it concerns you!"

"We're never going to solve this, are we, Liam? I don't want to fight anymore. I came here to make up. You're so upset and not once have you given me a good explanation about your erratic, drunken behavior last night."

"Erratic, drunken behavior? What the hell is that supposed to mean?"

"I've known you for almost a year now, and in that year I've only seen you drink a handful of times. I come here and find you almost buried in empty beer cans and alcohol bottles. What do you guys do when you're here, get drunk before you work on cars?"

"That's a low blow and you know it."

"Is it, Liam? Even Grandpa has noticed it. I know these past few months have been hell for both of us, but I always thought we could count on each other and not resort to relying on something else."

"I don't need you acting like this towards me, Jenny. I'm a grown man and if I want to have a beer once in a while with my friends, then I will. I'm not making a habit out of it. Most of those empty beer cans don't even belong to me, they belong to Joe. I shouldn't have to explain myself to you; you out of anybody should know me."

"I thought I did, Liam, that's why I question why you have started drinking more."

"This conversation is getting us nowhere. I don't have a drinking problem just like you don't have a relationship with

Johnny. You're taking this one-time last night and throwing it out of context. Here," he said as he handed me my car keys. "Your car is fixed. You can drive it home and I'll take Grandpa's."

I followed Liam back to the house. I couldn't believe how we were talking to one another. It hurt me beyond description. I yearned to go back to that dark place when I was in the coma. I wanted to wake up again and start all over with Liam, having everything that led up to this rift between us disappear.

We arrived at the house to be greeted by Grandpa. I remained in my car as I watched Liam and Grandpa talk. They were close in height, Liam only topping Grandpa by an inch or two; Grandpa's rugged hands glanced over Liam's broad shoulders. I could tell their conversation was over me. Grandpa's eyes darting towards me intermittently. After only a few minutes, Liam walked into the house as Grandpa made his way to me.

"Hello, Jenny, you doing okay?"

"Yes, Grandpa. I hope you don't mind me borrowing your truck."

"I don't mind at all, like I've always told you, all this belongs to you too; you don't need to ask or leave me a note. Although I do appreciate you telling me that you were gone. I must admit I was concerned to find you both out of the house so early in the morning."

My eyes went to the house. "What did Liam tell you?"

Grandpa's rugged hand squeezed my shoulder gently. "It's nothing, Jenny. He loves you so much, dear. You just need to go to him. I'm going to a horse auction; I'll be home this afternoon. But if you need me, just call me, okay?"

"I will, Grandpa, thank you."

"Don't mention it. It'll be alright."

Grandpa smiled at me as he got into his truck. I sighed heavily and looked into the front window to see Liam's shadow pass by. I knew he was waiting for me. I got out of the car and walked leisurely towards the house, carefully up the steps intentionally stepping over the broken one; still I could hear Liam's voice telling me to be careful as I walked over it. He was sitting on the floral sofa, a glass of water in his hands.

"So, are you just going to stand there or are you going to come in and sit beside me?"

I took his cue and walked over to the sofa, taking a seat on the opposite side of him. He turned to me and in the process scooted himself closer, his hand now resting on my leg.

"I did a lot of thinking while driving home from Joe's. I want you to know that I was trying to understand where you were coming from. I know I let you down and have no excuse for it. Maybe I did have a little bit too much to drink last night, but in all honesty, you still haven't given me a chance to explain. When Parker called me last night, I had all intention on telling him no. I knew you would be home soon, and I did plan on having a celebration with you, just like we had discussed. But did you know he heard from Kelli over the weekend?"

"No, I didn't, Liam."

"Well, he did. You know they've been having some problems. She told him she wanted to meet him. I swear, Parker spent longer than ever getting ready for her. He even cleaned his truck, but when he went to pick her up, flowers in hand, she told him she just wanted to give him back his spare key and class ring. He was devastated. She hardly gave him the time of day. They had been together since their freshman year, and that's how she treats him. He was crushed. That's when he called me. I couldn't leave him alone. He needed a friend, he needed me, Jenny. He's always been there for me, so I had to be there for him. By the time I got to Joe's, Parker was already drinking. I felt for him, Jenny because I know what it feels like. I know I've never lost you, but sometimes it feels like I have, so I had some beers with him. I really did just lose track of time. Parker was a mess, and I was just trying to be there for him, that's all."

"I had no idea, Liam. I always thought they would be together forever."

"Parker thought so too. But listen, this is about you and me, not them. You're right; these past few months have been a lot for us. I'm not trying to make any excuses, but I have had a few drinks now and then but don't hold that against me. I've been trying to work things out since that damn accident and during the time that I thought we were through. Hell yes, I drank. I drank a lot, but I'm not a drunk, and I'm not my dad. I don't want to hash this out anymore. What happened this weekend is done and over with, and I want to forget about it. I don't know why I'm having a hard time letting Johnny go. Maybe it's because every time I think I've gotten rid of him I have a damn nightmare. And I don't know why you had one last night, but I'm sorry you did. Jenny, I just need you to be on my side, I need to know that."

"But I've always been on your side, Liam, always. I'm sorry I didn't hear you out about last night, and I'm sorry that I was trying to defend Johnny's actions. I just want us to move on."

Liam pulled me to him, my head resting on his chiseled chest. His heart was beating hard against my temple as I closed my eyes. I felt the gentle nudge of my arm as I awakened; I groggily tried to lift my weary eyelids.

"Jenny, it's Grandpa. Have you been asleep for a while?"

"Huh? What time is it?"

"It's almost six in the evening."

I looked around for Liam, but he was gone. "Where's Liam?"

"I was going to ask you the same thing."

I felt a familiar but not welcome knot form in my stomach again.

"Did you two make up?"

I thought about our last moments together before I fell asleep. Things seemed to be fine. "I think so."

I checked my cell, but there were no messages. I called him only to hear his voice commanding me to leave him a message.

"Where could he be, Grandpa?"

"I'm sure he's just in town or something. I wouldn't worry, Jenny."

I tried to heed Grandpa's words but found it harder to do by evening. It was after eleven and there still had been no word from him. Grandpa had left again, and I was alone, only Blue to keep me company as I fell into an uneasy and restless sleep. By morning, I thought I would be awakened by the sound of Liam's voice as he brought me his famous pancake breakfast adorned with a lavender rose, but instead the only sounds came from Blue as he continually whined for me to let him out. The knot that had formed in my stomach last night had grown larger. I kept thinking back to our conversation on the sofa. Nothing Liam said to me led me to believe that something else was wrong. I lay back down, yearning to find my dark friend as I waited for Liam's return.

Chapter Nine
Gone Fishing

It was a dull and dreary Wednesday, hump day to most, but to me Wednesday signified that it had been nine days since I had talked or even seen Liam. I had left numerous messages on his cell, but all of them went unanswered. I even went to Joe's only to be told that they hadn't seen him since Parker had given Liam a ride to get his truck.

"I'm sorry, Jenny. Liam hasn't been back since then. He got in his truck and in all honesty I thought he was going back home. We were expecting him back to help load the car. When he didn't show up, that's when Joe started calling."

"He didn't say anything to you at all, Parker?"

"Not really. I asked him what his plans were, and he said he didn't know. He did say before leaving though that it was a great day to go fishing. I did think that was strange. I haven't known Liam to fish in years."

I sighed. "Thanks anyway, Parker."

"You're welcome. I wouldn't worry about Liam. He must just need some time alone to sort through this stuff with Johnny."

"You know about Johnny?"

"What do you mean? Of course I do. Everyone in town knows about the rift between Liam and him. That accident made headline news in this town."

"Oh, you're talking about that?"

"What else?"

"Nothing, Parker, it's not important. Hey, I wanted to tell you how sorry I was to hear about you and Kelli. I had no idea."

"Thanks, me neither."

"Are you doing okay?"

"I guess. It is what it is. I can't keep mulling over it, and apparently her plans were different than mine. I guess it's better to find out now that after I married her."

"Well, it still isn't right. She never shared any of that with me, but if she had I would have told you. You're too nice of a guy to have this happen to you."

"Thanks."

I started to leave when it dawned on me something Parker had said.

"Did you need something else, Jenny?"

"Parker, you said Liam mentioned fishing?"

"Yeah, why?"

"Nothing, it's just I think I know where he is. Bye, Parker and thanks again."

I hopped into my car and sped home as fast as I could. I jumped out of my car and ran towards the barn as I yelled for Grandpa. "Grandpa, are you here? Grandpa, where are you?" I continued to yell as I found nothing in the barn except for Sugar Dumplin' grazing on some hay. I ran outside only to run into him as he made his way to the back door of the house. "Grandpa!"

"Whoa, Jenny, where's the fire?"

"I'm sorry, but I need to ask you something."

"What is it, dear?"

"Can you tell me how to get to Serenity Hill?"

"Serenity Hill? Why do you want to go there?"

"Because I think that's where Liam is. I just saw Parker and he told me that one of the last things Liam said to him was it was a nice day to go fishing. Liam took me to Serenity Hill not too long ago, but he wanted it to be a surprise so he blindfolded me. I know that's where he is, I just don't know how to get there. Can you help me?"

"I can do better than help; I can take you there myself." Grandpa grabbed his coat and keys to his old Chevy and took me by the hand. "We can be there by dusk if we get a move on."

Our drive to Serenity Hill was silent. I was happy Grandpa didn't feel like talking, my mind was full of thoughts of Liam being there for the past week and not once letting me know about it. My knot had now taken over my entire stomach. I was sure that at any moment I was going to throw up from it. I focused my eyes straight ahead as Grandpa continued driving. He finally made the turn that led off of the main road and onto the dirt road that would end at Serenity Hill. I recalled the same motions of the familiar terrain as when I was blindfolded, and then in an instant, the old Chevy slowed down coming to a stop right before the ridge.

"I'm going to drop you off here unless you want me to come with you. I can see Liam's truck in the distance. I think he probably would rather just see you than both of us. I know he needs you more than me, dear." Grandpa gave me a gentle squeeze on my hand and the famous Larson wink for encouragement. I felt hesitant as I looked ahead. "Go on, Jenny, it's okay. I bet a Calhoun nickel on it." I snickered at Grandpa's remark. I never knew what that meant until I met Liam. He had once told me that Grandpa Mack regarded kisses on the cheek by pretty girls as Calhoun nickels. They were worth their weight in gold according Grandpa.

I leaned over and kissed Grandpa on the cheek. "Thank you."

"You're welcome."

Grandpa waited until I had made the clearing before leaving. I was only a few yards from the truck; Liam was nowhere to be seen. I realized how much I truly missed him as I touched his truck. I could literally smell him as I walked around it.

I felt almost betrayed as I wondered why Liam had been avoiding me; didn't he miss me as much as I had missed him? There was a time when an hour couldn't go by without him touching base with me, and now it had been over nine days. I had cried every night since then. My pillow continuing to stay damp as my tears never stopped falling on it. The night used to be my refuge, but these past nine days had eliminated that, leaving only my dreams that lead me away from Liam. Even my dark friend had deserted me in my slumber.

I walked towards the oak tree that sheltered his mom's final resting place, leaning down I noticed an envelope. There were no words on it, only a simply drawn heart in a misshapen form. It was Liam's drawing. I could pick out his style of writing from anyone's.

"I see you found my letter," Liam said as he approached me.

"Liam. I'm sorry; I wasn't going to open it."

"That's okay, it's just a note I wrote to Mom. I know it sounds pretty silly. It's not like she can read it, but it helps me to believe she can. You can read it if you want."

"No, that's for her."

"It's about you, how much I love you, how much I care for you, and how I never want to hurt you or be without you."

"Liam, why did you leave me and not tell me where you were? I thought things were okay between us."

"I don't know. I didn't plan on doing it that way. I just did. After you fell asleep, I fell asleep too. I had another nightmare that night. I woke up in a pool of sweat and this feeling of hurt. I was literally sick to my stomach thinking about Johnny and our fight. I know we made up, but I still felt awful. I told you this is where I go to clear my head, so I decided to do just that. I know I should have left a note, but once I made up my mind, I just left. I called Parker to come pick me up so I could get my truck, and I never looked back. I never meant to be gone this long. Are you okay?"

"Yeah, I'm fine. But I've missed you terribly."

"I've missed you too. How did you know to come here?"

"It was something you told Parker."

"What did I tell him?"

"You told him it was a nice day to go fishing. This is the only place you've ever told me you've been fishing. I just put two and two together. I told Grandpa, and he brought me here."

"I'm glad you came."

"Are you, Liam?"

"Yes."

"Why didn't you call me then? I would have come long before now."

"I saw your missed calls and listened to your messages. Actually I've listened to them over and over again, just so I could hear your voice."

"You could have called me to hear my voice."

"I figured you were mad at me for leaving the way I did, and I guess I just needed some time."

"Time? Time for what?"

"Time to think about us, about me, about you."

"Oh," I said softly as a huge lump formed in my throat, replacing the knot in my stomach. "So what about us?" I was afraid of what I might hear.

Liam stared at me intently with his deep blue eyes. Even in the darkness they stood out like two pools of iridescent water, shimmering in the night.

"Jenny, I've been dealing with my conscience. After all that you and I have been through I thought it would be easy to let go of my past, but it hasn't been that easy for some reason. That's why I've been here. I needed to get away from everything, including you."

"Your conscience?"

"You were right. I have been drinking. More than I thought until you made it clear to me. I didn't realize what I was doing, but after our argument, I looked back and instead of coming to you about the things that have been bothering me I tried to forget about them through a six pack. I thought it would be okay. The nightmares were not as bad when I drank. Things were improving, or so I thought. We seemed to be doing better, and I was opening up to you. But the nightmares are still there, I was too drunk to remember them. But the worst was seeing Johnny. It was the last straw. I'm sorry that I wasn't there for you when your car broke down. It should have been me. Seeing Johnny bring you home was too much for me to handle. As a matter of fact, I couldn't handle it. But it was also the fact that I let you down. I've always promised to take care of you, and I keep breaking that promise."

"Liam, that's not true. You've never failed me."

"Oh yes I have, Jenny."

Liam remained quiet as I carefully placed my hands in his. He squeezed them tightly.

"I love you, Liam. I'm sorry about our fight."

"Don't be. You had every right to be upset with me. I need you. I need you so much. I came here thinking that the next time we saw each other you would want to leave me. I think that's why I stayed away for so long. I was afraid that your calls were to let me know we were through. That's why I was avoiding you. I'm sorry, babe."

"Are you serious? After everything we've been through you think I would leave you over a stupid argument? Why would I want to leave you?"

"I guess in the back of my head I still think that you could do better than me. It scares the hell out of me, especially when I think of Johnny still being in the picture."

"I want you. Nothing or no one will ever change that, Liam."

I took my hands out of his grasp and wrapped them around his neck, forcing him to face me eye to eye.

"I love you, Liam."

"I love you too, Jenny. Forgive me?"

"Only if you forgive me?"

"What should I forgive you about?"

"For being so upset with you."

"Like I said, you had every right to be mad at me. I'm sorry for the way I've been acting lately. I don't need to do that, I just need you."

"Really, Liam?"

"Yeah really."

"So, you've been sleeping here the whole time?"

"Yeah, well almost. I went into town a couple of times."

"You did? For what?"

"To get some supplies and to check on you."

"To check on me?"

"I came to the house and stayed until our light went out in our room."

"Liam, do you realize how worried I was? Why didn't you come in?"

"I should have, I know. It was wrong. I just wanted to be near you, the way I used to sit in your driveway last year."

"I don't know what I'm going to do with you," I said as I leaned in closer to him.

"Well I have a few ideas, if you need some," Liam said with his crooked smile and the twinkle in his eyes that I had missed.

He looked over to his right, where in the distance, I could make out the shape of his tent.

"What do you have in mind, Mr. Larson?"

"Some long overdue making up."

Liam kissed me tenderly. I felt relief as he held me close to him. His touch, his smell, had been vacant from my senses, and I felt whole again as he carried me to the tent.

Chapter Ten
August 11th

We stayed together that night. I don't know if it was the location or because we hadn't been together for almost two weeks, but whatever the reason, the night was magical. Liam loved me unconditionally, and his extraordinary actions eliminated any doubts that I had been holding. All the misjudgments that had brought me here were diminished as soon as we were together. We talked about everything from what we wanted from each other to what we expected from each other as well. I told him of my concerns with his drinking, and he openly talked about his anger with Johnny. We didn't hold anything back this time. Everything from our lovemaking to our conversations was defined by a new awareness and appreciation for one another. Liam had promised to ease up on the drinking, and I had told him that I had been having that same dream every night since he left. He gave me his undivided attention, and when I finished, instead of witnessing anger or even jealousy I witnessed a genuine warmth and concern. The way it used to be with him. He wrapped his arms around me as though he was protecting me, knowing firsthand the struggle I was enduring.

"Jenny, I don't want you to be having this happen to you like it's happening to me. I would die a thousand deaths to take that dream away from you. I never wanted you to have to experience this."

"I think they're there for a reason. I think our answer to whatever is going on, lies in these dreams or nightmares."

"I don't know. That's far-fetched to me. I think I'm having them because I can't seem to let go of the past, and I think maybe, just maybe, yours are stemming from worrying over mine."

"You do?" I said, intrigued by his profound and interesting theory.

"Yes I do. I think somehow in your mentality, while you've been trying to help me, your subconscious has decided to continue the dream and finish it for me. Are you surprised by my theory?"

"No, not surprised, but I am impressed."

"Well good. Impressing you is something I strive for."

"You don't have to impress me, Liam. I'm already in love with you."

"Are you sure, Jenny?"

"Very sure."

"Good. Then there's one more thing we need to discuss."

"What?"

"Well, two things. I've been thinking a lot about you since you've returned from Glenville, I think you should sign up for some classes for the next semester."

"Really? Seriously?"

"Yes, really. I know how important this is to you, and I don't think you should be putting it off any longer. You've let me realize my dream of becoming partners with Joe; I think it's only fair that you start pursuing yours."

"I never doubted it. I know we always said I would go to school, but with everything that's happened, I didn't know if you still felt that way. You haven't said anything for such a long time. I thought maybe your feelings had changed on the subject."

"Not at all. I want you to do this. But there is something else I want to settle."

"Oh yeah, you did say there was something else."

"Jenny, I want us to set the date."

"Our wedding date?"

"Yeah, I want to marry you. I've always wanted to marry you. You know I'd marry you right now on this mountain if I could. I don't need the big wedding, but I know how important it is to you to have our families there. So I think we need to set the date so we can plan for it. Please, Jenny. Let's do this."

"You're right, we've waited too long as it is."

"So, when?"

"I don't know. I think if I can start school next semester then maybe we should plan the wedding for next summer."

"Next summer? Do you really want to wait that long?"

"No, but I think a summer wedding would be beautiful. Maybe we could get married at your place, behind the barn. It's so pretty there, especially in the summer. Or even better Liam, we could get married here. You just said you'd marry me here if you could, why don't we then? And I know this sounds a little weird, but it would be like your mom was here for it too."

"It's not weird at all. I love that you're thinking about my mom, and if that's what you want then yes. I don't really care where we get married, just as long as I get to give you my last name. I want you as my wife, forever. "

I threw myself on Liam, knocking him down to the ground. We rolled around in the grass as we kissed each other emphatically.

"You know that I can't get enough of you."

"I hope you mean that, Jenny, because you're my world. I don't need anything but you. I'd be lost without you."

"You're hopeless."

"For you, babe," he said as his blue eyes gazed into mine.

"So when next summer?"

"How about next week?"

"Next week? We can't get married that soon."

"Why not?"

"Well because I thought we had agreed on a summer wedding?"

"I know that's what you said but something very important happens next week."

"What?"

"It's the day you became mine. It's our one year anniversary."

"You remembered?"

"Of course, how could I forget that?"

"I don't know. I guess it's because I haven't heard you mention it. I thought maybe you didn't remember."

"You underestimate me. How could I not remember one of the happiest days of my life?"

"But we can't get married next week."

"Why not?"

"Because, there's not enough time. I don't even have a dress."

"Are you really serious?" Liam's intent look told me he was.

"Yes, I am. But I know you want more time to prepare, to do this right. It's enough that you want to marry me; I guess I can wait a little longer if you make me." He said, pushing me back down into the grass.

Liam's hands found their way inside my shirt, but I knew his intentions far too well by now. This wasn't foreplay; Liam was preparing to tickle me. He started slowly, making me believe his purpose was to seduce me, but I knew better. His face came down on me as his labored breathing continued. He was good, almost too good, but I was ready, preparing myself to attack back the moment he found my vulnerable spot. I found myself staring at him. It was always so easy for me to get lost in his baby blues. That was my weakness because once I did, I totally forgot everything else, and that's exactly what happened. I was watching him, but my mind had forgotten about his hands, in an instant I was laughing uncontrollably and trying to wriggle myself out from his firm but loving grip.

"Say uncle!" he demanded.

"No!" I forced out as I tried to breathe, still laughing incessantly.

"Say uncle!" Liam demanded again.

I couldn't, I wouldn't, and no matter how much I hated being tickled I didn't want him to stop. I loved every moment he shared with me, and I could have held onto this moment forever. But finally, I retreated and gave in, only to have Liam stop and just hover over me. He pulled my hair to the side as he came down to my face, and with the faintest of touches kissed the top of my head until he had made his way to my lips. We just gazed at each other knowing just how intense this moment really was. I held onto his neck as a huge smile graced my face.

"What, Jenny? What's the smile for?"

"I know the date."

"When?" he asked with bated breath.

"August 11th."

"August 11th, why?"

"Because you once told me the first time you saw me was on that date. And it's on the eleventh. It just makes sense, Liam."

Liam kissed me again as he hung above me.

"Then August 11th it is," he whispered contently.

Liam's arousal for me continued as he began to explore my entire body. His left hand moved to the back of my shirt as he held me in his protective grip. I wrapped my legs around him forcing him closer to me. We were methodical in our movements. The side of his face was next to mine, his overgrown stubble tickling me as his arduous breathing matched mine. I leaned into his face, teasing him as though I was about to kiss him. He reacted only for me to move away as I guided my lips to the side of his face. "Make love to me, Liam... please," I whispered.

By noon, the sun was set high in the sky and Liam and I were both totally exhausted from our lovemaking. It had been the triumphant end to what had started out as a very shaky and unstable beginning, both of us thinking the worst before allowing ourselves to realize the obvious.

"Jen?"

"Yeah." I contently whispered as I enjoyed Liam's feathery touch on my stomach.

"Are you happy we set the date?"

"Very happy. I know you seemed to push it more than me but I've always wanted it. I think the date is perfect. It suits us."

"Good, because I just want us to get on with our lives. I think about us growing old together sitting on the porch with our children surrounding us and our grandchildren, and I just can't wait."

"Our children?" I asked eagerly.

"Yes, our children."

"How many children do you want us to have, Mr. Larson?"

"I plan on us having at least a dozen, and out of that dozen, I do expect there to be a couple of girls." Liam's smile was huge.

"A dozen kids? Seriously, Liam?"

"I've never been more serious in my life. I want the two of us to be overrun with them. I think we deserve that after what happened in the accident. Children are a result of how two people feel about one another. I love you more than I can say, so it only makes sense that our love should produce a boat load of kids. I want our house to be filled with them."

"You are serious," I said softly.

"Dead serious, Jenny. I want to have as many children as possible, looking all like you." Liam pulled my hair to the side. "Is that alright with you?"

I smiled at him. "Yeah, it's definitely alright by me."

"Good, then." He pulled me to him. "Maybe we could get started right now."

Chapter Eleven
Just Like Old Times… Well, Almost

We left Serenity Hill that afternoon. Liam kept me close to him as he drove, his right hand securely placed as always on my left thigh. I reflected on how things were so confused and misconstrued when I first arrived, and now everything between us seemed to have a new understanding and clarity. Johnny's name wasn't mentioned at all except in the beginning. I didn't have the heart to tell Liam about the conversation Johnny and I had in his truck. Liam didn't need to know the details of Johnny's feelings towards me or how he insisted in staying in my life. I couldn't dismiss them though, for some reason. I realized that, but for now denying Johnny and what he meant was easier than facing it. Upon arriving home, Liam pulled to the curb and took my hand to help me out of my seat.

"You know I'm very capable of getting out myself," I said appreciatively.

"I know, but why should you if I can help you? What do you say we go to the game tonight? We could even go to Lougini's afterwards. It'll be like old times."

"I'd love to, Liam."

We took his camping gear and stored it back in the barn and proceeded to freshen up before the game.

"Do you think it's going to be weird watching the game from the sidelines tonight for you?"

Liam sighed heavily. "Yes. I think it's going to be very hard. But I am looking forward to seeing the team; they should be pretty good this year. And besides, last year when I was playing I could only watch you from afar, now I can keep you close to me. It's really the best of both worlds; I can watch my favorite team and hold my favorite girl." Neither one of us could contain our smiles.

We arrived later than we hoped at the football stadium to the normally packed house. There wasn't a seat to be found amidst the sea of blue and gold. The clock showed that there was a little over a minute left before halftime. The Yellow Jackets were up by three, but the Walton Tigers had the ball.

"Wow, looks like another close game," Liam said.

I looked around to see if I could find a seat for us while Liam kept his focus on the game. With everyone on their feet, it was hard to tell what was available.

"Liam, I think we're going to have to stand."

He didn't hear me. His attention was on the field.

"Huh? What did you say?" He was like a kid in a candy store as he watched the game; I could tell he really missed it.

"I said I think we're going to have to stand."

"I don't mind if you don't. Besides it's halftime. With people getting up to move around, we can find a seat."

I followed Liam down the steps that led to the front rows, holding tightly to his hand. Everyone we passed recognized him immediately and wanted to talk to him. It was last year all over again, and the fact that I was there didn't seem to matter. Spencer's all-American football hero had returned and was gracing them with his presence. He was beaming from ear to ear from the attention he was receiving. It didn't even matter that there was a game. Their football hero had returned and the crowd was adamant in letting him know how happy they were to see him. After everyone had their chance to speak with him, we were able to watch the teams re-enter the field, this time in seats that were graciously given up for us. As the teams came on the field, Coach Green looked up into the stands and immediately saw Liam. He gave Liam an exuberant wave that reminded me of a politician in a parade waving to his constituents. The game had turned into a nail biter. By the fourth quarter, with only a minute left, it looked like history was going to repeat itself. The Tigers had the ball on our 20-yard line and all they needed was to make a field goal to win the game.

"I can't believe this. We should have had this game," Liam said furiously.

The teams were in position, the ball was released and the Walton's kicker kicked the ball high, aiming it for our golden goal posts. It went straight up and left of center, hitting the left pole. The Yellow Jacket fans were going crazy with their premature excitement. But instead of the ball falling outside, it fell inside, giving the Tigers their second victory in a row over us.

"Dammit!" Liam screamed. "I can't believe they won again."

We just stood there, as the Yellow Jacket team walked off the field with their heads hung low. It was de ja vu' all over again. The crowd in the stands slowly packed their belongings and walked glumly to their cars.

"Do you still want to go to Lougini's?"

"Sure. Anything is better than this," Liam said as we left the field.

It felt like old times when we arrived at Lougini's as well. It too, like the football game, was packed to capacity. And again, it was as if Liam had never graduated. Upon arrival, everyone clamored to see him, to talk to him, to touch him, just to be near him. Most of them were football players who had played with him in the past, but there were still a few girls who seemed to forget that we were together. But it didn't matter to Liam, and to be honest, it really didn't matter to me either. We had been in Lougini's for over fifteen minutes and still hadn't made it to a table. As I waited for Liam to finish talking to everybody who approached him, someone had taken the only table that had become available. The look on my face caught Liam's attention immediately.

"I'm sorry, babe. I didn't mean for this to happen."

"It's okay."

"Why don't you sit with us? We've got plenty of room," Coach Green said, coming up from behind us.

"Thanks, Coach. But are you sure?"

"Definitely. We always have room for Liam Larson and his lovely lady."

"Thank you, Mr. Green," I said as he stood to make room for us.

We were surrounded by not only Coach Green and his wife, but three other football players.

"So Liam, how have things been for you since you graduated?" the coach asked.

"Very good, Coach. I've been keeping really busy."

"That's good to hear. I want you to know that Mrs. Green and I are so relieved that you have both recovered from the accident. That was one of the most devastating things that have ever happened to this town, and we're both just so happy that the outcome was good for both of you."

Liam smiled in my direction as the coach spoke. "Thank you, coach. I know there were a lot of people praying for us."

"You're welcome, Liam. I'm just glad you're both here. So tell me, what are you doing?"

"I'm working at Joe's Auto Shop."

"You are? That's great, but I thought you would be playing college ball somewhere. I know half the country wanted you."

Liam's glance returned to mine, this time without the smile. "I know, Coach. But I never planned on playing college ball, you know that, or for that matter, even going to college. Besides, the accident left me with a bum leg. I wouldn't have been able to play anyway."

"A bum leg? I never even noticed it."

"You can't," I chimed in. "He walks with a limp, but it's barely noticeable."

"I'm sorry to hear that, Liam."

"Don't be, Coach. I'm really happy. I'm not upset about it. It's not like that was the reason why I didn't play college ball. I had made that decision a long time ago. I want to help my grandpa on the farm and, as of this past month, I'm also part owner at Joe's Auto Shop."

"Liam, I knew you would do something great with your life. I just always thought it would involve football. You're one, if not the greatest football player I've ever had the privilege to coach. Your insight to the game is something that is truly rare. I could have used some of that insight tonight, that's for sure."

"It was a good game, Coach; it just got away from you at the end. It was anybody's game."

"Well, it should have been ours. You should come to our practices, Liam. I know the guys would love to have you there, and you could help me with the running backs."

"I'll have to think about that. Maybe I will."

"Just say the word. As a matter fact, just show up."

The crowd in Lougini's was in rare form. Half of Walton was there too, blatantly celebrating their victory against us. "So I hear you two are engaged?" Mrs. Green asked politely.

We looked at each other, both of us beaming as she spoke.

"You would be correct, Mrs. Green," Liam answered. "We just set the date."

"Oh, that's wonderful dear. When is the big day?"

"Next summer. August 11th."

"August 11th?"

The question wasn't asked by Mrs. Green but from a familiar voice coming from behind us.

"Well, if it isn't Johnny Bryant," Coach Green replied.

Johnny didn't acknowledge him. Instead, he looked at Liam and me, or more specifically just me.

"You set the date, Jenny?" He didn't seem to care that Liam was sitting next to me or that we were with a group of people.

"Yes we did, Johnny," Liam answered for me as he stood up from his seat. He stationed himself right between Johnny and me. "Do you have a problem with that?"

"No, no I don't, Liam. It's just that the last time I saw Jenny you two hadn't set the date. I guess I was just a little surprised that it's been set so soon after I saw her."

"Why would that surprise you? We are engaged. Wouldn't setting the date be the obvious next step?"

The tension between the two of them could have been cut with a knife. Johnny didn't oblige Liam with an answer. He was stoic toward him and only relaxed when he focused on me. I tried diligently to speak to Johnny with my eyes, imploring him to stop this nonsense. "Don't do this, Johnny." I motioned with my mouth. "Please don't do this." If he only knew the anger Liam was carrying and how the littlest remark could set him off. I didn't want to relive any of that, and I especially didn't want to relive it here at Lougini's.

"Why do you even care when the date is, Johnny?"

"I don't know, Liam. I guess I'm just curious like everybody else. But I don't understand where your anger is coming from?"

"There's no anger, Johnny. I just find it interesting that you would bee-line your way to our table after conveniently overhearing what we were talking about. That's all, friend," Liam said with an underlying tone of sarcasm to his voice.

Johnny remained stoic. In fact, neither one of them said another word. I could feel the stares of the whole table as the two of them carried on, neither one ready to relinquish or back down from the other. I believe everyone was waiting for the worst when Coach Green stepped in.

"Well boys, looks like this conversation seems to be over. Why don't we sit back down and just forget about this. There's no need for this, and I know you guys don't want to cause a scene." I couldn't believe what Coach Green said next. "As a matter of fact, Johnny, you can join us. I would love to hear what you're doing since you graduated."

Didn't he know the history between these two guys? Everybody else seemed to. Liam's lower lip was turning a nice shade of purple as he bit it. Coach Green motioned for both of them to take a seat. The last thing I wanted was for Johnny to sit with us and continue this sorted paw-wow. That ballsy who-gives-a-damn attitude of Johnny's was back in full force.

"Thanks, Coach, but I should be leaving. Congratulations, Jenny," Johnny said to me.

Johnny headed towards the small hallway by the entrance to Lougini's. Coach Green started asking Liam more questions, diverting his attention away from Johnny. I saw my golden opportunity.

"I'll be right back, babe."

"Where are you going?"

"Just to the bathroom, I won't be long."

Liam squeezed my hand as I left. I gave him a reassuring smile that this too would be okay.

The hallway was small and made an "L" shape to the left that led to the bathrooms. I waited impatiently for Johnny to come through the bathroom door.

"Jenny."

"What the hell was that?"

"What are you talking about?"

"You know damn well want I'm talking about. What were you thinking out there? Have you no idea how much Liam despises you?"

"I just wanted to say congratulations; that's all. I can't help it if Liam didn't want to accept it."

"How did you expect him to react? By giving you a hug? My God, Johnny, have you lost your freakin' mind?"

"Jenny, I didn't see any harm in what I did."

"You never do, that's the problem! You know damn well you were there to show Liam up. To make him and everybody else think that you still had the upper hand in this crazy mess between us. Is this some sick and twisted game of yours? Let's see how pissed off we can get Liam and Jenny before they explode on me? I thought you had changed. You told me you had changed. You haven't changed one bit, you're doing the same damn shit from last year. Why?"

"Don't you think you're over-reacting a bit? All I did was say congratulations."

"If it was that simple. You know you had an ulterior motive for coming over. It wasn't about saying congratulations; you were there for one sole purpose, to let Liam know that you weren't out of the picture. I know it, Liam knows it, and you for damn sure know it."

"Just because Liam doesn't like me doesn't mean I'm going to stop trying. I can't stay out of your life; I just can't, and I told you that when I brought you home."

"You can't, Johnny; you just can't act like this. There's too much bad history between all of us."

"I thought we were okay?"

"We are, I think. I don't know. You make me so mad that I can't think straight. I really want to try to be friends, but you're not making it easy for me. If you're going to draw a line, you know I won't cross it. I'll stand by Liam...always. And maybe, if this is what I can expect from you, we're not supposed to be friends. It's going to be too complicated. I need to trust you, and right now I don't think I can. You're like a live wire, unpredictable. I can't chance that with you, especially around Liam. I think you still think there's going to be something between us. There's not: no matter how hard you try, no matter how sweet you are, and no matter what you've done for me. I will always be grateful, but it doesn't allow you to come in and out of my life whenever you damn well please. Liam and I need to move on. We're planning a future together, and I can't let you destroy that."

"I don't understand why you are so angry."

"Angry doesn't even cover it."

"You know what I said about you being angry at me."

I pulled my hair in frustration. "Did you not hear one damn word I said to you? Leave me alone, please!"

Johnny looked truly hurt. "Jenny, I guess it was careless of me, maybe my approach was wrong. But something takes over when I'm near you, and it doesn't even matter if Liam is there. I know I've never had the upper-hand in this, but every time I'm around you guys I feel like I can't back down. I try, but when I see you with him, all I think is that you should be with me. I'll be the first to admit that I get extremely jealous. I know it's too late, but something inside of me won't allow me to stop trying. I don't care if you're marrying him or not. Honestly, I don't think it will matter, even when you're married to him. I'm in love with you, Jenny."

I already knew this. Johnny first professed his feelings when I was in the hospital, but this was the first time he had professed them to me when I could audibly hear him. Liam was only a few yards away from me and Johnny Bryant was telling me he loved me. Nothing seemed to make sense. I felt I was in a fog.

"Jenny, did you hear me?"

"I heard you, Johnny. But why?"

"Why?"

"Why are you doing this to me? Why now? Why here? You know how I feel about you. It's not the same for me."

"Jenny..."

Johnny grabbed my arms and pulled me to him. "Jenny, I can't hold it in anymore. I know it will probably never change your feelings for me. This entire time I've skated around telling you because I didn't want to hurt you. I knew you would be upset, but I think you've always known. Me telling you out loud can't come as a surprise to you, can it? I love you, Jenny, I love you."

Johnny took a step towards me, his face leaning down towards me.

"Please, Johnny, don't do this." My hand went up to block his face from mine.

I turned from him and walked away as he remained standing there. There was nothing more for me to say to him. Never in a million years did I think he would actually say it, even if I did know it to be true. I thought he would realize it could never be and move on with his life, holding on to that little secret forever, realizing in time that what he thought was love was nothing more than an infatuation, a puppy love that would fade away.

"Whoa, slow down. What's the rush?" Liam asked as he ran into me. "You're crying. What happened back there?"

"It's nothing, Liam. Let's go."

"Johnny," he said with venom in his voice. "Is he back there, Jenny? Because if he is..."

"Liam, it's okay. I'm alright. Let's just go." I pulled on Liam's arm, forcing him to follow me outside. He tried to resist as he noticed Johnny walking from where I had just come from.

"This does have to do with Johnny, doesn't it, Jenny?"

I breathed heavily. "Yes, it does. But it's alright now; I've taken care of it."

"Taken care of what? What's that supposed to mean? I don't need you fighting my battles, if that's what you were doing, especially if they involve Johnny Bryant. I can take care of myself and would actually like the opportunity to take care of Johnny. He's been a pain in my ass long enough."

"And you think this has been a joy ride for me?" I said back to him. "Stop it, Liam. I don't want any more fights. I don't want any more run-ins or looks or threats or anything that involves you and Johnny. I'm over it, and I'm sick and tired of it. I told him how I felt, and I told him to leave me alone. I'm done with it. I don't want to talk about it anymore." I said shouting at the top of my voice. "I just want to leave, with you. Please baby, just leave it. It's not worth it. Leave Johnny in there and leave with me. Concentrate on me, please," I said as I regained control of my voice.

Liam obliged. "You're right. I'll try and let it go. I don't want to think about that bastard anymore either. You are all I want to think about. I'm sorry about what happened in there."

"Don't be. You have nothing to be sorry for. It was Johnny's fault."

"You know he's still not over you. For him to be so blatant in front of me and everybody else just proves to me that things haven't changed for him."

"I know. But like I said, does it really matter? What matters is us. I don't care about anything or anybody but you and me. I love you, and we're getting married. My world is good. Let's just forget about Johnny. We have each other."

"You're right, babe," he said as he held onto me. "No more distractions."

"Hopefully," I whispered to myself as we left Lougini's.

Chapter Twelve
One Year

The following morning Liam and I drove over to my house. My parents had returned from their trip, and we were excited to tell them we had set the date. Aside from some tears, my parents were elated that we were moving on with our lives and making our plans. If we were going to do this, they thought it was about time. Grandpa Mack was just as happy for us as well, offering to help in whatever way we needed. He furthermore, insisted on paying for the wedding. Something my dad thought was quite generous of him but declined graciously. Liam seemed more excited than I had seen him in a long time. He had wanted this from the moment he had laid eyes on me. In his mind, August 11th couldn't get here fast enough.

October was flying by in frenzy. For starters, there was the Black Walnut Festival. Most of our friends who had been away at school had come in for it. I got to spend time with Kendra at the carnival, minus my sister. She was only a few months into her new position and being that she was across the country, she wasn't able to take the time off. Kendra and I made up for Ashley's absence by taking in every ride possible. Even though we knew the outcome would make us nauseous, we didn't care. But the most important part of the month was the one year anniversary of Liam and me. A year, when looking back in retrospect had been filled with so much emotion and drama that I couldn't believe that we had come out of it at all. I knew Liam was aware of the date, but I didn't really know how he intended on celebrating it. With the past few weeks leading up to it being so muddled with other distractions neither one of us had discussed it since Serenity Hill. I wasn't sure what to expect from him. But I should have known better to think that Liam would have let this day go without precedence. Little did I know how much thought and preparation he had actually put into it.

It was Saturday and Liam had told me to be ready by noon. He had planned the entire day by himself. He said that this was his gift to me, and whatever I had in mind of doing to forget about it.

The day was absolutely gorgeous, not a cloud in the sky, a beautiful fall day that seemed more like summer. Liam had told me he had somewhere to be early in the morning with Grandpa, so I made myself useful by tending to the horses and tidying the house up a bit. By eleven-thirty, I was finished and sat myself down on the steps being careful of the broken one to wait for Liam's return. By twelve-thirty, I was still sitting and there was no sight of Liam. By twelve-forty-five, I had resigned to the fact that he and Grandpa had become detained and wasn't coming. I was almost ready to give up when I saw Liam's truck rounding the corner that led to the house. He rapidly jumped out of the truck and was at my side instantly with a dozen lavender roses in his hand.

"Happy Anniversary, Jenny."

I remained quiet, only hinting that I was happy to see him with a slight smile.

"What?" he asked, confused.

"You're late."

"I know. I'm sorry. I had to finish something before I picked you up."

"You could have called me."

"I know, but if I did that, then I would have been even later. I really needed to finish what I was doing."

"What were you doing?"

"I can't tell you. It's a surprise."

This time Liam pulled my face to his as he cupped it in his hands and kissed me. "Don't be mad at me. Once you see what I have for you, you'll realize it was worth me being late. Okay? Don't be mad, it's our anniversary."

I kissed him back fervently, relinquishing my petty anger. "Happy Anniversary."

"Are you ready?"

"Definitely, I can't wait."

"Great, then let's go. We have a little bit of a drive ahead of us."

"What are you doing?" I asked as he picked me up in his arms.

"Taking care of you. I don't want you to have to do anything for yourself today. I'm taking care of everything and that includes you."

I began to giggle as he positioned me next to him in the cab of his truck.

"Here you go, my love. Oh, before I forget, there's one thing I forgot to do," Liam said.

"What's that?"

"This," he whispered softly.

I thought for sure that he was going to kiss me when to my surprise he didn't. Instead he leaned in to me, reaching behind my back and pulled out a blue bandana.

"This is for you, Jen."

"A bandana? Not again, Liam."

"I need you to put it on."

"Put it on? Why? You know we're still at the house. If you're thinking about doing something kinky, I suggest you wait, Grandpa could pull up at any moment."

"Just put it on, please."

"Liam, why are you doing this?"

"I told you I had a surprise for you. I want to see your reaction the moment you lay eyes on it."

"Whatever you have planned, I'll be surprised. You don't need to do all this."

"Yes I do, so humor me and please wear it."

I helped Liam tie it behind my head as he made sure there was no way I could see. His playful movements were amusing. He held onto my hand as he drove. I tried to imagine where we were going by envisioning what we should be passing, but after a few minutes the only thing I could tell was we were headed away from town. We drove for a long time before Liam's truck pulled off of the road.

"Do you have any idea where I'm taking you?"

"No, not a clue."

"Good. I will give you a hint though; I'm taking you someplace where you can touch the stars."

"Seriously Liam, where are we going?"

"That's all I'm telling you."

"For all I know, you're just saying that to lead me on, so I won't figure it out."

"No, I'm not. But no more clues, we're almost there."

"I'm glad. This bandana is itchy."

After about fifteen more minutes, Liam put the truck into park. My hands searched for Liam as I groped the inside of the truck cab. He was being peculiarly quiet. Not saying a word.

"Liam? Is everything okay? Are we here?"

"Everything is fine. In fact, everything is perfect. And yeah, we're here."

"Soooo, are you going to show me what the surprise is or are we just going to sit here, with me in total darkness, literally."

Liam didn't answer me; instead he took my hand and led me outside. We both stood stationery, Liam still unusually quiet.

"Liam..."

He slowly lifted the bandana from my eyes, but made sure I focused on him instead of our surroundings.

"I love you," he said affectionately.

"I love you too, Liam. Can I look now?"

"No. Not yet. Just look at me."

"Come on. You've kept me in suspense for hours."

"Okay, I guess I shouldn't keep you waiting. But you still can't look yet." He gently placed the bandana back over my eyes. At this point, I was thinking the surprise was just keeping me in the dark. But Liam took me in his arms and carried me to what I thought our destination was. I could feel the warmth from the sun as it struck my skin and there was a warm breeze that was floating in the air that when it hit me, sent a rush of euphoria through me. It felt good and intoxicating as I breathed it in.

"Okay, Jenny we're here."

My heart was pounding. I had been looking forward to this moment since he picked me up, but now that it was finally here I found myself becoming intimidated by the moment. Liam carefully took the bandana from my eyes. Just as I became adjusted to the sunlight, I found myself looking at an incredible sight before me. We were at Serenity Hill. The horizon was in front of us showcasing its magnificent painted sky. But what caught my eye was what was blocking part of the sky's view. In front of me was the most breathtaking gazebo I had ever seen, laden in lavender roses. It stood in a clearing near the cliff next to the old oak tree and trickling brook. I was speechless. All I could do was stare.

"You did this?"

"Just for you, babe."

"For me?" My emotions were getting the best of me as I tried in vain to hold back my tears.

"I love you, Jenny. I've wanted to do this for you ever since I first brought you here. I've been working on it in my spare time, hoping I could get it completed for today."

"You mean you actually made this?"

"Are you surprised?"

"Yeah, I guess. I know you're talented at fixing things, but I never thought you could do this. I thought all your talents lay in football and fixing cars. This is amazing, Liam." I touched the intricate woodwork.

"Grandpa taught me."

"Did he help you?"

"A little. I mean he didn't help make the gazebo. I did this all on my own in the barn, but he did help get the wood and materials for me."

"I can't believe you, Liam. It's so pretty. You never cease to amaze me." I was crying, unable to hold it back.

"This is only part of what I have for you, Jenny."

"What? There can't be more. I don't want anything else."

Liam took my hand and walked me inside the gazebo. The soft wind rustled the roses releasing their sweet scent on us. I closed my eyes as I inhaled it, taking in the moment. Liam led me to the center. The entire structure was painted in white except for the roof. It was a silvery blue. There were tiny holes sporadically placed in the ceiling, creating the effect of a starry night sky.

"Liam, it's breathtaking."

"I wanted the roof to look like the evening sky at Brush Creek Road. Some of my fondest memories are of us sitting there watching the sunset. You always said you felt like you could touch the stars. I wanted to make that real for you, Jenny."

"Liam, I don't know what to say. I can't believe you did this for me. I mean with everything that's been going on in our lives, when did you find the time to do this?"

"I found the time here and there, mostly at night when I would come home from Joe's or after helping Grandpa. I did a lot after you returned from Glenville. After our fight, I spent almost every waking minute working on it in the barn. I didn't know if we were going to stay together, but even if we weren't I wanted you to have this. Grandpa helped me bring it up today. That's why I was late."

"But I've been at the house for weeks. I never saw you working on anything."

"Believe me it was difficult, but I found my ways."

"I'm sorry I was mad. If I knew..."

"Shhhh... don't apologize." Liam held me close to him as he wrapped his arms around me.

"Liam, we're so close to the top of the world, I feel I could touch the sky."

"That's how I wanted you to feel, Jen. I wanted the gazebo to be here so you could feel like you were at the edge of Heaven. I can't imagine being any closer to it than here."

"I can never thank you enough for this, but I'm definitely going to try."

"You already have, babe."

We held on to each other and just enjoyed the solitude the gazebo brought us, Liam holding me close as we danced to our own music.

"I don't ever want us to stop dancing, Liam."

"Our life is a dance, babe. As long as we are together, the music will never stop."

"You're too good to me. I could stay here forever," I said after we finally sat down.

"I don't know about forever but how about tonight?"

"Are you serious? But we don't have any blankets or pillows or anything?" Liam gave me his famous, crooked smile.

"What did you do?"

"You didn't think I would bring you here unprepared did you? I have it all: blankets, pillows, food and...this."

Liam reached inside his pocket and pulled out a tiny black box.

"Liam!" I gasped.

"I know you know how much I love you, but I don't think you realize the extent of it. Ever since the accident, I thought I would never be the same again. I wanted so badly to fix things, to make things right, to take away the grief and go back to how it was before April 11th, but I couldn't. I did a lot of soul-searching while you were in the hospital, and I knew that I couldn't change things, but I wanted to make sure that if God answered my prayers and allowed you to come back to me that I would make your world a better place to live in. I promised God that. I didn't care about my world, because if yours was right then mine would be too. I know it took a while for me to live up to that promise. I kind of lost my way there for a while and I'm sorry for that."

"You don't need to say this. We're past all that," I insisted.

"Yes, I do. Something came over me, and I felt like you would be better off without me. I didn't want to hurt you anymore. And I know now that I was wrong in thinking like that, but at the time, I couldn't see straight and there seemed to be no other way. I know I've already told you this stuff, but the past month or so has been crazy for some reason, maybe it was the nightmares and seeing you with Johnny and even my drinking," Liam said slowly as he lowered his head. "I get crazy sometimes when it comes to you, and I know it's not always a good crazy. My jealousy over stuff is only because of my feelings for you. Like I said, I made a promise to God that I would be a better person, and I'm trying really hard to live up to that. I told you once that I wanted to make things right. That's why I wanted to forgive Johnny and move on with him, at least be friendly with him when I saw him, but it was too hard for me to do that. I tried, really. And I thought I was able to until I saw him bringing you home that night from Glenville. I knew then that it wasn't over for me, and from what happened at Lougini's, I would say it's not over with him either.

But that's not important. What is important is that I'm going to try again. I need to mean it this time. I believe if I'm right with you, then there'll be nothing but good for us. You know, like karma: if you do right then good things comes back to you. So, that's what this is about. I've been working every spare second on this for you but for me too. This gazebo represents so much more than just a present to you; it represents a new beginning for me to show you that I'm going to try my damnedest to make you trust me and for you to be proud of me. I love you, Jen, with all my heart and soul. I'm so sorry for how things have been. I know there's been tension between us, and the awkwardness of our arguing has just about killed me. I never wanted it and am sorry it's there."

Liam's gaze went to the floor as he took the box in his hand and opened it. I could hardly breathe as I watched him. His smile was so sweet and innocent, and his eyes possessed an unusual twinkle as they became masked in tears. His voice was quivering as he spoke. "Jenny, I promise to love and to hold onto you until my last dying breath on this earth, and when the fateful day arrives, I will continue to love you eternally forever more."

He slipped on my ring finger next to my engagement ring a plain silver band. It was demure in its simplicity and beauty, the only ornamentation gracing it was the words *Forever Jenny and Liam* inscribed on the inside of it. I stood there shaking almost uncontrollably as Liam kissed my hand. He in turn placed an identical band in my hand. "Here, Jenny, this is for me." I mimicked Liam's motions and slid the silver band on his ring finger. It fit perfectly. I couldn't breathe; my emotions were in shock as I gazed at our hands. "Before you say anything, I have one more gift for you." I looked at him in disbelief. He walked behind the gazebo and came back with a plain white box tied together with a blue ribbon. "Here."

"Liam."

"Please," he said as he pushed the box into my hands.

I carefully untied the ribbon, watching it float to the floor. Inside the box, I found the most beautiful white dress. I pulled it out and held it against my quivering body. It was understated in its beauty, showing a sweetheart neckline with lace that continued to the open back. The sleeves were short and capped at the top while the skirt fell effortlessly from its bodice as I imagined the layers of organza kissing my ankles.

"I don't know what to say Liam, it's gorgeous. Can I put it on?"

"Yes, definitely. I want you to wear it."

"I took the dress along with the ribbon and went behind the oak tree. When I appeared before Liam wearing it, I found him in a pair of black pants and a form fitting white button up shirt. Both of us were in our bare feet.

"Liam, you look so handsome."

"And you take my breath away, Jenny; the dress looks beautiful on you."

I walked toward him as he took both of my hands in his. "I wanted this day to be special, and I know this may feel like a wedding ceremony to you. Believe me I had thoughts of having a minister here, but what this represents is a promise ceremony from me to you that I will never take you for granted, will always love you, and be here for you no matter what the circumstances. Good or bad, babe, I promise to love you for who you are and for what you mean to me. This is my gift to you. This gazebo represents our love for one another and whenever you come here, I want you to feel that love, a place that welcomes you with open arms and forgives with those same arms. There is no sadness, pain, or guilt here, only love, Jenny."

I couldn't speak, but Liam could see in my eyes the joy he had just given me. His lips came to mine as he kissed me, tenderly, of course, and wiped away my grateful tears. "Thank you," I finally whispered.

"I meant every word I just said. You make me a better person, and without you, I would be nothing. I'm much stronger because of you."

We stayed there that night as Liam serenaded me with his guitar. We were wrapped in the blankets that Liam had brought, but more importantly, we were wrapped in our love for one another. Never had I been surer of anything in my entire life. Liam had given me something that was beyond the silver bands and beautiful dress; he had given me his word, his undying commitment that he would love me, protect me and be there for me today, tomorrow and into forever, on this earth and beyond.

Chapter Thirteen
A New Can of Worms

The next couple of months saw many changes in my life. For one, my parents finally closed the business. After a very heartfelt and painful decision they came to the conclusion that it was their only option. Dad's health had been deteriorating at a faster rate than we were prepared for. He gave full control to Billy and a few other people to run the store, something he had never done in the thirty years he owned the business. He had been diagnosed with hypertension along with a heart arrhythmia and had doctor's orders that he should retire.

It was heart-wrenching for my dad. He had built the store up from a tiny one room feed store into the business that it was known now throughout the state, supplying groceries to numerous smaller stores for over three decades. It was like losing a part of the family to close it, but with no other options, everyone agreed it was the right thing to do.

I guess the one good thing about retirement was Mom and Dad would now have more time for traveling. This couldn't have come at a better time for them with my impending nuptials and Ashley's prospering career. Besides, they had always wanted to go to California, and now they had no excuses not to go. I felt horrible that I couldn't step in and take over for them, but I knew I wasn't capable of handling such a tall order. I did have experience in running the store, but not enough. I knew exactly what would happen too; Dad would see me struggling and would want to help. This would be exactly the opposite of why we had him retire. It was the best for all of us to sell the store and let Mom and Dad move on.

And then there was Liam, of course. He and Joe were becoming inundated with business at the shop, being overrun with so many clients that Liam was afraid that they might have to turn down customers, something that clearly in their eyes was not an option. Their only option was to expand. Joe's shop was only capable of handling a few cars at a time, and at last count, all their lifts were in use, and eight more cars were in the wings waiting. There was a vacant building beside them; it was the perfect spot for them to expand their business. Liam and Joe had asked Parker to become a third partner. With no obligations now that Kelli was out of the picture, Parker was more than happy for the opportunity. He had sunk into a deep depression since Kelli had broken up with him. He still couldn't believe she was out of his life. It had come out of nowhere for Parker who had taken Liam with him to Charleston only a month earlier to look at engagement rings. The shop would be a welcome distraction for him and couldn't have come at a better time.

"I feel really bad about Kelli and Parker," I said to Liam as he replaced a tire on a 1965 banana yellow Corvette.

"Yeah, me too. I didn't see that one coming."

"I don't think Parker did either. Is he doing okay?"

"Yeah, I guess. We're keeping him pretty busy here at the shop, so he hasn't had a lot of time to think about the break-up."

"What about when he's away from here? They were practically living together. I bet he can't go back to his place without reminders of her."

"I guess. But from what he told me, she pretty much took everything she had before she left him. The place was almost empty."

Liam stopped what he was doing and gave me an intimidating look.

"What? Why are you looking at me like that?"

"I don't know, I guess I'm just wondering if you would ever do to me what Kelli did to Parker."

"You're joking, aren't you?" I asked, and Liam raised himself up to meet me.

"Yeah, I am. I know you wouldn't. I guess I'm just surprised as anyone about their break-up. I never in a million years would have ever called that one. I saw Parker and Kelli together forever. Kinda like you and me. I guess that's why I asked. "

"But we're different than them, Liam. You never have to worry about me leaving you. I think I've convinced you of that. To be honest, their break-up isn't as surprising to me as maybe it was to you."

"Why do you say that?"

"Well, because, I mean I really haven't known Kelli as long as you have, but in the short time I have I've gotten to become pretty good friends with her."

"And?" Liam waited for me to finish.

"I never told Parker this, and I feel bad because I actually told him I would have said something to him if I saw a change in Kelli, but it was after the fact and he was already hurting, so I didn't think it was necessary."

"What is it, Jenny?"

"It's just that, a lot of times she would talk about dating other guys and wanting to do things that Parker didn't seem interested in doing. I mean, I know Parker wanted to settle down here in Spencer and make a life with Kelli, but she's never wanted that, at least from what I gathered from my conversations with her. She's never talked about staying here. She's always wanted to leave Spencer."

"Then why wouldn't she have told Parker instead of stringing him along all this time?"

"I don't know. I can't speak for her, and honestly I didn't think it was any of my business. I do know she loved him, and it probably killed her to have to break up with him. But I think maybe she thought if she didn't make the break now she never would. I think what they had was a high school romance, and once that was over so was their relationship, at least in her eyes. Their break-up was probably inevitable. The fact that it happened now may have been a blessing in disguise. I think Kelli wanted something more than this town or Parker could give her."

"I hope you never feel that way, Jenny. That I'm keeping you here."

"Why in the world would you say or think that? We're different than Kelli and Parker. What we have is destiny, what they had for each other was lust," I said as Liam laughed. "What? Why are you laughing?"

"I don't know, I guess I find it amusing that you thought their relationship was based solely on sex."

"Well, it was, wasn't it?"

"Maybe most of it, but Parker did love her and wanted to marry her."

"I know. But I think Kelli was in love with the idea of being in love. Once that wore off, she realized that she and Parker really didn't have anything in common."

"Well, it's good to know that you feel our relationship is based on a deeper level than just the physical aspect of it. Although, I will say, I do enjoy that part very much." He pulled me to him.

"I must agree with you, Mr. Larson." Liam had gently pushed me down on the floor. It was covered in grease, but I really couldn't have cared less.

"Do you two need to get a room or something?" Joe had walked in.

"Sure, since you're asking. Do you mind taking over while I take my girl back to our place?" Liam said with a playful grin on his face.

"You know I have to go," I said.

"I know, babe, just me hoping, that's all. When will you be back?"

"I'm not sure, hopefully by nine, but long enough for me to sign up for my classes."

"I love you, girl."

"I love you too. See you tonight when I get back?"

"Yeah, I should be done here by nine too. I'll meet you at home. This time I promise that I'll have my cell on."

"Good. See you tonight. Bye Joe," I said as I waved to him.

"Bye Jenny," Joe replied back in his husky voice.

I arrived at Glenville's campus only to find that the line for class sign-up wrapped around the administration building.

"Ugh! This is going to take forever," I said under my breath. At this rate, I would be here until dark. I stood in line, and after only an hour I had moved a mere few inches. I considered if this was even worth it. The thought crossed my mind just to give up and wait until next year, but I was already here, and if I was to return without classes I knew Liam would send me back. He was going to make sure I went through with this.

"This line is never going to move," the woman said behind me.

"I know what you mean," I said to her. "I'd come back tomorrow if I knew my fate wasn't going to be the same as today."

"Your fate is already mapped out, my dear. You're destined to be here today." I knew that voice.

"Hello, Jenny," she said as I turned to greet her.

"Gertie!" I exclaimed as I gave her a huge hug. "Oh my God, I'm so glad to see you."

"How have you been, Jenny? You look great."

"I'm doing great. How are you?"

"Can't complain."

"What are you doing here? Are you here for Johnny?"

"No, not actually. It's for me."

"You? You're going to school here?"

"Yes, I am. Well, at least part time. I'm just taking a night class for now. They're offering a psychology class on how the mind interprets dreams. And since that's right up my alley, I thought it would be a good class to start with."

"A class about dreams?" I said inquisitively.

"Yes, Jenny. Why are you thinking about taking the same class?"

I paused. "No. I'm here for some business courses if I can get them before school starts. This line is taking forever."

"I know. I was here this morning; I left thinking that it would be shorter by now. I guess my woman's intuition is waning," she said laughing.

"It's really good to see you, Gertie. I've missed you."

"Same here, Jenny."

"So you want to take some business classes?"

"I think so, although your psychology class sounds very interesting. Maybe I should take it too."

"That would be great if you did. It would be nice to know someone, especially since I already feel like the odd ball because of my age."

"Don't be silly, Gertie. You'll fit right in. Age is only a number."

"Thank you, dear. So are you going to take the class?"

"I am now," I said with a smile.

"Wonderful."

"I think it might benefit me, to be quite honest," I said.

"You sound as if you have a personal reason to learn more about this subject."

"You could say I have a vested interest in it."

"Very interesting, Jenny. You never cease to keep me on my toes, hon."

"I seem to have that effect on you."

The line was finally moving.

"How have things been, Jenny? I haven't talked to you since this past summer."

"Good. I've been busy. Liam and I are getting married, and Liam is now part owner at Joe Michaels Auto Shop."

"Johnny told me that. He also told me that the wedding was this commimg summer. Is that true?"

For some reason, hearing Gertie ask me about the wedding made everything seem wrong and awkward, as though our impending nuptials was a bad thing.

"Yeah, Johnny would be right. The wedding is scheduled for next August, August 11th to be exact."

"The eleventh?" Gertie asked with wispiness to her voice.

"Yeah, the eleventh. I figured I might as well go with it. I can't keep ignoring it."

"I can see that dear, and as it should be. It will always be a part of you, Jenny. Just remember that although you are in control of your fate, forcing what should or should not be can cause unfavorable consequences. Continue to let the eleven be your guide, just don't read into things because you think they should be that way."

"Are you trying to tell me that I shouldn't marry Liam on the eleventh?"

"No, dear, not at all. I just don't want you to think that you have to make every decision based on that number. It will always be there. There's no need for it to influence your every decision. That should come naturally."

"I appreciate the advice, and I didn't set the date just because of it being the eleventh. That's the first time Liam noticed me. It's a very special day to him and to me too. We realized there wasn't a better day than that."

"Then it's meant to be, Jenny, I'm happy for the two of you."

"Thanks, Gertie. That means a lot, especially coming from you. You are very dear to me. I hope you know that. You taught me not to be scared and to believe in myself. This time last year I was scared to death of what the eleven meant. But now I know to look at it differently. I have you to thank for that. I don't know how I could have gotten through those months after the accident if it hadn't been for me hearing your comforting words."

"I can see you're a much stronger person than the sweet but somewhat timid girl I met in my shop last year. You've grown and it shows. You have endured a lot over your short time on this earth, not all of it being good, but you've been able to grow from the negativity and not let it bring you down. That's an admirable quality."

I didn't say a word, but she must have read my mind again because I was totally confused by her comment. Taking my hands into her white, wispy ones, she said, "Your karma my dear."

"My karma?"

"Yes, Jenny. Have you ever heard the phrase, what goes around comes around?"

"Yes."

"Your past can dictate your future. If your past has been unsettling and you as a person have had some sordid history in your past, well, the result of that sordid past could come back to haunt you in your future. Just as if you have done something good, then your future could be rewarded as a result of that."

"So, what you're really trying to tell me is that it will come back to bite you in the butt."

"Well I wouldn't have said it quite as eloquently as you, but yes, you seem to understand what I mean."

"My past up until last year has pretty much been boring, Gertie. I haven't done anything that I can remember that should affect my future in any way."

"I beg to differ, Jenny. You have led quite an extraordinary life, especially this last year. You tried in vain to make everything right for all parties concerned, whether it is with my son, or Liam or someone else."

I lowered my head as she spoke only to have her delicate hand raise it up to meet her intuitive eyes. "Listen, Jenny, I'm not trying to remind you of some of your more unpleasant memories. I'm only trying to tell you that I know what I'm talking about. Don't be afraid of what the future holds for you...and Liam. Your journey is destined to have many more bumps and detours; I'm only saying that the light at the end of the tunnel that you see might not exactly hold what you think."

"Is there anything about me that I can't keep from you?"

"Time will only tell, my dear," she said with a sing-song tone to her voice.

"Gertie, I'm so glad we've had this chance to talk. You don't know what this means to me running into you here."

"You act as though we would never see each other again, Jenny."

I paused, knowing full well that she out of anybody probably knew why I thought that.

"Honestly Gertie, I did. I don't know how much Johnny has told you about us, especially lately, but in a matter of speaking, I didn't see me seeing you anymore."

"Oh, I see. This has to do with Liam and Johnny, doesn't it?"

I nodded my head in agreement.

"Ahem," a voice from behind me said.

My back had been turned away from the line as Gertie and I had been talking. We were finally at the front, where a somewhat agitated clerk was becoming quite annoyed by my ignorance of him. "Oh, I'm sorry sir, I wasn't paying attention. Gertie, do you have some time? I would love to continue our talk. I can wait for you."

"Of course my dear, let's get our classes and then go for a walk. I think our talk is long overdue."

I was able to get into the Psychology class on Tuesdays, but the Money Management course was filled. There were no other classes available. So for this semester at least, I would only being taking the one course. I knew this would come as a shock to Liam, not only had I not gotten the courses I wanted, I was taking something completely different from what I had ever talked about and it was with his worst enemy's mother. I couldn't wait to unload this onto him. I could see the sparks flying already as he became unraveled.

"So tell me, Jenny, what's going on with Liam and Johnny that you feel that our friendship is at stake?"

"Gertie, I don't know where to begin. I thought everything from this summer after the accident was the start of a new beginning for all three of us. But it was all just a lie. Liam and Johnny both were covering up their true feelings between themselves for my benefit apparently. I think both of them wanted to let go of the hostility that had formed between them and led up to the accident, but for some reason neither one of them could. And with my injuries, I believe everyone was so focused on me that they felt the best thing was for me to believe that they had made up and were friends again."

"You mean they're not?"

"Not at all. In fact, I think it's worse than ever. I've seen a pure hatred grow between them in the past couple of months that I've never seen before. I'm afraid that at some point, they will again try to do something stupid because of their feelings. Johnny hasn't told you any of this?" I asked seeing Gertie's surprise.

"I'm sorry, but no. Johnny spends most of his time here in Glenville. He's only home occasionally, and even then I normally don't see much of him."

"I thought you guys were closer than that."

"We are, but this has been a very unsettling and hard year for Johnny. Not just with what happened with you, but there's been a lot of stress at our house as well." I gave Gertie a concerned look. "Jenny, I'm getting a divorce from Johnny's father."

"What? I'm sorry, I didn't know."

"There's no need for you to say you're sorry, there was no way you would have known. I tried to keep it as hush-hush as possible. It's okay though, it's been coming for years. Mr. Bryant and I have been living separate lives for a long time; it's a mutual decision. But it's still been very hard on Johnny. He hasn't wanted to accept it, and I must admit that Mr. Bryant and I could have probably picked a better time to have told him. It was right after your accident, dear. I didn't mean for it to happen like that. We both knew what Johnny was going through and the guilt he felt. But he accidentally overheard us one night talking about it and well, it just came out. That's one reason Johnny moved in with his friend, Jake."

I stood there dumbstruck as she told me this, realizing that Johnny had to be going through his own personal hell. "I don't know what to say."

"Dear, there's nothing to say. It's alright and for the best. Anyway, I believe Johnny will come around. He does call on a regular basis, and it's not like I don't ever see him. He still helps when he can at *The Spiritual Ship,* and he was home for Thanksgiving. But as far as what's going on with the three of you, I really can't help you. He hasn't said anything at all to me about you or Liam."

I found that somewhat odd. Gertie had always been Johnny's confidante. He told her everything, and for him not to mention the rift that was still going on between him and Liam seemed quite strange to me. "Well, it probably doesn't even matter anyway. I'm being selfish telling you about my petty problems when you're going through all this."

"Jenny, I want you to talk to me. If I can help you, I want to. That's what I do, dear, and you've become far too important to me for me not to help you. In a way, I might know you better than you do. I just mean that your life is not ordinary. You have special circumstances that make you stand out, like your number eleven.

Please, Jenny, I want you to always be able to talk to me. I'll try to help you in any way I can. Don't let what's going on between Liam and Johnny interfere with what you need to take care of in your own life. Your soul is just as important, maybe more. Only if your soul is gleaming, will you."

"That all sounds good, Gertie, but I think that's easier said than done. What's going on with Liam and Johnny and I guess me too, is so much more complicated. Everything seems so out of hand and messed up. I don't know if things will ever be right."

"Jenny, can I ask you a very personal question? And if I may ask, will you answer it honestly without holding back?"

"Sure," I said, doubting what I was obliging too.

"How do you feel about my son?"

"How do I feel about him? I like him. I think he's a very nice guy, and I will always feel indebted to him for what he did for me."

"That's not what I mean, Jenny, and you know it. How do you feel about my son? Do you have any feelings for him like you do for Liam?"

I felt like I had just been hit by a two ton truck. Never did I think Gertie, of all people, would ask me such a question. "Gertie..."

"Deep down, Jenny do your feelings for Johnny go any deeper than just the platonic friendship you say you have for him?"

"I don't think I can answer that."

"Can't or shouldn't? I'm not trying to put you on the spot with this, but I know my son pretty well. I don't think he would be this upset if he didn't feel you have feelings for him that are stronger than you are willing to admit. I believe some of my son's frustrations lie with the fact that the girl he's in love with might have feelings for him too."

"Gertie, he can't be in love with me. How can he be in love with me when there's never been anything between us? I've asked him this myself. I truly believe this is just a game with him, nothing more."

"Did you ever think that it was possible to carry feelings for more than one person? I think deep down you have stronger feelings for Johnny than you're willing to admit, and possibly, that's where some of your frustration is stemming from."

"What a thing to say to me! You're wrong."

"Just hear me out. I'm not trying to cause anymore grief in your life. I'm just trying to enlighten you."

"But you're saying it like you already know I do."

"Jenny, do you forget who you are talking to? I see how you react when Johnny's name is mentioned, and more importantly, I see the warmth in your voice when you say his name. It's nothing to be ashamed of. I know that you're in love with Liam, and I'm not trying to persuade you otherwise. I just think that maybe, and I mean maybe, you should think about what I said."

I didn't or maybe couldn't respond. All of a sudden, I wished I had never run into Gertie. She was stirring up a new can of worms that should have been left un-open.

"Gertie, you're wrong. I do have feelings for Johnny, but they're not like that. What we share is special, but it nowhere compares to what I share with Liam. I will always be obliged for what Johnny did for me. I know I wouldn't be here talking to you if he hadn't been there for me that night. But, the only thing that came out of that was a mutual respect and friendship for one another, at least for me."

"Be that as it may, Jenny, but I know what I'm saying. I am a woman myself; I may be a little be older than you and even though my marriage didn't work out, I do know what it is to be in love and feel that extra something special because of him. You may deny it now, hon, but I truly believe under this tough exterior you are trying to display, there is a part of you that feels that extra something special for Johnny too."

"But Gertie, I can't be in love with Johnny when I'm in love with Liam."

"Jenny, it's been known to happen before, to have feelings for more than one person. And I never said you were in love with Johnny, I said I could tell you felt something for him more than you were willing to admit. You were the one that said love." I looked away feeling ashamed for some reason. "Listen, Jenny, I'm sorry I've made you uncomfortable. That was never my intent. Johnny is my son, and when he's upset, it transcends to me. He's hurting, and I know it's partially because of his feelings for you. I've needed to tell you this for a while but never thought the timing was right until now."

"I guess I understand, Gertie, but can I ask you something, if that is alright?"

"Of course. What is it?"

"You said that you could tell that when I speak of Johnny that my emotions seem different."

"Yes, that's right."

"But how could you say that when this is the first time I've seen you since I visited you in your shop? That was almost a year ago. And I know that you couldn't have seen or heard it then in my voice. In all honesty, this time last year, I literally loathed Johnny. I detested the mere ground he walked on."

"You're right, but you forget I did speak with you over the summer. Besides, reading people is part of my business."

I again became very uncomfortable. She seemed to have the innate ability to read me better than I could read myself. "Do you think you're saying this because of how close I feel to you and that Johnny is your son? I mean maybe this could be wishful thinking on your part that Johnny and I could get together?"

A smile arose on Gertie's face. "Jenny, I'm not saying this for my benefit. Don't get me wrong, the mere notion of you being Johnny's girlfriend would be very pleasing to me, but this is for his benefit too. Jenny, you must realize by now how he feels about you. I do believe his feelings for you in the beginning were, candidly speaking, more physical, if anything. But I know my son better than anyone else, and I have seen how his eyes light up at the mere mention of your name. I saw how he was when you were in the hospital. He was beside himself, and it was very hard for him to keep even an arm's length distance from you while you were there. But he had no choice with Liam being present. He knew he was crossing a line if he visited you too often. That is why he made his visits with you infrequent, and eventually he saw it was best not to visit you at all."

I had nothing to say. All this was more than I was expecting. I was just supposed to come here and sign up for a couple of classes and be on my way. I felt smothered. Feelings I thought were nothing more than gratitude were now surfacing to be something much more. Johnny was a friend, that was it. We reached the parking lot, and I stood there dumbstruck as Gertie seemed undaunted by what was said. I knew she meant no harm, but she was causing more stress for me. I tried to be aloof to it, but that was next to impossible to do with Gertie.

"Listen, Jenny, I don't want any ill will between us. We're going to be seeing a lot of each other now that we're in school together. I didn't want to keep this from you anymore. I care deeply for you, and I know you've got a lot going on mentally. I just wanted you to be conscious of where some of your frustration may be coming from. That's all. Maybe I am wrong on this. It's been known to happen," she said with a slight laugh. "But I couldn't go on without bringing this up. Just think about what I said. Mull it over. You're feelings for Liam are probably spot on, but it doesn't hurt to consider Johnny's. He deserves the truth from you, even if it's not what he wants to hear."

Gertie embraced me with a gentle but firm hug. Our eyes met as she pulled away from me.

"It was good to see you, Gertie," I said as she still held onto me.

"It was good to see you too, Jenny. I'm looking forward to our time together."

"I'll see you soon."

"Bye, dear."

I stood there as she walked away. There were countless people passing me, but I didn't notice any of them. There was no way in hell that she was right about this. She was just looking out for her son like any mother would. But in the back of my mind, I also knew better. I had always second guessed myself when it came to Johnny. I knew all along his feelings for me, but I couldn't act on them. I loved Liam. But Johnny was always there, Gertie was right. Johnny did care for me; he did love me, and I... "This is crazy!" I said out loud as I covered my face with my hands. All I knew was that I needed to get home to Liam, put this afternoon out of my head, and concentrate on the road ahead, the road that included Liam and I on it together and nobody else.

Chapter Fourteen
Not Again

The drive from Glenville was a blur. I knew I had feelings for Johnny, but they were purely based on gratitude, a friendship born from his selfless acts and never giving up attitude towards me. How could I not be indebted to him after what he did for me? But Johnny's stubborn attitude had caused problems. Not only was he not getting the message to back off with his feelings towards me, but his behavior had me question my thoughts for him. And because of that, I really didn't like Johnny. I didn't need to question my own feelings when I knew all along how I felt. It was just more mind games on Johnny's part, or was it? I couldn't allow myself to think otherwise. To do so, would only mean heartache... for Johnny.

It was ten when I arrived home. It was dark inside except for a small table lamp that illuminated the living room. As I walked up the steps, being careful not to fall into the broken one, I could see through the window Liam sitting on the floral sofa. My heart leapt at the sight. That alone was my validation of where I belonged. As I entered the door, Liam rose to his feet and was at my side in seconds to take me in his arms. I never grew old of Liam's playful mannerisms. It was one of Liam's most irresistible traits that I loved so much about him.

"I thought you would never get here," he said with his body pressed against mine. "I don't know if I'm going to be able to stand you being away from me, babe."

"It's only going to be one night a week. You'll be fine. I was only gone for the afternoon."

"Technically, you were gone the whole afternoon and part of the evening. You said you would be home around nine; you're over an hour late. I should be mad at you."

"Mad at me? How can you be mad at me?" I said as I caressed the nape of his neck with my hand.

"I'm not mad, babe, but I am going to reprimand you for being an hour late."

"You are, are you?"

"Yes I am," he said as he swept me off of my feet and into his arms.

"It's really not my fault. The line for registration was a mile long."

"Did you get the classes you wanted?"

"Well, not exactly." I could feel my blood pressure rise as I was about to tell him who I had run into. The last time Liam and I spoke of Gertie he had told me never to see or mention her name again. Informing him that I would be having a class with her for the next few months would not sit well with him.

"What happened, were they already filled?"

"Yeah, they were. I think I should have registered earlier. But I did get into one class."

"What is it?"

"A psychology class."

"Psychology?" He mimicked me.

"Yeah."

"Why psychology?"

"I don't know. I guess when I was reading over the class descriptions this one intrigued me. It's more about analyzing dreams and the unconsciousness than anything else. And with our history, I thought it might be interesting, besides there was nothing else for me to take."

Liam just looked at me.

"Maybe this class can help me make sense of the dreams we're having."

"Jenny, really? Come on. I'm not letting my stupid dreams or yours run our lives, and that is exactly what they're doing if you feel compelled to take a class about them. Why didn't you sign up for something that would be more suited to your major?"

"Because I don't know what I want to major in."

"What about the business courses?"

"They weren't available, and I didn't see any harm in taking this course. Besides, who knows, maybe I'll like it well enough that I will want to pursue something in this. And one of my soul reasons for ever wanting to go into business was so I could someday take over for my dad or at least help him. Now that he's closed the business I don't know if I want to pursue a career in that anymore."

"Well hell, Jenny, if you want to take a psych class, then go ahead. It's not up to me anyway. Who knows, maybe you'll end up learning something about our damn dreams after all. Besides I'm just happy you're home where you belong. Like I said you were gone way too long for me today."

"I'm home now."

"Yes, you are." Liam's eyes were a contented color tonight as if everything was right in his world. Even though I knew I should, I didn't see the need to tell him about Gertie and spoil a perfectly good evening.

"I love you, girl."

"I love you too, babe."

The next morning I awoke to the smell of coffee and pancakes wafting up from the kitchen. I rolled over in bed, bringing the covers to my face. Liam's scent smothered me. I inhaled it deeply as it took me back to last night.

"What is this?" I said as he walked into the bedroom, placing a tray of misshapen pancakes and slightly burnt bacon in front of me.

"Breakfast."

"You're spoiling me. It's going to be pretty easy for me to get used to this if you keep it up. Is this what I should expect every morning as Mrs. Liam Larson?" I picked up a piece of bacon and examined it closely.

"This and so much more, Jenny." I was still staring at the bacon. "We have forever for me to improve on my cooking skills," he said, nibbling my neck.

"Forever?" I whispered back to him.

"Yes, Jen." He moved the tray away from me and made himself comfortable.

"What about breakfast?"

"Oh yeah, that's why I came up here. But last night was so nice; I thought there was still some unfinished business that we should take care of."

"Unfinished? I can't imagine we forgot to do something last night. As I recall we pretty much covered all the bases," I said with a slight grin.

"Yes. But a couple of those bases still need some of my undivided attention."

Liam was being an incurable romantic lately, insatiable with his ways. He was being so open with me now, and I felt like I was taken a huge step backwards in our relationship by keeping Gertie a secret from him. Of all times, I knew I shouldn't be thinking about Gertie, but I was. My sub-conscious was letting me know that my little secret was wrong, and the guilt I was feeling over it was proof. It was eating away at me. I hadn't even lied to him about it, I just didn't mention it, and I knew I should especially since it was Gertie.

"We're not going to get much done today if this continues," I said, reciprocating Liam's actions.

He sighed heavily as he rolled over on his back.

"Hey, I didn't literally mean for you to stop. Come back here," I said with futile results.

"I know, Jenny but you did remind me of something that needs to get done today."

"At work, or here on the farm?"

"At work." Liam looked at me as though there was more to this than just a muffler that needed to be replaced.

"What's going on?" He sighed again. "Liam?"

"Jen, don't be mad at me for what I'm about to tell you okay? Promise me?"

I hesitated. If this had been the first time he had ever said those infamous words to me I would have said yes without hesitation. But because our history had been laced with intermittent lies my immediate uncertainty was only to be expected.

"Liam, what's going on?"

"Please babe, promise me first," he said again sitting up in bed.

"Okay, I promise. But I can't promise you that it will last if I don't like what I hear."

Another sigh echoed from his mouth.

"Fair enough," he said.

"You know I've been really busy at work lately especially since the holiday season. You know, customers wanting us to customize their cars and trucks." He stopped to wait for my reaction.

"Yeah, I know, honey. That's all good. What's wrong with that? That only means business is good."

"Right. But it's not just cars and trucks we have been working on."

"Oh?"

"Liam, what else is there?"

"Motorcycles, Jen."

"Motorcycles?" I said. I recalled hearing Liam talk to Parker and Joe regarding some motorcycles they had been restoring for a man from Glenville.

"Well, you know we worked on some bikes for this guy a few weeks ago, and in doing so Joe realized I really had a knack for them. I've never owned or even ridden one in my life, but for some uncanny reason, I knew everything about them. It was instinctual. So noticing my interest, Joe thought I should learn some more about them. He owns a couple and brought them in the other day for Parker and I to take a look. He's got some classics, Jen. A '67 Harley Fat Boy that is just amazing. The body of it is a cherry apple red with black trim on the bottom. And when you turn it on, I swear it purrs like a kitten."

Liam's eyes lit up as "67 Harley Fat Boy" rolled off his tongue.

"You seem really excited about this."

"I am, Jen. I mean I still love working on trucks and cars especially mine, but never did I think I would feel the same rush as I do with these motorcycles. It's amazing, and to ride one, well I can't even begin to..."

"Ride one? You mean you've been riding them also?"

"Yeah, Jen. I mean what's the point of fixing them up if you can't test drive them yourself. And Joe didn't care. As a matter of fact, it was his idea that Parker and I give them a spin."

I became silent as I stared straight into Liam's eyes. I knew exactly where this conversation was going, and in my mind, I was already beginning to wonder about the repercussions of motorcycle riding.

"Jen, say something please."

I couldn't talk, I just stared at him in total confusion. Even though in my mind I knew exactly what I wanted to say, it wouldn't come out. Maybe it was the shock from hearing him tell me. After the accident, I thought he would stay away from anything that would put him in harm's way. Was he really willing to do it all over again with no regard to us?

"Jen?" he whispered softly again. "Please talk to me."

"I know what you're about to say, Liam. I'm sorry I'm not being vocal, but I'm trying to grasp this, trying to understand why you want to go down this road again that almost cost us our lives. I'm trying to understand why you would want to put me through that hell again." I didn't quaver or raise my voice. I kept it level and even toned, but the stare from my eyes clued Liam in instantly that I wasn't happy about this.

"What do you mean 'go down the same road'? It's not going to be like that at all. That race was a death match between Johnny and I; you know my skills at driving are very good."

"Yes, driving a truck, Liam, not a motorcycle. This is totally different. The chances of you getting seriously hurt go up exponentially on a motorcycle!"

"Is this your personal belief or do you have some sort of scientific data to back up your statement?" Liam asked with a slight grin on his face. He was trying to lighten the mood, but I wasn't seeing the humor in it.

"I'm being serious. Stop smiling at me like that. Do you realize that a motorcycle is nothing more than death on two wheels? You, of all people I would think, would be thinking more rationally about riding one of those death traps!" I was beside myself. I couldn't believe he was serious about this. Anyone else, I could understand, but not Liam, not after what we had been through the last year.

"Calm down. You're overreacting."

"Overreacting? Liam, be serious. How or better yet, why would you want to ride one of those?"

"They're not half as bad as you're making them out to be."

"Tell me this then: when you rode Joe's motorcycle, did you just ride it around town at a normal speed?"

"Not exactly. I mean Parker and I didn't cruise the main drag if that's what you're asking."

"Then where did you go?"

Liam turned away and sighed heavily. He fidgeted with some knick-knacks on the bedside table. Seconds turned to minutes, and the minutes ticked slowly by as I waited for Liam to answer something I already knew.

"We took them on Ripley Road."

"Ripley Road? Are you kidding me?"

"I'm not kidding. I know it's not what you want to hear, but it was the best place to test them. You can't appreciate those bikes unless you push them and put some speed underneath you."

"Test them? Why do you have to test them? I thought you were just joyriding? What's there to test drive?"

"To see how fast they'll go," he said.

"Why in the hell are you testing them for Joe on Ripley Road? You know how hard it is for me to even go on Ripley Road. I intentionally go a different direction just to avoid that road, and you are racing again on the same stretch of pavement that almost cost us our lives just because Joe wanted you to test drive his motorcycles? Why didn't he do it? Why you? You know why!" I answered my own question. "You know what I think? I think it was your idea all along. You wanted to do it! Joe had nothing to do with it!"

"You have to understand that racing is something I've always done. Last spring, I thought I would never want to race again, but when I rode the motorcycle it all came back. I missed it more than I thought. It felt so good to be going fast. My adrenaline was on a high again, and I felt good. I didn't feel upset or anything that I've been feeling since the accident. I knew then that I couldn't give it up. I need this, babe. If anything, just to make me feel alive again."

"Dammit Liam, that's the stupidest thing I've ever heard come out of your mouth."

"Why are you so angry?" he asked as he tenderly placed his hand on me.

I automatically shrugged away. "If you don't know, I'm not going to tell you. We've been through so much shit over the past year, and I really thought in the past few weeks we had made some headway, that we had turned the corner, and were moving on, but this comes with complete disregard to me. I can't support you in this asinine stunt. Do you really expect me to put on my rally cap and cheer you on to victory as you plow down the same road that almost killed us? And it's not even the fact it's on Ripley Road, it's the fact you've decided to race again. If you really love me, you won't do this. You don't need to be going one hundred miles an hour to feel alive. That's just an excuse."

"Jenny...I guess I never thought..."

"You're damn right you never thought about it or me!"

"But honestly, you're really jumping to conclusions. You're acting like I've already started racing, when in fact, I've only test-drove them. I never said I was going to race. It was you who implied that."

"So, you're not?" I asked coolly.

Liam just sighed. "Jenny…"

"That's what I thought. I wasn't implying anything. Looks like I was just stating the obvious."

"Please try to understand that I'm not doing this for any other reason than I just love to race. I would never put myself or especially you in harm's way again, but you know ever since the accident, something's been different with me. I just thought it was the blame I was placing on myself, but honestly, babe, as soon as I got on that motorcycle I felt something that I thought had died with me that night. I felt like me again. I felt like the guy you first met and fell in love with. I know I promised you I would never hurt you again, and I mean to keep that promise, but this has to do with me feeling whole again. If I can feel that way, I'm going to be a better person for you. Maybe this will help with my nightmares, I don't know, but I do know I felt something and can't explain it. It's just in me, and I don't think I can let it go. You can't ask me to give up one of the few things I love."

"And what about me?"

"That goes without question, I love you. I love you the most, more than anything."

"Then why would you want to put me through that worry again? Wondering whether or not this would be the time when you didn't make it. How is that fair to me?"

"Jenny, I promise you with my very last breath that nothing is ever going to happen to me. For Christ sake, I know what it feels like to almost lose the only person that means a damn to me. I don't and won't let you feel that pain I had to endure. I'm not out to kill myself. I just want to get back out there again. I need this, Jenny. I've needed to do this for a long time I think. I really believe this will help me."

"Help you? What do you mean by that?"

"I mean that I've been scared since the accident. I think I've lost some of my self-confidence, and I don't know, maybe some of the nightmares I've been experiencing are a result of being scared. Listen, I've never been scared about anything in my life except for two times. The first time was the night my parents died, and the second time... well... that's when I almost lost you. I need to get over this. I need to move on from what happened, and I think the only way I can is by getting back out there and racing again."

"But you don't need to prove yourself anymore, Liam."

"Not to you, but to me. I know you're trying to help me. I know you're there for me. But you know what I've been going through since the accident, even with the stuff I've confided to you. Hell, you went through the worst of it, and thank God you've managed to emerge almost unscathed from it, but I haven't. Having you by my side has helped me more than you'll ever know, but it obviously hasn't been enough for me to get rid of this feeling I have deep down inside of me or release me from the nightmares."

"Why do you think riding a motorcycle will cure all of this? If you need some sort of adrenaline rush, why don't we go to an amusement park and get that same feeling on some damn roller coaster that goes 100 miles an hour?"

"You know that's not the same as what I'm talking about. I just know that when I was riding I felt a rush of emotion that I haven't felt in a long time. It was like an old friend coming back for a visit. All the feelings that made me do it before returned, and it felt good, really good. When I was riding, things seemed right with me again. I didn't feel any of the doubt or worry, and maybe most importantly, I didn't feel scared. Listen to me, please. I love you with all my heart and soul. There's nothing, and I mean nothing in this world that I wouldn't do for you. You're the most important person in my life. Why would I want to jeopardize everything, especially after the hell we've been through? But, babe, the time since the accident has been very hard on me."

"And it hasn't for me?" I was feeling somewhat slighted.

"Of course it has, probably more so. I just meant that I don't know if I can give something up that is such a part of who I am? Just like you, I could never give you up. You make me complete, but I'm realizing, so does racing."

"But why, Liam? After everything that has happened, why go back there? What's more important here, you trying to relive your glory days or us? What if something would happen? There's no guarantee that if you start racing, even for the fun of it as you so casually put it, that you won't have an accident. Last spring is still too real for me. I can't go through that again, and hell, I'm still not over it. Just the worry alone almost drove me crazy. Plus, do you remember how you acted after the accident? I do. Because to be quite honest, you still act different sometimes. How could any of this be good? How in the hell could you be racing again be a good thing? And to add insult to injury, let's try killing ourselves on a motorcycle this time since your truck didn't get the job done!"

"Jenny..." He went for my arm.

"Don't Liam!" I cruelly shrugged him away from me.

"Just let me finish."

"What else is there to say? Oh, I know, does the winner get the girl this time?"

"That's not fair, and you know it."

"It's not fair that you didn't talk to me about this first, but you seem to be okay with that. Don't you think I should have some say in whether you kill yourself or not?"

"I am trying to talk to you about this. That's what this whole conversation has been about. That's why I brought it up to you." Liam grabbed me from the waist and wrapped his arms around me, hugging me tightly. "I love you, Jenny, so much. I need you to back me on this, please. I need to get over what's keeping me from moving on, from acting differently as you say I do. I can't run from this. I need to face it and show to myself that I can conquer it. I promise that things will be different. Last year, it was all about Johnny and trying to see who was the bigger man. I was so hell-bent on proving Johnny was wrong that I lost sight of you. That's not the case anymore. I just need to prove to myself that I can do this. Plus, I love it, babe. I need this. It's who I am. And it's a part of me that you fell in love with last year. I need to get that part back."

Liam's calming voice made me want to believe him. I had known him long enough to know he was telling the truth. I didn't want to rush to judgment, but I could tell he meant it. The mere thought of him racing again was turning my stomach inside out, but I had to at least hear him out on this. He wasn't hiding his feelings, and as I thought about what he said, I realized that he could be right. This daunting wall had been built up by him, and I couldn't seem to break it. Maybe the answer was to do what had helped build it up in the first place. I couldn't hold him back from this. He had to do this whether I supported him or not.

"Jenny, I promise you that I won't let anything happen, but please don't make me promise not to race again. It would be like asking me never to breathe. I need to know I can get out there again and make what was wrong right again. Please don't ask me to give that up because you know if you say the word I will, that's how much I love you."

I stood there, knowing that my word held more credence than anything else with Liam. One nod of my head in either direction would determine our fate. Either I allowed him to continue with this insane quest, or I stopped it before something serious happened. I hesitated. I wanted to hold the key that opened the door to reveal that our future together was secure and safe, no more grief. We'd been through enough to last a lifetime. I wanted reassurance that our fate wasn't going to be tested anymore, but there was no way to know. As I thought about it, I knew whether he had my blessing or not he would never be truly happy until he could figure this out on his own. I had to let him know I was okay with this, whether I was or not. At least then he could carry on knowing he had my support. He was waiting for my impending answer with bated breath. I wanted to say no, to tell him to return the bikes and forget about racing. He would do it in a heartbeat, but I couldn't hold that sort of power over him. I wasn't like that, and I wasn't going to turn into that sort of person. He didn't need my approval, but he was asking for it. I would have to suck it up again, give him this, and pray that this was the answer we were both looking for.

"Are we good, babe?" Liam asked.

"Yeah, we're good. I'm not happy about this and you damn well better be careful, but we're good with this."

My heart felt heavy, the same way it used to feel when I thought something bad was going to happen, how it felt on April 11th.

.

Chapter Fifteen
The Gift

It was three days before the New Year, and aside from Christmas, I had hardly seen Liam. He had been busy at the shop. It seemed odd to me, being the time of year that the shop would be bombarded with so much business, but as I was to find out, the business wasn't coming from their normal customers. This time the customers happened to be themselves. They were working on two motorcycles of their own. Liam, with the influence of Joe, had bought himself a 1972 Harley Davidson Ironhead. It was, according to Liam, a diamond in the rough. It needed extensive repair and a paint job, but Liam had reassured me that after his hands had been on it for a while the bike would come out looking like a million bucks.

His energy for the past few weeks had been concentrated almost solely on this project. Furthermore, the races had begun in Spencer again. Even after many protests from people who thought that after my accident there should be some sort of mandate against them to protect future incidents from occurring, the races were in full force. Of course the cops were on the heels of every teenage boy within the three county radiuses, watching and observing their actions as though they were under radar. It didn't matter, for every two steps the police made they were still always a step behind when it came to the races.

Liam had been chomping at the bit. He had worked on at least six different cars, preparing them for the impending races. And even though Liam knew my disdain towards the races, he had tried to explain to me that being a part of them was moving forward instead of looking backward. It was killing him that he wasn't a part of it, but that was until Joe asked him to test drive a couple of the motorcycles for an upcoming race. It was Joe's idea that motorcycles should be incorporated into the racing. As he saw it, it only meant more business for him since nobody else in the area worked on bikes. And of course it didn't take Liam long to jump on the bandwagon, especially now that he had my reluctant approval to race them.

I was sitting on the front step in front of Liam's house, fiddling with the broken step with my shoe when Liam came home.

"Hello, my love," he said with an engaging kiss.

"Hello. How did things go at the shop?"

"Great. I've got most of Parker's bike torn apart, and I started on mine tonight. It's going to be a dream, Jenny. I can't wait for you to see the finished product."

"I can," I said with some disinclination.

"Not again. I thought we were over all that."

"We are. I'm sorry. It was just another futile attempt on my part to voice my feelings about it. That's all. Forget I mentioned it. What do you want to do tonight?"

"I don't know. Did you have something in mind?"

"No. Not really."

"Why don't we take a drive to Glenville?"

"Glenville? Why do you want to go there?"

"I guess I would like to see where you'll be going to school, and also I need to go pick up a part for my bike."

"Oh. So going to see my school is only an afterthought to you getting your part?"

"No, of course not. But why not kill two birds with one stone. Besides, I think we need to get away from here for a while."

"You do, do you?"

"Yes, I do. I've neglected you, and I'm sorry."

"You don't need to be sorry. I know you've been busy. It's okay."

"No, it's not. And with my schedule only becoming busier and you starting school soon, we'll have even less time together. Besides, it's almost New Year's Eve. There's no reason for us to stay here. We deserve to have some alone time, so while I get my shower why don't you pack a bag for the both of us?"

"Anything in particular, you want me to bring?"

"You just need to bring yourself. You won't need any extra clothes while we're there."

"I won't?"

"Not if I have my way with you," Liam said, kissing me tenderly. He bolted up the few steps that led to the front door and ran inside taking the inside stairs two at a time. While he showered, I packed our bag and called my parents to inform them of our plans. Before I could put our bag in his truck, he was by my side again.

"You don't waste any time."

"Not when it comes to spending time with you. Are you ready?"

"Definitely."

"Then let's go."

Glenville seemed asleep when we arrived. The last time I was there, the whole town was hopping, but because of the holiday break, most of the students had gone home.

"It feels like a ghost town. There doesn't seem to be anybody here."

"Well, at least not many students."

We pulled into the motel parking lot and checked in. It was still early, so after some freshening up we decided to check out the downtown and grab a bite to eat. It was eighteen degrees outside and there were a couple of inches of snow on the ground, so our walk led us straight to the nearest bar, which happened to be *The Dock*. The last time I had been there I had ran into Johnny on this very same deck that I was standing on with Liam. I had this innate feeling that if I turned around I would see Johnny behind me. A chill ran up my back at the thought of it, and it wasn't from the frigid air that stroked my skin. Upon walking in I instantly realized why we didn't see too many people in Glenville. They were all inside.

"Wow, this place is packed," I said looking around.

Liam took my hand and maneuvered us around some people until we found a small table in the far corner of the establishment.

"What would you guys like to drink?" Asked a young man with tattoos covering every part of his exposed body.

"Two beers," Liam said as the guy looked straight at me. Within minutes, the tattooed guy had returned with two large glasses brimming with the pale ale.

"Can I get you two something else?"

"Yeah, can we see a menu?"

"All we serve are burgers and fries."

"We'll have two burgers with everything on them then."

The guy gave me another look. I found myself squirming in my seat as he continued his obvious stare on me.

Liam must have noticed it too.

"That will be it," Liam said, hoping the waiter would get the message to move on.

"What's up with the tattoo guy? Do you know him?"

"How would I know him?"

"You have been here before; maybe he's an old boyfriend that you're keeping a secret from me."

"You can't be serious? I've only been here one time. Besides, all my boyfriends I keep hidden back home."

"Not funny, Jenny," Liam said as he brought my chair closer to his. "There better be no other boyfriends." I just giggled. It was nice to see Liam get jealous over me without the threat of a fight ensuing over it.

The tattooed waiter returned with two greasy hamburgers smothered with everything on them, and placed them in front of us.

"Will there be anything else?"

"No, but thank you," I said.

We began to dive into our greasy hamburgers when a burly man with a long beard came to our table.

"Are you Liam Larson?"

"Yes, I am." Liam tried to choke down the bite of hamburger he had just taken.

"Hi, I'm Toby Raines. I thought I recognized you. I've seen you race." I rolled my eyes in the other direction. "You're really good. Are you the new co-owner of Joe's shop in Spencer?"

"Yes, I am."

"I like Joe. He's been working on my stuff for years. As a matter of fact, he just finished a couple of motorcycles for me. I didn't think Joe would ever find anyone to help him out, but it makes sense that it's you. You're a legend around these parts. I heard you were in a pretty bad accident last year, I'm glad to see you've recovered."

Liam gently squeezed my leg from underneath the table as Toby finished his sentence.

"Um, yeah, it was bad, but I'm doing fine and so is my fiancée, Jenny. She was in the accident too."

"I'm sorry to hear that, it's good to meet you." He put his rough hand out for mine.

"Nice to meet you too." His hand felt like sandpaper with huge calluses covering it.

"Well, I don't want to take up your time, but I've heard through the grapevine that you're into motorcycles now." My eyes rolled again. I could see where this conversation was going and I really didn't want to have any part it.

"I am, but just repairing them for now."

"You don't race them? I must have gotten my information wrong."

"Well, not yet. I do plan on racing them. I just bought a 1972 Harley Ironhead not too long ago. It needs a lot of work before I can put it on the road."

"Ahh, that's a great bike you have, a classic. They're one of the best, especially for racing. So, you are into racing them?"

Liam gave me a quick glance before answering. "I do. I just need to get my bike working. Why do you ask?"

"I own a parts store right out of town. My specialty is selling hard to find parts, especially for bikes. But my real business is overseeing the underground racing circuit in the area," he said in an undertone.

"Really?" Liam's eyes lit up like a Christmas tree and his smile was as wide as Toby's girth.

"Do you have anything I might be interested in?" I wasn't quite sure if Liam's question was referring to parts for the bike or for information on the racing circuit, but by their mannerisms I would bet he meant the latter.

"I think so. Maybe you can come by and I'll show you what I've got if you're going to be in town for a while."

"We're actually here for a few days. I could come by tomorrow."

"That would be great. I'm right off the main road about a mile west outside of town. The place is called The Body Shoppe. There's a huge sign of a half-naked woman holding a bunch of tools in her hand with the shop's name on it. You can't miss it or her for that matter," he said, spitting out a hefty laugh.

Liam laughed with him until he caught my reaction.

"Here's my number if you need it. I'll be there all day. Just stop on by when you can, I'm always there."

"Sounds great, I'm looking forward to it, Toby."

"Me too. I think you're gonna like what I have to offer you."

Liam could tell I wasn't the least bit happy. "I'm sorry about that, babe, but I can't let an opportunity like this pass me up; it'll be good for business."

"Business? It sounds like it was just about helping you, not the shop."

"Well it is, but any of this will be good for the shop."

"I thought this weekend was going to be about us."

"It will be, and it is. This is only a minor little detour that will only take a few hours out of our time together," he said, trying to sound appeasing.

We finished our hamburgers, and while Liam paid the bill, I went to the bathroom.

"Are you ready to go?" Liam asked as I exited the door.

"Yeah, I just need to grab my coat."

"I'll meet you outside. I saw Toby was on the deck when I paid the bill, I want to make sure I have the directions to his place right before we leave."

I went back to our table and grabbed my coat. I noticed a small white piece of paper folded neatly in half with messy scribbling on it. I didn't remember it being there before.

"What is this?" My name was written in a haphazard manner on the top of the paper.

I unfolded it slowly looking around to see who might have left it. I didn't recognize anybody in the bar and aside from Liam and Toby, who I just met; there wasn't anybody in here who should know me.

I need to talk to you. Meet me tomorrow while Liam is with Toby. Please, Jenny."

"Excuse me…" I said to our tattooed waiter, who was back to clean our table.

"Yeah, is there something else you want?" He wasn't the most pleasant person and seemed annoyed that I was still there.

"Do you know who left this note? I went to the bathroom and when I returned, I found it here on the table."
"Maybe it was your boyfriend."

I sighed. "No, it's not him. Did you notice anybody? It would really help me."

"Look, I'm just here to wait tables and serve beer. I'm not being paid to see who leaves you love notes."

I scoped the room out cautiously, looking for the person I thought left me the note. I didn't see Johnny anywhere.

"Well tell me then, do you know a guy by the name of Johnny Bryant?"

"Johnny? Of course, most people here know Johnny, but if you're asking because you think he left you the note, you'd be wrong. He hasn't been in here all night. I haven't seen them in here for a few days."

"Them?"

"Yeah, him and his girlfriend."

I felt my heart drop to the pit of my stomach. The fact that Johnny had a girlfriend should have no effect on me at all. In fact, I should be glad that he finally got the message and moved on, but that's what was bothering me. He had finally moved on.

"Well, thank you anyway." I glanced at the note again. I had crunched it into an almost unreadable condition. Who would leave me this then? I dismissed the notion and crumpled the note up even more and stuck it in my coat pocket.

"Ready?" Liam said after saying goodbye to Toby.

"Yeah, whenever you are." We started our walk back to the motel. The entire time I hardly heard one word Liam said to me. I looked around every corner to see who might have left me the note. I didn't know what to do. I was supposed to oblige this person by meeting them tomorrow. It was irrational to do it and a little absurd, but my curiosity had the best of me. I needed to know who wanted to talk to me.

"Are you okay, Jen?"

"Of course, why?"

"You just seem pre-occupied and quiet. Are you upset about tomorrow?"

I instantly thought about the note. "What?"

"Are you upset with me meeting Toby tomorrow?"

"Oh, that. No, I'm over that. I understand that's going to happen. I'll be fine. I think I might walk around the campus or just wait in the room while you see him."

"Stay in the room? I thought you were going to go with me?"

I frowned. "Honestly, I love you to death, but I really don't want to stand around and wait for you while you and Toby talk about bike parts. It's fine. Besides, this will give me a chance to look around and familiarize myself with the campus."

"If you're sure."

"I'm very sure. Let's hurry up, I'm getting cold."

"I know exactly what to do to warm you up."

"I'm sure you do," I said as Liam drew me closer to him. We made our way back to our room.

The next day I woke up in bed to find myself alone. There was another note, this time on the pillow next to me and with handwriting I recognized.

I love you, babe. Last night was just what I needed...you to myself. I won't be gone long, enjoy yourself. Miss me, I already miss you. Love, Liam.

I grabbed his pillow and held it tight to my chest as I inhaled his scent. I decided I would just wait there for him. Last night's note was unimportant, and I settled on the fact that I didn't need to know who wrote it. From my view, I could see the snow falling outside. I went to the window to get a better look when I saw Johnny staring back at me from the motel parking lot.

"Johnny," I softly whispered. Johnny wrote the note. I knew it.

He smiled widely at me and motioned for me to come down, putting his hands together in a prayer manner, as if he was pleading with me to not let him down. I hesitated and then nodded yes, motioning to him to give me five minutes. I quickly ran a brush through my hair and brushed my teeth while I threw on the same clothes I had on from last night. He was waiting by the stairwell as I walked down.

"Hi, Jenny," he said sweetly, almost too sweetly, as though he had forgotten our confrontation at Lougini's.

"Hi, Johnny. You left the note? I asked my waiter last night if it was you, and he said you weren't even in there last night."

"I wasn't, per se. I had a friend leave the note for me. I didn't think it would go over too well if Liam saw me there."

"Yeah, probably not, but how did you know we were there?"

"I saw you guys walk in. I was across the street."

"Oh, I see. But how did you know that I would be able to get away to even see you?"

"Oh, that. I know Toby. He's a friend of mine."

"He is? Johnny, did you put Toby up to this? I mean, was this visit out to his shop legitimate, or was it just to get Liam out of the way for a while?"

"I'd like to take credit for it, but I'm not that good. I saw Toby before he went to talk to you and Liam last night. He was talking to me and noticed you guys walk in. He had mentioned then he was going to go introduce himself, that's when I thought of the note. Toby left it when he came over to your table."

"He did? Really? So...can I ask what this is about?"

"I needed to see you."

"Needed?"

"I wanted to see you. You look good. How are things?"

"Good. What about you? I heard you have a girlfriend?"

Johnny's head lowered. "Yeah, she's nice. I don't know if she's officially my girlfriend, but she's someone who helps me pass the time."

"Pass the time? You need help passing the time?"

"Yeah, Jen...to help me forget about you."

"That's not fair."

"Maybe not, but it's the truth."

"I think I better go."

Johnny reached out and grabbed my hand. "Don't. I'm sorry. I shouldn't have said that, but I've wanted to see you for so long, and when I saw you guys last night I had to do something. Please, I know you have some time. Can we go somewhere and talk?"

"Talk about what? The last time I saw you, you acted like a complete jackass, do you remember that? Do you think that I can just forgive your actions because you have feelings for me? Nothing's changed, Johnny. I'm still marrying Liam, and you guys still hate each other."

"Listen, I'm sorry about what happened at Lougini's. I wasn't in the best frame of mind that night, and I guess I let my feelings get the best of me. There's no excuse for that, but you have to understand that it's really hard for me to be quiet when I see you. I knew if I was to walk into that bar last night, the chances of all hell breaking loose were pretty good. I didn't want that for you, so that's why I asked Toby to leave the note."

"Just because we're standing here right now doesn't change things though, Johnny."

"I know, but can we please try to be friends, the way it started last summer. I've given in to the realization that Liam isn't going anywhere, but I don't want to be absent from you either. I need you in my life, whether you feel that way or not."

"This sounds like the same old broken record to me. It's not going to work. I can't be friends with you as long as I'm with Liam, and Liam's always going to be there."

"You do want me in your life then, right?"

I just looked away. I didn't know how to answer that. How could I say yes when every fiber in my body was telling me no?

"Jenny, I think about you night and day. You're my first thought in the morning and the last thought at night. I wonder if you're happy, sad, what you're doing, and if you're with him."

"Johnny..."

"I know exactly what you're going to say already. It feels like we've had this conversation a thousand times, and it's mostly because I won't give up. Every time I think I'm ready to throw in the towel, something inside of me tells me not to. As long as you're on this earth, I'm always going to try. I know that you feel by staying friends with me you're lying to Liam. I'm not asking you to change your ways, but I want us to be the way we were this summer. I was so happy. I felt that no matter what we would have something, something that I could cling on to when I'm down."

"What's that supposed to mean?"

"I don't know. Just like you, my life hasn't been a bed of roses lately either."

I was reminded of my conversation with Gertie.

"I'm sorry. I saw your mom not too long ago. She told me about your dad and her. I'm sure that's really hard."

"Are you talking about the divorce?"

"Yes, isn't that what you meant?"

"No, but thank you. I knew they were headed for divorce years ago. They just took their time realizing it as well. I'm fine with their situation. They're much happier, and the fighting is over. We're all better off."

"What did you mean then when you said that it made you feel good to think about me when you're feeling down?"

"It's nothing, not important. Forget I mentioned it. What I don't want you to forget is me."

"Johnny, this is so hard, harder than you can imagine and much harder when you talk to me like this. Liam despises the mere ground you walk on, and if he even had an inkling that I was standing here with you, I think he would try and kill you on the spot. I do want you to be a part of my life, but I don't see how it will ever work. We can never be just friends. Liam won't allow it, and I can't do this behind his back."

"Doesn't he want you to have friends? I'm sure he talks to other girls. You both haven't given up having friendships with the opposite sex, have you?"

Johnny's tone was cynical.

"Of course not, Johnny. But none of our other friends have the history that you have with Liam or me."

"Fair enough, but I think you're just scared to live. Who said you had to give up your life just because you're getting married."

"I'm not giving up my life. As a matter of fact, I'm making it better. I have a life outside of Liam. You just don't know that because you don't know me."

"That's what I'm trying to fix. Listen, I know you feel uncomfortable talking to me outside your motel room, but I'll be around tomorrow night, come meet me."

"It's New Year's Eve. There's no way I can meet you. Liam will be with me the entire night."

"Do you want to remedy this, make us right?" He asked and I didn't answer. "Do you, Jenny?"

I remained quiet. Johnny was becoming annoyed by my silence, but the fact remained that by me saying yes to him only meant that I would be subjecting to go down a path I didn't know if I could return. Liam and I were finally moving forward and working things out. His nightmares seemed to be under control, and aside from his new found hobby, we were both looking forward to our impending wedding.

"Jenny, dammit, stop this," he bellowed with frustration. "Listen, I have an apartment on the outskirts of town. It's right across the bridge on the left side. The building is brick with brown siding on the side. I'm in apartment 2B. Please come see me before you go back home. Nothing has to happen. I won't corner you or keep you prisoner, if that's what you're afraid of." He paused for a moment. "I...I just have something for you."

"Why don't you give it to me now?"

"To be honest, I didn't think you would take my note seriously. I didn't think I would see you today, so I didn't bring it." Johnny looked at me with his intentional brown eyes. "So can I count on you to stop by tomorrow?"

I slowly nodded. "This is crazy, Johnny."

Johnny just smiled. "Until tomorrow." He took my hand and gently kissed it.

I stood there wondering what I had just done. What was this all about? What was I doing? But I didn't have much time to mull over it. Within minutes of Johnny leaving, Liam's truck pulled in next to me.

"What are you doing outside in this freezing cold, Jen? You look like you're in another world standing out here."

"I don't know. I guess I was just star gazing."

"In the middle of the day? Those must be some brilliant stars you see?" He looked up in the sky to see for himself.

"So did you have fun with Toby?"

"I did. He's got some amazing stuff. You have to see it."

"What's the verdict then?"

"Verdict?"

"Yeah, did he give you a schedule of races?"

Liam knew I was right on target about why he really went there.

"Yeah, he did, but it's okay, nothing to worry about. You'll see. So how was your day? Did you take a walk around the campus?"

"No, I decided to stay here."

"What were you doing when I pulled up?"

"Nothing, just deciding on whether I wanted to take a walk or not, that's all."

"I've got a better idea. Let's walk upstairs to our room. I can tell you everything that happened to me, and then we can decide whether we want to leave the room for the rest of our time here."

"You're good with staying inside with me until the New Year?"

"Yes. But we can come up for air tomorrow night. We've been invited to a New Year's Eve party at Toby's place."

"Is that at his shop or his house?"

"His shop. They're one and the same actually. He has a little place behind the shop that he lives in. I got the impression you didn't like Toby last night, but he's a really nice guy and just because he's involved in racing doesn't mean he's a bad person."

"I know. I'm sorry, just me being apprehensive I guess. I'll try not to rush to judgment in the future."

Liam took my face in his hands and kissed me hard. "Let's go upstairs. We're spending too much time here in the cold when we could be under the covers keeping warm."

The night with Liam should have been magical, but instead of concentrating all my energy on him, my mind went to Johnny. I kept playing the scenario over in my head on whether I should show up at his apartment. His ultimatum made me apprehensive and angry, but I wanted him back in my life. I missed his presence and seeing him earlier made me realize that, and that scared me. I didn't want to feel happy to see Johnny; I wanted to feel disgust, to be over him. Why couldn't I just say no to him anymore? Where was my backbone? I had it last year; it was always easy for me to dismiss him, but not anymore.

I felt as though I was cheating on Liam too, and the worst part was I hadn't done anything...yet. How in the world would I feel if I actually did go and see him? And what did Johnny have for me? It wasn't my birthday, and I couldn't imagine he had a Christmas present for me. There was no reason for him to give me anything. Maybe there was nothing for him to give me. Maybe he just said that to lure me to his place.

I lay in bed staring at the discolored ceiling. Liam was fast asleep, his right arm stretched over me while he softly snored in my ear. I loved him more than life itself. I couldn't see myself with anybody but him, so why in the world was I going to see Johnny tomorrow? I continued to stare blankly at the ceiling until the morning light made its presence. Liam softly stirred as his right arm never once left my body. It was as if he knew even when he was asleep that I needed his touch against me. I softly kissed him on the lips only to have him draw me closer to him.

"I thought you were sleeping."

"I was." He entangled his right leg into mine, forcing me to roll over to face him.

"I love you, Jenny."

"I love you, too."

"Last night was nice. Did you sleep well?"

"Yes," I lied. "What do you want to do today?"

"Stay here with you, under the covers with your body against mine."

"You might get hungry."

"Don't think so."

"Liam?"

"Yeah?" He snuggled me closer.

"Do you still want to go to Toby's party tonight?"

"Umm, yeah don't you?"

"Sure, I was just asking."

"We don't have to stay the entire time, but we should make an appearance."

"I guess, but we really don't know him, or for that matter, anyone else that will be there."

"True, but I think Joe and I are going to be doing a lot of business with him for the shop. It'll be good, if only for that. Which reminds me, I called Joe yesterday about a couple of parts Toby had. I need to meet Joe at Toby's but just for an hour, well, maybe a little longer than that, but I promise it won't be any more than a few hours. You can go with me. We can be back before it gets dark or at least by late afternoon," he said, trying to make it sound as if it his whole day wouldn't be spent at Toby's.

I saw my opportunity. "No, you go."

"Are you sure?"

"Yeah, positive. I'll get a chance to see his place tonight. From what it sounds like, once in one day will be plenty. You go, and I'll stay here and pack our bag for our trip home tomorrow."

Liam left for Toby's a little later that day. It had begun to snow. I watched Liam from our window as he was removing the new layer of snow from his windshield. He gave me a smile and a wink as he waved goodbye. I waited, watching patiently until his truck was out of sight. I would have to act quickly if I wanted to get to Johnny's and back before Liam returned.

The snow was falling heavier by the time I left the room. Trying to make great strides to make up time only put me further behind as I made my way through the heavily snow laden streets. I came to the bridge and looked across it; Johnny's apartment was directly to the left as he had said. The two-story building was hard to miss. It was outlined in multi-colored Christmas lights and fake snow was painted on all the windows. I thought I noticed one of the curtains on the upper window move slightly as I approached it, possibly Johnny I thought. Scoping it out I realized the entire bottom was apartment 1B; the only stairs leading to the second floor was on the right side leading to a door with 2B tacked onto it, Johnny's apartment.

I took a huge deep breath and proceeded up the rickety, wooden steps. I stared at the door, hoping it would willfully open without me knocking on it. I looked around; the town looked deserted, not that it really mattered. It was just me being a habitual worry wart that made me keep checking. There was a Christmas wreath that looked like it had seen better days encircling the doorknob. I slowly tapped it, hoping that if Johnny didn't answer I could still say I was here. But he heard it and eagerly swung the door open to greet me.

"Jenny, you came."

I didn't say a word, only giving him a complacent look. Johnny motioned for me to come in as I took one final glance behind me before entering. The room was remarkably large. There was not one but two overly stuffed couches facing each other to the left of me, and to the right was a small eat-in kitchen littered with various pizza boxes, empty beer cans, and dirty dishes strewn across it. To the far side of me was a small bathroom, and to the left of that was Johnny's bedroom. I didn't have to second-guess that, his large bed was in plain view. My mind comprehended every little detail as I scoped Johnny's apartment. I hadn't moved since entering, my feet firmly planted into the floor as soon as I had stepped in.

"You know you can come all the way in. You don't have to stand by the door."

"Oh, sorry." I continued to peruse the place as I followed Johnny cautiously to one of the couches.

"Sit down."

I looked at the couch. It was covered in potato chip crumbs and other leftovers.

"Sorry about that," Johnny said as he quickly swept the crumbs off of the couch and onto the floor with his hands. He then motioned with the same hands for me to sit down.

"I'm glad you're here. I didn't think you would show up."

"I told you I would come."

"Yeah, I know but I can honestly say I didn't believe you until I opened my door. Thanks."

"For what?"

"For keeping your word. It means a lot."

"Whatever for?"

Johnny sighed heavily. "I don't know. I'm just happy you're here. You have a million reasons not to be here, I'm just happy that you were able to find one reason to come."

"I'm here because you asked me to come here, Johnny. If you haven't noticed, I'm a little nervous about being in your apartment."

"There's no reason to be."

"Yes, there is. Liam. If he ever found out about this, I can't even begin to imagine the holy terror he would ensue. I'm risking a lot by even talking to you, much less being in your apartment."

"I know. That's why it means so much to me that you showed up."

I remained quiet, Johnny and I just staring at each other.

"Where are my manners? Can I get you something to drink… or eat?"

"No, I'm fine."

Johnny, on the other hand, got a beer for himself. He took a large gulp of it before sitting back down next to me. I moved closer to the edge of the couch, but Johnny sat down beside me.

"Johnny, can I ask you what this is about? I've been here for almost fifteen minutes now, and you've shown me no indication oof why you wanted me here."

"Can't two old friends just visit with each other?" he said, taking another huge drink of his beer.

"Of course, if we were considered that. I don't even know if I can classify us as friends at this point, Johnny. I started to stand up only to have him catch my hand."

"Jenny, please sit back down. I have something for you."

"You didn't have to get me anything."

"I know, but I wanted to."

Johnny went to his bedroom and returned placing in front of me a green envelope. It was crinkled and torn in one corner, as though Johnny had been keeping it in his back pocket.

"Open it, Jen."

With a heavy sigh, I carefully tore the envelope to reveal its contents. By the weight of it I thought maybe there was nothing inside, a riddle that Johnny wanted me to solve. But before disregarding it I felt a small piece of paper stuck in the inside corner. I pulled it out carefully. It was a red heart made out of construction paper. It was small in size, easily fitting in the palm of my hand. The edges were roughly cut with one side of the heart a little larger than the other. It looked like a small child had cut it out instead of a grown man.

"I know it doesn't look like much, but there's a lot behind this heart."

"It's very sweet Johnny, but I don't understand."

"Do you remember last summer when I came to visit you on your porch, and I signed your cast?"

"Yeah, I do. I remember it very well."

"Do you remember what I wrote?"

I did. "You wrote that I had an unbreakable heart and that I would always hold a place in yours, but Johnny, nothing's going to change by doing this. Don't you understand that? I'm engaged. I'm marrying Liam next summer. Whatever happened to you saying that you would finally relent when Liam proposed to me? Do you remember saying that? Well, there's a ring on my finger now, and you're still not backing down."

"I can't, Jenny. Believe me, I've tried, but I can't stay away from you. I need to convince you to give me a try before you marry Liam."

I sat there in utter disbelief. I couldn't get through to Johnny, and I didn't know how to anymore. I held the small red heart in my hand, clutching it so tightly that I almost tore it in half.

"Why, Johnny?" I said, speaking only above a whisper.

"Because I'm in love you."

Tears began to fall from my eyes. Johnny's hand carefully approached me to wipe them away. I went to turn my head, only to have Johnny to take my chin and turn it directly to face him. Before I could react, he was kissing me. My gut reaction was to push him away from me, but he wasn't allowing me to move. He forcibly wrapped his arms around me, holding me secure in his embrace as he kissed me passionately. I tried not to kiss him back, but I could feel his emotions or better, his love as he touched me. He secured his lips around mine, making sure I wasn't deprived of their softness or sweet taste. The kiss lingered, and finally after Johnny had felt I had received his message, he released me, our breathing heavy as we stared into each other eyes. I could see contentment and happiness, no remorse or regret.

"I love you, Jenny."

"Johnny…"

"Please don't be mad at me, Jenny."

I wasn't mad at him. In times past I would have been, and I should be madder than hell now, but I wasn't. Instead, I felt relief and guilt at the same time for enjoying the moment as much as I did. I pulled my hair back, dropping the small and fragile heart to the floor. We both bent down to pick it up, our eyes meeting each other's instantly; he again pulled me to him, kissing me so hard that we both fell to the floor. Johnny was leaning over me, his hands exploring my upper body as I tried hopelessly to stop him. He was being tender and erotic, and in those few moments, I felt more from him than any amount of words he had ever spoken to me. I could feel his love for me permeate from him as our lips touched, and only when he released me once more was I able to wrangle myself into a sitting position. Johnny never stopped touching me though, no matter how much I tried to put distance between us, he continued to make sure some part of our body was connected. I didn't say a word, I only stared at him. My eyes trying to speak what my inaudible mouth couldn't. He moved in closer, my initial reaction again was to brush him off but instead of kissing me this time he placed the paper heart against my beating chest.

"Johnny, you can't do this to me."

"Please don't push me away, Jenny."

"I'm a married woman."

"Not yet."

"I might as well be. This is wrong, so wrong. I've got to go, Johnny. Liam will be wondering where I am."

Johnny looked at the floor in defeat as he sighed heavily. "I can't seem to get through to you can I, Jenny?"

"Don't you think it's the other way around?" Johnny stared at me in puzzlement. "Me, Johnny. I've been trying for over a year to get through to you that we're not going to happen."

"Do you really believe that, Jenny? After everything, you still showed up at my door today. If you were so hell bent on having me out of your life, why are you here?"

"I told you already. I came here because you asked me. I do care about you, but in a different way. I can't let what just happened, ever happen again. You took advantage of me. You have a hold of me for some reason. A piece of me can't seem to let you go, and I don't know why. But I do know that this, what's going on with us right now can't anymore. I love you too, Johnny, but not in the same way you love me. I love you for being there for me, for being my friend through hell and high water, but that's all."

"Jenny, I need you in my life. I need to know that you want to be in my life and have me in yours. I don't care about Liam or what he thinks. I'm willing to fight for you."

I stood up, Johnny rising with me.

"Does this have to do with your mom?"

"My mom?"

"Yeah, I saw her a couple of weeks ago when I was registering for classes. We had a long talk and most of it was about you. Did she put you up to this?"

"That's absurd, Jenny. I don't need my mom helping me with you, or anyone else for that matter," he said with a pissy tone to his voice.

There was a light from outside that was shining in through the living room window. It cast a shadow against Johnny's face making it appear more fragile. His strong features looked shallow, and his complexion seemed pale. It was the first time I had noticed since I had arrived. His eyes seemed different too, as though he was carrying a horrible secret behind them that they were trying to convey to me.

"Are you okay, Johnny?"

"Okay? Where the hell did that come from? I just professed my love for you, kissed you passionately, and then had you tell me that my love for you means nothing more than a friendship to you, oh…and to top it off you think my mom is behind this. Yeah, I would say, all things considered, I'm just fine. Thanks for your concern. I know it's coming straight from your heart," he said as he grabbed the paper heart from my hand and threw it to the floor.

"I don't know what you expect from me, Johnny. Do you want me to break up with Liam?"

He turned back to me and looked me squarely in the face. "Yes. Yes, I do, Jenny. That's exactly what I want you to do."

The answer seemed so obvious to Johnny as he answered me, like I should have realized this all along too.

"I can't, Johnny."

I turned away again, heading towards the door only to have Johnny slam it shut in front of me. He took hold of me tightly and kissed me again. I didn't realize I was crying as I felt the wet liquid hit my cheeks. He slowly let go of me, only for me to realize that it was his tears that were falling on me. He led me back to the couch. I knew better than to follow him, but I went anyway. He pulled me close to him as we sat back down. He touched me poetically, his fingers telling a story as they glided against my trembling skin. I finally pushed him away from me, if for only a moment, so I could breathe. And then and only then did I realize what was happening.

"Johnny, we can't go on."

"Yes, we can, Jenny. Please don't deny me the only thing I've ever wanted, the only thing that keeps me going. Don't resist this; you know you want this too."

"I can't, and I don't."

"Yes, you can, Jenny. I love you."

"No, you don't, Johnny. You don't even know me."

"I know you better than you think. Better than you might know yourself, Jenny. I know you're confused and you have been for months. I know in your heart of hearts you have thought about me, that you have thought about us, that you have thought about us being together. I know you feel something for me. I've gotten to you; you're just too caught up in believing otherwise to admit it. I feel it. I felt it when we touched, when we kissed, so don't try playing innocent with me because I'm not buying it. You can't look me in the eye anymore and tell me that I disgust you when your body, your heart is telling me something completely different. You want me just as much as I want you."

I looked away from Johnny, almost in shame.

"Tell me I'm wrong, Jenny. Tell me everything I just said doesn't hold any value, because if you do, if you can honestly sit here and tell me there is nothing going on between us, then I will for once believe you and finally leave you alone."

"How dare you, Johnny. You've been taunting me for a year now. Never giving in or giving up. Until I finally have to give in to you because I have no other choice but to. You broke me. I don't want this, but how am I supposed to continually ignore your intentions when you won't let me? How much am I supposed to take before you make me wonder myself about us? Whether I want to or not. I do think about us. I won't lie about that, but it's your fault that I do. You've placed those thoughts in my head with your never ending relentlessness with me. I look at you and see a breath of fresh air. I see no more worries or troubles. Liam is supposed to be that breath of air for me, but for some reason, it hasn't been that easy for us anymore. But I can't breathe you in because the moment I do I lose everything."

Johnny was quiet, but only for a brief moment. "Then just breathe, Jenny. Breathe me in for once in your life. Don't think about what you should do. Do what you feel, what your heart feels."

"I can't. You know I look at you and think about the what-ifs, the might-have-beens, but then I see Liam and know what is. No matter how you feel about me or me you, there will never be any comparison to what I feel for Liam. It's…"

"Don't tell me Jenny, destiny, kismet? Come on, Liam's your first love. Every girl feels that way with their first." Johnny's callousness to my feelings was hurtful.

"You're a jackass, Johnny. I need you to stop confusing me and stop thinking about me. My head and heart was clear before today."

"Were clear, Jenny? I'm sorry, I can't believe that, and I can't keep denying or apologizing for my feelings for you. You can't marry Liam, not until we have a chance. It'll be a mistake."

"I'm not making a mistake by marrying Liam."

"You don't know that," he said.

"Yes I do, and I know it because we have gotten close. Even after what just happened between us, my feelings haven't changed. I still love Liam, not you, and I really believe that you don't love me."

"But I do, Jenny. I've tried to avoid you, hoping that would help, but it only makes me want you more. I've tasted you, and I can't get your taste out of my mouth. I want more. That's why it was so important for me to tell you how I felt tonight and to give you my gift."

"But I can't give you anything in return."

"You've already given me something, Jenny, you just don't realize it."

"What?"

"You gave me this... time. Because no matter what happens to us, I will have known for at least an hour, you allowed yourself to open up to me and feel something greater than the hatred you always say you feel, and if that's all I ever get from you, I can die knowing that you really do care for me. I love you." He touched the now crinkled red heart and tightly squeezed it. "I don't want you to leave without this. It's yours. It's always been yours."

He turned and walked away from me. I got up and opened the front door and gasped as the cold air hit me like a ton of bricks. I didn't look back; I knew if I did I would see Johnny, and I couldn't bear to look at him again. My heart and head were aching. I felt confused and very alone. I walked briskly, holding the little heart tight in my hands. I didn't want to lose it. Turning the corner to the motel, I could see Liam's truck. He had made it back before me. I quickly put the heart in my coat pocket and wiped my face of tears one more time. Liam would be waiting for me to return to him. I walked slowly to our room as my thoughts went to Johnny. I could see Johnny looking out the window of his apartment. He was looking for me, waiting for my return.

Chapter Sixteen
The Aftermath

Toby's New Year's Eve party was in full swing by the time Liam and I arrived. His tiny place was packed like a can of sardines with people who were engulfed in the holiday spirit. There were more people at this party than I had ever seen. He was right though; there was no way of missing his place. The girl holding the tools was as large as she was offensive. It didn't take Toby long to spot us. He bee-lined his way to us as soon as we entered.

"Liam, you guys made it! Fantastic."

"I told you we would be here. You remember my fiancée, Jenny?"

"I sure the hell do. How are ya darlin'?" He hugged me tightly.

I was set back by his unusual greeting towards me. "I'm fine. Thanks. This is some party you have."

"Thanks. It's not much, but we try. It seems to get bigger every year. Hell, I don't even know half the people here myself, but in my opinion, the more the merrier," he said as he chugged a can of beer.

"We?"

"Me and my girlfriend, Gina." Toby began scoping out the room, trying to locate her.

"She's around here somewhere. I'll have to introduce you two later. She's probably socializin' or something. You guys go grab yourself something to drink, make yourself comfortable, and I'll catch up with you later. Enjoy everything. Tonight my house is your house and every other vagrant here," Toby said, laughing as he walked away chugging what was left of his beer.

"Wow. He's a character," I said somewhat aloof.

"Jenny, he's nice. You just have to get to know him."

"And you know him now? You only met him yesterday."

"True. But I've spent a lot of time with him since we got here."

"That's for sure," I said under my breath.

"You'll like Gina too. I think you two are going to be good friends, especially since we'll be doing a lot of business with Toby."

"You guys made a deal?"

"Yeah, we did. Didn't I tell you?"

"No."

"I'm sorry, babe I must have forgot. We sealed it today when Joe came over."

"Oh."

I immediately crossed my arms, sending Liam the message that I wasn't too thrilled about his new-found friendship with Toby and his girlfriend Gina. I just couldn't see how any good could come from this.

"I'd like a drink."

"Sure, I'll go get you one." Liam never even realized that I was upset.

As Liam left to get our drinks, I maneuvered my way through the crowd as I found my way to an empty corner to wait for his return. I wanted to go so badly. I never felt so out of place in all my life. It was New Year's Eve. I should be having the time of my life, but because Liam felt inclined to mix business with pleasure, I found myself in a corner, by myself, people-watching a bunch of drunken strangers crawl all over themselves.

"Having fun?" A voice said from around the corner.

"Johnny!"

"Hi, Jenny long time no see."

"What are you doing here?"

"Remember, I told you Toby is a friend of mine. I've been coming to his New Year's Eve parties for years. I should ask you what you are doing here to be quite honest. Are you and Liam good friends with him now?"

"Well, I'm not. But Liam seems to be."

"Oh, I see. You don't seem to be happy with his newfound friendship with Toby."

"I'm not. I know what Toby does, and I don't like it."

"You mean you know about the underground motorcycle racing?"

"Yes, I do."

"So, are you trying to tell me that Liam is considering racing again?"

"Considering is not the operative word. He is doing it. He's already got a bike he's working on. That's why he's been talking to Toby so much; he's buying parts and getting information from him regarding the races."

"I'm surprised. I thought after last spring, racing would be the last thing on Liam's mind."

"Just think how I felt when I found out. I thought he was joking, but looks like the joke is on me."

"I'm sorry. I know this must upset you."

I just looked at Johnny. He had no idea.

"Thanks. Hey, I know this is going to sound kind of rude, but I really don't think I should be talking to you. Liam could come back any minute."

"Don't worry. Liam hasn't seen me, nor do I plan on him seeing me. Besides, right now, he's out back with Toby and Gina talking. If I know Toby, he'll have Liam absorbed in one of his many racing stories for the next few hours. Did this afternoon have any effect on you?" Johnny moved in closer to me, backing me into my corner.

"Johnny, I can't talk about what happened this afternoon with you now."

"Why?" Johnny said in a roguish manner.

"You know why. This isn't the time or the place for this conversation."

Johnny sighed. "You're right, but you can't you look me in the eye and tell me that this afternoon didn't affect you somehow."

"It did, Johnny, but that's all I'm saying. I already feel more confused than I should. I need to forget about it and think about what's going on right now."

"And what's that?"

"Do you think every single thought I have is about you? I need to focus my energy and my attention on Liam right now, and if I know him, no matter who's talking to him, he'll be returning to me soon."

"You seem pretty confident about that."

"I am. Now please, I'm asking you to go before Liam gets back and all hell breaks loose. I'd like to see the New Year come in without worrying whether or not I'll be spending it in the hospital because the two of you can't control your anger."

"But back in my apartment..."

"Johnny we're not back in your apartment, and what happened back in your apartment won't happen again. That was you taking advantage of my vulnerability. You're skating on thin ice by doing this."

"I'm not worried about the ice breaking. Are you telling me you would be more receptive to me if we were alone in my apartment?"

"Oh my God, you just won't take the hint will you? I wasn't expecting what happened to really happen. You confused me, and I shouldn't have let it go as far as it did. I want an understanding from you that you will back off."

"Jenny, I told you I loved you this afternoon. Did you think that was just a pick up line so I could get my way with you? I meant it. I need you to know that there is someone else out there who thinks the world of you and who is willing to lay there life on the line for you."

"What's that supposed to mean?"

"I mean that I'm not going away, and I don't care how much you say you love and care for Liam or how much you think you two are soul mates. I'm here to prove you wrong. I'm here to prove to you that I'm real. All I ask is that you give me a chance. That's it."

"What about your girlfriend, Johnny?"

"You mean Charlene? She means nothing to me. I told you she was just somebody to pass the time with."

I felt more confused than ever before. I didn't know what to think of Johnny's feelings for me. It didn't seem to matter to him at all that Liam was only yards away. He just wasn't giving up.

"I can't just leave Liam for you. I don't think you realize what you're asking of me."

Johnny's eyes moved quickly from mine and to the left of me.

"I'll see you soon, Jenny, I promise," Johnny said sweetly as he squeezed my hands.

I turned to see why Johnny's exit was so abrupt, and then I saw Liam coming up from behind.

"There you are. Here's your drink, babe. What are you doing in the corner all by yourself?"

"Where else should I be? You've been gone forever. I don't know anyone here. What else was I to do? Start making out with one of Toby's friends until you decided to come find me?"

Liam could tell I was more than a little annoyed.

"I'm sorry. Toby started talking to me, and I couldn't get away."

Just like Johnny said he would, I thought to myself. "About motorcycle racing?"

"Yeah, how did you know?"

"Lucky guess."

"Look, why don't we stay just for another hour or so and then go back to our room and bring in the New Year the right way, just you and me."

A faint and half-way appeasing smile came across my face when from behind Liam's right shoulder I saw the approach of five long blood red fingernails creep up from behind grasping Liam's shoulder tightly.

"Gina!" Liam said as he turned to see who was touching him.

"Toby and I wondered where you went," she said.

So this was Gina, I thought to myself. She was quite striking with long black hair and huge doe-shaped green eyes that were outlined in coal-black eyeliner to match her hair. Her lips were as red as her nails, and she wore an off-the-shoulder black sweater with skin tight black jeans.

"Gina, this is my fiancée, Jenny."

"Hello," I said in my coolest but sweetest voice.

"Jenny, it's so nice to meet you. Liam has told me so much about you. She definitely is a looker, Liam. I can tell why you can't stop talking about her," Gina said with a closed grin.

I could tell she was as fake as her scarlet nails. She slowly leaned into me as she brushed my hair to the side. "You have quite the catch yourself, if you don't mind me saying," Gina whispered, as her alcohol-laden breath reached my nose. I could hardly keep from choking as her breath encircled me. She straightened herself up and gave me the closed grin again. "So Jenny, Liam told me you will be taking some classes here at Glenville."

"Yes, that's right."

"That's great. I'm sure we'll be seeing each other. I go to school here also."

How great, I thought sarcastically. All three of us stood there in a communal moment of awkwardness.

"Well, I better go mingle. It was nice meeting you, Jenny. I'm sure we're going to be seeing a lot of each other. I can't wait to see you at the races."

I just gave her a syrupy smile as I watched her walk away. "She's a real treat," I said to Liam.

"That didn't sound very sincere."

"It wasn't meant to be."

You haven't even given her a chance. Don't be so judgmental."

"Are you kidding, Liam? Do you know what she whispered to me? She told me what a catch you are. I think this relationship you are going to have with Toby is going to be just swell. I can't wait for it." I threw down my drink and stormed outside, Liam behind me as I left a trail of my tears for him to follow.

"Jenny, what's wrong? Did I miss something in there?"

"Not just in there, Liam, but our whole time here. I thought this weekend was supposed to be about us, about you getting away from work and us being together before I start school, but the entire time we've been here it's been about you and Toby and setting up new deals and underground racing. And the time we have spent together has been overshadowed by conversations of Toby. Why did I even come? You didn't need me here, you have Toby and, from what it looks like, Gina too!"

Liam wrapped his arms around me. "I'm sorry, baby. I didn't realize how bad it was. Let's go back, okay?"

"I don't want to go back in there, Liam. Don't you get it? I hate it here. I hate Toby and from what I can tell, I hate Gina too. I hate the idea that you're doing business with him and that you're going to be racing with his blessings. I want to go."

"Then let's go back to the motel."

"I mean home, Liam. I want to go home."

"It's New Year's Eve, Jenny." I didn't say anything as I continued to let my emotions take control. "Okay, let's go home."

We drove back to the motel in silence and gathered our bags. The silence continued as Liam packed the truck and we left the motel. As we drove through town and crossed the bridge, my eyes became glued to the second floor as we passed Johnny's apartment. There was a light on in his window. Liam remained focused on the road as the snow fell in heavy flakes. The weather was becoming worse and with the new snowfall, visibility was limited. Even with Liam's truck, he was being extra careful. It was

11:45, fifteen minutes until the New Year. We were a few miles out of town when Liam pulled to the side of the road.

"What are you doing?"

"I'm not driving anymore until we settle this. It's almost midnight, and I have no intention ringing in the New Year with you mad at me. We seem to fight more than we make love," he said with a tender note to his voice. "I'm so sorry, Jenny. I totally lost my head while we were here. I didn't realize it until you brought it up to me that I had been neglecting you. That was never my intent."

He was being sincere. "Are you sure, Liam? Did you have this already planned?"

"What do you mean already planned?"

"I mean, did you think you could kill two birds with one stone by bringing me along for your business trip? You had me believing one thing while all along you had ulterior motives. This was never about you and me. It was always about meeting up with Toby, wasn't it?"

"No, not at all."

"Think about our time there. As soon as we arrived, within hours Toby was at our table. Then I was pretty much left to take care of myself while you took care of business. I was just sprinkled in here and there throughout the weekend for good measure, so you could say you were with me."

"I don't know why you're getting so upset with me. I'm trying to better myself and build a future for us. You don't think the business is going to grow by itself, do you?"

"No, of course not. But you know how I feel about you racing again. I don't like it. I'm only going along with it because I know you're not changing your mind. I don't think you need to build your business around you racing again. What's wrong with just fixing the damn cars like you used too? Who said you had to become part of the problem again!?"

Liam knew I was right.

"Jenny, I've messed up this year. And all I've been trying to do since the accident is make things right with you, and I'll be damned if I'm still not messing things up. You're right. I talked to Toby a few days ago. He asked me to come over to look at some stuff. I knew you wouldn't be happy with it, and because we haven't had a lot of alone time together I thought bringing you along with me would help make up for the time I've been away from you. I never meant for you to be stuck in the motel room while I was trying to conduct business for the shop. You're the most important person in the world to me, and everything I'm doing is for you. I want to make something of myself so you'll be proud of me. Your feelings are the only thing that has ever mattered to me, Jenny."

Little did he know that I wasn't cooped up in the motel room.

"Liam, you don't have to prove anything to me. Don't you understand that? You never have. I've never held you accountable for the accident, and I don't think any less of you because of it. What else do I need to do to convince you of that? My God, the accident was almost a year ago, and you're still hanging on to that shit. Is it really that important to you to prove that you're man enough again by racing?" He looked at me in shock. "I'm sorry, that came out wrong."

"So you don't think I'm man enough anymore, huh?"

"I never said that."

"You just did!"

"No, I didn't, Liam. I said is it that important to you to race again to prove to yourself that you're a man again. I've never felt that way about you. It's always been you with this hang-up. I've been ready to move on from this for a long time. I've been offering my help, wanting to be there for you through these nightmares and feelings of depression, but you only let me in so far before you draw a new line that you won't let me cross. What else am I supposed to do? We can't keep coddling this behavior, Liam. It's not normal."

Liam was gripping his steering wheel until his knuckles were as white as the snow that was falling before us. His eyes were straight ahead. Huge flakes melted instantly as they hit the warmth of the truck's windshield. We had only been sitting here for a few minutes, but in that short amount of time the road had been cloaked with a white blanket of the new fallen snow.

"It's not normal for me to still feel like I'm responsible for everything either, Jenny. I know you're here for me. I know I can count on you. But I have to do this for me. I've told you that. I've come to see that now. Don't you think I wonder why you've been able to move on and I can't? You've said you're experiencing strange dreams just like me, but it doesn't seem to faze you. All I see anymore is you slipping away from my grasp, and it's my fault. I can't hold onto you, my hands struggling to hold you, to keep you close to me, and you still slip through my fingers. It's in slow motion, and I can see your look of disappointment as you fade away. Wondering why I can't help you, why I can't save you, and then you're gone. Your face full of disappointment is etched into my brain forever, and the only way for me to get rid of it is to get back out there again, to prove to myself that I have some control and that I can finish the race. I haven't finished the race yet. In my mind, we're still lying there on the blacktop only inches from the finish line. I have to finish this, Jenny. It's the only way for me to move on, the only way." Liam's voice softened as he spoke. The pallid white of his knuckles slowly turned to its normal pinkish color as the blood flowed back into his fingers.

"So this has nothing to do with me or even Johnny?"

Liam looked at me, turning his focus from the falling snow.

"Yeah, I guess, partially. It is about you, but getting you back. I still feel as though there is a gap between us. No matter what we've done, or more importantly what you've done to help me, I feel like there is still something missing, and I don't mean how I feel for you. That's never been the question. I love you more this minute than I did the last, but until I can wake up without any guilt or feelings of emptiness, then I feel at least I'm still holding onto you by a thread. You're ready to slip away just like you are in my nightmare. And as far as Johnny is concerned, it's all about him. You know that's what this is all about. He is the nightmare, Jenny. He's the one who takes you from me, and the thing is I don't have to be asleep. I live it with it whether I'm asleep or awake. When I'm losing you from my grasp and you're slipping away, it's Johnny who's pulling you from me." Liam became peacefully quiet for a moment only to become unsympathetic in his tone.

"Jenny, I know he was at the party tonight. I saw him talking to you."

"You did? Why didn't you say something?"

"Would it have mattered? What was I supposed to do there at Toby's? To be honest, for one of the first and possibly only times I didn't want to cause a scene with him. It just wasn't worth it. I'll have my day with him, but it wasn't going to be tonight."

"What do you mean by that?"

"I really don't know what I mean by that, but I have to do something."

I gave him a disconcerting look.

"I just mean that at some point, I'm going to have to confront him. I know why he's mesmerized by you, Jenny. It's for the same reasons I am. You're intoxicating, and I would die in a heartbeat to make you happy. I used to think that he was just looking at you as another notch in his belt, a one night stand if you will, only because that was the sort of reputation he carried at Walton, but it's different with you. I can see it in his eyes when he looks at you. I'm not saying I'm okay with it. I'm not, you already know that, but my past tactics with him haven't worked. You're my life, Jenny. I won't let him come between us, so I need to take care of him. I just don't know how yet."

Liam seemed thoughtful and insightful as he spoke this time about Johnny. The animosity that he normally carried about him wasn't there. There was a new level of maturity that Liam possessed that I had never seen in him before. This time last year he would have been at Johnny's throat if he had seen him talking to me, but not tonight. I admired Liam's new trait but still wondered if this was a new ploy to throw me off so I wouldn't worry about another bloodbath between the two of them.

"Can't you see that these damn nightmares are just a grim reminder to me of what I almost lost? And who I almost lost it too? I know things haven't been smooth sailing for us, no matter how hard we've tried, but I love you, babe, more than anything. That's the only thing that hasn't changed for me. I know it might seem like I feel differently, but I'm more in love with you now than ever before. I hope you know that. Everything I'm doing, whether it is working at the shop, conducting business with Toby, or even deciding to race again is because I love you. I know that might sound strange, but it's the truth."

"You're racing because you love me? That is the most ridiculous thing I've ever heard, Liam."

"No, it's not. I'm racing because I need to prove to myself I can. I'm showing myself and maybe a few other people who have doubted me since the accident that I'm okay."

"I've never doubted you," I said, placing my hands on Liam's.

"I know, but I've doubted myself. I need you to trust me and give me some space with this. Please let me fix this the only way I know how. Let me get rid of my demons, babe."

I pulled Liam to me and hugged him tightly. The smell of his body was invigorating to me. I inhaled it deeply. He reciprocated by holding me just as tight. There was no question in my mind that Liam was the only man I loved. I wanted him and nobody else. I made a promise to myself that night that no matter how hard Johnny tried to steer me differently I wouldn't allow him to interfere with my feelings anymore. I would be stronger. "Do what you have to, Liam. Just be careful, for me. I would die if you left me."

"Don't worry, Jenny. I'm never leaving you...."

He looked at the clock in his truck. It was half past midnight.

"Happy New Year, darlin'."

"Happy New Year."

"Let's go home and celebrate," he said as his lips molded into mine.

Chapter Seventeen
Kendra's Turn

    Happy New Year, or should I more appropriately say Happy busy New Year. If I thought Liam had been busy before; I had been rudely awakened by just how busy Liam really was. He was engrossed with new business for the shop. Even though there were three of them working, they were overwhelmed with customers because of the racing that was happening. It was in full swing again. All the cars, whether they were from our neck of the woods or not, came to the shop for detail and design. Word had spread quickly of the quality workmanship the shop was doing, and between Parker, Joe, and Liam they had their hands full with new clients.

    Of course, the other tidbit of news was the venue for the races had changed, not surprisingly since that always seemed to be the case last year, but this was largely in part due to the accident, but also, and just as importantly, because the cops were more than ever trying to keep the races from happening. They were patrolling most every weekend to catch a race before it happened. They were going to bring an end to them if it took every officer they had to do it. Every back road from Spencer to the county line was being patrolled, and because of that, most of the races were being conducted in neighboring counties and on any given night. There could be two or three races a week, with upwards to twenty or more participants. This was averaging close to sixty cars a week, and all of them were coming to Joe's Auto Shop.

It was no wonder that Liam and the boys had been scrutinized and interrogated by the police on a regular basis. The only saving grace, if you could call it that, was the motorcycle work the shop was handling. The police had no idea the bikes were being repaired and detailed for impending races. To them, the shop had just hit a bit of good fortune and all the work that was coming in had no bearing on the races. It was a nice cover up for Liam, and it allowed him not only to continue their work for the races but for Liam to work diligently on his bikes.

I had started my first week of classes at Glenville. I was thankful for this diversion since Liam was so busy. It was good for me. I missed not seeing him but was trying to understand. The talk we had on New Year's Eve enlightened me to why he was putting so much of his time and energy into this racing craze. I will never fully agree with it, but at least I'm not harboring any negative feelings towards him because of it, at least I was trying to convince myself of that. I was becoming the jealous wife to his mistress, and that wasn't who I was, besides there was still Johnny to think about. I hadn't told Liam anything of what had happened while we were in Glenville. I knew I should, but I couldn't bring myself to do it. I had a sinking feeling that my decision would come back to haunt me later.

My psychology class was interesting, and aside from Gertie, who was a constant reminder of Johnny, I was enjoying it immensely. I hated that, though. Gertie had always been the light in what normally seemed to be dark days for me, and I missed that. Now she was just the reminder of something I needed to forget.

"So what do you think of Professor Rollins?" Gertie asked me upon leaving class.

"I like him I guess. It's kind of hard to say so early in the semester."

"Well, I think he's wonderful. The way he talks about our dreams being a conduit to our next life is just fascinating to me. If this is any indication of what the rest of the semester will be like, I can't wait for it."

"Well, well Gertie if I didn't know any better I would believe you have become smitten with our teacher."

"Smitten? More like head over heels, Jenny. I'm not a kept woman anymore, and I do have eyes. And those eyes have found Professor Rollins eyes to be dreamy."

"Oh my God, Gertie I can't believe you just said that. That is the corniest thing I've ever heard come out of your mouth. I do believe you're out to become the teacher's pet. I never would have thought that of you," I said, giggling.

"Come on, Jenny, just because I'm an older woman doesn't mean I don't have desires, and just because you're engaged doesn't mean you can't look."

"Well, he is cute, but I'm happily satisfied. You can have Professor Rollins. He's all yours."

"Thank you, Jenny. Besides you already have your hands full with Liam and Johnny."

I stopped walking and looked at Gertie in bewilderment. Her no holds bar attitude towards me was almost too much for me to handle. "Why would you say that to me?"

"Because it's true, Jenny."

Gertie's candor sometimes was too forthright.

"Listen, I know you're only being honest with me. Maybe even looking out for me, but you of all people knows that nothing is going to happen between your son and I. Aside from me trying to mend some broken fences and just be friends, I'm not pursuing anything with Johnny."

"But there's already something going on between you two. I've sensed it from the beginning, and I've seen it in Johnny in the past couple of weeks. His demeanor the past week is much happier, and I can only attribute that to you. Have you seen him recently?"

I didn't know how to answer that. I didn't want anybody to know that I had seen him.

"I've seen him around."

"Remember who you are talking to, Jenny."

I just sighed. I hated the fact that sometimes she knew me better than my own mother. "Gertie, it's not important if I saw him. What is important is Liam, not Johnny," I said, trying to sound adamant.

"I know, Jenny. It's what you've always said, but I know that's not the whole truth. I'm not going to rehash our past conversation, but remember, whether you think you are or not, you're still toying with my son's feelings. In his heart, he believes you care for him and much more than you let on to others. Your little facade to fool people is only fooling yourself, my dear."

I remained quiet as she spoke. Gertie knew she was going too far. "I'm sorry, Jenny, I didn't mean to come off like this. It wasn't my intention to be so blatant, but I care about you too. I will try in the future not to bring this stuff up to you. I know it's not really any of my business, but it's hard for me to remain quiet when I know what's going on, especially when I have the innate ability to see more than most people. I will try harder, I promise. I enjoy our time together, and I don't want it to be ruined because of my meddling nature."

"Thank you, Gertie. I know you mean well. I just want to figure this out on my own. I know I can come to you, but let me make that decision, okay?"

"Yes, definitely. Well, I've gotta go, Jenny. I still need to pick up a few things at the bookstore for this class. I'll see you next week." Gertie placed her long, spindly fingers over mine and squeezed them tightly; the content, happy look she had possessed changed immediately to a look of worry and confusion. She didn't say anything as she turned to walk away, but I could tell she felt differently when our hands touched. I tried to shrug it off, but being who she was, I knew there was always a reason for her disposition. She had a gift that exuded from her whether she tried to hide it or not. It worried me. She knew things. That was part of her gift. I knew I should go after her and ask her what she saw, but I was distracted by my cell ringing.

"Dawg! What are you doing?"

"Kendra! I just finished class. What are you doing?"

"Nothing really, I thought about going down to *The Dock* and wondered if you would like to join me."

"Yeah, I'd like that. I can meet you right now."

"Great. See you in a few."

I thought I would find Kendra with her friends, but to my surprise, she was sitting in a booth by herself. She greeted me with open arms and a beer as I sat down.

"Hey friend, how are you?" I said as she handed me my mug.

"I'm great. It's so good to see you. How were your holidays?"

"They were wonderful."

"I'm guessing you spent them with Liam?"

"You guessed right. How was yours?"

Kendra paused. "They were nice."

"Did you see anyone in particular?"

Kendra paused again. "Umm…yes."

"You're acting strange, Kendra. What's going on?"

"I never could hide anything from you. I guess I'm acting strange because of who I saw over the holidays."

"And who would that be?"

"Tony."

"Tony?! Really?! "

"We're back together, Jenny."

"You are? That's great." Kendra wasn't sharing my enthusiasm. "Kendra? This is great, right?" I was puzzled by her indifferent behavior.

"Yeah, I guess."

"Excuse me if I'm reading you wrong, but shouldn't you be a little happier than this?"

"I'm sorry, Jenny, it's a little more complicated."

"Why? What's going on?" Kendra's eyes were welling up with tears as her forefinger methodically traced the rim of her beer mug. I reached out and placed my hand over hers. She was trembling and her hands were ice cold. "Kendra, what is up with you? I'm sensing you didn't call me down here just to have a beer."

"No, I didn't... Jenny, I'm pregnant."

My mouth dropped to the floor as nothing came out of it except air. I didn't know if I should say congratulations or not. She was visibly upset. I held my congratulations and instead went over to her side of the table and hugged her. She reciprocated by holding on tightly to me. A familiar feeling I had grown accustomed to from times when I was upset and just needed to feel Liam's touch on me. I sat down next to her embracing her as she held on to me.

"Kendra, does the baby belong to Tony?"

"Uh-huh," she said in between her subtle sobbing.

"I'm guessing this wasn't planned?"

"No, Jenny. Oh my God, what am I going to do? I'm only eighteen years old. I can't have a baby now."

My mind went back to when I was in the hospital and Liam was telling me that I had lost our baby. How I wish I could be pregnant right now, and hearing Kendra wish she wasn't, it was hard for me to understand the pain she was feeling.

"Does Tony know, Kendra?"

"Yeah, I told him over break."

"What does he have to say?"

"Jenny, he's so happy. He asked me to marry him. You know he never wanted us to break up. It was me. I wanted space. I wanted a chance to enjoy college life and do what I wanted. I wanted some freedom, just like every other person who goes off to college. I guess this is what I get for wanting too much." Kendra's tears began to free fall at a rapid rate. "Jenny, what am I going to do? This will ruin everything. I wanted to do so much before I became a mom. I had plans. I wanted to see the world. How am I going to do that with a baby and a husband?"

"It could be a lot worse, Kendra."

"Huh? How?"

"You could be going through this all alone. It sounds as though Tony wants to be a part of this."

"Yeah, I guess." Kendra let out a huge sigh as she placed her hands over her face and bent her head backwards. I sat there motionless, not knowing what to do next for her. I wanted to console her, and I was trying, at least the best way I knew how. If it could have been any other problem, my bedside manners would have been more believable, but this was different. It was so hard for me to fathom her feelings when I wanted so badly to be in her shoes. So many nights I had laid in bed as my hands caressed my barren stomach, knowing that at one point those hands could have been moving over a baby, a baby that Liam and I had created. Instead, it was just a void inside of me, no life, the way I felt so much of the time. I looked over at Kendra, she was almost beyond consoling. Her emotions were so surprising to me. I knew this was a shock to her, but I never imagined she would be this upset over it. Sure, it would cause a setback, but I firmly believe things always happen for a reason, and this baby was there for a reason.

"Kendra, I know this isn't what you want to hear from me, but this could be a blessing in disguise."

"What, Jenny? How can that be? This is going to destroy everything I've ever wanted to do with my life. I'm not ready for this. I'm not ready to be a mom or a wife. I'm not like you Jenny, I don't want to settle for the first guy I fall in love with."

She knew instantly that she had said the wrong thing to me. I turned away from her, hoping that I could will myself not to cry. Or more importantly, not to lash out at her with something I knew I would regret later.

"Oh my God, Jenny, I didn't mean that. I'm sorry. It's just that…"

"Kendra, it's okay."

"No, it's not. I'm just so upset. I never meant to say that. I don't even believe it. I don't know why it came out. You and Liam have something special. You always have, and when I do dream about settling down, I always imagine myself finding someone like you have. You're lucky, Jenny, and I want that too…I just didn't want it so soon. That's all."

"But it's not always luck. Liam and I definitely have had a rocky relationship since we've been together. Sure, we love each other, but sometimes that doesn't seem like it's enough. We've had so many obstacles to overcome that I wonder if we're not being tested for something bigger that just hasn't happened yet."

"You mean like seeing the number eleven?"

"Yeah. I still don't know if I've figured that one out. I've just come to learn to accept it. It's obviously not going away, so I just try to deal with it in a positive way. I know we're both young. I know to someone looking from the outside in it might appear that I've fallen for the first guy, but you at of all people know that's not true. I can't explain it, but Liam and I were brought together even before we met. It was timing. And whether we met last year at a football game or ten years from now, we were meant to be together. And obviously you were meant to be a mom, whether it was ten years down the road or now. We can't always control our destiny, sometimes we just have to hang on and accept it for what it is and go with it. That's how Liam and I are. Everyone thinks we're the luckiest couple on this earth, but if you really look hard and look deep into our relationship, you know that every day we fight for each other. Nobody said it would ever be easy, Kendra."

"I know. But you guys have been able to weather the storm and it's because of the love you both share for one another. That's what I meant. I see how much you two love each other. It was apparent from day one, and it's even more apparent now, especially with what you guys have gone through. Most boys would have walked away, but not Liam. You guys are in it for the long haul, and that's what I want too… but one day, a long time from now. How can this be a blessing, Jenny?"

"It just is, Kendra. You know ever since Liam and I have been together I've been more aware or better in tune to my surroundings. I don't mean literally, like where I live. I mean theoretically. Things happen for a reason whether you want them to or not. It may not be what you had planned, but some of the best laid out plans are those that you have no control over. You can't always be in command of your life, no matter how hard you try. Sometimes there's a higher force that knows what's best for you, and the only thing you can do is follow it and trust your instinct. You have signs and it's up to you to notice them and read them for what they are. I believe this baby was meant to be. It could be your sign that a change was necessary in your life."

"But Jenny, Tony and I hadn't even spoken in months. We got together by accident one night a couple of months ago at a party. It was good to see him, but I didn't expect for us to sleep together that night, though. It just happened. It was just one time, Jenny. And we were careful. There were a hundred other times last year when I should have been pregnant because of our carelessness. Why this time?"

"Like I said, it was timing. You said yourself you hadn't been in touch with him. If this baby was meant to be then the powers that are made sure you and Tony would meet up again. I truly believe that, Kendra."

"Jenny, I'm so sorry. I just realized what I've been doing. How can I be so selfish?"

"What are you talking about?"

"I'm acting like a spoiled brat about not wanting this, and I totally forgot about you losing your baby. I keep messing things up, first with being pregnant and now with my friend. I didn't want our visit to go like this."

"It's fine, Kendra, that's what friends are for. It is hard, but you know I've accepted what happened to me a long time ago. Don't think you can't talk to me about your baby without worrying over me. I'm a tough cookie. And besides, I'm happy for you, really happy. And I want to be here for you."

"Jenny, I'm so glad you're in my life. I feel like we've reconnected. I knew we always had our friendship, but after leaving for school, I think I forgot how important it was to me."

"It's always been there Kendra. I'll always be your friend. But the question that remains to be answered is what are you going to do now? Have you told your parents?"

"Hell no. No one knows but you and Tony. I could hardly bring myself to tell you guys. I don't know how I'm going to tell my parents. They'll be devastated. If I thought my world was collapsing, theirs definitely will after I tell them they're going to be grandparents."

"I don't think it's going to be as bad as you're making it out. They'll be upset, but after the initial shock wears off, they're going to be fine. They love you. There's nothing you could do that will change that for them. They're going to be there for you, just like I am and, more importantly, like Tony will be."

"I just don't know if I love Tony. I mean I love him. But I don't think I'm in love with him. And I know I don't carry the same feelings for him that you and Liam share for one another." Kendra paused for a moment as she wiped her tear-stained face. "Can I tell you something, Jenny?"

"Anything."

"Do you want to know one of the real reasons Tony and I broke up this summer?"

"You mean there's more to it than what you've told me?"

"Yes. I mean that was a big part of it, but it was because of you."

"Me?"

"Well, you and Liam. Last summer after you and Liam separated, I watched you guys. Even with everything you two had just gone through, the accident, you almost dying, the separation, I could still feel the love between the both of you. It was amazing. I think I saw what Liam was trying to convince you of in the beginning of your relationship. The love he had for you was so deep and sincere, and then what I saw from you. I mean you were so skeptical of him in the beginning. Do you remember that? You loathed him, and then all of a sudden I saw you look at Liam differently. It was as if someone had taken the blinders off. Your eyes lit up at the mere mention of his name. It didn't take me long to see that you felt as deeply for him as he did you. This love was in you as well. It just needed you to find Liam before it could show itself. What you two shared was so much more than just a high school romance. It was and is the real deal. I knew I didn't have that with Tony. Did you know that I saw a lot of Liam when you two were separated?"

"You did?"

"Yes. I didn't want to let you know because I thought it might upset you even more than you already were. Tony was spending a lot of time with Liam, and usually I was with Tony. So I was seeing a lot of Liam too. He was a mess, Jenny. All he could think and talk about was you. He was so worried and concerned for your welfare. It didn't matter that you were mad at him; he always wanted to make sure you were okay. He would drive by your house late at night and sleep on your street just to be near you. It baffled me that someone could feel that much love for someone at such an early stage in their life. I mean, we had just graduated from high school. Most of us were wondering what was next for us, but not you two. I could tell that it was different. I was scared to death about what the future held for me and if Tony was to be a part of it, but when I saw you and Liam and how you guys knew and I mean really knew that your futures were to be one, I knew I had to make sure for myself. I was looking at Tony in a whole new light. I felt trapped all of a sudden. He was smothering me and I didn't like that. So when it was time to leave for college, I knew the best thing was to break it off. I wanted to experience life and find love the way you found love with Liam. I didn't think I could do that with Tony."

"But you must have still felt something for him or you wouldn't have been so willing to be with him, Kendra."

"It was like seeing an old friend. I didn't know anyone at the party, and when I spotted Tony, my heart skipped a beat or two. We began talking like we never had before, I mean really talking. We sat on the couch and gave each other our undivided attention. We talked for hours and not just about us but weird shit like global warming and politics. I didn't even know Tony knew what global warming was," Kendra said, laughing. "Everything just felt right that night. It was like we both had matured. Then at the end of the night when the party was over, he offered me a ride back to my room. But we never made it. Instead, we ended up at the motel. It was so magical, Jenny. We had missed each other so much, and it felt good to be together again. But..."

"Kendra, there's no but to it. Just because you think you have something different from what Liam and I have doesn't mean what you and Tony have isn't special. You two are different from us, and it shouldn't be the same as what Liam and I have. You guys have your own destiny and in that your own magic. You said the night was magical, and through that love and magic the two of you created more love." I placed my hand on her stomach.

Kendra took both of her hands and placed them over mine. "I can't believe I have a life growing inside of me. I'm so scared."

"It's okay to be scared, Kendra. I just don't want you to be scared for the wrong reasons. I know this is going to alter what you thought you wanted in life, but maybe you were going in the wrong direction and this baby is going to put you back on your right path. Talk to Tony. If he wants to be with you, don't shut him out. It's the worst thing you could do right now. You think you're scared, just think how he must be feeling."

"But that's just it, Jenny I have been thinking about that. What about his football career? How is he going to be able to continue playing and be a dad and a husband and go to school all at the same time? It's impossible."

"It's not going to be easy, but you're never going to find out if you don't allow him to try. He did ask you to marry him."

"You don't think he said that just because it was the right thing to do?"

"I don't know. I can't speak for Tony. All I do know is you have to at least give him a chance to be there. This is his baby too."

"Maybe, I don't know. Everything seems so complicated now." Kendra wiped the tears from her face again as she wrapped her arms around her stomach and rocked back and forth.

"Tell me something. How did you know Liam was the one? You've never doubted your feelings for him. If anything, I've seen your love grow even stronger. How did you know, Jenny, after such a short time that you had found your soul mate? I mean, how do you know he's the one, the only one?"

"I just do, Kendra. It's so hard for me to explain, but I love Liam more than life itself. Even through all the hell we've endured, my love for him has always been my base, my rock, or better yet, my stronghold. And I know he loves me just as much. I don't know how else to explain it. Sometimes you just know, and that's how it is for us."

"Even with Johnny, Jenny? I mean I know he still has feelings for you, strong feelings."

If she only knew, I thought to myself. "Yes, Kendra, even with Johnny. I do have feelings for him, how could I not after everything. He's been such a part of my life too. I feel gratitude and a deep friendship towards Johnny."

"I think he would hope for a little more than a little gratitude, Jenny."

"I know, but it would be too painful. Don't forget, if it wasn't for Johnny, the accident probably never would have happened. Liam will never forgive him for that."

"Well, I think it's beautiful what you and Liam have. Like I said, it's what I want. I just don't know if it will be with Tony, even with the baby. I can't all of a sudden feel something more for somebody just because I'm having his baby, and so far, my feelings are more confused than ever towards Tony. That's what I'm worried about. I don't see them changing any time soon."

"You have to have faith. Don't judge him yet, Kendra. Remember you're both in this. I know you're feeling confused, but so is he, I'm sure of it. Everything you have told me he's going through too. Give him a chance. You might feel differently once the two of you have a chance to talk this out."

"Yeah, I guess you're right. You're always right, Jenny. You're the voice of reason. Thanks."

"You're so welcome, friend." I looked down at our table and the two mugs of beer that had gone untouched.

"So I'm guessing the beer was to throw me off with your news."

"Yeah. I didn't know if I was going to be able to tell you tonight or not. So, I didn't want you to wonder why I wasn't drinking. I've seemed to have grown a reputation here for my partying. I guess that'll change now."

"It's going to be okay, Kendra."

"I hope so." Kendra paused before speaking again. "I love you, Jenny. You're my best friend."

"I love you too, dawg."

We left *The Dock* that night promising we would stay better in touch. I waved goodbye to Kendra as she drove away. She was on her way to meet Tony. She had called him right before we left, asking him if he would go with her to break the news to her parents. I didn't know how things were going to turn out for them, but I envied her. No matter how bleak she thought her future looked, she was still entering a chapter in her life that I wasn't. I held on to my stomach as I drove home. I yearned to feel my baby inside of me. I never even had the chance to experience those feelings; it was taken away from me before I could. Kendra said I was lucky. In my mind, she was the lucky one.

Chapter Eighteen
Stolen Kisses, Stolen Moments, and a Cardiologist

The second week of classes was in full swing, and even though I was only carrying one subject, I was bombarded with homework. I was spending much of my week in Glenville even when I didn't have class. Most of my schoolwork required in-depth research, and the local library in Spencer didn't carry the materials that my homework required. Liam and I were like two ships passing in the night, neither one of us happy with our conflicting schedules that kept us apart, but we did our best and kept in constant touch with our cells. He was still spending most of his time at the shop. If he wasn't working there, he was helping Grandpa on the farm. Grandpa had decided to retire after Liam bought into Joe's shop. He knew Liam wouldn't have the time it took to keep the farm running the way it should, and Grandpa had succumbed to the realization that he was too old to do it by himself.

So with much reservation Grandpa had sold all his horses except for Sugar Dumplin'. He kept her for me. I had grown attached to her. Grandpa's retirement was bittersweet for Liam. He always saw himself with Grandpa as they worked on the farm side by side and growing it into a horse farm they both could be proud of, but you couldn't do that unless both parties were willing and able. Grandpa wasn't able anymore and Liam didn't seem to be willing.

I was more or less living at the college library. I honestly thought that the homework would come gradually as school progressed. Never did I believe I would have as much in the first few weeks as I did in the first semester of high school. It was overwhelming, and I felt grateful that Liam understood my constant absence.

"Having fun?" The voice from behind me whispered.

"Johnny, what are you doing here?"

"I'm here to do homework, just like you." He sat his books and himself down next to me.

My body became tense.

"What are you studying?"

"It's psychology."

"Oh yeah, the class you're taking with Mom. Are you working on the paper due next week?"

"Yeah, I can't believe Professor Rollins is expecting us to write a twenty-page paper so soon after the semester started. I don't even understand the subject yet, and he's expecting us to explain why we dream the way we do. I have a good feeling I'm going to flunk this."

"You, not do well on a homework assignment? Come on Jenny, aren't you the girl who has never gotten a B in her entire life?"

"That was before college."

A huge smile came across Johnny's face as I spoke. In an instant, I felt the warm touch of his hand over mine. "Johnny, please... don't do this." We both looked down as his hand slid off mine.

"I'm sorry, Jenny. I guess that was a little presumptuous of me. It's just that it always feel so natural for me to touch you." I remained quiet. "Well, I guess I should find this book I need for English class. You think you have it bad, I have to write a paper on *Moby Dick*. I knew I should have paid more attention in high school. I totally paid a girl to write that paper for me last year. I guess that's what I get for trying to skate through my high school years without trying. Payback is always a bitch." Johnny gathered his books as I looked onward. I didn't want to make eye contact with him. "Oh, before I forget, I know you'll probably say no, but I wanted to invite you anyway. I'm having a party for my birthday in a few days, and I would really like it if you could be there. I know you probably won't, but it would mean the world to me if you did come."

I just shook my head back and forth. "Johnny, you know I can't do that."

"I figured that. I just wanted to make sure you knew you were invited. You are the only one I really want to be there," he said softly. "Anyway, if you change your mind, I'd love to see you. You would make my birthday if you were there." Johnny looked at me with his big brown eyes. I couldn't help but stare back at him. I knew my answer, but in my mind I was trying to think how I could justify being there, if for anything, just to wish him a happy birthday.

"I'm not changing my mind, Johnny. I can't."

"Well then, why don't you just wish me a happy birthday now and I won't get my hopes up about you coming to my party?" He leaned down to face me.

I found myself still staring at him when it struck me what he was saying. "Oh my God, Johnny, today is your birthday isn't it? It's the eleventh!"

"Yeah, it is. I'm the ripe old age of nineteen. Can you believe it? I feel like an old man."

"Happy Birthday," I said sincerely as we embraced. Johnny enthusiastically welcomed my gesture by reciprocating with an even tighter embrace. The moment lasted for what seemed like hours as we both declined to relinquish ourselves from one another.

"Thank you, Jenny. Like I said, I feel like an old man."

"Yeah, right, nineteen is pretty old. You'll be collecting social security before you know it."

Johnny didn't seem to want to share in the levity that he had begun. Instead he sat down, pulling me with him.

"Are you okay?" I asked.

"Yeah, I'm fine, just tired. I've been driving back and forth from Spencer a lot to help Mom with her shop. The first of the year is always busy for her. So with school and helping her, I haven't gotten a lot of sleep."

"If you don't mind me saying so, it shows. You look really tired. You should slow down a bit. Why don't you just sleep at your mom's instead of making the drive every day?"

"Because all my classes are in the morning. I scheduled them that way so I could be available to help Mom in the afternoon and evenings."

"Well, I know your mom doesn't want you to run yourself ragged. You could work something out so you're not making that drive every day. That seems a little excessive."

"Maybe, but with Mom going to school also, she needs me to be there. Besides, I don't mind. It keeps me busy and from...."

"And from what?"

"It keeps my mind off you, Jenny. Ever since New Year's Eve I can't help but think of what happened between us."

"It never should have. I was upset with Liam, and instead of just dealing with him, I let my guard down with you. I didn't mean to lead you on."

"You mean what happened between us didn't mean anything to you at all?"

I didn't answer him.

"If you say it didn't, Jenny, then I know you're lying. I could feel something when we kissed. You can't kiss me like that and expect me to believe you don't have any feelings for me. We've kissed before. There was feeling behind this one."

"Johnny, I can't do this anymore with you. Can't we just be civil with one another and move on from this? You have so much to offer. Any girl would love to be with you. Why do you want me, the one girl you can't have? I thought you would be tired of this. Why do you keep trying? Hoping against hope?"

Johnny just looked at me as I poured out my soul to him. He didn't flinch or even shift his position. Instead, he grabbed my hands and brought them up to his lips and kissed them softly. A reaction I wasn't expecting from my tirade.

"What, Johnny?" I whispered.

"All I have is hope, Jenny. If you take that away from me, then I might as well lay myself down and die. Give up. That's why I moved to Glenville. I never thought you would show up here, and when you did, I found myself looking for you, watching every door open to see if it was you coming through it. I would wait at the welcome center in hopes I might see you, and when I did I would watch from a distance, knowing that I shouldn't be watching you but still never able to take my eyes off of you. To see you, even for a minute, made me happy and gave me more hope. It never has mattered to me that you keep refusing me or that you've sworn yourself to Liam." Johnny's eyes fell from my sight as he focused on our still entwined hands. He looked tired, very tired. "I know the truth, but I also believe in the what-ifs and maybes, Jenny. That's where my hope lies."

He became silent for a moment. "Well, I've gotta go. Like I said, I have a paper to write too, and I am tired. All I really came over to do was to invite you to my party. I'm sorry about the kiss." He turned to walk away, only to return his gaze upon me. "Actually, I take that back. I enjoyed the kiss. I've always enjoyed kissing you, even if they have been stolen. It's been a long day, and by the looks of things, it's going to be a long night for me as well. Don't worry about my party, like you would anyway. I know you can't come. I just wanted to extend you the invitation. I'll see ya around." Johnny turned and walked away from me before I had a chance to speak. It was the first time he had ever done that. I was always the one trying to leave him. This wasn't like him. His goodbye was too casual and too easy.

That night I lay in bed with Liam's body securely next to mine. He was already asleep by the time I made it home. He must have been exhausted from his day. He hardly budged when I crawled in beside him. His only acknowledgment of my presence was his movement closer to me as we both settled in. Our time together had been scarce since the New Year, neither one of us relinquishing our priorities to make time for the other. We spoke often on the phone and would talk briefly in the morning before our days forced us to depart from each other's side, but the long and lingering nights that I cherished were nothing more than a memory for which I yearned. Our lives were clouded by priorities that did not care how precious our time together was. It had been stolen from us by a thief with its own selfish goals that to me, seemed to revel in the separation it had taken from us.

    I snuggled closer to him and pulled his arms over me in a protective manner, cherishing the stolen moment as I closed my eyes only to have them open prematurely. I couldn't sleep or didn't want to. The night had become estranged to me. It was an uneasy reminder of an unfamiliar and dark place that I did not want to visit and tried in vain to avoid. I looked at the clock. It was 3:29, and I was no closer to sleeping than when I had first laid my head down. My mind was distraught as thoughts of Johnny consumed it. I turned to look at Liam. He looked peaceful as he slept. His slumber was quiet and a reprieve I was happy he had found. His nightmares had all but vanished. He hadn't had one for over a month. We didn't understand why. Nothing significant had changed with Liam. He still carried the same animosity towards Johnny and the same guilt from the accident. If anything, we both felt the nightmares should be more prevalent than ever before, but for some reason, they were not. The only thing I could attribute to the absence of them was his new found interest. It was all he thought about. The past few weeks Liam slept, ate and breathed anything and everything that had to do with motorcycles and racing them. To look at him you would have no idea of the strife that he was bearing, the burden that buried him daily as he struggled to break free from the unseen shackles that enslaved him. His mentality was always in a state of torment.

    I wanted to wake him and let him know that I was home, but I couldn't. His contentment while he slept had been few and far between, and it would be selfish to deprive him of this. Right now, everything was right in his world, the way it should be. I, on the other hand, lay there wide awake afraid to give into the slumber that my body craved. How I wish I could will myself to the familiar darkness that I had learned to love so much. Ever since the accident, I had welcomed my dark friend as a sanctuary that I could go to when my mind could no longer bear my reality. It had accepted me, my weaknesses, my strengths, and my desires, never questioning me, only understanding me and embracing me with its shadowy, murky attendance.

Lately when my eyes no longer saw the light, I didn't see my dark friend. Instead, I saw turmoil and chaos. I was being pulled in two different directions: one towards Liam, the other towards Johnny, but unlike my reality where my soul belonged to Liam, my dream pushed me towards Johnny. There was an urgency that beckoned me to him. I couldn't pull myself away from it. Just like the tide that pulls you into the dark waters of the sea, with no control, I was being pulled towards Johnny. I was losing sight of Liam as he lay in the carnage of the accident, his voice screaming helplessly for me as I vanished in front of his bewildered eyes. The only thing clear to me was Johnny as my body relaxed into his, his calming voice reassuring me that this was right, that he needed me more than Liam did. I felt relieved at the sight of Johnny but still totally confused as I searched in vain for Liam. I only found the darkness.

But this wasn't the same friend that I had grown accustomed to seeing when my eyes closed. No, this was a presence that unbeknownst to me was being issued to lure me into its shadowy depths, beckoning me to follow it as it pulled me farther away from what was comfortable to me. The more I resisted, the more it drew me into its abyss. I felt smothered as I tried to find my way back to Liam. My heart grew heavy, and there was an unfamiliar tugging that told me that I needed to let go of my fears and allow Johnny to lead me away from the carnage. Johnny's eyes grew soft as he nestled me against his chest. Relief swept over him. Still, I looked futilely for Liam. I no longer heard his frantic pleas for my return or see his sweet face as pain and fear overtook it. He had faded away, just as I had. I only saw Johnny and felt the release of anxiety from his body as we continued to drift. I didn't understand it nor did I want too; it frightened me. Confusion overtook me. I screamed for Johnny to release me, but he ignored my frantic pleas. Instead, he held me tighter, afraid that if he let go, I would be gone.

A feeling of trepidation filled me as my journey began with him. I did not know where we were going or why, but as the passage began into the unknown and the truth was about to be revealed, I would always wake up startled by what my subconscious wanted to portray to me and afraid of what I might see. That is why I dreaded sleep. I was afraid of the journey with Johnny. My dark friend who I welcomed with open arms and felt so at peace had turned itself into a betrayer that I desperately tried to avoid.

I nestled my head deeper into my pillow as my gaze returned to Liam: my love, my soul mate. I brushed his hair out of his eyes and watched as he softly murmured. He unconsciously pulled me closer to him. Liam was all I ever wanted. I was at peace and felt fulfilled when I was with him. My desires were for him alone. My conscience was clear when I was with Liam, and I did not understand why it became muddled when Johnny was before me. I knew where I belonged, so why didn't my dreams convey that same message? A feeling of emptiness and loss overcame me as Liam held onto me. I had almost given in to the unwanted sleep when Liam's lips were upon mine.

"Hello, babe. When did you get home?"

"Hours ago."

"I've missed you," he said, with his eyes still shut.

"Me too."

I nestled my head into his body as the tips of my fingers traced the outline of his chiseled chest. It was now past five o'clock.

"Can't sleep?"

"No. I've been awake most of the night."

"Why?" Liam pulled my chin up so our eyes met. The sleepy vision he had previously engaged was gone. He seemed to be as wide awake as me.

"I don't know."

"Do you want to talk about it?" he asked as if he knew there was a reason for my conscious state.

"No, not really. How was your day?"

"Busy. We worked on six cars and three more came in when I was leaving."

"That's a good thing, right? I mean being busy is good."

"Yes. But it's not giving me much time to work on my bikes."

"Oh."

"Jen, is this still a sore subject with you?"

"It's okay."

"Well since we're talking about this, there's something I need to tell you."

"What?"

"There's a motorcycle race coming up, and I'm going to be in it."

I pulled away from Liam and lay prone on the bed. My eyes fixated on the ceiling above me as I tried to concentrate on the small cracks while Liam talked to me.

"Listen, Jen, you knew this time was coming. I'm ready for this, and aside from some tweaking on the bikes, they're ready too." A small tear slid down the side of my face. "I have to do this."

I remained tolerant in my position as I began to imagine the cracks in the ceiling as a road that led away from where we were. I thought of myself and Liam traveling down its path and into the light. We were happy. A feeling of joy swept over us as the new dawn approached us. All the drama that had coated our lives over the past year was nothing more than a mere illusion of our minds. We were excited as we walked into it, but the excitement was abruptly ended as Liam's voice deafened my vision. What I thought I was imagining was just that, my wild imagination taking Liam and me away. Liam's voice reminded me of my reality as he informed me of his impending race.

"Jenny, aren't you going to answer me?"

"Huh?" I said as I pulled my gaze away from the ceiling and into Liam's blue eyes.

"Aren't you going to answer me?"

"I'm sorry, what were you asking me?"

"I want to know if you are going to watch me race?"

"Oh. "When is it?"

"This Saturday, it's going to be in Glenville. The actual place and time haven't been told to me yet, but Toby said he would let me know in the next couple of days."

"I don't know, Liam. You know how I feel about this."

"You also know why I'm doing this and why it's so important to me."

I sat up in bed as I cradled the blankets closer to me. "How many races are there?"

"Two."

"I have to think about it. It's hard for me to say yes to this, a lot harder than it must be for you to race. You're going to have to give me some time."

"Jenny, I love you. I feel like the past few weeks have turned us into strangers. I miss seeing you. I miss being with you. Please say yes. I want you there. You're my support system, my refuge."

My refuge, I thought to myself. That was the first time in a long time I had heard those words part from Liam's lips.

"I don't know, Liam."

"It's just a race, Jenny."

Just a race? I thought to myself, just like our accident was supposed to be just a race.

"What, Jenny?" He asked as though he had no idea what he had just said to me.

"Just a race, Liam?"

"Yeah, just a race," he said, coyly.

"There's no way what you're doing is just racing. Maybe a year ago, or even two years ago, it would have been just another race, but not now, not today. This race as you so casually refer to it is the reason why I've been so upset lately. You know I've never agreed with this, even when you told me your reasons behind it."

"Jenny, I think you're making this out to be more than it really is. It would be different if I had never raced before. Are you forgetting the experience I carry?"

"Experience? Are you kidding me, Liam? You've never raced motorcycles before!"

"Just because I'm on two wheels instead of four doesn't mean I don't know how to handle myself. Come on, have a little faith in me."

"Faith? That's all I've ever had for you. Ever since I've known you, I've put my faith in you. I love you, and I don't think you need to race again to get rid of these demons you say you still carry. I think you've been able to move on from the accident months ago, but you're using that past guilt as a crutch so you can race. You know deep down inside how I feel and that I would never approve of you racing just because you wanted to keep doing it, so instead, so I would feel pity for you, you tell me it's to help you heal, to help you move on. Well, I don't believe it. I think it's a bunch of crap, but I'm going along with it because I do love you. So don't ever tell me I don't have any faith in you. Lately, that's all I seem to have." I turned away from him and got out of bed before he had a chance to speak. When I looked back, his head was down and his arms crossed. "What? You don't have anything to say to that?"

"What do you want me to say, that you're right? I can't do that. You're wrong. I can't believe you just said that to me. Where in the hell did that come from? You know that I didn't make any of that up. Do you really think that little of me to think that I would use you in such a way? For my own sake? I don't need pity, Jenny. Never have and never will. For almost a year now I've wrestled with the decision I made last year that almost cost you your life. I almost died that night with you. When you were in the emergency room and doctors and nurses were scrambling over you trying to save your life and our baby's and they told me you were dying, I started to die too. I've loved you from the moment I set eyes on you, Jenny. I couldn't bear the thought of you leaving me and it being my fault."

"But it wasn't your fault, Liam."

"It was, Jenny. You weren't behind the wheel. Johnny wasn't behind the wheel. I was. Don't you know me anymore? I thought after everything we've been through together, you of all people understood. But after what you just said, I don't know if that's true. I'm trying to get better, and whether you believe me or not, racing is going to help me get better. I need you to believe in me, but if you can't seem to do that and think that this all a game that I'm putting on for you for my own selfish reasons, then so be it. It's not going to change how I feel about racing. I'm going to race next Saturday whether you want me to or not. I'm going to get over this the only way I know how. My nightmares are real, you know that!"

Liam rose from the bed and walked out of the room without batting an eye in my direction. I stood there, wondering why I said what I did. It wasn't like me, and to be honest, I didn't even feel that way. I knew Liam was being sincere with the torment he still carried. I had seen it, I had felt it, and I had witnessed the nightmares myself. He couldn't have made those up. The way I talked to him made me think of Johnny. I continued to stare at the empty hallway that Liam had just occupied. His footsteps were heavy, and his slight limp was apparent as I heard him walk outside. He could never hide his anger, and when he was mad, it was conveyed through his whole body, even in his walk. The madder he was, the stronger his step became, and by the sound of what I heard, he was madder than hell.

Through our bedroom window, I saw him talking to Grandpa Mack, who was letting Sugar Dumplin' out to pasture. Grandpa's hand went on Liam's shoulder as in a gesture of reassurance. I noticed Grandpa's eyes move away from Liam and towards the bedroom window. I knew they were talking about me. In the far corner of the room on a chair was a bride's magazine. The pages were curled upwards from the many nights I had scanned through it, gazing at the numerous bridal gowns it carried. I wondered now if it was all in vain, time wasted on something that would never happen.

Looking out the window once again I noticed Grandpa helping Liam lift one of the bikes in the back of his truck. Liam was gone in minutes. He didn't even come back to say goodbye. It was so unlike him, but then again, it was so unlike me saying what I said to him.

The next week was hell for me. Liam had decided to better prepare himself for the impending race that he should work on his bike with the help of Toby. He needed a clear head and thought maybe this would be best for me too. He was coming home, but it was at all hours of the night. I didn't really want to be there by myself, but even when Liam showed up, I felt alone in our bed. His last words to me before leaving was that he loved me and hoped he would see me at the race. I still didn't know if I could be there. I missed my home and found this time the perfect opportunity to see my parents. I missed them and decided I would stay with them for that period of time.

It was good to be home. Aside from the holidays, I rarely saw them anymore. The store was closed and seemed like a ghost town as I passed the warehouse that led to my house. Only a year ago, the street was busy with delivery trucks and customers frequenting the store, but today the only sign of life I found was the occasional car that would drive down the street as a shortcut to the next street. Dad's health remained in question, even after the closing of the store he still seemed to be extremely tired.

"Mom?"

"Yes, hon."

"How's Dad doing?"

"He has his good days and his bad days, dear."

"Is he going to be okay? I mean is his heart alright now?"

"Not really, Jenny." Mom put down her paperwork and scooted next to me as she placed her hands on mine.

"Jenny, your dad is sick. His heart isn't well."

"Why haven't you told me about this?"

"Because we didn't want to worry you. You've had a pretty traumatic year yourself. I don't want you to worry. Dad is seeing a very good doctor, and he assures us that with the proper precautions, your dad will be fine."

"What does that mean, proper precautions?"

"Well for one thing, it meant closing the store. And we did that. The other thing is to keep stress to a minimum for your dad. He's also on medication to reduce his blood pressure. I don't want you to worry, Jenny. We're doing everything we're supposed to do."

"I'm sorry, Mom."

"Why are you saying that?"

"I feel like I haven't been here for you. I mean with Ashley in California I should have taken more responsibility and been here for you guys. I'm sorry."

"Don't be, Jenny. And you have been here for us. Seeing you healthy and happy and the love you and Liam have for one another has been wonderful for us to watch. We're just happy that you're okay and that you and Liam are getting ready to start your future together. You have so much to look forward to, and it makes

Dad and me so proud. Tell you what, Dad has a doctor's appointment tomorrow in Charleston, why don't you go with us? We could go shopping and out to eat afterward, just like we used to."

A smile came across my face. "It sounds great. Besides, I would like to meet Dad's doctor. I think it would help me."

The next day was Thursday: two days before Liam's first motorcycle race and two days before Johnny's birthday party. The doctor's office was located in an old Victorian house located in the old part of Charleston. Dr. Thompson's office was decorated in an out-of-date off-white and peach design. The walls were covered with multiple pictures that when aligned with each other made one giant flower that looked like it was going to jump from the borders that were confining it at any moment.

In the waiting room, there were two peach sofas and an old chair that looked like it had come from a second-hand store. It had been badly reupholstered in a peach and white fan pattern to match the décor. An odd smell lingered through the room that reminded me of the hospital, not the stark, clean, sanitized smell but more the sick smell that emanates from the ill patients. I held on tightly to my stomach as a knot began to form. I hated that smell ever since Liam's accident at Christmas last year. You would think after the year I've had the smell wouldn't bother me, but it did. It was a ghastly smell that reminded me of death.

"Honey, why don't you sit with Dad while I sign him in?"

"This shouldn't take long, just a couple of tests, and then I can take you and Mom shopping and out for a nice dinner," Dad said as I sat down beside him.

I squeezed his hands as the knot in my stomach grew larger. After Mom signed Dad in, she opted to sit in the badly upholstered chair next to us. Besides us, the only other person in the room was an elderly man who carried an oxygen tank with him. His focus remained forward, looking neither at us nor towards the front desk. He breathed in and out in a regulated fashion as his oxygen tank took count of each breath. I found myself in a trance as I became hypnotized by his breathing pattern. In and out he breathed with no irregularities, as though he had been practicing his skills for years. I found myself becoming mesmerized by him, an unexpected distraction, and a relief from the nauseating smell. The grapefruit size knot in my stomach slowly shrank down to the size of a lemon.

"Mrs. King?" the nurse said. "We need your insurance card."

"Oh, I'm sorry. Jenny, can you take this to her?"

"Sure." I walked to the front desk and handed the nurse the card.

"If you can wait just a second, I'll make a copy of it."

I smiled appeasingly as I waited patiently for her to return. My eyes drifted from side to side. I looked down at the sign-in sheet to see where Mom had written Dad's name in: Henry King. Appointment time: 11a. I glanced up at the clock it was 11:11, doctors were notorious for making their patients wait, I thought as I drummed my fingers on the counter. I wondered if Dr. Thompson was even seeing a patient right now, he was probably in his office having a snack while his patients waited tolerantly for their name to be called. I glanced back down at the sign-in sheet to see who was before Dad. Only two others: Mrs. Mary Gordon and Johnny Bryant.

"Johnny Bryant?" I whispered aloud.

"Excuse me, did you say something?" the nurse said as she handed me the insurance card.

"Uh, no, sorry, just thinking out loud."

I looked at the name again. This had to be someone else. It couldn't be the same Johnny I knew. Besides, we were at a cardiologist office. There would be no reason for the Johnny I knew to be here. It had to be someone else who just happened to possess the very same name. I sat back down slowly when the nurse opened the door.

"Mr. Garrison, Dr. Thompson will see you now."

Mr. Garrison, whose eyes never ceased to look anywhere but forward, immediately looked towards the nurse as he carefully maneuvered off the adjoining couch. He grabbed the cord that attached him to the oxygen tank and proceeded towards her. He walked slowly as he took his companion with him, the nurse held out her hand to help him as they disappeared behind the door. It was only the three of us now, the room deadly quiet since Mr. Garrison was no longer here to entertain us with his patterned breathing. I stared at the door, my thoughts still on Mr. Garrison when the door swung open again. Great, I thought, finally Dad's turn. But instead of a nurse saying, "Mr. King, Dr. Thompson will see you now," a young man walked out, a young man who just had a birthday, a young man who I knew, a young man who just so happened to possess the name of Johnny Bryant. Our eyes locked into each other's immediately, he was just as surprised to see me as I was to see him. He didn't say a word to me though but turned briskly to face the nurse.

"Here's your prescription, Johnny. We'll see you next month. Please call the office if you have any questions regarding your new medication."

He didn't respond, only nodding as he turned away. His surprised gaze returned to me.

"Hello, Jenny," he said calmly.

"Hi, Johnny." I didn't know what else to say. I was still shocked to see him.

I guess he didn't know what to say either. Instead, he gave me a small smile and walked away, hesitating only for a moment knowing full well that I would want to know why he was there. I immediately went to follow him only to have the nurse open the door again.

"Mr. King, Dr. Thompson will see you now."

Chapter Nineteen
Grandpa

Dad's visit with Dr. Thompson went routinely, nothing had changed and nothing new to surprise us, but I was still surprised, not by Dad but by Johnny. I couldn't understand why he would be there. It didn't make any sense, it wasn't as if he was there for someone else, I remember the nurse distinctly saying his name. It was his medicine. What was going on with Johnny? Maybe I wasn't supposed to know, but he had invaded my life for the past year. I felt I was inclined to know what was wrong with him, but at the same time, I didn't think I was going to be able to handle anymore. How much can a girl take before she implodes? I dropped my parents off and promised them I would call soon. Liam had left me a message that he was home and wanted to see me. Upon my arrival, I found him sitting on the front stoop, his foot balancing on the broken board.

"Hi," he said.

"Hi. Why aren't you at the shop?"

"I wanted to see you. How is your dad?"

"He's okay. Nothing's changed. The doctor wants to see him in a month for a follow-up."

"I'm glad he's not any worse, Jenny."

"Yeah, me too."

"I didn't mean to leave the way I did. I don't have a reason for it. I'm asking you for your support and then I go and leave."

"It's alright, Liam. Besides, this week gave me a chance to spend time with my parents. I needed that, and I think they did too. Listen, I never meant to come off so cold to you. I know what you have been going through and it was pretty heartless for me to say what I did. I'm just scared, Liam. I'm having those same feelings I did last year before the race, and it scares me to death. I don't want anything to happen to you."

"I know you are, and I understand, but I am going to be fine. I've already tested the bike, and it's riding like a dream. I really think you would be proud of me, and I know I want you to see me race. I want you to be at the finish line, babe." Liam rose from his sitting position and grabbed my hands. "Maybe it would help you too, if you could see me do this."

Liam kissed me tenderly but with a passion I hadn't felt for a while from him, his arms bringing me closer to him as the kiss continued. I could feel his pulse beating in his neck as my hands wrapped around him. I wanted this to last. I wanted him to pick me up in his arms and carry me to our room and make love to me. I wanted him to tell me that I was all he needed, that he was a fool for believing that racing would solve any of his problems. But he didn't.

"I love you, Liam. That's why I'm scared. I don't think I can watch you race. It's too soon for me. If something would happen..." Liam didn't let me finish.

"Nothing's going to happen, Jenny. It's just a race, and from what Toby told me, it's a piece of cake. Hell, there's not even a bend in the road. It's a straight shot down a dirt road. It'll be over before you can yell my name." His crystal-blue eyes were softer than I had seen them for a while.

"I want to believe you, but I can't promise you anything. I'll do my best, but don't be mad at me if I'm not there."

Liam sighed heavily as he released his tight grip on me. He was disappointed. "Okay. I guess I have to live with that." He kissed me again lightly on the forehead this time as he got into the truck. "I have to get back. I'll be staying with Toby until Sunday. I'll keep my phone on so you can reach me. I better go, though. I still have to pick up Parker and Joe. I love you, Jenny."

I smiled as he drove off. I saw him place his fingers to his lips as he placed them on his rearview mirror. I reciprocated the motion as he disappeared around the turn. I stood there, knowing full well in my heart that I wasn't going to be able to watch him on Saturday night. My heart grew heavy as his truck disappeared. I turned and walked inside the house, Blue following me close behind. I heard Grandpa Mack in the kitchen. I didn't feel like talking, I wanted to go upstairs and crawl under the blankets and sleep until Liam returned to me. My mind wanted to forget about everything, Liam, Johnny, and the torment I was feeling for having any feelings at all for Johnny.

"Jenny, is that you?" I didn't even make it to the second step.

"Yes, Grandpa, it is."

"I thought so. I just poured myself a cup of coffee. Why don't you join me?"

I didn't want to; I just wanted to escape to the bedroom. "Sure, Grandpa, I'd love a cup."

Grandpa had just sat down at the table with two cups of coffee in his hands. He gently placed the porcelain cups with their blue rose detail on the table as he pulled out a chair for me.

"Here you go. I don't know what you like in yours, but here's the sugar and creamer. So, how are you, my dear? I haven't seen much of you lately. Did you have a nice visit with your folks this week?"

"I did. It was good to spend some time with them."

"How is your dad?"

"He's doing okay. The doctor said everything looked good, but he still doesn't want him to do any work. It's really hard for my dad to just sit around and do nothing. That's not like him."

"I understand. That's the same way I felt after my heart attack."

"But you slowly started working again, Grandpa. I mean, I know you don't do the stuff you used to, but you still do a lot more than what we ever thought you would be able to do."

"True, but it's taken a year for me to come back, and even now I'm not doing half of what I used to. That's why we got rid of the horses, Jenny. Liam and I both realized it was time."

Grandpa hadn't taken one sip of his coffee, only stirring it incessantly with his spoon.

"Did I tell you that Mom and Dad are thinking of moving?"

"No. Where to?"

"Down south, possibly South Carolina. They both have wanted to live there ever since I can remember. Dad has gotten a lot of his produce from the farmers markets in Columbia and

Charleston, and they've talked about moving there every year. The only reason why they never did was because of the store, and now that I'm not living with them anymore and the business is closed, they think it's the perfect time to make the move, not to mention that Ashley is in California."

"What about the apartments?"

"Billy is going to manage them, besides they pretty much take care of themselves, and I guess Billy is a pretty good handyman. If anything goes wrong, Dad knows he can rely on him."

"Are you okay with their decision, Jenny?"

I paused. I really wasn't, I would miss them terribly, but I knew it was the best thing for them. "I guess so. Even Dr. Thompson thinks it's a good idea. All Dad thinks about is the business. He's surrounded by it, it's just a reminder of what used to be. It's killing him to see it so vacant and empty. He's been depressed ever since it closed."

"I figured that. It's hard to see your dream vanish before your eyes. Your dad worked hard to build his business. I think they're doing the right thing by moving, though. I've thought about moving myself."

"You? Where, Grandpa? This is your home."

"It's not really. It's Liam's home...and yours. Besides, I haven't made up my mind fully on the matter, but I am seriously considering it. After you and Liam are married, the two of you are going to need your space to build your lives together. You don't need me in the background."

"That's not true, Grandpa. We want you here always."

"I know that, but this has been a very hard year for the two of you. Just because I haven't seen a lot of you doesn't mean I haven't been watching you guys. The both of you have been hurting. I know you love each other, but you've both been in a lot of pain. I can see it every day. It's been a struggle for me not to get involved. I know you need each other, but there's been a wall between the two of you for months now."

I just looked down at my coffee. Grandpa placed his rugged hand over mine.

"Jenny, what's going on?"

"I don't know, Grandpa. I really don't know. I don't know if it's Liam or me, but no matter how hard we try to break down that wall, there's another one that goes up. I don't agree with his racing, and he still's going through with it. I don't understand it. He knows how it makes me feel, and I still have these dreams from the accident. They are so real to me, and it just brings everything back from that night like it just happened."

"Wait a minute: I thought Liam was having the dreams? You are too?"

"Yes. I've been having them for a while now. It's so weird because mine start where Liam's leaves off. It's like I'm seeing what Liam can't."

"Does Liam know about them?"

"Yes. He doesn't understand why I'm having them either. I haven't talked much about them to Liam, he's been so busy, and besides, Liam hasn't been having his nightmares lately."

"What's lately? I've had to wake him from them every night this week."

"What do you mean?"

"I mean Liam has had a nightmare every night this past week."

"I thought he was staying at Toby's?"

"I thought so too, but he came home every night in hopes you would be here. He didn't want to go into detail with me, but he said he understood why you were at your parents' and not here. I knew he was feeling bad, and I thought he was at least calling you, but if this is news to you, then I'm guessin' he never made the calls."

"No, I never heard from him. We really didn't talk much this week, and the couple times we did, he never mentioned the nightmares. He only talked about the upcoming race. That's one of the reasons why I stayed with Mom and Dad. He said he was going to be in Glenville."

"Well, he's had one every night, and from what I heard, they're just as bad as ever, maybe worse. I'm just surprised he didn't call you."

"Why are you surprised?"

"Well, because they seemed really bad. He kept screaming your name. I would find him in a bed of sweat, shaking uncontrollably, just like always, but at the same time, ten times worse. I thought for sure he would want to at least hear your voice after one of them. I tried to help him, Jenny, but you know there's nothin' I can really do for him. It's you that holds that gift. I would end up just sitting with him while he went through it. He would jerk away from me telling me he had to find you before it was too late. When he finally would wake up, he just laid there with tears streaming down his face. He kept apologizing for putting me through this. I told him not too, but he still carries so much guilt. He thinks he has lost you even though you're right here with us. He feels like that accident took a part of you away from him that he can't ever get back. I don't know what to do, Jenny. I thought the two of you had a handle on this. They're not getting better. In my opinion, they're getting worse, and now to hear that you're having them too, well I'm a little worried for the both of you."

The two of us just sat there staring at our now ice-cold coffees, neither one of us interested in drinking them.

"Jenny...have you guys thought about seeing a counselor?"

"I brought it up to Liam months ago, but he won't have anything to do with it. You're right, he is stubborn and proud. He's not bending when it comes to that. He doesn't want anyone to know about the nightmares or the fact that he still has issues with the accident. Everyone in town thinks that their all-American boy is just fine and so is his girlfriend, and that's how he intends on keeping it. Have I ever mentioned to you about my friend, Gertie?"

"Gertie Bryant?"

"Yes, you know her?"

"Of course, that's Johnny's mom. She owns the psychic shop in town. She's a very nice lady. I've known her and Gary for years. I was sorry to hear that the two of them got a divorce. Why do you ask?"

I sighed before speaking, knowing full well that what I was about to say to Grandpa could never be taken back.

"I've become good friends with her. She takes a psychology class with me at Glenville, but I knew her before then." I sighed again, nervous to go on. "Grandpa, did Liam ever tell you why the accident occurred last April?"

"A little bit. You know, for as long as Liam has lived with me he has told me everything. As a matter of fact, I knew all about you before we even met, but as far as the race and the accident, he hasn't told me much. But that doesn't mean I don't know, Jenny." I gave Grandpa a peculiar look. "I know about Johnny. Hell, I think most of Spencer does."

"Oh," I said in dismay.

"Jenny, Liam loves you more than life itself. You changed him from the very beginning. I'm not telling you something that you don't already know, though. I'm not sure what kind of hold you two have on each other, but I do know it's stronger than anything I've ever seen before. The love you share seems to transcend time and space, and I think that's why these months since the accident have been so devastatingly hard for him. He doesn't want anything to come between the two of you, and no matter how hard he's tried to convince Johnny of that, Johnny doesn't seem to want to go away. I told you he shares most everything with me. Well, even though he hasn't shared a lot concerning the accident, he has told me that the reason for the race was Johnny. You're a beautiful woman, Jenny. Liam's afraid that Johnny might wear you down eventually. It's been almost a year since the accident, and from what I've seen and heard, Johnny is still around."

"Grandpa, I love Liam."

"I know that, dear, and Liam loves you, but Liam also knows that Johnny loves you too. What does this have to do with Johnny's mom anyway?"

"We became friends last year. I went to see her for some advice, and ever since then a friendship has developed. Liam doesn't like it, so I try not to talk about her to him. He doesn't even know that we have a class together. I hate keeping that from him, but I really like her, and I don't want to lose her friendship. She's been there for me, even when my mom couldn't. Mom is so worried about Dad that I don't want to worry her more. So, I've turned to Gertie."

"I see."

"The reason why I mentioned her is because of the gift she has. I know a lot of people don't believe in that sort of stuff or in her, but she truly has a gift. I think she might be able to help Liam and me with our dreams. A few months ago I brought her name up to Liam in hopes that he might agree just to go and talk to her, but he won't. I know it's because of Johnny. He won't see a psychologist, so I was hoping he would at least see Gertie. I was thinking that maybe, just maybe, if he opened up to her, she could resolve some of the unanswered questions regarding our dreams. I don't think racing is going to be the answer. I think the racing is only going to make things worse."

"Jenny, can I ask you a serious question?"

"Of course you can."

"Do you have feelings for Johnny?"

My heart stopped as those words fell from Grandpa's lips. I took a deep breath. It was as if Grandpa knew something too. "I do, Grandpa, but they're feelings of gratitude. How can I not have feelings for him? I know maybe I shouldn't, but I do. Believe me, I have tried to convince Johnny to leave me alone, but he won't listen to reason. I don't know what to do because deep down I would like to have a friendship with him. No matter how hard I've tried to exclude him from my life he keeps popping back in it, and because of that, I've grown to like him. He pulled me from the wreck, and I will always be grateful to him for that, and I know that's where Liam's nightmares stem from. He couldn't do that, and it's eating him up inside." I lowered my head into Grandpa's hands. "What am I going to do? I love Liam; I don't want to lose him, Grandpa."

"I know you do, but you've got to understand that Liam can't have Johnny in the picture. That should be obvious. No matter how innocent you think your relationship might be with Johnny, it's not. It would be different if you were speaking about Parker or Joe or any of your other friends. They've never tried to take you away from Liam. I'm not saying your feelings for Johnny are clouding your judgment towards Liam, but I do believe you're not seeing the whole picture, the picture Liam is seeing."

"What are you saying then, Grandpa?"

"Maybe there's a decision to be made, Jenny."

I remained quiet, knowing Grandpa was making sense.

"Jenny, did you realize Liam is still drinking?"

"What? He told me he had slowed down. Do you mean he's drinking more?"

"Yes, Jenny. He's been drinking a lot from what I can tell. I thought he was done with that, but I've noticed some empty beer cans and whiskey bottles in the barn. I know he's trying to hide it from me. He knows I would be upset, especially with the whiskey. That's what his dad used to drink, and that's what finally did his dad in."

I looked at Grandpa in disbelief. I knew he had been drinking more than usual, but I hadn't seen him drink for a while. "He told me he had stopped." I felt awful. I should have known everything that was going on in Liam's life, and lately that hadn't been the case for either one of us.

"I don't think he wants you to know, Jenny, but he needs you more than me. I know this boy like the back of my hand, and if he thinks racing again might help him get over these nightmares then let him try it, but make sure he's not drinking while he's doing it. He even turned down an interview with Coach Green because he wanted to work on his bike. But you knew that."

"Coach Green?"

"Yeah. Don't tell me you didn't know about the job offer?"

"No, Grandpa. Liam never mentioned it to me."

"Coach Green called him right before Christmas. He wants Liam to be his assistant next year for the varsity football team."

I felt blind-sided. Why would Liam keep such important news from me? This was great news, and he never even shared it with me. I really didn't know what to think anymore.

"I love you, Grandpa. Thanks for the talk."

"I love you too, Jenny, and you're welcome."

Things didn't make sense anymore to me. Liam and I seemed to be living together but separate lives from each other. It didn't matter if we loved one another or not. Right now that didn't seem to be enough for us.

Chapter Twenty
The End

It was half past midnight on Saturday when I arrived in Glenville. Bad weather had set in, and besides from some movement inside *The Dock* the town looked completely deserted. Only the die-hards would come out for a drink on a snow packed night like this, I thought.

I knew before going to see Liam, I had to see Johnny first. I needed to get some answers from him and to let him know that it was over for us...even as friends. Not that I was allowing there to be anything more between us than the friendship, but if I allowed it to continue, I knew the consequences would be detrimental for all concerned. I cared for Johnny, but I loved Liam more, and his love was more important to me than any feelings I might carry for Johnny. My need to finish this with him was stronger than times past. Maybe before, there was a part of me that didn't want to end it between Johnny and me, but even that was gone. I would admit that I was going to miss Johnny's presence in my life, but in time, I knew that too would pass.

Liam was spiraling out of control, partially because he thought he was still losing me. I had to make sure he knew that he was never in jeopardy of that. He was my priority. His drinking had begun again. I wondered if Toby and Gina had anything to do with that. Liam certainly seemed to like their company and the business they were giving him, not to mention Toby's advice on motorcycle racing. In Liam's fragile state of mind, it wouldn't take much to persuade him to have more than a beer or two. Toby and Gina were bad news, and I needed to get Liam away from them before any more damage occurred.

It seemed weird knowing Johnny wouldn't be a staple in my life anymore, but looking at the whole picture, I knew I wasn't being fair to myself, Liam, or Johnny. Maybe it wasn't right to tell Johnny right before his party, but he was a big boy. He could handle it, and besides, I didn't know when Liam was racing. I needed to get to him before he made the biggest mistake of his life. I pulled my car into a parking spot next to Johnny's white Bronco. I sat there in the cold for what seemed like hours, trying to get the nerve up to walk the flight of snow covered steps that led to Johnny's front door. Any chance of me backing out of this and driving away was gone as soon as I heard the tapping of Johnny's hand on my frosted window.

"Hello, Jenny," he said, as I rolled down my window.

"Hello."

"I saw you pull in. Are you here to see me?"

"Yeah. I need to talk to you."

"Okay. Why don't you come up? I was just coming back from *The Dock*. Jake Pittman and I were starting the party a little early by having a few beers in celebration of my birthday."

"Happy Birthday, again."

"Thank you," Johnny said, as he opened my car door.

"I thought I would see you at *The Dock* tonight. Liam is there with Toby and Gina."

"He is?"

"You seem surprised. Are you not here with Liam?"

"Not tonight. He came to spend the weekend with Toby. I'd rather not talk about it if you don't mind. It's kind of a long story." Johnny gave me a familiar glance that I knew too well. He already knew why Liam was here.

"No, that's fine. I just brought it up because usually where Liam is you are too."

"Yeah, usually," I said quietly as we walked into Johnny's apartment.

"Here, have a seat." He brushed off a new dusting of potato chip crumbs from his sofa.

"I see you're still just as good a housekeeper as the last time I was here."

"Some things never change. So what's going on, Jenny?"

"I think I should be asking you that."

"What do you mean?"

"I mean, why were you at Dr. Thompson's office the other day? I've tried calling you numerous times and you haven't returned any of my calls. What's going on?"

"Oh, I thought that's what this was about. I was hoping you were here for something else," he said, as he gave me a suggestive look that I did not find amusing. "I was ignoring your phone calls because I didn't want to talk to you about it. You never call me, and since Thursday I've had at least a dozen from you. I knew it wasn't because you missed me. Anyway, it's not important why I was there, and I don't want to bother you with it."

"Not important? I see. I guess it's normal for a nineteen-year-old boy to be visiting a cardiologist. I hear it happens all the time." I stood up to walk away only to have Johnny grab my arm. He looked defeated.

"Well," I said.

"It's common if you're a nineteen-year-old boy who was born with congenital heart disease."

"What? Are you kidding? Is it serious?"

"I don't know, I guess it can be. I have something known as Coarctation of the aorta. In layman's terms, it's the narrowing of my aorta. I was born with it but didn't have surgery to correct the problem until I was eleven years old. As a result of that, I now have high blood pressure and need to see my cardiologist periodically for my blood pressure medicine."

"Why didn't you tell me?"

"I never thought it was necessary. Why? Do you actually care?" Johnny asked in a sympathetic tone.

"Of course I care. I had no idea."

"I'm fine. Like I said, I was born with it. I've lived with this problem all my life. I have to go in periodically for check-ups. That's what I was doing when you saw me Thursday. My blood pressure has been out of whack for some reason, so Dr. Thompson wanted to try a new blood pressure medicine on me. It's nothing really."

"Of course it is."

"Well, you're in agreement with my mom and Dr. Thompson. I hate going to the doctor, probably because I've had to go so much in my life. I used to go to them on such a regular basis when I was a kid. As I got older and things seem to be as normal as they could be for me, I stopped going altogether. Mom would pressure me though, especially when I started playing football. The doctors told my parents when I was young I would never be able to play contact sports, but I made such a remarkable recovery from my surgery that they allowed it. They were cautious, but they gave the okay for it. I loved it so much that I was willing to do anything they said in order to play. I would stand on my head if they told me to," Johnny said with a soft chuckle.

"Anyway, by the time I hit high school, I pretty much stopped going to the doctor unless it was for a sports physical, and even then I tried to snake out of it. I didn't have any problems, so I didn't see the need for the visits. I was playing hard and playing well. I started exercising and lifting and was in the best shape of my life. When I did see my doctor, he said everything seemed great with my heart, but about a month ago, I started experiencing some dizzy spells. I brushed it off, but one night at Mom's shop I was unpacking some boxes for her when I fainted. That's all Mom had to see. She made the appointment the next day. Dr. Thompson ran me through a series of tests and through them discovered that my blood pressure was remaining high. So, as a result, you are now looking at a nineteen-year-old who has to take blood pressure medicine. So much for my youth. I'm an old man now, Jenny." Johnny chuckled again at his own expense. But I didn't. I was taking this much more seriously.

"I can't see the humor in this at all, Johnny."

"Why, because I called myself old? It's no big deal. So I'm on blood pressure medicine. People take medicine every day, besides it could be worse: I could be dying," he said as he continued to laugh at himself.

"That's not funny either, Johnny!"

Johnny put his arms up in self-defense at my remark. "Whoa, girl! I didn't mean to get you so riled up! If I knew your reaction to my health would do this to you, I would have told you a long time ago. I like it when your temper flares. It makes me think you just might really care for me."

I looked at him in disbelief, not knowing if I wanted to punch him or hug him. Johnny could see my concern and hesitantly as if he was waiting for me to react, put his arms around me. I couldn't deny the fact that I had come to love his touch against me. I hugged him back as tight as I could, holding on to him for as long as possible, knowing our time together was coming to an untimely end. Johnny knew something was different with me this time too. He could sense it.

"Are you okay, Jenny?"

"Yeah, I'm fine. I was worried about you. I needed to know that you were okay, Johnny."

"I am. I promise. But there's more to why you are here, isn't there? You normally don't show up at my doorstop at all, and for you to show up at midnight must mean something can't wait. Am I right?" I just looked away. "What is it, Jen?"

My eyes had become full of tears, but I could still see the warmness in his chocolate brown eyes as I returned my gaze to him. They were sincere and honest as they looked directly into mine. Johnny had never lied about his feelings for me, not even once, but I felt as though I had been lying to him all along by leading him on. I could hardly bear to tell him what I must. I knew it would be the end of a friendship that I had grown to count on, but it was time. He needed to let go of me. But maybe more importantly, I needed to let go of him because as much as I thought I wasn't holding on to him, I was. I was playing with his emotions by allowing him to believe that through our friendship he still had a chance with me. It was a selfish act on my part.

"Johnny, I'm here to tell you good-bye."

"Good-bye? You just got here. Where are you going?"

"I'm letting you go. This is it. I want you to move on and find somebody. You have so much to offer that it's selfish of me to let you think that there could be anything between us."

"You've never really done that. It's always been me trying to convince you, I thought."

"Yeah, I know, but I've always allowed us to have a friendship, even if I didn't believe in it. I can't do that anymore. It's not fair to you or to Liam. I truly care for you, and I always will. We have something between us that no one can ever take away from us, and I will always hold you close to my heart, but my heart still and always will belong to Liam. I love him, Johnny, and he's suffering right now because of me. It's killing me to see him like this, and as long as you're a part of my life, Liam's never going to be able to move on. I know you guys were good friends at one time; can't you go back to that time and remember what you once had, before I came into the picture? You wouldn't want a friend of yours to be in so much turmoil as Liam is, would you? If you can't do it for me, do it for a friend, a friend that once meant a lot to you. Please let go of me, for Liam's sake."

Johnny stood up at walked to his window.

"So this is really it then? The end."

"No, I would rather think of it as a beginning for you, Johnny. I know you love me. I do, really, but it's not fair to you for me to string you along. Even though I've told you from day one there could never be anything between us, there still is, and whatever that is can't go on any longer. Please try and understand that after tonight, I need you out of my life for good, forever."

I walked over to him and placed my hand on his shoulder. He grabbed it with his hand and held on to it tightly.

"Liam is a damn lucky man, Jenny. I hope he realizes that." He gently squeezed my hand before walking to his bedroom door. He turned to make eye contact with me, only to give me a despondent look.

"Johnny?"

"Jenny, would it be too clichéd to say thanks for the memories?" I smiled, knowing to speak at this moment would cause a flood of emotions that I couldn't control. "I thought so. But I do want to wish you and Liam a life full of love and happiness. You guys deserve it, and I mean it this time. I'll be seeing you, Jenny."

He closed his bedroom door behind him. I stood there alone in his room, knowing that a chapter of my life was over. I took one more look at the empty room that was decorated so poorly with mismatched furniture before gathering my coat. Outside Johnny's window, I could see the snow was falling heavier now, a new layer covering the old one. It was almost symbolic as I thought of the new start that awaited Liam and I. I opened the door to take in the fresh air, the feeling of relief and excitement that encompassed me just seconds earlier was now overshadowed immediately by the sight that took my breath away.

"Liam! What are you doing here?"

"Don't you think I should be asking you that, Jenny?" he said as the snow whipped past his face. He stood there in a frigid stance in the freezing elements. Liam wasn't wearing a coat, only an old flannel shirt that was only half-way buttoned up, exposing his chiseled but semi-frozen chest. The cold air took my breath away but not until I had time to breathe in the horrible smell of alcohol that was projecting from Liam's mouth. He was madder than hell as he stood before me, but worst of all, he was drunker than I had ever seen him before. He tried to stand still, but the icy wind that continued to whip its way through us made him waiver from side to side.

"You're drunk, Liam."

"And you're a liar, Jenny. You know I didn't want to believe it. I saw your car parked over here and for the life of me I tried to convince myself that it belonged to somebody else. It can't be my Jenny. She would never do that to me. She knows how much I despise Johnny, but I had this God-awful feeling in the pit of my stomach that I was wrong. I tried to brush it off, hoping that you were here to see me, you know, maybe show a little support for your man before he raced. But then I thought, if that was true, then why weren't you beside me? I waited and waited for you to walk through that damn door at *The Dock,* but you never did. I could see your car as I looked out the window, and I continued to pray to God that it belonged to somebody else, but then I should have known not to pray. None of my prayers ever do come true. I walked to the window and I couldn't believe who I saw standing as pretty as a picture in Johnny's window. I still didn't want to believe it was you, so I had to make sure even though you promised me there was nothing going on between you and that jackass, knowing that being here with Johnny would be the worst possible thing you could ever do to hurt me, but I was wrong. I guess I've been wrong about a lot of things, but mostly I've been wrong about you." Liam wasn't yelling, but the look in his eyes was enough to beat me down, to kill me from the inside out.

"You don't understand, Liam. There was nothing going on here. I was telling Johnny good-bye, to leave me alone. I told him I love you. It's always been you."

"That's true, Liam," Johnny said, coming from behind me.

"You bastard!" Liam finally screamed from his cold-hardened lungs. "You stay out of this! I'm tired of you meddling in my business! I guess I'm the fool but never again. You can have her, Johnny. You win!" Liam slurred as his arms flew up in the air. He was swaying from each side as he tried to keep his balance and make his point. I reached for him only to have him jerk away from me. It was the worst feeling ever to have Liam refuse my touch. If he were to fall down the flight of snow-covered steps, I knew he would kill himself.

"Leave me alone, Jenny."

"You don't mean that, Liam. I love you."

"Love? How in the hell can you use that word so loosely? You don't mean it so why say it?"

"Because it's true. You know that. You're just drunk. You're not thinking straight, and you're letting the alcohol control what you say. You know it's never been Johnny."

"It seems it's always been him, Jenny. He's always been in the picture. I guess I was just blind to the obvious. I guess I should have seen it the night of the accident. It was him all along, your knight in shining armor that saved you from the guy who almost killed you. It looks like those nightmares held more truth behind them than I was willing to give them credit. No wonder you wanted me to see Gertie. It's his mom for God's sake, just another chance for you to be close to him. Damn girl, you've played me. Victory to the loser, you both deserve each other."

I couldn't speak for crying. It felt like a thousand bees stinging my cold, brittle face as the salt from my tears hit it, but that was nothing compared to the pain I was feeling in my heart.

"Please, baby, don't do this. It's not over. Try to listen to me," I begged him.

"I'm not listening to you. Gina was right. She said you would be here."

"Gina?!"

"Yeah, Gina. She and Toby both have had my back since I've met them. They seem to genuinely care about me and my racing, unlike you. She was the first to notice your car tonight. She was the one who told me I should come here and see for myself. I'm glad I listened to her. Who knows how long you were planning on keeping this going on."

I grabbed the railing to protect myself from also falling down the flight of steps that were continually reminding me of their presence. The wind was whipping through my body as it blinded me with its authority. "They don't care about you. All they care about is how much money they're going to make off of you. Don't you see that? It's as plain as day. They know your reputation for racing. They know how good you are. That's all they care about, Liam. They don't care about you. They're just using you, babe. I'm the one who loves you, who cares for you. I've been the only one in your corner from day one. You've let them brainwash you."

"Nobody tells me what to do, Jenny. I can control my own destiny. Destiny. Ha! What's your stupid eleven have to say about that?" Liam said as he pulled out a small, silver flask from his back pocket and took a huge gulp from it. I went to grab Liam only for him to yank his arm away from me again. I could hardly see him through my tears. How I wish I had never shown up tonight. I could have just called Johnny, but no, I had to do it in person. If Liam would only believe me, but he was past believing anything I had to say. "Liam, I did come here to see you. Ask Grandpa Mack. Why else would I drive to Glenville in the middle of a snowstorm at this hour? It was to see you. I only came here to say goodbye to Johnny. You've got to believe me. You know me better than that. I would never deceive you like this." I was pleading with Liam at this point, but nothing I said could penetrate.

"That's what you always say, Jenny. You're only seeing Johnny to tell him to leave you alone. How many damn times does the boy need to hear that before it soaks into that stupid brain of his?"

"You're right, Liam," Johnny said, interceding again. "She has said it to me lots of times, but you know as well as anybody that I never accepted it. I kept pursuing her anyway for my own selfish reasons. I was always hell-bent on making her mine because I couldn't let her go. I wanted her for myself. It didn't matter that she loved you. I thought I could change her mind, but I couldn't man. Believe me I've tried, but she only wants you. Nothing I do seems to faze how she feels about you. Liam, she loves you with her heart and soul. I know that now. If you would just believe what she's trying to tell you, you would see she's telling you the truth. I'm done trying, Liam. You said I win, but I could never win this game. She's always been yours. She wants you and nobody else. And that's the truth."

Liam stumbled on Johnny's small porch, supporting himself by grabbing on to the rickety, wood railing as he took another gulp from the silver flask.

"What's going on with you, Liam? I've never seen you drink like this."

"It's a time-honored family tradition that I'm just carrying on, Jenny."

"This isn't you."

"Maybe it's always been me. You seem to want to show your true colors; maybe I'm just showing mine."

"You don't mean that, Liam. Please, let me take you home. We can talk there."

"I'm not going anywhere with you. Besides, I've got a race to get ready for, or did you forget that?"

"Listen, man, you don't need to do this. You're messing up here. I know you don't want to believe me, but dammit, Jenny's telling you the truth. We were once friends, try to remember that. Nothing happened here, no matter how badly I wanted it to. She just came here to say good-bye to me. Don't screw this up. She loves you," Johnny said in my defense.

"Get out of my face, you bastard. We were never friends."

Liam glared at me. His blue eyes hardened as they threw daggers into my soul.

"I'm going to Toby's. I don't ever want to see you again. You're dead to me, Jenny."

"Don't do this, Liam. Please talk to me. We can work this out. I love you so much, baby." My words came blubbering out. Liam never turned around. He staggered down the flight of steps and walked across the road and vanished into the falling snow.

"I have to go after him, Johnny."

"He's not going to listen to you tonight. He's too drunk. You better wait. I think maybe I should be the one to talk to him. It should come from me. Right now he thinks you've lied to him. Let me try to get through to him."

"He's not going to listen to you either, Johnny. I've got to do it."

"Don't be stubborn now. You've got too much at stake."

"I've got to try. I can't be here. I'm sorry."

"Where are you going in this blizzard? You're a mess. You're in no condition to be driving yourself in this weather. Let me take you if you're so hell bent on doing this tonight."

"I can't, Johnny. It would just make things worse."

I left Johnny standing there as I made my way to my car and drove off. I had no idea where I was going as I sat idle at the green light as it waited for me to move. Johnny was right though, I was too upset to be driving, especially in this weather. I would never make it. I glanced to my left; Liam's truck was still parked at *The Dock* right next to Toby and Gina's bright orange Camaro. I pulled into a parking spot at the far side of the bar. I waited and waited as I watched for Liam. It felt like an eternity before I saw him walk out, swaggering from side to side as Toby helped him to his truck. There was no way on earth he should be driving, but Toby guided him along with Gina to the passenger side. Gina followed Liam while Toby got behind the wheel. Thank God I thought to myself, at least he won't be driving. I could have sworn Gina saw me, her sinister eyes glancing in my direction as she gave me an evil and satisfied smirk.

I wanted to follow them but knew that I wouldn't be able to talk to Liam tonight. Toby and Gina would make sure of that. Still, I needed to make sure that he was going to be okay. I waited for them to get some distance from me before I proceeded behind them. It was almost impossible for me to see. You would think that Liam's huge black truck would be easy to spot in these white out conditions, but it wasn't. The snow was coming down at such an alarming rate that I could hardly see two feet in front of me, much less that huge black Ford F-150 truck. I tried to stay calm as I made my way through the same tracks as theirs, but even after a while of doing that, I was becoming disoriented in the blinding snow. The weather seemed to have it in for me too. It was literally suffocating me with its blinding snow, and I had no idea where I was going. I felt stupid for not knowing where Toby lived, but I had only been there the one time and the roads of Glenville were still very new to me.

I cried aloud as I hit my steering wheel. My car slid out of control, and I found myself careening into a deep embankment as the snow never relented in helping to bury me inside my vehicular tomb. I didn't care at this point. Liam said I was dead to him, and at this very moment, I felt dead. I wanted to be dead. At least then I wouldn't be feeling the pain that was killing me. I felt numb and had become a baron shell that possessed no life in it. I closed my eyes as I became mesmerized by the falling snow. Darkness surrounded me as I gave in to my weakened condition. I succumbed to my long-lost dark friend as it led me away from my pain and into the oblivion of peace and tranquility. I felt comfort here, and the torment of my reality became less as I drifted farther away. It was the last thing I felt before I heard his voice. He had come after me, but to my shocking dismay as my eyes opened themselves and gazed upon the frosted windows, I did not see Liam but Johnny. Once again, Johnny had come to my rescue.

"She's over here, Jake!" Johnny yelled. I could hear the pounding of Johnny's fists against my window as he pleaded with me to open the door, but it was stuck, frozen solid from the cold. Johnny took a large meal rod and told me to look away as he broke the window to my car. He pulled me out and cradled me in his embrace as my shivering body gave in to his warmth.

"It's going to be okay, Jenny. I have you," Johnny whispered in my ear as he placed me in his truck. It was just like my dream. Jake wrapped me in a heavy wool blanket as he made room for me to lie down. I laid in a fetal position as my body shook uncontrollably. It was daylight now, the sun shone brightly against the sapphire blue sky, but the sun's warm rays did nothing for my body that had become permanently frozen inside.

"She's freezing, Johnny. We need to get her to a hospital."

"No!" I tried to bellow out between staggered breaths. I implored Johnny, pleading with my eyes for him to listen to me.

"Just drive for now, Jake." Johnny sat beside me as he wrapped his arms around me. I could slowly feel myself begin to thaw as the warmth from his body transferred itself onto me.

"What were you thinking, Jenny? You could have died if I hadn't have found you."

"I'm already dead, Johnny."

"I'm taking you back to my place."

"No. I can't go there. I want to see Liam."

"Liam is at Toby's."

"I know. I have to talk to him. I have to make him believe me. I can't do that if I'm at your place. I shouldn't even be with you now. If Liam would see me, it would only justify what he already believes. I have to do this without you. Please, Johnny, please." My voice quivered violently.

Johnny knew I was right. "Okay, but you're going to have to use my truck. Your car needs to be towed."

"I can't drive your truck. Liam knows it."

"She's right, Johnny. You can use mine, Jenny," Jake said. "Liam won't recognize it."

I acknowledged Jake with an endearing and grateful smile.

"Well, you can at least come back to my place to warm up. You're an ice cube. Liam won't even know you're there. I'll make sure of that, and besides, you can't go there now. I'm sure he's passed out, and he'll probably be that way for hours. You won't do yourself or anybody else any good by going there at the crack of dawn."

I was reluctant to listen to his advice but knew he was right. I would wait. I would wait for Liam to have a clear head, and then I would approach him. He would have to see how stupid last night was, and when he did we could put this terrible misunderstanding behind us.

Walking into Johnny's apartment seemed so surreal to me. Only hours before I was sitting on this very same potato chip covered couch explaining to Johnny that Liam meant more than anything to me. Now I sat here pondering if I would ever see him again. What a complete one-eighty my life had done. How in the hell could this get so blown out of proportion? None of it made any sense to me, but neither did Liam's behavior. He was drunk, drunker than I had ever seen him before. He wasn't even himself. The Liam I knew seemed to lie dormant behind those crystal-blue eyes that I loved. I was scared.

"How are you feeling? Are you okay?" Johnny asked as he handed me a cup of coffee.

"No. But should I be? My whole life ended last night, Johnny. Everything that means a damn to me is gone."

"That's not true. Liam just needs to come to his senses, that's all. He was drunk and obviously not in the right frame of mind to understand what we were trying to tell him. It'll be different today, you'll see."

"Johnny's right, Jen. How could Liam or anyone else for that matter understand anything with that much alcohol running through his veins?"

"Did you see him drinking, Jake?"

"Of course I did. Johnny and I both saw him."

My gaze on Jake immediately went to Johnny. "Johnny?"

"Yeah, Jen, he was putting away a few too many last night."

"Why didn't you tell me? I could have avoided that whole fiasco if you would have said something to me. I could have gone to him instead of him finding me here and thinking the worst."

"Jen, I never had the chance to."

"You never had the chance? My God, Johnny, I sat on this couch for twenty minutes. When were you planning on telling me?"

"I wasn't. I guess I didn't think it really mattered. I thought maybe..."

"You thought maybe I was just here for a secret rendezvous with you? Let Liam drink himself to death, it doesn't matter as long as I can have some time with, Jenny. Am I painting a pretty clear picture of what your intentions were?" I said with disgust.

"Of course not, Jen. You've got it all wrong. I did think in the beginning that you might be here for me, but it was never my intentions to keep something like that from you. I told you I saw Liam at *The Dock*. I told you that when you were sitting in your car. If you were so worried about his drinking, you had every opportunity to go save him then, but you didn't. You came up here with me." Johnny's retaliation to me broke my heart in two. I should have never come upstairs last night. I should have gone straight to the bar and helped Liam.

"I've gotta get out of here. I can't stay here anymore."

"Where are you going?"

"Where do you think, Johnny?"

"Jen, it's still too early. He's not going to be ready for you. It'll be like waking a rattlesnake from its sleep. You're gonna get bit. Please, I'm asking you for your sake and Liam's too, wait it out a while."

I heard everything Johnny said, but it literally went in one ear and out the other. He grabbed my arm in one last attempt of desperation. It didn't work. I was out the door before either Johnny or Jake could stop me.

I couldn't wait any longer. Liam was planning on racing tonight and in the state of mind he was in, I was scared to death it would be the end of him. Time was not on my side.

Chapter Twenty-One
The Confrontation

I stood in the harsh cold as I pondered my next move. I had no idea where Toby lived and to make matters worse, I had no way of getting there. My car was still in some ditch off some God-forsaken road between here and nowhere. I felt conquered and beaten before I had even started.

"Here, these might help," Jake said as he came from behind me and handed me the keys to his truck.

"Thanks, but I can't, Jake. I don't know when I'll be back, and I'm not sure what's going to happen."

"I know, but I also know that you have no intention of going back to Spencer until you have seen Liam. Since Johnny's truck will be too obvious, the only alternative is to take mine. My truck's brand new, and Liam doesn't know it. It's the only choice, Jenny."

"Why are you doing this for me?"

"I'm not. I'm doing this for Johnny." A curious look came over my face. "Look, I know I don't really know you, but I do know Johnny. He's been my friend for a long time, and I would do anything for him. He's in love with you. If anyone knows that besides you, it's me. I've been the one who has listened to him talk about you day in and day out over this past year as he tried to forget about you over countless six packs and sometimes," he hesitated, "another girl. Damn, he thought things were gonna be different after last summer, but Liam didn't want any part of him, and to be quite honest, Johnny didn't want anything to do with him either. So my good friend just stood on the sidelines and watched you from afar, waiting and hoping for the impossible to happen. I think he always knew that your heart belonged to Liam. He just couldn't compete with what you two have, but Johnny has always been a dreamer. That's why he never gave up, but dreams don't always come true, and maybe that's why he's willing to help you now. I don't know the reason behind it, but I do know he can't stand to see you in pain. He wants you to be happy, even if that means helping you get Liam back. And like I said, I'd do anything to help my friend out, so here take my keys and do what you need to do. Toby lives about five miles west of here. Turn left at the light and follow the road until you see his sign for his shop. You can't miss it."

"Thank you, Jake. I don't know what to say."

"You don't need to say anything. Remember, I'm doing this for Johnny. He doesn't need this in his life right now."

Jake owned a brand new, candy apple red Chevy Silverado. It looked as if he had just driven it off the lot. Aside from the snow on it, there was barely a speck of dirt to be found on his bright new, shiny toy, and the new car smell awakened my dead senses as I sat behind the black leather steering wheel. I put the mammoth truck into drive. It came easily to me. I had driven Liam's truck so many times that Jake's truck was a piece of cake for me. The size did little to intimidate me. In fact, it empowered me, and I felt stronger as I drove out of town. My fear of facing Liam diminished the more I accelerated. Maybe it was the feeling Jake's truck gave me or maybe I just realized I had nothing to lose, but whatever the reason, I felt confident that all would turn out. That was until I turned down the road to Toby's shop. Then all the anxiety and fear that had just eluded me, returned with a vengeance.

Gina was standing in front of the shop, looking straight at me as I pulled in. Her arms crossed in front of her chest and her long, red fingernails tapped her forearm as I approached her.

"What are you doing here?" she said cynically as I exited the truck.

"I'm here to see, Liam. Where is he, Gina?"

"You're wasting your time. He doesn't want to see you. Didn't you get the message last night?"

"I don't believe you. Liam loves me. He'll want to see me."

"What's going on out here?"

"It's nothing, just Jenny trying to start up some more trouble."

Toby appeared from the side door to his shop. He resembled a homeless man with his dingy gray t-shirt splattered with stains and his grossly torn jeans covered in the same matter. His hair was standing on end, and as he came closer to me, I could smell the alcohol as it lingered from his body.

"Toby, please, I want to see Liam. Can you tell him I'm here?"

"He doesn't want to see you, Jenny. I'm sorry. You need to let this go. It's over between you two. Besides, he's got a big race tonight, and he doesn't need any distractions, especially from you. We've had to move the races inside my warehouse because of the weather. We've got a lot to do without you interfering. He needs to focus, and he can't do that if you're bothering him. I'm not going to get him so you can mess with him now."

"It's okay, Toby. I can take care of this," Liam said as he appeared from the same side door that produced Toby only moments earlier.

"What are you doing here, Jenny?"

"Liam, please can we talk?"

"I don't think we have anything to say. I said all I needed to last night, and you pretty much showed me what you needed to tell me by being at Johnny's."

"You have it all wrong. I was there to tell him to leave me alone. You know I love you. It's always been just you. Why are you acting this way towards me now?" Liam averted his eyes from mine and went towards his two new best friends. "Is it them? Are you letting them persuade you?"

"You need to go, Jenny," Liam said with no emotions, as I wore mine on my sleeve.

"No. Not until we talk. You owe me that much, and not with them listening to us."

"I don't owe you a thing, Jenny."

"Yes, you do!"

Liam approached me quickly as he grabbed my arm and pulled me away from Toby and Gina.

"What do you want from me? I have loved you from the moment I saw you. I have put up with this shit with Johnny for far too long, and I'm tired of it. What do you expect me to think when I see you in Johnny's apartment? Huh? I am tired of playing games with him over you. If you want him that badly, then he's all yours. You said you went to tell Johnny goodbye, why? Why do you need to keep convincing him to leave you alone? The only reason I can think of is you've been seeing him behind my back all along. Your excuse to tell him to leave you alone is just a lie. You got caught Jenny, and that's why you said it. You needed to cover your ass. You had no intention of leaving Johnny alone, just like he's never had any intention of leaving you alone. I feel like I've been racing against him for your affection since the beginning. Well, I'm done racing. He's won. I've got other races to worry about, and they don't include you or Johnny. If you want him in your life so much, you can have him. There's no room for the both of us."

The smell of alcohol saturated my senses as it wafted from his mouth.

"You're still drunk, Liam. This isn't you talking."

"Dammit, Jenny! Quit trying to judge me. For God's sake, you're not exactly an angel yourself! And so what if I've had a few beers? There's nothing wrong with it. You're not my parents: they're dead, remember!?"

Liam's voice had risen to a fever pitch as he yelled at me. I felt myself unintentionally backing away from him, only to have him squeeze my forearm harder as I took each step.

"You're hurting my arm, Liam. Please baby, stop this. Please come home with me. We can work this out," I said as my weeping went uncontrollably. He had become a stranger to me. "We've always been able to talk things out. I didn't even know about your job offer with Coach Green. You always told me everything. We've never had a problem until now, and it's because of who you're hanging out with."

"You mean Toby?" A sickening laugh came from Liam as he gulped down the last few sips of his beer before crushing the can and throwing it into the snow.

"Yes... and Gina. Ever since you've been associating with them, your whole demeanor has changed. You don't care anymore about anything. You said you needed to prove to yourself that you were a man again by racing. What good is that going to do if you end up losing everything?"

"What else do I have to lose, Jenny? I've already lost you, and I didn't even get on that damn bike yet. Johnny already took care of that for me. The bastard! And as far as the job offer, I didn't want to take it. It was as plain and simple as that, and I don't have to tell you. You seem to have no problem in keeping things from me."

"You're insane! You've got so much to look forward to, what about our future? Why would you want to risk everything for a cheap thrill?"

"That's why you think I'm doing this? For a cheap thrill? You don't get it do you? Hell, you've never gotten it. I'm doing this for me. I need to move on. I need to get past the hell this past year has brought me. And now I guess I need to get past you too."

Liam looked right through me with those last words. A cold of epic proportions shot through my body as I remembered him telling me that I was dead to him. His eyes were ice. There were no feelings behind them, only a hardened glaze that seemed unscathed by my presence.

"Umm... I don't mean to interrupt this little party of yours, but if you want to race tonight, we've got a lot of work to do," Toby said with a callous and insensitive tone to his voice.

"Don't, Liam. Please, I love you. Don't do this. Come home with me." I reached out to grab hold of him. He looked down at my hand as he paused momentarily, and in that instance I thought perhaps, maybe I had gotten through to him, but as his gaze returned to mine I knew I hadn't. His eyes were colder than before.

"Go, Jenny. I don't want you here."

Those seven words severed my heart. I fell to my knees as I dissolved into my own hysteria, desperately trying to hold on to Liam's hand as he forcibly jerked it away from me.

"You heard the boy. You need to leave, girlie. You're not wanted here," Gina said as she knelt down beside me, her gum smacking hard between her scarlet red lips. She was laughing sadistically as she got up and put her arms around Liam and led him away from me.

"Jenny, you should go," Toby said as he helped me up.

"I don't understand, Toby."

"Liam's got a big race tonight. I told you having you here is only going to distract him. He's got to focus."

"It's just a damn race, Toby. He doesn't need to do this."

"He's good, Jenny. There's going to be some people here who can help him if they like what they see."

"Help him? What are you talking about?"

"I've got some sponsors coming in from Ohio. They've heard a lot about Liam and want to see him in person."

"But he's never raced motorcycles before."

"You wouldn't know that to see him ride. I don't think it matters what he rides. He knows how to handle himself. He's got a future in front of him. He's going to make us a lot of money, but he can't if he's being held back. You're holding him back, Jenny."

"Us? What do you mean he's going to make us a lot of money? You're using him. You only want him to help you. Dammit, Toby you can't do that to him!"

"I'm not doing anything to him. He's a big boy who can make up his own mind. I don't need to influence him. He wants this as much as I do. You heard the boy; it's time for you to leave."

Toby held the door open to Jake's truck as I sat myself behind the wheel. I watched Liam talking with Gina and Toby. In front of me stood a man I didn't know, a man I didn't recognize anymore. I tried to understand how things fell apart so quickly in the past couple of days, but in my head nothing made sense. The only thing that did was Toby and Gina was somehow controlling Liam for their own benefit, and for some reason, Liam was allowing them to do it. I continued to stare as his focus remained on the two of them and only shifted in my direction once. He glared at me for what seemed an eternity, and in that time, I saw Liam, my Liam, as his gaze returned to the man I knew and loved. The hardened glaze was gone and replaced by the gentle and loving blue eyes that adored me It only lasted a moment. As soon as it came, it diminished, a flicker of light that was swallowed immediately by an obscurity I couldn't identify.

I drove back to Johnny's apartment in a trance, my body and mind still numb. I was trying to comprehend the demise that had just taken place. The only emotion I seemed able to produce was the never ending tears that hadn't stopped since Liam found me at Johnny's apartment. My life had come to an end. I didn't know how I would be able to move on from this day. I wanted time to freeze, so I could too. A life without Liam was a life not worth living. I had reached Johnny's place. He was holding the door open for me. He stood there as the wintery weather shrouded us both with its icy touch. It didn't even faze me. I was already numb to it. Johnny held my door as I sat there, my body unwilling to move from its spot.

"It's over, Johnny."

Johnny remained quiet. There wasn't anything for him to say, and he knew it. Instead, he did the only thing that came so naturally for him when it regarded me; he brought me to him and held me tightly. "Why don't you come upstairs for a while? You've been through a lot. I'm not going to try anything if that's what you think. I just think you need to rest, and maybe I can help you through this. I'm here for you if you want to talk about it."

"There's nothing to talk about. He doesn't want anything to do with me. He told me himself. Did you know Toby's bringing in potential sponsors to watch him race tonight?"

"No I didn't, but it doesn't surprise me. That's how Toby operates. He's always looking for the next big thing. I'm sure that's what he's seeing in Liam. I'm so sorry. This is all my fault."

"No, it isn't. It's mine. I want to go home. I don't want to be here anymore."

"Let me take you then. Jake and I got your car while you were gone. We covered your broken window so you can drive it home, but I don't think you should be by yourself right now."

"No, it's okay. I'll be fine. Besides, I really don't want the company. I have a lot of thinking to do, and I'll do it better if I'm alone."

"Jenny, I wish I could take back last night."

"You and me both, but I don't think that's important anymore. Funny thing though..."

"What?"

"Nothing really. I was just thinking on my drive back from Toby's about last year. This time last year, Liam and you were preparing for the race. He was willing to die for me. He loved me that much. I must have done something really bad for my luck to change so drastically in a year. I was racking my brain out trying to remember what I did to cause this. I'm sorry that I ever tried to be friends with you. It's only caused me problems."

"You don't mean that. You're just upset."

"Yeah, I do mean it, and yeah, I am upset. But if I hadn't tried to work things out so we could all be friends, then I wouldn't be in this mess right now, and Liam and I would be happily in love and planning our wedding. It isn't fair, and it isn't right. Karma's a bitch, and it's come back to bite me in the ass big time."

"Jenny..."

"Don't, Johnny. I don't need a pity party. I'm sorry I'm being so cynical to you right now, but that's all I've got left. Liam's drained everything else from me. He said I was dead to him, and that's exactly how I feel. I want you to know that I do wish you all the best. I hope you find everything you want out of life, and I wish you good health, but this is the last time I'll ever see you. You're only a bitter reminder of what I've lost."

I handed Jake's keys to Johnny as he handed mine to me. I didn't even look at Johnny as I drove away. As a matter of fact, I didn't even look back. I kept my focus on the open road in front of me, the road I drove alone.

Chapter Twenty-Two
Little Boy Lost

I felt dazed as I drove to Spencer. My thoughts were consumed with images of Liam as he repeatedly told me we were through. *You're dead to me Jenny,* kept rambling through my head. How could he say that to me? And more importantly, how could he mean it? He couldn't. Those were Toby and Gina's words, not Liam's, I was positive of it. They were poisoning Liam with their entrancing and lucrative promises of an encouraging future in racing, but what was even more baffling to me, more than even Liam being distant to me, was that Liam never wanted that sort of attention. He shunned away from it. It was his for the taking in football. He was the best damn football player Spencer had seen in years, and he didn't want any of the notoriety that accompanied it. He wanted to play his game, and that was it. The perks that came with his local celebratory status didn't faze him, especially after we met. So, why now? Why now did he crave the attention from something he normally detested? Something else was driving him to this behavior, and I knew I still needed to try and reach him before it was too late for both of us.

The events of the past forty-eight hours were swirling in my head as I made my way up Liam's driveway. The soft, amber light that always welcomed me as I approached the house created an uneasy feeling that made me want to vomit at its sight. A feeling of grief grew inside me. I wanted to close my eyes and never wake up again. The nightmares that Liam and I experienced were nothing in comparison to the hell I was living. Maybe those nightmares were an omen to this. He said I was always being taken away from him, but Johnny was the rogue perpetrator that was behind the nightmares, and in reality, it was me who was the villain. Johnny, at least in my opinion, was not in the picture anymore, no matter how much Liam wanted to think otherwise. I inhaled sharply as I thought how this tragedy had unfolded.

    I slowly made my way towards the broken step that led to the front porch and to the entrance of my once tranquil domain. I was scared. This house wasn't home anymore. It felt foreign to me. I was a stranger within these obscure and placid walls, but as I allowed myself to continue, I felt some relief as detailed and comprehensive images engaged me as my mind drifted back to a happier time. The laughter, the numerous talks, the love that Liam and I shared deluged me, and once again, the warm and welcome familiarity of this home embraced me. I felt I could breathe again as this place accepted me once more. I needed to know I belonged here, even if Liam made me think otherwise.

    "Jenny, dear, is that you?"

    "Yes, Grandpa," I said, startled as he found me still lingering in the hallway.

    Without hesitation, he came to me and hugged me, unknowing of the turmoil that I was about to beset on him. "How are you, my dear?" The silence I allowed answered Grandpa's impending question immediately. My face was inflamed and swollen from the immeasurable tears that had been flowing from it. "What's wrong?" I didn't know what to say or even where to begin. I couldn't find it in me to tell him that it was over between Liam and me. I didn't want to because by saying it meant that it was true, and I couldn't bring myself to believe that either. It wasn't true.

This was just a fork in the road between us. "Is Liam okay? Are you? Where is he?" He said as the questions flowed from the tip of his tongue.

"He's not here, Grandpa. He's still in Glenville."

"Oh, what's wrong then? Is this about your dad?"

"This isn't about him." I looked away, not able to face Grandpa as his temperate gaze held itself on me.

Grandpa gently turned me to face him as he spoke tenderly to me. "Jenny, something's really wrong, isn't there? Did you have a talk with Liam? Is this about his drinking?"

"Grandpa, Liam and I have broken up." I hardly got the words out of my mouth before collapsing into his arms.

"Jenny, that can't be."

"It's over. It's really over this time."

I knew I had to tell Grandpa the whole story, or it wouldn't make sense to him. Hell, I knew the story, and I still didn't understand it. We made ourselves comfortable on the floral sofa in the living room, and I began my tale. We sat for hours as I explained in length every minute detail that had led up to the past couple of nights. Grandpa never interrupted or judged me. Instead, he listened with an open heart and, more importantly, an open mind. I was shaking violently as I released my emotions, unable to hold anything back. The pain I was enduring was more than I could possibly bear. I had become nothing more than an empty shell, my body carrying nothing more than the pain and misery that sustained me. Grandpa reached for me. His strong, rugged arms embraced me as I succumbed deeper into his shelter.

"Can you ever forgive me, Grandpa?"

"Whatever do you mean, Jenny? What do I have to forgive you for?"

"For being stupid, for not listening to Liam from the very beginning. It's my fault that Liam doesn't want to see me anymore."

"He loves you, Jenny."

"I don't think so, Grandpa."

"Did you hear him say that?"

"No. But he pretty much said everything else that would make me believe that. What am I supposed to do?"

"You're as strong and stubborn as you are beautiful, Jenny. Fight for him, be there for him because if you don't, no one else will. Make him see the truth. This year has been so hard on him. He's carried more demons on his shoulder that he can't shake off, and that's why it's so easy for other people to influence his decisions. As much as he tries to portray this strong person, inside lies a weak and vulnerable man. Never question his love for you. It's still there. It's just being smothered by this negative energy that's entered his life. I think he knows the truth, but in his weakened mental state, he can't believe it right now."

"I'm afraid, Grandpa. I don't think I can handle Liam rejecting me again. You don't know how it hurt to hear him talk to me the way he did. I've never heard him talk like that to anybody, much less someone he was supposed to have loved."

"I was afraid that this might happen."

"What do you mean?"

"Only that this day was coming, and it was coming long before you entered the picture. Liam's been a very focused and driven young man ever since his parents' deaths. He had to be because that's the only way I would have it. I made him that way because I knew the hell he would fall into if he didn't have something to motivate him. That's why I drove him to play ball. If he was doing something, then he didn't have time to think. Your mind can be your best friend or your worst enemy, and in Liam's case it was the latter. Nobody should ever have to witness what he did, especially an impressionable young boy such as he was. And in Liam's case his mind was against him from the beginning. I could tell his behavior was different right after the funerals, but to be honest, I chalked it up to him losing his parents. The pain he sustained only grew. It never went away or even diminished a little. I used to find Liam yelling and screaming, kicking and hollering as he would slam things in his room. He didn't seem to care. His eyes were inexpressive, just dull and gray, no life behind them at all. At the time, his grandma was still alive, but you know she didn't last much longer after her Jessica died. Only then did I see the power behind Liam's anger. He was only six years old, but he held more resentment against the world than anybody I ever knew. He hated everybody, including me."

"Did you try to get him some help, Grandpa?"

"Of course I did, but it didn't work. He didn't want it. I didn't know what to do. One day he would seem to be moving on, and then the next, well...I can tell you there were more of the bad days than good. I didn't give up on him, though. I love that boy, and I knew if I could reach inside him I could help him. I spent all my time with him. If I had to work then, he had to work. Luckily for me, most of my work was on the farm so I could keep him near me. That's where Liam fell in love with horses. I made him help me day in and day out, but it still never seemed to be enough. I would find him crying out every night for his mama. He loved her so. She used to sing him to sleep at night, and I would find him in a corner of his room, rocking himself back and forth with his eyes closed as he hummed the songs she used to sing.

This went on for over a year. I was at my wit's end, and then one day, when we were at the feed store, Liam found an old football outside in the parking lot. He became mesmerized by it. I swear once that pigskin touched Liam's hands he became a different boy. He never let that football down. We would spend hours in the evening just tossing that ball back and forth to each other. It was some of the best times of my life with the boy, and as time passed, I saw a change in his behavior. He seemed to be a different person, and I attribute it to that football. He had a purpose. He wasn't always thinking or blaming himself for his parents' death. I got him on one of those recreational football leagues, and he just took off. It was like he was born with a football in his hand. Even the coaches said they had never seen such a natural. I didn't think anything would ever replace the love he had for the game, but that was until you entered his life, Jenny." Grandpa gingerly placed his rugged hands over mine and squeezed them tightly. "You have also changed my boy for the better. You have made him a better person, and I thank God for you every day."

"But he's not that boy right now, Grandpa."

"I know. That's because you're not in his life anymore and neither is football. He is slowly spiraling backward to the way he used to feel as a little boy. The hatred and pain he used to carry has arisen again, and what you are witnessing is that little boy lost. That's why when I tell you not to give up on him, I mean it. I can't do it for you. This is still between you and Liam. Listen to your heart. Let it speak for you, and remember, timing is everything. I can feel Liam's pain, but I can't help him anymore. You're right, he's not that little boy anymore."

"You know I came back here to gather my things and leave. I don't feel like this is home for me anymore, Grandpa."

"This will always be your home, Jenny. You know it and so does Liam. We just need to remind him of that."

I hugged Grandpa tightly. He was my only peace during this violent storm I was enduring.

"I love you, Grandpa, I really love you."

"I know. I love you too, dear. Listen, we have to stick together through this, but I can't get involved. Liam's not going to listen to me."

"I'm just scared. I've never seen him act like this and I don't know how to handle it. I don't want to make things worse and drive him even further away from me."

"I think you forget the power you have over my boy. You can do this, Jenny. Just be patient and never let him forget that you love him. He'll come around, I promise."

"I wish I could believe you, Grandpa." I held on to him even tighter, feeling that if I let go I might lose him too.

"I've gotta go hon, but I'll be back. If you should need me, I want you to call me."

"I will, I promise, but I'm not going to be here when you return. I can't, especially if things aren't fixed between Liam and me. He's not going to want me here."

"I know that, but I want you to know that you can stay here. This house is your home."

"I can't be here when Liam returns. He's racing tonight, and I'm sure he's returning home tomorrow. He was only supposed to be gone this weekend. I can't imagine what he would do if he found me here. You didn't see the look in his eyes towards me."

"Well you do what you think is right, but if you do leave, I don't think you'll be gone long. This little hiccup will pass quickly. You just wait and see."

Grandpa's presence had renewed my faith that things were going to somehow work out. I still didn't know how but at least I had some hope, which was more than what I walked in with. The next few hours I spent in Liam's room, our room. It was so easy for me to lose myself in there. I had to come to my senses and gather some of my things, just in case Liam should come home sooner than expected. I was mentally drained from the weekend. There was a hole in me that seemed to be swallowing me from the inside out. Every time I thought I could move on, I took a step backward. It was the only time since I had known him that I was frightened of seeing him. My suitcases lie next to me on the bed, still vacant as I tried to fill it with my belongings. The task was cumbersome, and the only thing I wanted to do was go to sleep. This room had become my sanctuary, and I wanted to encase myself with the way it made me feel as I drifted away into my dream world. Instead of sleeping, I arose from the bed and left the room, leaving my empty suitcases where they lay. I didn't look back. I couldn't.

I arrived at my house only to find it empty, as it had been for the past few weeks. Mom and Dad were in the Carolinas per orders from Dr. Thompson. My bedroom looked unappealing as I entered it. The anxiety was only compounded when I noticed the numerous bridal magazines still strewn across my bed, grim reminders of what would never be. I fell on my bed, the magazines flying into the air as my body dropped. It was half past eleven o'clock. Surely Liam had finished the race and had probably won it by now, I thought. I could see his face light up with enthusiasm as his eager fans rallied around him, and of course, his most recent entourage, Toby and Gina would be in front of the pack, impatiently waiting their turn to get to him. The offending thought was enough to lull me to sleep, and I was almost there when the incessant sound of my ringing phone interrupted it.

"Hello," I said, wearily.

"Jenny, it's Jake."

"Jake?"

"I'm at the hospital in Glenville. You need to get over here as soon as you can."

I didn't even bother asking Jake any more questions. I made it to Glenville in record time, my emotions steering my way as pure adrenaline kept me awake. My mind was racing with thoughts of Liam bloodied and unconscious, lying on some hospital gurney as I entered the emergency room. Please dear God not again, please, please not again.

Chapter Twenty-Three
Not What I Expected

The emergency room was filled to capacity upon my arrival. The scene was all too familiar to me. I observed the mayhem of sickness and brutality as patients moaned and groaned as they waited peevishly for help. The looks in their eyes did nothing to the personnel who looked as though they were victims as well, a migration of doctors and nurses with impending trepidation on their faces as they tried to help each individual who thought their needs were more important than the others. The somber scene made me ill as I scanned the room for Liam. Everywhere I looked there were patients, each demanding the attention of anyone wearing a white coat and stethoscope. It was a sea of blood, pain, and misery that seemed to be pulling me into the middle of it.

"Jenny, finally you're here," Jake said with relief in his voice.

"Jake, where's Liam? Is he hurt badly?"

"It's not Liam, it's Johnny."

"Johnny? I don't understand?"

Jake pulled me to the side of the hallway as he led me to an empty seat. "I called you because it's Johnny who's here. He went to see Liam after you left, Jenny. He wanted to try and get through to him before he raced. He thought maybe if he could make him believe him, Liam wouldn't race and possibly even go back to Spencer to see you. But..." Jake's voice trailed off.

"But what, Jake? What happened?"

"Well, when he arrived at Toby's, Liam told Johnny to get the hell away from him. Liam was angrier than I had ever seen him, and just as drunk too. Johnny could hardly get a word in edgewise. Liam was on some kind of hell bent tangent as he threw every obscene word and gesture towards Johnny. It didn't help matters either that Toby was there too. Toby is Johnny's friend, and he had to pick a side. He didn't want to go against Toby, but he had no other choice. He had to for your sake, Jenny. Johnny didn't back down from Liam's insinuating remarks. He tried adamantly to talk some sense into him. He was determined to make Liam hear him, but he wouldn't have anything to do with Johnny. It got ugly, and it got ugly fast. Before I could do a damn thing to help either one of them, Liam started throwing punches at Johnny, and then Toby did too. It was the two of them against the two of us. Johnny didn't want it to end up like that. He wanted to talk to Liam, not fight him, but Liam had other ideas from the moment he saw us. I knew this wasn't a good idea, but Johnny thought differently.

"But what happened? Why is Johnny here? Did Liam..." I hesitated as I began to ask what I thought I already knew. "Did Liam hurt Johnny? Is that why Johnny's here?"

"No, it's his heart. I don't know what happened. We were fighting, but there were no direct punches. It was just a bunch of sloppy hands flying in every direction. Liam was so drunk that he couldn't hit himself if he wanted to, but I saw Johnny fall to the ground. Liam wasn't even near him. Johnny was holding his chest, and I knew right then it was his heart. I picked him up and rushed him to my truck. I was going to take him to the hospital myself, but Liam had already called 911."

"Liam?"

"Yeah, Liam."

I was baffled. Liam loathed Johnny. He detested him, and by all accounts he should have done nothing.

"I can't explain why he did it unless the Liam we used to know realized it was the right thing to do."

"Is Liam here, Jake?"

"He was, but he heard me call you. He didn't want to see you. I don't know what's going on with him, Jenny. He's messed up, and I'm afraid for him."

My heart sank, hearing Jake say that to me.

"How's Johnny?"

"I don't know. I haven't seen him, and I haven't been able to talk to anyone yet. They took him away as soon as we got here. I know his parents are here."

My hands went over my face as I collapsed into myself. "Jake, I need to see Liam, but I've got to make sure Johnny is okay."

"I know, Jenny," Jake said as he put his hand on my shoulder.

"Jenny, is that you?"

"Gertie!" I exclaimed as I embraced her. "I'm so sorry about Johnny. Have you seen him?"

"Yes, I just did. They're taking him to ICU right now."

"Is he okay?"

"Well, I don't know. They're running a bunch of tests, but we won't know anything for a while. They want to keep him here for a few days." The words fumbling from her beautifully contoured mouth as she tried to keep her composure. "Jenny, I know why Johnny was with Liam tonight. He explained everything to me. He wants you to know he's sorry, and he doesn't want you to blame yourself for what's happened to him."

The hole in my stomach seemed to grow larger as the night progressed. "Gertie, this is my fault."

"Walk with me, dear. I think we need to talk. Will you excuse us, Jake?"

Jake nodded his head as Gertie took my hand in hers and led me away.

"Gertie, you don't need to say anything to me. I can handle this on my own. You should be with your son right now, not with me. Your concerns shouldn't be about me."

"But that's why I'm here. My thoughts and concerns are with my son, but his are with you. Johnny's heart is in trouble, but it's partially because it's broken. Listen, you know that I know the struggle you have been enduring with Liam and Johnny. You have lived more in your young eighteen years than most people do in a full lifetime, and may I add, more in this past year than most. You know from the moment I met you I felt a connection to you. I love you as though you were one of my own, and because of my son's feelings for you, that connection has grown stronger. I can't tell you without being honest to both of us that I didn't see this coming. Liam has been on a road of destruction since the accident."

"You mean you knew things would end up like this? Why didn't you warn me? I could have helped Liam before any of this happened."

"Honey, I may be able to see the future, but even I can't always predict the outcome. I saw Liam full of torment and rage. It doesn't take a mind-reader to figure out he was in trouble. Anyone who relies on himself solely without the help of friends and family will always find themselves in a bad place, and that's exactly where Liam is right now: a bad place. This rage he carries didn't start with you. He's been carrying it for a long time, but I'm afraid if he doesn't get the help he needs, it will end soon, and the ending will not be good."

"But you could have told me this. I never in a million years thought he would self-destruct like he has. Did you know about the drinking or Toby and Gina?"

"Jenny, does that really matter right now? Don't you think your concern should be what your next step should be?"

"I don't know what I'm supposed to do. I know I love him, Gertie. I want to fix things with him. This past year has been nothing but a roller coaster for us. You know, to be honest, I think a lot of people wanted to see our relationship fail. I mean we had a lot of supporters, but most people didn't understand why it was so easy for us to love one another. I think we sometimes questioned it too. It was easy from the very beginning. I never thought I would love someone as much as I do Liam, especially at my age, but I've learned through trial and error and from you that sometimes our future is already laid out for us. We just need to understand and accept it.

I never thought I would have to fight for Liam's love. Toby and Gina have drawn a huge wedge between us, and for some reason Liam is allowing it to happen. I know he had been drinking more this year, but honestly, I never thought it would get so out of control. The way he's talked to me these past couple days are hard for me to take or explain, but I do know it's not my Liam. It's someone else, and by all accounts, I'm putting a lot of the blame on Toby and Gina. They're using him, and I can't get through to him.

He sees me as the bad person. He really thinks I've been cheating on him." I paused before continuing knowing what I was about to say, Gertie probably already knew. I felt ashamed. "Gertie, I….."

"I know, dear."

"You do?"

"Of course. Do you forget who you are talking to? Besides, I am his mother. It is hard to keep things from me whether you tell me or not. I'm pretty good at figuring things out. You're both so easy to read."

"I didn't mean to develop any sort of feelings for him beyond just being his friend, but he was so persistent with his, and to be quite honest, he had become a breath of fresh air to me. There were so many times when Liam and I would be having problems, and I knew I could turn to Johnny, and he wouldn't care what it was. He was just always so happy to make me happy. Maybe I shouldn't have relied so heavily on him, but it was nice. I knew it wasn't the same as what I had for Liam. Liam is my life. I would die for him. I love him that much."

"I know, Jenny, I know. Johnny knows that too. That is why we need to fix his broken heart by helping you mend yours. He wants you to be happy, and he realizes that happiness lies with Liam. I know that's why he went to see Liam. You're the only one who can get through to Liam, but trust me when I tell you that you have to do it soon. I wasn't lying when I told you Liam was on a road to self-destruction. He's in trouble, and you need to help him find his way home, back to you."

"Mrs. Bryant?" The nurse interrupted.

"Yes."

"Your son is in his room now. He's asking for you."

I grabbed Gertie's hand and squeezed it. "Please, can I see him first?" I implored.

"Go ahead, tell him I'll be in to see him soon. I think I'll get some coffee."

Johnny's room was another grim reminder of why I detested hospitals. The antiseptic smell that hung in the air, as well as the smell of cafeteria food that remained lingering in the walls, was enough to make me want to gag. It was foul to my senses, and the smells triggered flashbacks that I wanted to forget. Johnny slumbered quietly as I tiptoed my way to his side. He was covered in starched, white sheets. The only exposed part of his body was his upper chest, and it was completely laden with wires that led to the adjacent machines that were melodically beeping.

"Hey there, you're not my mother," he said, sweetly as he tried fervently to open his eyes.

"I asked your mom if I could come see you first." The silence became difficult as the two of us looked intently at one another.

"Jenny?"

"Johnny, why?" My hand was resting on top of the sheet that protected his.

"Because."

"Because? Just because?"

"Yes. Just because. I love you, and you know that, but I can't stand to see you hurt anymore. I look at you, and I see pain. And that's exactly what I saw when Liam came to my apartment. I knew you loved him, but I had no idea how much until this weekend." My head lowered as though I should be ashamed of what he was revealing to me. "I don't want you to be unhappy, and I'm going to bear this cross until I can make things right between you and Liam. Maybe this downward spiral he's on isn't all my fault, but I do know that I'm to blame for the majority of it."

"No, Johnny."

"Yes Jenny, I am. If you would only look back, you would see it all started with me, and it's going to end with me as well. I need to make things right. I deserve what's happening to me. Mom used to tell me that a person needs to make themselves a good example to others, and in doing so, good things would happen to them. Well, I pretty much screwed my luck up when I decided to become a pig-headed, stubborn jackass. What goes around comes around, and I guess I'm getting my due. I'm okay with that as long as I can make things right with you and Liam."

"Johnny, do you honestly think your condition right now is a result of some sort of bad karma because of your feelings towards me? That's utterly absurd."

"Maybe it is and maybe it isn't, but it makes as much sense as your number eleven. Listen, Jenny, I'm not claiming I have the answers to any of this, but at least I can try to do what's right. It's not even about you anymore. Liam used to be my friend, and I crossed the line. I know that now. I have to do this before it's too late for both of us."

"Too late? What's that supposed to mean? It sounds like you're trying to make your peace, Johnny. Are you okay?"

"As good as a guy can be with a broken heart."

"Johnny..."

"It's alright, Jenny. Sorry, I didn't mean for it to come out like that, bad choice of words. I have something called Endocarditis. I've developed an infection in my heart. It's just one of the many consequences that can happen with having congenital heart disease."

There was more silence between us as I gave Johnny a genuine look of concern.

"Don't give me that look. I'll be fine. You don't need to feel sorry for me."

"I don't feel sorry for you. I care about you. I can't help but care for you. We've been through too much."

"Don't, Jenny, please, for me. It's not healthy for either one of us."

"Please stop talking like that."

"Like what?"

"Like this is it, the end, like you are dying."

"Maybe I am, Jenny."

"That's not funny."

"I didn't mean for it to be."

Johnny sighed heavily. "I'm sorry, that was cruel to say, but sometimes I feel like it. I've had to overcome a lot in my life, mostly because of my heart condition, but nothing has compared with trying to overcome the challenges I've faced since meeting you. I was hell bent on winning you over. I knew in my damaged heart that you were to be mine. Maybe it was the competitive spirit in me, but I couldn't get you out of my head. It didn't matter that Liam and you were together. I knew that, and you, of course, knew that. Hell, you were all Liam ever talked about when I saw him. That's why when we finally did meet, that day in English class, I knew who you were, but I had no idea that you would literally take my breath away. And since then, I've been dying a little bit every day."

I didn't know what to say. I looked at him as he lay helpless in the starched, white bed. I knew I couldn't allow my pity for him to dictate my emotions. No matter how much I cared for him and no matter what he said to me, it still didn't change anything. "I love you, Johnny… but…"

"I know, but you aren't in love with me. Only Liam holds that honor."

"I'm so sorry, Johnny. What you said to me means more to me than you'll ever know, but I can only look at it as though it's coming from a friend, a good friend, but nevertheless a friend. I don't even know if I still have a future with Liam, but I have to try. I just want you to know that I do care for you, and I always will. What you did for me tonight assures me that our friendship will never be fleeting. I know I can always count on you. I'm just sorry that I don't think you'll be able to count on me."

"It's okay, Jenny. That's the way it should be anyway. I'll be fine. Like I said, I've overcome a lot, and I'll be able to get over this as well."

"I have to go."

"I know. Be careful. You're dealing with a wounded man who can't see the trees for the forest."

"What do you mean?"

"I mean that Liam is so caught up with the anger that's in him, he can't see you. He can't see that his salvation is right in front of him. Just be careful."

"I will. I promise."

I left the hospital without even saying goodbye to Gertie or Jake. I sat in my car as the snow fell steadily on my windshield. The scene was too familiar to me. It took me back to Johnny's apartment when Liam found me there. This snowfall seemed to be a sign that nothing had changed, that I shouldn't try to see Liam or even persuade him to see the truth. Grandpa Mack told me to give things time, and right now I thought my next move was to do just that, give Liam some time.

"Where are you going?" Jake said as he opened my car door.

"I'm going home, Jake."

"Home?"

"Yeah. I thought about going to see Liam, but I don't think it's a good idea. If he didn't want to stick around after learning I would be here, then I know his attitude hasn't changed."

"So, you don't want to see him race?"

"Race? I thought the race would have been canceled?"

"No, it's still on. It got moved because of the fight."

My heart dropped. "No, Jake I can't. Besides, I'm the last person he wants to see. I need to figure this out before I make my next move, and I can't do it tonight. I need some time."

"Be careful, Jenny."

"I will. Thanks for calling me. Hey, will you do me a favor?"

"Sure, anything."

"Will you let me know how the race turns out?"

"Are you sure you want to know?"

"I love him, Jake."

"I will then."

I drove back to Spencer feeling more depressed and alone than before. I held on to my cell tightly as I hoped against hope for a call from Liam that I knew would never come.

Chapter Twenty-Four
Life Goes On

The winter had been harsh since I last seen Liam. I kept to myself mostly and found that the foul weather was contributing to my miserable life. My parents were in the process of moving to Myrtle Beach. Although they were extremely upset with my circumstances, Dad's health took priority with them, and I had convinced them that my situation wasn't half as bleak as it seemed to be. I was becoming a great liar. I half-way believed it myself.

I had made the decision to stay at my house while Mom and Dad were in transition. I had the house to myself for the most part, which considering my state of mind I thought was a good thing, but on the contrary, it was the worst possible situation for me, something my friends had realized. I was inundated with phones calls from Kendra, Parker, and surprisingly even Jake. All of them made sure I didn't spend too much time alone. Kendra was now in her sixth month of pregnancy and learning how to juggle school, becoming a new mom, and being a single parent. It hadn't worked out with Tony. In the end, she had decided that no matter how much she cared for Tony, that there wasn't enough love for her to want to marry him. What had happened between them she had concluded was an act of fate, but it was her fate and not Tony's.

Parker, on the other hand, had become the brother I never had. He came over nightly to check on me. I think he also knew that I would want to know about Liam, so he had become my confidante and conduit, allowing me to keep in Liam's life without literally being there for Liam. I thanked God for this. I was going crazy not knowing how he was doing. The business at the shop was booming, but according to Parker, Liam was distancing himself from it. Ever since he had met up with Toby, he was becoming less and less involved with the shop. I couldn't figure it out. This was Liam's dream. He had put all his savings into it. According to Parker, when Liam was there he was more concerned with when the next race was and his next beer. My heart sank every time I heard this.

I can't begin to say how many times I had picked up my phone, just staring at it as I mentally tried to call Liam. It had been weeks since our falling out. I had no idea that life could move on without the world stopping, but my friends were reminding me that life did go on, and they were keeping me from sinking into pity and demise.

I seemed to have another ally in my corner: Jake. He had made it a point to check in on me regularly. I never quite understood why he had become so concerned but realized that it partially had to do with Johnny. I hadn't spoken to Johnny since that night in the hospital. I knew he was worried about me, so I was positive that Jake had become Johnny's confidante as well. Jake asked me too many questions for a guy who seemed to have nothing in common with me, but I realized it was because of Johnny's interest in me that Jake was doing this. That was fine because, in return, I was able to keep tabs on Johnny's status as well.

Jake had turned into a good friend and kept his word by calling me that very next day after Liam's first motorcycle race. Liam won of course. I already knew that, don't ask me why, but I just knew. The would-be sponsors who came there the night before had gone home after the fight between Liam and Johnny. They didn't get to see Liam win the race, and for some reason I was gratefully relieved, but through the grapevine I had learned that they would be returning. Liam had been in over a dozen races since then and had won every single one of them. He was hell on wheels according to Parker, and there wasn't a person within the state who came close to beating him. Word was spreading quickly of his success. It seemed he was moving on. Our relationship, in my opinion, was more over now than it had ever been. He had found his new love and was pursuing her with all the same emotion and tenacity that he had done with me.

The consequence of that was I really didn't seem to care about anything anymore. I stayed at home and stared at the ceiling as I wished my life away. I even dropped out of school. It meant nothing to me, and because Gertie was there, I didn't want to be there either. She reminded me too much of what I was trying to forget. I knew I was slipping into a deep depression, but I had no control over it. Nothing seemed to matter to me now that Liam didn't care about us. From all that I had gathered, Liam never even mentioned my name anymore. How could someone who used to think I was his entire reason for existing drop me off of the face of the planet with no regard? Most nights I cried myself to sleep as I waited for the next day, only to repeat my miserable behavior. I beckoned for sleep as I slipped into the darkness that I yearned for on a nightly basis. It was my refuge. Days turned into weeks, and weeks turned into months.

It was soon April, April 10th to be exact. The next day would be the one year anniversary of the horrific accident that in my opinion had been the catalyst to the demise of our relationship. I knew exactly what I would be doing the next day, and wondered if Liam would be doing the same thing. I always wondered what he was doing. He was my one singular thought night and day. I lay on my bed and gazed at my clock. In only minutes, it would be one year, one year that had changed my life forever. The grandfather clock echoed in the background as I counted down with it to midnight. "One year, babe," I whispered.

****

"Hey, Liam what are you doing?" Parker asked, somewhat agitated.

"Nothing, why?" Liam seemed to be in his own little world. He played carefully with the beads on his leather bracelet. His thoughts went to Jenny as he remembered her giving it to him on their first Christmas Eve.

"We have to finish this car before tomorrow. Joe is going to kick our ass if we're not done with it. Come on, get with the program. All you do anymore is just mope around."

"Leave me alone, Parker. You have no idea what I'm going through."

"Are you joking, man? Everyone between here and kingdom come knows what you're going through, and if you're not smart enough to realize it yourself, you're going to lose the best damn thing that ever happened to you, if that hasn't happened already. You need to go over to Jenny's and apologize your butt off before she decides you aren't worth it. I don't know what kind of damn hold Toby has on you, but man, you screwed up when you allowed him to enter your life. I've never known you to be a drunk, but that's exactly what you've turned yourself into and a stubborn one at that."

Liam raised his fist towards Parker only to have Parker do the same. The two of them just stood there as neither one of them wanted to back down. Throughout their friendship, the two of them had thrown many punches together but none at each other. Parker looked stunned and confused as he watched Liam's actions towards him. He knew that the guy standing in front of him wasn't his best friend. Parker took the higher road and carefully backed away.

"You don't know what the hell you're talking about," Liam yelled at him.

"Yes, I do! Who do you think has been trying to pick up the pieces since you made Jenny's life a living hell? It's been me! She loves you, man. Get over yourself and go make things right with her! I know you're not a drunk, and that's why I don't understand why you're doing some of this crazy shit. You're stronger than that, Liam!" Liam didn't respond. It was like Parker was talking to a brick wall. He just raised his hands in defeat. He didn't know what to do. And as far as Liam was concerned, the only gesture he made towards Parker was to raise his next beer in a toast as he gulped it down to the last drop. Deep down, he knew he had changed. Liam could tell that he was spiraling out of control but felt as though it was past the point of no return. He wanted to tell Parker that he knew what he was trying to tell him was the truth, but too many words had been spoken, and he knew that it was pointless now. Instead, he turned and walked away. He looked at his watch…"One year, babe," he whispered to himself.

"What did you say?"

"Nothing, man. It doesn't matter anyway."

"God, Liam what has gotten into you? I used to know you, but I can honestly say I don't anymore. I mean, I'm your best friend, and I'm trying to figure out what happened to you. One day you tell me you're the luckiest guy on the earth, and then the next you tell me that's it's over between you and Jenny, and you don't even want to talk about it with me? And to make matters worse, you would rather spend more time in Glenville with Toby than here at the shop. I thought this was what you wanted? What changed?"

"Like I said, you wouldn't understand."

"I understand that there is a girl who is worried sick over you and cries in my arms every time I see her as she wonders what went wrong. I understand that there is a girl who loves you more than life itself and feels like her world has just ended. And I understand that there is a girl who never cheated on you! Do you understand that?!" Parker's voice was escalating with each word he spoke. "Liam, you love Jenny. You used to tell me that nothing was impossible as long as she was in your life. What's different now?"

"I'm not good enough for her, Parker. There, I said it! Do you feel better? You finally got it out of me! She's better off without me. I'm just going to bring her down. I'm no good to anybody. She should be with Johnny; at least she won't have to live with the demons I have to live with every single day of my life. He's always been the hero, her savior. Why should it change now?!"

"Man, you're crazy, Liam. You've really gone off the deep end this time. Stop being so pathetic and feeling sorry for yourself. You think the whole world revolves around you. Well, it doesn't, and it's about damn time someone told you that. There's someone else in this picture, and you're about to lose her...forever! Hell, I don't know why Jenny still wants you. If I were her, I would have dumped your sorry ass a long time ago!"

Parker threw his wrench down as it echoed in the shop. He left Liam there alone as Liam slumped himself on an overstuffed couch in the corner of the shop. Parker was right. He was feeling sorry for himself, but he knew that it was his fault for the mistakes since that fateful night, and in his mind, it was too late. The damage was done. Liam slumped further into the couch as he began to relive April 11th all over again.

****

Jenny didn't sleep much that night. She tossed and turned as she kept having the same dream that had haunted her for months. They were only seconds away from winning the race. The smile that Liam wore lit up his entire face as he turned to look at Jenny. She stared back at him with the same smile. Her emotions were just as high as the excitement and euphoria exuded from both of them. The scene outside portrayed a contour of people who lined the sides of Ripley Road as they made their way to the finish line. Everyone screamed at the top of their lungs as the rain beat down on their drenched bodies. Even though Liam was topping eighty miles an hour, Jenny could make out every person that cheered them on as they passed. It was a glorious feeling, but the scene that would happen next would make her feelings change instantly. In one split second, a turn of the head, the euphoria that was exuding from both of them was gone, replaced with fear and panic. Nothing could prepare them for what lay ahead of them. There it was. It had evaded everyone's sight, a presence larger than life as it stood undaunted as the black truck barreled towards its magnificent frame. There, right in front of them, was a deer that at the time seemed impervious to the situation at hand as it sauntered his way on to the road.

    The crowd was also clueless to the events that were about to unfold in front of them, but Liam and Jenny knew that fate was stepping in. It was too late for Liam. He knew what he had to do, but would it work? He instantly turned his steering wheel, overcorrecting it in order to miss the monster that stood between him and the finish line. Time seemed to stop, but time wasn't on Liam's side. His beautiful F-150 that had never let him down couldn't adhere to his owner's commands of turning fast enough to miss the deer. It clipped the deer's antlers, sending the shaken creature running for its life and sending the F-150 into overdrive, careening out of control as it flipped over and over again before finally coming to a rest on its top. Liam and Jenny both lay there in their blood as the screams from the crowd resonated from above them. Neither of them heard it. The noises from around them were muffled from their own screams. Liam frantically screamed for Jenny as he tried to reach her. Jenny panicked as she slipped in and out of consciousness, screaming for Liam to come to her. The dream was so real, every detail so vivid as though it had just happened. She felt helpless as she watched it play out in front of her.

    Jenny was finally awake, only to find she was lying in a pool of her own sweat and hearing her voice scream for Liam. Her body lay fetal as it trembled, and she cried intensely. She needed Liam. She needed him desperately.

Hours had passed before she even attempted to arise from her bed, and when she did the world seemed callous to her feelings. Life was going on. She looked through her baby blue curtains that revealed a world untouched by her ordeal. Cars and pedestrians moved about their business, unaware of the torment and pain that she was enduring. Didn't anyone know? Didn't anyone care? She thought to herself as her curtains fell softly into their place. The house symbolized Jenny's life at present as she made her way through it. It was empty, only a few remnants remained to remind her of the life she grew up in, just as there were only remnants of memories to remind her of the once blissful past she shared with Liam.

The entire day became an ode to April 11th as it replayed itself repeatedly in Jenny's mind. She clutched her stomach as she tried to eat her toast. She gagged as she forced herself to swallow it. A queasy, unsettling feeling came over her as she pushed her plate away from her. It was the same ill feeling she felt exactly one year ago. The vile taste lingered from her half-eaten breakfast and remained with her as she drove towards her destination. Her stomach grew weaker as she focused on her journey's end. She knew where she was going, but to get there she had to drive down the one stretch of road she had intentionally avoided for exactly three hundred sixty-five days. She never took it anymore. It brought back too many horrible memories to her. It didn't matter if her destination needed to take her on it. She would always find another way around it, anything not to have to drive on the one stretch of road that haunted her very soul more than anything.

But today was different. Today she wanted to go down this road that held so much pain for her, and as she drove past the familiar landmarks that reminded her that she was close, her stomach began to churn even more uneasily. The bend up ahead closed in fast, much faster than she was prepared for, and before she could take another breath, she entered Devil's Bulge. Her heart raced as she slowly drove into it. She could visualize Liam's truck as it made its way around the bend and then effortlessly as usual, as though the truck had a mind of its own, it made the kiss your ass turn with such ease that if you didn't know any better you would have thought the turn had been carefully choreographed.

Jenny took Devil's Bulge with much greater caution and restraint than Liam would have. She drove slowly as she recalled herself sitting next to Liam as he calculated the bend with ease, and as she finally made her way through and began to exit the demon curve, she exhaled deeply knowing she had conquered one demon only to confront another. The stretch of road that stood in front of her held more apprehension than Devil's Bulge ever could. She braked immediately. She didn't think she could do it. Her will weakened. What little confidence she carried quickly diminished as she sat idle in the road. She realized that at any moment, another car could come up from behind her and collide into her, but she seemed oblivious to the looming danger. It didn't matter, just like nothing else did in her world.

She stared blankly at the open stretch of black asphalt in front of her. This was Ripley Road. It taunted her, mocking her fear as if it had been waiting for this day since the infamous accident. *What are you waiting for? Are you scared, Jenny? Come on, I won't hurt you; I'm just a piece of pavement. Don't let me stop you. I've been waiting for you. You knew we would meet again. It was only a matter of time. You're not going to let me stop you, are you, Jenny?* There seemed to be a sinister, evil laugh in its teasing as its inanimate voice echoed in her ears. Jenny shook her head violently as she tried to toss the voice from her head. Her knuckles grew pasty white as she gripped the steering wheel with a fervent hold, and then and only then, with a nod to her rearview mirror, as though she was blaspheming Devil's Bulge, Jenny gunned the gas pedal to the floor as her speedometer quickly crept past the sixty-mile per hour mark.

"Don't stop there. You know you can go faster. I can handle it, but the question remains...can you? Maybe you can do better than your boyfriend. He can't seem to handle anything!"

"Damn you!" Jenny floored it this time, throwing caution to the wind as she flew up the road that taunted her. She knew she was closing in on the stretch that almost killed her, reaching a speed of over eighty miles an hour. "Take that, you bastard!" She said, laughing in a malevolent and threatening tone. She felt empowered as she took on the road that mocked her every move. She threw her head back in triumph as the end came near, knowing finally she had beaten one more demon, but alas, in the end it was the road that would have the last laugh. Gripping her wheel as the road pushed her car out of the way, making it slide out of control and crashing into an embankment at the very same spot that Liam's truck had gone off exactly one year ago today. Her emotions gave in as her malevolent laughter turned into a heartbreaking gasp for air. She was exhausted from her ordeal, realizing that this stretch of ordinariness still had a hold on her.

"This isn't fair, why did you do this to me?" she bellowed at the road that seemed unyielding to her pain. Jenny carefully put the car back into drive and moved forward. She didn't look back but could have sworn she heard the road hiss as the wheels rolled over it. The rest of her drive was insignificant after that, yet she was still nowhere near the resolution she was hoping to find on this day.

Life was moving on. Even the sun was brighter than usual, casting a beautiful ray of light directly into her path without a care that her world was crumbling around her, or it would be more forgiving to her needs and cast its glow elsewhere. Everything around her wanted her to remember that fateful night. The smell of gasoline engulfed her senses just as it did one year ago as she lay in her semi-conscious state. She rubbed her hands across her left arm as she felt the indentations that were grim reminders of the shards of glass that had embedded into her skin. A shiver ran up her spine as the taste of blood entered her mouth. She was choking on it as she vainly tried to yell for Liam's help, his reach just short of where he could touch her, so close yet so far away from her. As she turned off the main road and carefully made her way down the beaten dirt road, she realized she was covered in a cold sweat, effects from the nightmare that replayed itself to her. She finally came to a stop as the dusty road turned into a pasture of grass. She was finally here... Serenity Hill. She exhaled.

****

Liam drove quickly as he made his way out of Spencer. He knew where he should be going: Jenny's, but he didn't dare go there. He was afraid. He knew deep down that nothing had happened that night between Johnny and her, but he allowed his enfeebled mental state to do the talking for him. As a result, he had lashed out at the only person that had ever meant a damn to him, and he did it in such a way that he knew she would never take him back. He believed she had had enough, enough of his temperament, enough of his unforgiving behavior, enough of his self-pity, and enough of him. Period. No, for all the notoriety he had received throughout his high school career and all the so-called friends he thought he had made, Liam had never felt more alone than today. Life was going on without any regard to him. He had screwed up royally with Jenny, the only person he had ever loved or who had loved him. She always saw the good in him and always believed in him no matter what, but he couldn't handle that. Life was too good. Even after the horrific accident, she stood by him, and he couldn't handle that either. This was the only way he knew how to handle anything in his life, by running away and letting go. He looked at his unopened beer can and became sick at the sight. He didn't want this, and as a result of his revelation, he crushed it, making the contents explode around him. The sheer release of it also made his emotions explode as he slammed on the gas pedal and sped faster away.

****

Jenny sat in her car, feeling helpless and more alone than ever. She thought for sure that she would feel some sort of comfort. Serenity Hill, of all places, always brought her feelings of belonging and reassurance, but instead she felt an impending fear of anxiety and unease as she reflected upon the hill in front of her. Aside from Brush Creek Road, it still was one of the most beautiful spots she had ever seen, the closest thing to Heaven. She inhaled deeply the sweet scent the hill provided as she got out of her car, wiping away the remnants of tears that still lay on her face. A gentle breeze enveloped her, and for a moment made her forget her troubles. She walked cautiously forward, looking in vain for the sight she wanted to see more than anything, but he was nowhere to be seen. She knew she wouldn't find Liam here, but deep down in her heart, she had hoped he would be here waiting for her like so many other times before.

She carefully made her way to the edge of the hill that overlooked the vast valley and high peaks. The ground was soft and gave way to her as she walked softly on it, leaving her footprint depressed into the ground. She instantly looked for a second set of prints, only to be disheartened. The wind grew as she made her way to the edge of the cliff, the edge of Heaven as Liam used to call it. The sight before her was breathtaking and at the same time unusually unpleasant. Nothing held any credence to her anymore, not even the majesty of this place. She walked away from the view and found herself standing in the gazebo. Her hands outlining the intricate woodwork as she imagined Liam's hands touching the same spots as he methodically worked on her gift.

Jenny sat there for hours. Reflections of her time with Liam inundated her senses. She could visualize him and smell his sweet scent as though he was only inches from her. The cruel wind surrounded itself with his presence although he was nowhere to be seen. She could feel him against her as his gentle touch embraced and comforted her, but her mind was only playing tricks on her as it always did, and she opened them only to have her reality validated. She came here looking for what she had been missing...peace, comfort, and more importantly, love. Instead, she found more heartbreak and sadness. Liam's words still echoed to her: *"You're dead to me, Jenny."* She cried aloud. She walked away from the gazebo that brought her no comfort and lay on the soft ground that welcomed her body, and she closed her eyes to find the tranquil darkness that had always been there for her. In minutes, she was asleep.

****

Liam made his way down the beaten dirt road. He drove without caution, not caring about his well-being or anything else for that matter. The road ended abruptly in front of him to display the newly soft spring grass. He parked his truck and slowly stepped out. Normally he would have driven all the way to the top of the hill, but not today. Today he wanted to take the walk on foot. Serenity Hill had always been there for him, and today of all days, he wanted to embrace every part of it. He closed the door but not before he put a small, white envelope in his back pocket. The smell of the new grass immersed his senses as he made his way forward. He looked ahead; he had just made it in time. The sun was peeking over the horizon, illuminating the view and all its glory before him. He fell to his knees as he thought about Jenny. She loved it here almost more than he did. She used to beg him to bring her here just so she could see the sun rise above the peaks of the hills. She said it was the most awe-inspiring sight she had ever seen, and if she never lived another day in her life she would feel contented knowing that they had gotten to share in one of the most beautiful sights God had ever bestowed upon them. His tears flowed freely as he realized they would never share another moment like this again. He felt the burden of the world on him as it buried him within. He looked all around him. The beauty that Serenity Hill encompassed was nothing compared to the beauty that Jenny held, and it wasn't even her physical beauty. It was the beauty that she held inside her that Liam missed the most. He looked for her, hoping against hope that possibly she would be here too. He knew what this day held for her, and it troubled him that she was enduring it alone. He had failed her again, he thought to himself.

He fell to his knees again as he spoke. The words were inaudible, but he knew she was listening. She always listened to him, no matter how much distance came between them. He stayed there for hours as he succumbed to his despair. The hopelessness that surrounded him only grew heavier as he realized that the grief he bore was of his own accord. Serenity Hill brought no comfort to him as well. No one could fix his mistakes but him. As he continued to stare at the grey tombstone, he knew that it was probably too late. His destiny had been laid out before him, and it was of his own choosing. He had made the fool's choice, and there was no turning back. He had to leave, but before doing so, he carefully took the envelope and kissed it tenderly as he gently laid it on the ground by his mom's grave. He walked away but not before going to the gazebo. He felt burdened as he stood in the middle of it. There was no comfort or joy that he promised Jenny she would find here, only sadness and loneliness.

****

It was late afternoon when Jenny awoke in a daze. The comfort and solitude she longed for still evaded her. The sleep she sought was uneasy and restless, and she knew that what she was hoping to find here could not be found. Liam was gone. He never showed. Never did she think she would have to relive this day all alone. Her world was an empty, dark shell that rejoiced in her misery. She had concluded it was her payback that had led her to this. This is what she deserved for trying to care for someone else. This was her penance for allowing Johnny to be a part of her life. She had made her choices, and her path had been laid out before her. She knew she would have to walk it alone.

Her body ached for Liam's presence, for his touch as she rose from the soft ground she had become used to. She wanted the ground to swallow her now and put her out of her misery, but instead it beckoned for her to rise and move on. She was ready to leave Serenity Hill now that she knew she wasn't going to find the comfort she had sought, but before her departure she walked over to the familiar tree that protected and sheltered the grey tombstone that held residence beneath it. She bent down on bended knee as she cried, her hand tightly grasping the cold, hard marble. She spoke softly and then tenderly kissed the grey granite before rising. She was ready to leave, knowing that this would be the last time she would be here. Before her exit, she noticed the small white envelope that had secured itself between the tombstone and a patch of woodland violets. There were no words on it, but she knew instinctively that it was hers to open, and when she did her body failed her as she collapsed to the ground.

Chapter Twenty-Five
A Punch to the Gut

    The small rectangular envelope looked innocent enough, but my heart pounded as I tried to bring myself to open it. I knew the contents would reveal what I was hoping to avoid: the truth. My hands trembled feverishly as I carefully lifted the flap to find multiple pieces of blue paper neatly folded in a tri-fold manner. My heart pounded even more aggressively as I noticed the familiar handwriting that was etched upon its surface. Only Liam wrote with such haphazard and rushed regard. I didn't want to read what I already thought I knew, but the contents beckoned me to as I held the cerulean paper between my fingers. I already knew that it was over between us, having it in written form only endorsed it for me. I took a deep breath, knowing the inevitable was before me and then proceeded to read, my heart still pounding at an uncomfortable rate.

    Dear Jenny,

    Where to begin...I've stared at this paper countless times, only to walk away from it every time. Each time that I thought I had found the courage to begin, I would stumble with my thoughts and realize I couldn't continue. It's funny how a grown man could be scared to death of something so small and trivial, but this paper, I knew, after I would begin would hold so much meaning behind it. It's been months since that night outside of Johnny's apartment, months that we have spent apart, months I have spent contemplating what to do, and months wondering what the hell went wrong. It's not easy for me to write this, especially on this day, it's a little past midnight on April 11th, one year exactly since our horrible accident. I know you are suffering right now because so am I, and I'm sorry that we are apart. I never wanted this day to come with you having to endure this alone. We should be together, but something's been unraveling for a while now and the timing of this just sucks.

    I'm trying to understand what happened, but it's so hard for me too, Jenny. I've loved you from the first time I laid eyes on you sitting on the hill outside of school that late summer afternoon. In that instant, I saw my future. Everyone thought the passion we had for one another was too much too soon, but we both knew better. It couldn't be explained, but we knew we were made for each other. We were soul mates or better yet, kindred spirits. I never was one to believe in anything before you came along, I had no reason to. I love you so much, Jenny.

    My heart breaks knowing I can't hold you right now. I would lay my life on the line for you, but I can't seem to get past the regrets of my past. That damn accident seemed to be the catapult to our demise or more or less mine. Everything after April 11th has been nothing but heartache for us. It should be so easy for us to be together, but for some reason, it isn't. I've tried to get over things so we could move on and have a life together, but it's been harder for me than I thought. And it doesn't help to know that there is someone else who seems to love you as much as I do. I've often thought how things would have been between us if Johnny never had entered the picture, if he would have stayed away, but then again, he seems to have been placed in your life at least for a reason, so I'm sure it was only a matter of time before the two of you met. I know you have told me numerous times that you harbored no feelings for him, but he was relentless with his, so how can I blame you for not sheltering something for him, whether it was platonic or not. I tried to overlook them, knowing the gratitude you felt for him was something any human would feel, but what I thought was nothing more than an innocent friendship, I realized now was merely a façade of Johnny's true feelings for you.

He's always seemed to be there for you, waiting in the background, waiting for me to mess up, and waiting for his opportunity. I don't know if it's my past that has caused me so many afflictions or the fact that I can't seem to be the man I should be for you. You know you are my everything, my world, but I can't be yours until I can release myself from these demons that have tormented me. I can find no peace or comfort in my life. I used to look forward to each new day knowing that I would be seeing you, but now I can't stand the day or night because you are nowhere to be found.

I find that I have too much time on my hands, and with that comes more self-pity, self-pity that I try to wash away with my drinking and with my racing. When I race, I forget the pain. I feel like the all-American football hero that Spencer used to hail me as. I'm strong again, invincible. I feel like the boy you fell in love with, not the person I have become, someone who can't seem to find closure. Jenny, I know it doesn't make any sense. I promised you I would never race another day in my life, but I never dreamed I would be plagued with so many demons that I couldn't erase. I need to get over them, and that's why I'm doing this. Nothing else seems to help, not even you. I need to regain my self-worth. I'm no good to you as I am. You know that no matter how many times we have talked about the accident I still place all the blame on myself. I need to feel like the man I used to be, and racing seems to be the only answer to my dilemma. When I was given the opportunity, even though I knew you would disapprove of it, I couldn't refuse. I never meant to shut you out, but the more I drank, the more ashamed I became of myself. I never wanted to be like my father, but that's who I see when I look in the mirror.

 I write this letter to you with much sadness and heartache. I want you to know that no matter what has happened between us that I will love you forever. My love for you has never left me. It only grows stronger with each passing day, and I hope that no matter what, you can still feel my love for you. I never meant to hurt you. Please forgive me for all the broken promises I made to you. I truly meant to keep them. Maybe a stronger man could have, but I don't seem to possess the qualities of such a man. I'm just a broken man with a past that won't leave him alone. These past few months that we have been apart have been the hardest thing I have ever had to endure. My life is empty without you. The nightmares that plagued me have never left me and only validate the guilt I am supposed to carry.

 Ever since my parents' passing, I have been beset with loneliness. Not even Grandfather Mack could fill the void, and believe me, he tried. But in you, things were different. I saw everything that had been missing in my life, in you I saw happiness and hope, and I saw the love that I had been searching for all my life. You filled the void that no one else ever could or ever will.

 You are and will always be my soul mate, my kindred spirit. I do not blame you for Johnny's part in all this, that blame falls on me as well. I am a jealous man when it comes to you, and Johnny seemed to thrive on that. It only made things worse and made me realize how vulnerable I really am. I hated the bond that the two of you formed. I wanted to be your savior not Johnny. You've told me time and time again that you held no feelings for him, but it would take a blind man not to see the bond the two of you made, intentional or not. It was just one more punch to my gut. I wanted to give you the world, but instead I felt I had taken the world away from you. I'm so sorry. If I could take it all back, I would do it in a heartbeat. I would do anything for you, Jenny.

 Once my drinking became heavier, I could tell I was becoming more withdrawn from you. I couldn't stop myself, and I felt ashamed when I was with you. I knew I should stop, but I couldn't. You tried to help, but I was in denial. Dad could never stop either, and we both know what happened to him. And because of that, I needed to distance myself from you. I was afraid of the monster I was becoming.

I thought I could turn away from the racing and drinking and even the influence of Toby whenever I wanted and return to you a stronger man, but instead I became the pawn in my own game. I'm sorry, Jenny. I never wanted to be like my father. I despised the very ground he walked on, and the more I tried not to be like him, the more I've turned into him. I raced to forget the heartache, and I drank to forget everything else.

Everything shifted after April 11th, my world's axis changed. You are my angel. You tried so hard with me, but I resisted you, and because of my selfish actions, I fear I have lost you forever. My weakness became my comfort. I've always been perceived as a strong and indestructible person, but in retrospect, I now see it was you who was the strong one. I needed you much more than you ever needed me. I thought I had the world at my feet when I played football. Everybody wanted me, adored me, and craved for my attention, but I never understood it nor wanted it. I was content with this, that was until you entered it. Then and only then did I realize how empty my life had been.

You completed every aspect of me. You gave my life purpose. I could always be myself, you were my refuge, but in the end, I allowed even that to slip away. I know Johnny loves you, and as weird as it sounds, I'm okay with that. I've accepted his feelings towards you. I know they are not going away, and it doesn't bother me anymore. What does bother me are my actions that led to the night outside Johnny's apartment. I never wanted you to see me in that condition or for me to be in that condition. I never thought I would sink so low. I know why you were there, and I'm sorry that I didn't believe you. I can't seem to let go of the demons that plague me. I've tried, my love, with every fiber of my soul, but they have a hold on me and aren't letting go. They possess the strength I lack.

You aren't with me now, and I miss you so much. I wish I could make things right between us. That's all I think about. I would give up everything to have things the way they used to be between us. Those happy times seem like a lifetime ago. I want to be the man you fell in love with, and my quest is to find him again. You can do so much better than me, Jenny.

From the beginning of our relationship, I have been the fortunate one, the lucky one to have you by my side. Thank you for that. I can feel your presence all around me. It comforts me, and your love is what fuels me to conquer my fears. I can only hope that you feel my love as it surrounds you. I love you, and with each breath I take, I always will. Maybe you knew all along our relationship would be riddled with problems and that's why you tried to resist me in the beginning, but I wouldn't give up. I had to have you in my life, and I still do. I just can't live without you, Jenny. I don't know how I'm going to go on without you in my world. Life has no meaning without you in it, but I promise that I will never do anything to make you be ashamed of me. Your love, whether we are together or not, will endure me. Kindred spirits are linked together forever, and I know that someday, whether it is tomorrow or a hundred years from now, we will be together again. I want you to have the life you deserve. Please be patient with me as I try to find the person you fell in love with. I'm still out there. I just got lost along the way.

I'm so sorry that I can't be with you right now, another broken promise that I intend to make right. Please believe me when I tell you that I'm embracing you. I love you, babe, more than life itself. I hope you can feel my love for you, it's never died. Please don't give up on me.

Your eternal love,

Liam

I read the letter multiple times, memorizing every word as I could hear Liam speak them. I had cried a million tears since Liam entered my life, some happy and some sad, but none fell harder than those I shed while reading his letter. Every syllable echoed in my mind as I stared at the words. Liam was hurting as much as I was, but for all the good this letter did, it still did not rectify the obvious. We were still apart, and I felt numb as I stared vacantly at the letter. My heart raced as anger began to deluge me. How was I supposed to perceive this letter? Did Liam think this would make me feel better, that this was his way of apologizing? I couldn't stand it. He was running away instead of facing me. He was making this all about him and not realizing the torment I was still enduring. I felt so alone as I crumpled the blue pages and threw them to the ground. This did nothing for me except make me feel worse. All Liam needed to do was to come to me, but he didn't even have the decency to do that. After everything we had been through, and of all days, he gives me this damn letter. I left Serenity Hill, barreling away from there as fast as I could. I didn't stop until I had reached Joe's. I didn't know if I would find Liam there, but I had to start looking somewhere. It was late, and except for a couple of lights that illuminated the back room, the place looked completely deserted. I yelled for Liam allowing my anger to control my voice.

"I know you're here, Liam. I'm not leaving until we talk!" I screamed. I waited impatiently for him to appear. My voice echoing as it hit the walls of the shop.

"Liam! Dammit come out and talk to me right now!" I demanded again.

"He's not here, Jenny," Parker said calmly as he entered from behind a closed door.

"Where is he? I need to talk to him, and I need to talk to him now."

"I don't know, Jenny. I haven't seen him since early this morning. He left right before sun up. He didn't tell me where he was going, but honestly, that's not surprising anymore. You know as well as I do that he doesn't do anything by the book. I don't know him anymore. I thought possibly because of what day it is, he might come looking for you. Haven't you seen him today?"

My anger subsided with Parker's question. "No, I haven't seen him. I was hoping to. I went to where I thought he would be, but I didn't find him. Instead, I found a letter he wrote me."

"A letter?"

"Yeah." I lowered my head, and Parker could tell from my demeanor that I didn't want to go into detail about it.

"Jenny, I'm sorry. You know if I knew where he was I would tell you. Are you doing okay? I know what today is. Is there anything I can do for you?"

"No, Parker, but thank you. I'm doing alright, considering. It's been really hard. I'm not going to lie to you, but I'm handling it, just like I've been handling everything else in my life lately."

"You know, before Liam left this morning, we got into a pretty bad argument."

"Really, what was it about?"

"I think you might already know."

"Me?"

"Yeah. I've tried to talk to him ever since you two had a falling out, but he never wanted to listen. I guess I just had enough of his stupid behavior, so I let him hear what I had to say whether he wanted to hear or not. Apparently he didn't want to hear it because after I was done he left in an uproar, and I haven't seen him since."

"Stupid behavior, Parker?"

"You know he's not been acting right for a while now. I mean if I'm going to be honest with you, he's been a different person since the accident. I don't know what's changed in him so much that he can't handle. I know about his dad, and it's scaring me to see him drink the way he does. And now the way he's hanging out with Toby and this reckless racing, well it's like putting matches to gasoline. They don't go together, and eventually you're going to have a fire. That's what I'm afraid is happening to Liam. Toby is bad news. He doesn't care about Liam except what he can use him for. He has Liam racing death matches just so he can earn a few bucks off of him."

"You can't be serious?"

"I'm afraid I'm dead serious, Jenny. Liam is supposed to race again tomorrow night. It was going to be tonight, but Liam told Toby there was no way in hell he would do it tonight. I was hoping he would find you. I've told him countless times how sad you are, and I know it's bothering him, but something's keeping him from you. I'm just afraid it's the alcohol."

"I've got to find him, Parker. Do you have any idea where he might be?"

"I wish I did, but no."

"I've got to go then. I can't wait around here for him."

"Be careful. If Liam is drinking…"

"Don't worry, I will be. I have to find him, though. This has to stop."

My first thought was to drive to Glenville. Maybe he had changed his mind and decided to race, but in my heart I knew that wasn't true. I knew he wasn't there, not on this day. I drove aimlessly for the next hour as I searched for Liam, he seemed to be a ghost, and there was no trace of him as I searched the town. I was at a loss when I found myself at Liam's house. Liam wasn't there either. The only person to greet me was Grandpa. I fell into his arms as he met me at the door. I was drained of my will and exhausted from my ordeal.

Chapter Twenty-Six
Twist of Fate

"It's over, Grandpa," I said, blubbering into his worn plaid shirt.

"Jenny, hon, what do you mean? Please come in and sit down." Grandpa led me inside to the familiar sofa that held so many fond memories for me. "Did you talk to Liam?"

I shook my head back and forth as I tried to speak between my incessant crying. I couldn't believe I still had tears to fall. "No, Grandpa. I went to Serenity Hill thinking I might find him there, but instead I found a letter."

"A letter?"

"Yes, it was next to Jessica's grave. I thought I would find him there, you know, because of the day, but instead I found a letter that has me even more confused. I don't know what to do Grandpa. He doesn't want me in his life anymore."

"That's not true. That boy loves you dearly. He's just troubled right now, and he doesn't know what to do about it. His love for you has never wavered, but I am concerned for his welfare, Jenny. To be honest, I didn't think it was going to get this bad with him. I thought the nightmares would end and he would be able to move on and plan his future with you, but that hasn't been the case."

"I know, and it's all my fault."

"Now listen Jenny, it's not your fault. I was afraid for this. There is nobody here to blame, not even Liam. This goes beyond anything Liam could even control or understand."

I looked at Grandpa with a perplexed expression. He in turn sighed.

"I guess I need to explain myself. I have something to tell you, and when I'm done, I think you will realize that Liam and I share more in common than our looks or our last name. Did I ever tell you how I received my limp or this scar on my face?"

"No," I said, intrigued.

"It was the year of my eighteenth birthday. My dad had just bought a brand new cherry red Ford pick-up truck, and I was bustin' at the seams to drive it. We didn't have a lot of money back then, and this was the first new truck my dad had owned in over twenty years. It was his baby. He took care of that truck with a tender hand and a tender foot. He never went over the speed limit when he drove it, and always, and I do mean always, he would wash it down after driving it. He loved that truck, but being a teenage boy, all I could think about was driving it as well as showing it off in front of my friends. I begged my dad to let me take it out. I would ask him every Saturday night, and every Saturday night Dad would say no.

I was relentless in my pursuit and kept asking, hoping that he would have to say yes sooner or later if only to just shut me up about it. I had just had my birthday and graduation was in less than two months. Mom and Dad told me that if I could pull out at least three A's on my final report card, the truck was mine for the taking that first weekend after graduation. I know I don't have to tell you how excited I was to hear them say that. If you didn't know, Jenny, school never agreed with me. Maybe that's where Liam gets it from. I would rather be hanging with my friends or working on the farm with the horses. I never liked being confined to a chair having to learn things. I wanted to be doing things. So, bringing home one A was a feat in itself, much less bringing home three. I thought I'd never know what it would feel like to sit behind the wheel of that beautiful truck, but I wanted to drive it so bad that I could practically taste it. It was driving me crazy, so for the remainder of the school year I worked my tail off on getting good grades, and when my parents received my final report card they not only saw three A's gracing the page but four. They were ecstatic for me and just as surprised as me, and being who they were, they kept their word, telling me the truck was mine to drive that first weekend after graduation.

    I couldn't tell my friends fast enough. Next to being outside in the fresh air, I loved being behind the wheel of a truck. I guess that's another trait Liam gets from me. Anyway, that weekend couldn't get here fast enough, and when it finally did arrive, I was ready for it, and so were my two best friends. The three of us cruised Spencer for hours that Friday night. I took care of that truck as though it was my own, making sure I didn't go too fast or go too slow for that matter, just like my dad did. It was everything I had dreamed of. It purred like a kitten and handled like it was made for me. My friends were in awe of it as much as I, and by the time Saturday came, the three of us had planned to cruise the town again. But this time we felt we needed to do a little more showing off, and that's exactly what we did.

    I remember the night well, just like it was yesterday. It was a hot, summer night, and Dwight Campbell was having a party to kick off summer. Everybody was going to be there. I couldn't think of a better way to arrive than in my dad's cherry red pick-up truck. When we got there, we were the talk of the party. All my friends wanted to look at it, and most of them wanted to drive it, but, of course, I told them that privilege belonged to me and me alone. Needless to say, there were a few guys though who thought I was being a little too much of a show off with the truck and thought I should be put in my place. The truck was fast, Jenny, and I didn't mind telling everybody that. For those who didn't like what I had to say, well they were the ones who thought I should be taught a lesson. You know, I might be quite a bit older than you and Liam, but nothing much has changed in regards to being a teenager and having parties. What goes on now went on then as well. There were boys and girls making out and plenty of alcohol was to be found. And of course, there were the races."

I immediately interrupted Grandpa. "You mean the same races that…"

He didn't let me finish. "The same ones, Jenny. Like I said, some things never change. It's only the time that makes it different. Well, I don't like admitting this, but I had been drinking at the party and probably a little too much. We all were; we had just graduated, and we were celebrating our newfound freedom. I guess I let the alcohol do the talking for me because as soon as I was challenged with the truck, I didn't back down. His name was Miles Becker, and he was meaner than a rattlesnake. He was the school bully and was always in trouble, and if he wasn't in trouble, he was looking for it. Normally I knew to stay the hell away from him, but having that truck made me feel empowered, like nothing could happen to me. Probably some of the same feelings Liam has felt before, if I know that boy, which I think I do." Grandpa paused for a moment before continuing, intertwining his fingers the same way I had seen Liam do a thousand times as he reflected on his thoughts.

"Well to go on, besides being the school bully, Miles was also the richest kid in town. His parents owned the local five and dime store in Spencer. They were some of the nicest folks these parts had to offer. They were geniuses at business but lousy at being parents. Miles was an only child, and while they built their store up they kind of forgot about their son. To make up for their busy lifestyles, they spoiled the kid and gave him money to appease him. He was left alone most of the time to do what he wanted, and what he wanted was to get into trouble. By the time he became a teenager, he was one of the most hated kids in the town. No one wanted to be around him, and those who did only did because Miles would bribe them with free stuff from the store and sometimes even his money.

So like I was saying, he challenged me. I do believe the boy was jealous. It was ironic in retrospect, the rich kid jealous of the poor kid, but I had something he wanted, and he was going to make sure that if he couldn't have it, he was at least going to make sure it looked inferior to what he had. Miles drove a black Chevrolet pick-up. I won't lie, it was a beauty, but it paled in comparison to my dad's truck, and Miles knew it. He challenged me to see who had the fastest truck. In all honesty, I tried to talk him out of it in the beginning, but like I said, the alcohol did most of my talking. Dwight's house was located off of the main road a couple of miles out of town. We decided the first to make it to the main road would be the winner. The winner got bragging rights, and the loser, well, he just lost his dignity. I knew it would be dangerous, but like I said, that truck made me feel empowered, I knew I could win it. I had no doubt.

Miles had two friends who decided to race with him, and so to make it fair, my two buddies decided to race with me too. We both got in our trucks and drove parallel to each other to the starting point; Dwight started the race by shooting his dad's shotgun in the air. We were neck and neck for most of the race, neither one of us backing down. I knew the alcohol was playing a big part in my behavior. I had my two buddies with me, and we were yelling at the top of our lungs as we saw the finish line in sight. I guess I kind of forgot what I was doing, or maybe I was drunker than I thought, but I had begun swerving back and forth on the road, maybe hoping I could push Miles off the road and then the race would be mine. But my judgment was impaired, and I swerved a little too far. The wheel started shaking as I grasped it tightly. I remember my knuckles were bone white as I tried to straighten her out, but it was too late. The truck was on its side coasting to the finish line on its two right tires. My buddies were screaming for me to bring her down, but I couldn't. The truck flipped over as I passed the finish line. I don't remember anything after that. I woke up in the hospital days later to find myself with a broken hip and a huge cut down the side of my face." Grandpa looked away as he became somberly quiet.

"I'm so sorry, Grandpa. How horrible for you, and how horrible for you to have to relive that with Liam as well. It's uncanny the similarities between our accident and yours. It must have been awful for you when you found out about our accident."

"It was, Jenny. Something I'll never forget. You know Liam doesn't even know this story."

"He doesn't? But why? He must wonder about your limp and how you got your scars."

"He thinks I was born with the limp and the scars came from falling off a horse into a bed of barbed wire. That's what I want him to always think, Jenny. He can't know the real truth."

"I won't tell him, I promise, Grandpa. But why don't you want him to know?"

"Because, Jenny, it would devastate him, especially now. He's way too fragile to know the truth. You know how much he detested his father. I saw him grow up with that anger, and I saw that anger grow as he grew. I vowed to myself that he would never know the truth about me. It's not that I just don't want him to know, it's because of our history. I was a drunk too. He's trying so hard not to be like his dad. If he knew I had the same problems and what happened to me in that accident, I don't think we could ever save him."

"What else happened that night, Grandpa?"

"I lost one of my best friends that night. Lee West was his name, and he was my very first friend. He was thrown from the truck when it flipped over, killing him instantly. I never got to say good-bye to him. His funeral was held while I was still in the hospital. I never took another drink after that, Jenny. It took years for me to recover, and I'm not talking about my physical injuries. I mean mentally. Lee lived on the same road as me, and I had to pass his house every day. It just about killed me. It wasn't until I met Liam's grandmother that I started feeling normal again. She saved me, so I know what you mean to Liam. It's the same feelings I carry for my Eleanor." Grandpa squeezed my hands in his as his blue eyes became hazed in tears.

"But what about Miles and his friends? And didn't you say you had two friends with you?"

"Miles' truck went into a ditch. He and his friends didn't even receive a scratch. And yes I did say I had my two best friends with me. My other friend received a concussion and a broken arm. He was pretty lucky. We didn't speak for years after that night, neither one of us able to look at each other without thinking about Lee. It wasn't until my wedding to Eleanor that I saw my friend again. I had invited him but really didn't think he would show. He surprised me the night before my wedding, though. We talked until the sun came up. I still hear from him from time to time. His name is Ott Banner. I saw him about a year ago."

"I remember his name, Grandpa."

"That's right, Jenny. And as far as Liam is concerned, Ott is just a good ole' buddy of mine from years ago and nothing more. You know, years later, after my Eleanor and Jessica died, I found a letter from Jessica that she had written to me. It was about a month after her funeral." My mind went back to the vacant room in Grandpa's house. "I was putting away some of her stuff in storage when I found it. I gotta tell you, it brought me to tears after I read it. My Jessica was going through a whole hell of a lot with Liam's father. People say that the apple doesn't fall far from the tree, and although my sweet Jessica never took to the bottle, her husband sure did. She knew her fate I think even before Allen did. She knew she would never see her Liam grow up, and she wanted to make sure that I took care of him. And, Jenny, that's exactly what I'm trying to do, but now I can't do it alone. I need your help." I stared at Grandpa with heartfelt eyes as I recalled reading Jessica's letter. I wanted to tell Grandpa I knew about it, but it didn't matter. He had told me, and that was good enough.

"Well, that's my story, Jenny. I hope it doesn't change how you see me. I will tell you this, no matter how bad it seems between you and Liam, don't give up on the boy. He needs you, even if he doesn't think so himself. Part of his problem is his stubbornness. If you were to leave him now, I would lose my boy for sure. I've almost lost him already. He's hanging on by a thread. I know what he is going through because it's the same stuff I went through when Lee died. The only person who helped me was my Eleanor, and believe me, I fought her off too. I didn't think anybody could help me. It was her strength and resiliency that saw me through, and it will be yours that will see Liam through. She never gave up on me, and I know you won't give up on Liam either."

"Grandpa, may I ask you something?"

"Of course."

"I know where Jessica is buried, but why isn't Eleanor buried at Serenity Hill? Or is she? I just remember Jessica's grave."

Grandpa sighed as he twiddled with his fingers. "Eleanor isn't buried, Jenny." I looked at him, confused. Grandpa took in a huge deep breath as he looked to the sky and closed his eyes. "No, she didn't want to be buried. This farm, our home, was her favorite place on earth and when she knew her time was near, she told me she never wanted to be far from me or this place. After her death, I had her ashes spread over this homestead, the way she wanted it, the way it should be, at least for my Eleanor. This way we're close to each other, and I know she's where she belongs." He opened his eyes and brought them to me with a smile on his face. "My Eleanor is always in my heart, but she's also always around me. That's why she's not at Serenity Hill. Our Jessica wanted to be buried at Serenity Hill because that place brought her so many wonderful memories, memories that included a time when she was in love with Allen before he turned into the monster that killed her. She hated that man at the end, and I hate him for what he did to my family. The whole town knew the drunkard Allen Greer was turning into, and that's one reason why you won't see Jessica's married name on her tombstone or why Liam doesn't carry the Greer last name. The Greer name brought nothing but heartache to my family. Liam carries the Larson name because that's how Eleanor and I wanted it and Liam too."

"Grandpa, I never knew. I never even thought to ask Liam about why his last name wasn't the same as his dad's, but it makes sense. I know how much he hates him." I paused before continuing, wanting to change the dismal mood that had been generated. "I do want to tell you that I think it's beautiful what you told me about your wife and Jessica and where they wanted their final resting place to be. It's a beautiful tribute to them. You know, you are one of the most honorable and loving men I have ever met, and what you just shared with me makes me love you even more. You and Liam do share so much, but it's not the negative stuff that I see, it's the strength the two of you possess that I admire the most. That's why it frustrates me when Liam won't let me be there for him. I believe in him, Grandpa, and I don't understand why he doesn't believe in himself." I paused as I reflected on what I should tell Grandpa. He had shared so much with me; I knew I had to share this with him. "Grandpa?"

"Yes, Jenny."

"Has Liam told you about Johnny?"

"You mean about the reason for the race that led to the accident? I told you I already knew about that."

"Yes, but there's more."

"You mean the fact that Johnny is in love with you too."

I stared at Grandpa in astonishment. "You know?"

"Yes, Jenny. I've known for quite some time now. I might not be the brightest bulb in the socket, but it's not hard to see what Johnny feels for you. He wears it on his face the way Liam does."

"Did Liam tell you anything?"

"He's told me some stuff. If you mean about the night at Johnny's apartment, no he didn't. I found that out through Parker."

"Parker? I don't understand."

"Parker just told me a few nights ago. Jenny, I've been just as worried about Liam as anybody, and I knew something was wrong, especially after you went back to your parents' house. When Liam wouldn't talk to me about you, I knew something was seriously wrong, and that's when I started noticing the empty beer bottles in his truck and in the trash. He wouldn't talk to me about that either. Every time I asked, he would become mad at me and walk off. His demeanor changed drastically. I noticed he was spending a lot more time on the phone with some guy named Toby, and he was always talking about racing motorcycles. It was then I knew I had to get involved. He vowed to me when he was in the hospital that he would never race again. When I heard him setting up races with this Toby guy, some punk I had never in my life heard him mention before, I knew there was a problem. He was spending less time here and more time away, and I knew it wasn't at Joe's or with you. Joe would call me on a regular basis asking if I had seen

Liam. Liam barely stayed here, and when he did, he smelled of alcohol. It just about killed me to see him self-destruct because I was seeing me at the very same age right after Lee died. And his nightmares, I told you they're just as bad as ever. I mean, I haven't seen Liam much at all these past couple of months, but the times he did sleep here, I couldn't get a wink of sleep from the screaming he was doing. But this is stuff you already know.

You're a very beautiful, young woman, and Liam knows that. It would take a blind man not to see the beauty you possess, but what makes you so beautiful is what comes from here." Grandpa pointed to my heart. "Liam saw that and so did Johnny. I'm not saying I condone Johnny's behavior. It's been wrong of him to pursue you the way he has, but you really can't blame him, and you can't blame yourself. Parker told me that after that night at Johnny's, Liam was a complete mess, the worst Parker had ever seen him, but Liam told Parker that he believed you when you told him why you were at Johnny's. But in Liam's eyes, he had to put on that front, even if it meant hurting you in the process. He couldn't allow himself to act any differently in front of Johnny either. It was the alcohol talking for Liam that night, and just like it got me into a boat load of shit, it did for Liam too. I lost my friend over it, and Liam was losing you. That's why he hasn't been able to see you face to face, and I'm sure that's why he wrote you the letter instead of talking to you in person. I don't know exactly what happened at Johnny's or what was said, but I do know that no matter what words or actions were conveyed between you two, Liam didn't mean it.

He's drowning, Jenny, and not to sound corny, but you're his lifeboat." Grandpa held on tightly to me as he allowed me to weep. I didn't want to be alone on this day, and if Liam couldn't be with me, I was so glad that his grandpa could. "I want to tell you that it's going to be okay, but you know as well as I do that I can't say that anymore and truly mean it. All I can say is that you and Liam share something very special, and if you believe in each other like everybody else believes in the two of you, then you'll both come out of this together. The way it should be."

    I fell asleep in Grandpa's arms that night, his words echoing in my ears as I drifted off to my familiar dark friend. Only this time, I couldn't enjoy the solitude that the darkness brought me. It was interrupted by my dreams.

Chapter Twenty-Seven
A Stranger's Plea

It was the same as always. I was lying on a bed of glass as the smell of gasoline consumed my every sense. Liam was a few feet away from me, and the panic in his eyes was scaring me. I knew this was bad. The truck was still hissing, and the tires were still turning, but we were not moving. Liam and I were trapped by the black beast as it failed in its quest to beat the white Bronco. I was screaming for Liam to help me and, out of desperation, tried to wrangle myself from the dashboard that was determined to keep me it's prisoner. Liam's hand reached for me. The look of frustration swept over his face as his attempt failed. I wept profusely as the enormity of the situation made itself clear to me. I screamed to Liam for his help, but it was muffled by his own screams for me. *"Please, Jenny just reach for my hand. I'm right here baby. I'm not leaving you!"* Liam cried.

"Liam, I'm scared. Please help me, it hurts, please don't leave me!" I cried back to him, but neither one of us could help the other. Both of us were trapped and beyond each other's ability to give comfort. Liam's face blurred to me, he became more distant, and his voice began to trail off. *"Liam, don't leave me! I'm begging you, please don't go!"* But it was no use. He was hardly visible to me anymore. I was becoming surrounded by a veil of darkness. It

was surreal to me. I had the strangest sensation that there were people trying to help me, but I couldn't make them out. I struggled to grasp my reality, but I was becoming weaker by the second, and the darkness that was settling in on me was winning its battle. I was so tired. I knew I couldn't fight it off anymore, and then and only then, when I was ready to accept my fate, did I feel *his* embrace around me.

I knew this dream, or nightmare as Liam referred to them; I had dreamt it a million times before and so had Liam, but as always, where Liam's stopped mine continued. It didn't matter that I knew the voice that saved me. I had always hoped that just once the voice would be of Liam's, as his arms embraced me and carried me to safety, but it never was the case. It was always Johnny's voice that reverberated in my ears. It bothered me to know this because my heart lay with Liam, but my subconscious seemed to lay with Johnny.

Dreams are a funny thing, and not until recently did I put any stock into them. I never had any reason to before, but I never had so many unanswered questions either. I knew I loved Liam; there was no doubt in my mind of that, but why was Johnny still there? Johnny had confessed his feelings for me and he had kissed me not once, not even twice, but numerous times since he entered my life. And still I rejected him, but I had become weak and doubted myself like Grandpa had noted. Maybe because of the distance that had grown between Liam and me, I wondered what it would be like to be with Johnny, and maybe that was the real reason I snuck off to see him the day Liam and I came to Glenville and why I saw him the night Liam found me at Johnny's apartment.

But my feelings were validated that night. I knew that Johnny was nothing more to me than a friend. It had always been Liam, and I was ready to leave Johnny behind once and for all and continue my life with the man of my dreams. My hopes and dreams were about to come true. I would help Liam fight his demons, and we would succeed and conquer all that life put in front of us. I was ready to accept eleven's fate for us too and make sure our karma was surrounded by a good aura, but I never had the chance because Liam found me at Johnny's and because of the tension between us, he thought the worst. It was my fault, and there was no way for me to take it back. Liam was beyond reason and wouldn't listen. His drunken behavior only solidified his actions, and being the stubborn and proud man that he was, he wouldn't allow himself to look like the weaker link even if that meant hurting me in the process by his unusual and callous tone towards me in front of Johnny. He considered me dead, as he put it. At that moment, I became a ghost to Liam.

My dream continued. The voice I heard beckoned for me to respond to it as I desperately tried to stay in my unconscious state. "I'm right here, Jenny. You're safe now. I won't let anything ever hurt or harm you again. You'll never be in danger with me by your side." His voice reassured me. His embrace on me was strong, and the comfort it held for me made me relax, knowing that things were going to be okay, or so I thought. This time, as I relinquished to Johnny's presence, I was surprised by a stranger's voice that resonated in my ears. "Jenny, you have to listen to me. Please open your eyes and listen. You have to go back. Liam needs you. He's going to die if you don't return to him. Please, Jenny, listen to me. I need you to help him. He loves you so much my dear. Please, before it's too late. He's lost without you, and he can't seem to find his way back to you. Go to him. Help my son find his way back to his one true love, you...Jenny." Her voice was melodic and sweet in its tone. I opened my eyes to find that I was looking at Liam's mom, Jessica.

I knew I was dreaming, but her image was so real to me. I found myself looking straight at her as though she was really standing before me, her long, dirty blond hair flowing wistfully around her porcelain face as her eyes danced with the same blue flecks as Liam's. She was more beautiful than I had ever imagined her. Her hands reaching out to me, and she smiled softly as if she was telling me it was going to be alright. I cautiously placed my trembling hand in hers, knowing I was holding the hand of a ghost, but the warmth of her touch comforted me immediately.

"Walk with me, Jenny. I've been waiting a long time for this moment with you."

Her hand tightened around mine as she led me away from my darkness. The light ahead of us was unusually bright but blanketed us with its warmth. I felt dizzy and confused. I looked behind me to bid farewell to Johnny, but in my attempt to do so, I found myself staring at Serenity Hill instead of the scene of the accident. Liam was gone too, as well as his truck and mayhem that the accident produced. There was nothing behind me except the sound of trees rustling in the breeze and the horizon that led to what I had once told Liam seemed to be the gates to Heaven. It was even more beautiful than what I had remembered, everything shown in a more brilliant clarity. Liam's mom continued her walk with me as she led me down a narrow path abundantly lined with moss and woodland violets.

"I'm confused." My voice quivered feebly, but her immediate smile reassured me.

"It's alright my dear. I understand, but you have no reason to be scared or confused. I'm here to let you know that it is going to be alright but only if you help Liam. He's lost without you. He is going down a very dangerous path. His beliefs are muddled with outside influences. You need to go to him, Jenny, before it's too late."

"I want to help him, that's all I've ever wanted, but he won't let me. He doesn't seem to love me anymore."

"He loves you more than you'll ever know. That's why he hasn't been able to return to you. He's embarrassed by the person he is becoming and feels that you are ashamed to be with him. He wants you back and needs you. He just doesn't know how to make that happen. The accident changed my son, and only you can make him return to the man he was, the man you fell in love with. You need to prove to him that nothing else matters except the love the two of you share for one another. Then and only then will he be able to conquer the demons and let go of his past. The separation that the accident caused between you two needs to be dissolved. He needs to be with you. Help him find his way back to you before this path leads him to the point of no return. His path has always been with you, help him remember that."

"I'm still confused; I don't understand why you didn't go to Liam yourself. He is your son. Why me?"

"Liam and Grandpa were right about you. You carry the heart of an angel, and it's pure through and through. You possess a quality that allows you to see what others can't. You can look beyond the obvious, and that's why I came to you. You can see what others can't. Your mind is open to what others close theirs off to, and it is easy for you to believe, and you believe in Liam. He has closed himself off to this, his nightmares are toxic, and he won't allow himself to go beyond them. You, my dear, want to look beyond and find the answers. They have always been there, guiding you and Liam. You have the gift to see beyond what's really there. You are receptive and willing to believe in me, even though you know I only exist in your heart. I can't reach Liam; only you can my dear. Please go to him and help my son. I have always been there for him, but his love lies with you. The two of you were joined together before you took your first breath. Your spirits are fused from a realm beyond the life you are aware of, it's kismet. That's why it hurts so much for both of you now. Your love runs deep."

"I'm still scared, I don't want to lose Liam, and I'm afraid he won't want to see me. He was so bitter the last time I saw him."

"Trust me, Jenny."

Her pace had become measured and deliberate, but still she graced the path we walked on with an ethereal ease, carrying me alongside her. We had come to a fork in the path. She stopped short of it and turned to face me, cupping my hand into hers. The feel of her skin was like nothing I had ever felt, as though a thousand butterflies were amusing my skin with their delicate wings.

"I have to leave you now, Jenny, but I will always be with you, just as I am with Liam. I promise our paths will cross again."

"Please, you can't leave me now. I need your help. I can't do this by myself. Liam needs your help."

Her beautiful smile graced her face once more, reassuring me once again.

"I will never leave you or Liam. I love you both so much, Jenny. You can do this, trust in yourself and the love you and Liam share. It's much stronger than you realize and can't be broken. Believe in this, Jenny, and go to my son. Help him find his way back to you. You're both lost and need the support of each other. There is no greater entity than the power of love, and you both possess the most special kind, the undying kind, my dear."

Her hands tightened around mine once more before she released me. She pointed me down the path as she took the other. I wanted to follow her, but she nodded for me to go on. "Tell Liam I love him."

I yelled after her, "Wait, don't go. There's so much more I want to ask you, please wait!" I continued yelling as I found myself struggling to release myself from the uncomfortable grasp that held me.

I woke up in a panic. My arms were wrapped around my body as if I was trying to wrestle myself. I sat up and pulled my sweat-ridden hair away from my face. I couldn't believe what I had just dreamed. It was Liam's mom. She was so real to me; I pinched myself to make sure I wasn't still asleep. I could still see her and feel her satin hands as they held mine. I looked around the room. I was alone, only Blue by my feet as he slept, unaware of my unconscious tirade. My body trembled horribly as I tried to rationalize what had just happened. I yelled for Grandpa.

"Jenny, what's wrong?" Grandpa ran to me as I continued to bellow out his name in my fear-struck voice.

I ran to him, forcing him to hold my weakened body. "I had a really bad dream, Grandpa."

"Jenny, honey, calm down. Tell me what the matter is. What was this dream about?"

"Oh my God, I saw Liam's mom. She spoke to me!" I screamed as my body began shaking.

"What, Jenny? What are you saying? Listen, you're stressed, and your emotions are playing with you, sweetie. Jessica couldn't have spoken with you. You're just overly tired with everything that's going on in your life right now." Grandpa was trying to foster my fears when all he was really doing was frustrating me more.

"She came to me, Grandpa, in my dream. I know what I saw. I have to find Liam. I have to help him before it's too late!"

"Jenny, honey, Jessica's dead. She's been gone for years now. You know that. It was just your imagination. You've been so tired and caught up with what's going with you and Liam that you're allowing your imagination to play tricks on you." Grandpa was tender in his words, but I knew what I had dreamed. She was real.

"But she did, Grandpa, she really did. I know it sounds crazy, but I saw her and not only that, we talked. She held my hand for

God's sake! I can still feel her touch on me. I know this doesn't make any sense, but I'm telling you the truth. I've been wrestling with this for months now, trying to understand why I've been having this dream, and then tonight when it came to me instead of seeing Johnny, Liam's mom appeared before me. She told me I needed to help Liam before it's too late."

"Too late, Jenny? Are you talking about the discussion I had with you?"

"I don't know, Grandpa. I'm not sure what she meant, but I do know I have to find him, and I have to find him soon. I've had this unsettling feeling inside of me ever since the night at Johnny's, and it's only gotten worse, and now this just validates my feelings even more. If I don't find Liam and try to talk to him, I think something terrible might happen to him. Please, Grandpa, you have to believe me." The last two words rang in my ears as I heard Liam's mom telling me the same thing. Believe. Maybe that was the key to this, we hadn't lost our love for one another, but we had lost our belief in each other. "I have to go, Grandpa. I need to find Liam."

The look in Grandpa's eyes made me think that he finally believed me about his daughter, that she had come to me. "Then go, dear, but please be careful. I don't like this though; I don't like this one single bit."

I hugged him tightly before leaving. He had always been there for me. The wind was wicked, and the sky was dark with billowy grey clouds cloaking the horizon before me as I left the house. A storm was approaching, a sign perhaps of what could be in store for Liam and me.

Chapter Twenty-Eight
Brush Creek's Chance

    I don't know what pulled me in my direction, maybe it was just my gut instinct, but out of the few places I presumed Liam to be, I found myself driving towards Brush Creek Road. We hadn't been there together for a long time. The place seemed foreign to me as I passed the familiar landmarks that led me to our spot. The actual sight sent a wave of emotions over me as I recalled the numerous times that Liam and I had spent there, but the sight that was the most familiar yet foreign to me was seeing Liam's truck, parked in the exact spot he always parked it with me, overlooking the horizon that made up the skyline of Spencer.

    I walked carefully as I saw Liam's shadowy silhouette leaning against the side of his F-150. He didn't even flinch as I made my way towards him. His eyes focused straight ahead on the horizon as the sun began to hang itself in the sky. I approached him cautiously. If his letter was truly any indicator towards what he was feeling lately, I knew this could be a mistake. I had played out this scene a thousand times in my head, but I shook as I thought of the consequences. Liam was my life as much as I was his. Every word he wrote in that letter I felt, but for some reason Liam had lost sight of that. That didn't matter anymore. I had to reason with him. My dream was too real, and I knew that I had seen Liam's mom. A twig broke beneath my foot, and the pop resonated in the air. Then and only then did Liam turn his head in my direction.

"Hi," I said in a calm, guarded voice. He didn't speak but only stared at me, almost as if he was looking through me instead of at me. It had been months since I had seen him. His appearance astonished me. His once beautiful crystal-blue eyes that danced with flecks of color were now less than ordinary with a dull glaze covering them, and his hair was disheveled as it hung limply on his broad shoulders. His face was worn and tired. The softness that normally infused it was gone. A hardened, calloused image of a much older man appeared before me. "Liam? Aren't you going to say anything to me?" Moments passed and Liam remained quiet as his stare penetrated me. "Liam?"

"Jenny," he said, in a very soft and frail tone. "I didn't think I would ever see you again."

I just stood there. I came with such a plethora of emotions that I didn't know how to take his comment. I came with worry and anger, but as I gazed upon Liam, both of those disappeared and were replaced with pity. I had heard the rumors that Liam had changed, and I had witnessed it to some degree myself, but nothing prepared me for what appeared before me.

"Aren't you going to talk to me? Liam, please we have so much…" But before I could finish he finished for me.

"So much what, Jenny? Love? Happiness? Hope? What do we have so much of? I don't think we have anything, except maybe an overabundance of bad luck. Why are you here, anyway? Did you not get my letter?"

"Yes, I got it. I found it right where you left it."

"Then you must have read it."

"Yes, I did."

"So why are you here?"

"Because I love you."

Liam's head lowered. "You know, I've been sitting here most of the night. After I left Serenity Hill, I didn't know where to go. I thought about going back to the house, but I didn't want to encounter Grandpa, so I just started driving around town. I drove by the high school and then even went to Walton, but wherever I went, I always seemed to end up back on your street. I sat in your driveway for hours. I just wanted to be near you. I kept thinking about one of the first times we were together. Do you remember? It was after your competition at the Black Walnut Festival. It had been pouring, and you were soaked to the bone. God, you looked beautiful that night, even though you didn't think so, but you had me mesmerized. It was one of our first dates. You wanted to go home to get cleaned up, but I didn't want you out of my sight. We came here; do you remember?"

I nodded my head.

"I love you, Jenny," he said with a sympathetic tone.

"Then why aren't we together?" I implored him.

Liam didn't answer. Maybe he was trying to think of a good enough answer for me, or maybe his hesitation was his answer. I knew I didn't know why. In my mind, we should be together, but as I stood before him, only inches from each other, I had never felt farther away from him in my entire life.

"If you read the letter, then I think it explains everything. It answers that question."

"You mentioned in your letter that you knew that there was nothing going on between Johnny and me. If you know that, then there's no need for this separation. I told you from day one that I am here for you and always will be. I need you. I want to help you like I've always wanted too. We can beat this drinking together. You're a strong man, and you don't need it."

"But don't you see Jenny, you can't help me, nobody can. I'm not the Liam you fell in love with last year, and honestly, I don't think I'll ever be that man again. I've tried for over a year to get past the accident, and I can't. If anything, things have only gotten worse for me. You don't need a drunk in your life, and from what people are telling me, that's what I've become. I guess it was only a matter of time before my dad came back into my life. I never wanted to be like him. That's why we can't be together. My dad killed my mom. I'm becoming the mirror image of him, and if that's right, then I could hurt you again. You're better off without me, no matter how much we love one another. Maybe that's why Johnny has always been there. Maybe he was the sign, the meaning behind the eleven. He's your destiny, Jenny, not me." Liam's dull gaze continued to stare through me.

"You can't mean that, Liam. How in the hell can you give up so easily on us?"

"Give up? Really? You think I've given up on us?"

"What else am I supposed to think? You keep pushing me away. I don't know what else to think. What was I supposed to take from that letter? If you love me like you say you do, then we shouldn't be standing here having this infantile discussion. People have problems every day, but if they really care for each other, like I know we do, then they stick together and work it out. They don't give up on each other. I need you; don't you think I'm suffering too?"

"I know you're suffering, Jenny, but it's because of me. I've broken so many promises to you, and this one I'm going to keep. I promised you that I would never let anything ever happen to you again after that horrible night, and if we stay together, you will get hurt. My dad killed my mom, and if I'm turning into him, then I can't be near you. That letter represents how I feel and who I've become."

"Who you've become?"

"I'm different, Jenny. I can't be the man I need to be for you. I can't seem to let go of my past, whether it's letting go of the accident or letting go of the drinking. I know I haven't been as honest with you as I promised you I would be, but I can't seem to stop going down this path I'm on, and if I allow you to go with me then it's only going to bring us more pain. Like I said, that's one promise I will never break. I won't hurt you, Jenny."

"Liam, baby please, I love you. If you think this has to do with the racing then just race. I want you to be happy, and if racing makes you feel good again, then I want you to do it."

"I've been racing for a couple of months now, and I'm doing really well. It's funny, even though we've been apart after every damn race, I still look for you in the crowd, hoping against hope that I will see your beautiful, angelic face looking for me, but I never did. Instead, I've only found a bunch of people who want a piece of me. Maybe that's how it's supposed to be. Anyone I've ever really cared about I can't seem to keep in my life. It's only fitting that I should lose you too."

"You haven't lost me. You said in your letter that we are kindred spirits, and I know that to be true. We're meant to be together forever."

"You shouldn't believe everything you read, Jenny. We might be soul mates, but it seems we're not meant to be together. I think Johnny might hold that honor."

"I know it's us, and I know that because I believe in us and because I was told that as well."

"By who? Your parents, Kendra, my grandpa?"

"No, by someone who you love very much and who loves you...your mom."

The expression on Liam's face was priceless. I couldn't tell if he believed me or thought I was the craziest person on this earth, but either way, I had his attention for what I thought was the first time in a very long time.

"What did you say?"

"I had our dream last night, Liam, except instead of seeing Johnny take me away, it was your mom who took me by the hand." I paused before continuing. Liam just stood there as he slowly took a step backward from me, his face frozen in disbelief. "She was beautiful, Liam and so real to me. I can still smell her and feel her touch on me. It wasn't just a dream."

"I don't believe you. You're just messing with me because you know how important she is to me. That's so cruel of you, and I really don't appreciate it. I bore my soul to you when I told you about her and now you're telling me she's coming to you in some damn dream. That's really sad, Jenny. I never thought you would be the type of person to toy with my emotions and stoop so low. Why you? If this is true, then she should have shown up in my dream, not yours!"

"I don't know why, Liam, but I'm telling you the truth. Maybe it's because of the way you're acting lately; maybe she knows that I'm the only one who can reach you. Liam, she knows what you're going through. She sees you."

"This is really good, Jenny, even for you. First it was your number fetish, and now you're seeing ghosts. You're one for the books, girl. I can't believe you're using my dead mom as some sort of tactic to get back at me."

"I'm not. If you would just put down this wall you have built up against me and just listen to me... Jenny, your fiancée, the girl who loves you and who I know you love, then you would know I'm being honest with you. Look into my eyes. I would never try to hurt you through your mom. I'm the only one who knows the pain you carry over her death. She's afraid for you, Liam. I know that's why she came to me. She knows that something terrible is going to happen if you don't change, and I can only guess it has to do with your new hobby and maybe your new friends."

Liam did as I asked and looked into my eyes that were beseeching him to believe me. "What kind of trouble, Jenny? Are you talking about my motorcycle racing? I told you, I'm good. I'm not going to go and have another accident if that's what this is about. I'm the talk of the town, maybe even the state. Hell, Toby says there are people as far away as Ohio who want to race me. Nothing's going to happen. Maybe you should see for yourself, and then you'll understand why I'm racing again. Until I can feel whole again, I'm never going to be the man you need. I can't stop now, Jenny."

"Damn it, Liam, what do you have to prove? Are you still trying to beat Johnny? My God, he's not even in the picture anymore!"

"Are you sure, Jenny? He still loves you, and I can only guess he'll never give up."

"I guess that's your cross to bear then, Liam. If I haven't convinced you by now that there's never going to be anything between Johnny and me then I'll never get through to you. I'm only human, and the feelings I have had towards him have been ones of gratitude. You know that. I will admit that I may have been confused there for a while, but it was only because you seemed to be so distant to me. My heart has never wavered over my feelings for you, and I know that because I've had the opportunity to see how I could feel with Johnny, and there was nothing there…ever. I came here to warn you not to do something stupid. I know I saw your mom, and she knows something's going to happen to you. Please, if not for me, think of her before you race again."

I spoke those last words calmly as Liam looked on. My heart was heavy. I went there thinking a myriad of thoughts and carrying just as many emotions. I was leaving with only one of each. It was over, and I was forever heartbroken. "I guess this is it then. I've nothing more to say except I love you, Liam, always have and always will. Good luck, and maybe if you could do one thing for me, just please be careful." I placed my hand on his. He didn't grab it the way he used to. Instead it remained on top of his, by itself, alone, the way I felt and the way it seemed our lives would be from each other, alone.

"Jen?"

"Yeah?"

"It's not what you think. Remember what I said in the letter, it's me, not you. I just need time."

"I guess I know that now."

"And I do love you. This isn't over for us. I still can't live without you. I just need to find the boy you fell in love with." I didn't answer him, but I didn't think he expected me to. He knew that I felt we were better off together than apart. This was his decision, not mine. "Maybe if you ever feel like it, you can watch me race."

I nodded my head. "Yeah, maybe." But we both knew I wouldn't be there. "I'll be seeing you, Liam."

Liam didn't respond but did grab my hand tightly as he looked earnestly into my eyes. They were filled with tears and so were his, both of us realizing the enormity of what was happening between us. He didn't want me to leave, but I knew that I couldn't stay under the circumstances. He couldn't let go of his demons yet, so I reluctantly let go of his hand.

"And for the record, I know the boy I fell in love with is still inside of you. You just need to believe like I do." I waited for Liam's response, but of course, there was none. "I guess I'll be seeing ya then. I love you, Liam."

"I love you too, Jenny." His voice carried as I closed my car door.

We looked at each other one last time. I implored him with my eyes to tell me not to leave, but he only stood there as my car backed away from him and drove off.

Chapter Twenty-Nine
Remnants of Me

    I should have felt much worse as I drove away from Brush Creek Road. Normally I would be crying a river of tears, but after everything, that river had finally run dry. There was nothing left in me. I truly had become an empty shell. I didn't know what I was going to do. The road before me was clear with no detours to interfere or change my path anymore. The life that Liam and I had was nothing more than a memory now. It seemed our dance was over. I pulled up to Liam's house, relieved to see that Grandpa's truck was gone. I didn't want to explain to him the outcome of my failed attempt. It really wasn't important though, he would soon find out once he realized that I was gone.

    I walked solemnly inside to find the smell of Grandpa's coffee still lingering in the air. Its smell enticing me as my permanently numbed body tried to ignore it. I inhaled it deeply in hopes that in times of my despair I could reach back into my memories and remember how good this house always smelled. My feet became attached to the floor, unwilling to move forward as they should. I forced myself to continue onward but not before taking in the room to my left. This was the room that first welcomed me, the room that made me feel at home like I really belonged there. I felt melancholy as I recalled my first visit.

Everything looked the same; the only difference was the addition of numerous pictures of Liam and me that now graced the fireside mantle. The grandfather clock echoed in the background as it reminded me that time was moving on and so should I. I already knew this. I left the pictures as they were. I didn't need them to remind me of my time with Liam. I had my memories for that. My intent and hope was that Liam would gaze upon them and remember what we once had and possibly still could.

I took my time as I climbed the stairs that led to the second floor. At the top, I began to turn to my left but decided to leave the unoccupied room alone. There was no need to disturb its eternal silence and the secret it held. I instead turned to my right and walked down the familiar hallway that led to Liam's bedroom. The door was shut, waiting for me to say the secret word that would allow me entry. I closed my eyes as I mimicked Liam's gestures as he would kick it open while holding me close to him. The feeling wasn't the same as the door opened and allowed me access to what had been a haven for me. The room felt unusually cold and desolate as I made my way inside, my footsteps echoing loudly against the hardwood floor as they informed me just how alone I really was in here. I shivered as I ached for his embrace one more time. I sighed heavily as my eyes perused around the room. Scene after scene played before me as I saw Liam and me engaging in each other's presence. My heart became heavy and burdened as I realized that we would never share any more moments in here. There would be no more laughter, no more talks, no more endless gazes, and no more each other.

The room was dark except for the streaks of light that came streaming through the window, enlightening me of the new day approaching. The darkness was rolled away by the sun's warm rays. In the meadow, Sugar Dumplin' sauntered her way up the hill as she took intermittent stops to feed on the dew-dropped grass. I would miss her breathtaking presence that I had grown so accustomed to seeing. I turned from the window and from her and took one more glance of the room. I glided my fingers across Liam's desk to his end table and finally his oak bed, allowing my hands to run through the rivets of the wood. Liam's pillow was askew on the bed, and I brought it to me, breathing in his scent that still remained forever on it. I held on tightly as I begged God to reverse the tragedy that was unfolding, to change the clocks and allow time to take Liam and I back to a place where we were together again, the way it should be. Instead, the room remained the same, and the silence deafened my ears as it reminded me that I was still alone.

I decided to leave everything here, even my belongings. They were a part of my time with Liam, a part of my past that I couldn't take with me. I put the pillow down and walked away with my head hung low. I couldn't hold it high. I wasn't proud or happy about what was taking place. I was angry and sad for allowing this time between Liam and me to be so fleeting and that the guarantee of us being together for always was nothing more than a façade that held no credence. I closed Liam's door. As I held onto the tarnished, bronze doorknob, my mind told me to let go of it, but my heart begged me to not. The hallway looked peculiarly longer than before, and my heart grew heavier.

I descended the stairs slowly as they creaked beneath my feet for the last time. I didn't look to either side but kept my focus forward as I opened the front door. The sun was nearing the top of the painted sky as I heard Liam's voice, "*Watch your step.*" He said in my ear as I walked down the damaged, wooden plank. I smiled nostalgically at the gesture. The wistful touch of Blue's touch was against me now. He was pleading with me for my attention. I patted his head affectionately and rubbed his long ears as he playfully forced his face into my hands. "Go now. I'll see you around, friend," I said as he continued his relentless regard towards me. My mind beckoned me to look at the house just one more time, but I just couldn't. I had been able to restrain myself thus far, and I wasn't going to break down now. Instead, I got in my car and drove away, adjusting my rearview mirror in order not to see the house as it summoned for my return. I had left.

The next few weeks, I tried to acclimate myself to my new life, a life without Liam. I had decisions to make, and I needed to make them soon. My parents were gone, and our business was closed. Aside from the apartments that my parents instructed Billy to take care of, there was nothing left but our house. Since Ashley was in California, my parents had given it to me. It was mine to sell or keep, my choice. I knew I didn't want to stay there. I felt Liam's presence around me there, and I couldn't stand it. Even the phone calls I was being inundated with from my friends were driving me crazy. My phone rang constantly, everyone checking in on me, but none were from the only person I needed to hear from, none were from Liam.

"Hello," I said, in a solemn tone.

"Jenny, it's Kendra. Where the hell have you been?"

"I've been here. I just haven't been answering my phone, that's all."

"Are you alright?"

"I guess, Kendra, as good as I can be. I'm just trying to move on. How are you?"

"I'm good. Just a couple more months, and she'll be here."

"She? You found out it's a girl?"

"Yeah, I couldn't wait, besides Mom wanted to help decorate the nursery, so we needed to know what color to go with." Kendra gave an unusual, eerie pause. "Hey, Jenny?"

"What, Kendra?"

"I just wanted to tell you how sorry I am about you and Liam. I still can't believe you two aren't together anymore. It just doesn't seem real."

"I know, but it is real, Kendra, too real."

"What are you going to do now?"

"I haven't decided, but I think I'm going to get out of town for a while."

"Have you heard from anyone, Jenny?"

"You mean, Liam?"

"Well yes, or Johnny."

"No, Kendra, once I left Liam that was it. I've gotten a couple of messages from his grandpa, but I haven't returned them. I know I should, but I can't. I'm afraid I would lose it, and I'm really trying to be strong right now. I just hope he'll understand. And as far as Johnny, I haven't talked to him in a long time."

"So you don't know."

"Know what, Kendra?"

"Johnny's in the hospital again."

"What?"

"I don't know any of the specifics, but Parker told me that it's got to do with his heart."

My heart sank as Kendra's last words rang in my head. I didn't want to see Johnny, but I knew I couldn't leave town without knowing if he was going to be okay.

"Kendra, I can't talk right now. I need to find out what's wrong. I'll see you around."

"Okay. And, Jenny? Just in case I don't see you," as if Kendra knew this would be our last conversation, "I want you to know that I love you. You're my best friend, and I just wish I could have been there more for you."

"I love you too, and you have been here for me, besides you've got more important things going on in your life. We will see each other again, someday." I paused as I tried to regain my composure. "Bye, Kendra."

"Bye, Jenny."

The phone clicked as Kendra's farewell lingered in my ear. I knew I needed to see Johnny before my departure. I had to do this. I took my time as I drove to the hospital only to find myself driving to Gertie's instead. I hadn't seen her for months, and I was wondering why she had made herself scarce to me. *The Spiritual Ship* still looked the same to me as I approached it. The window was still covered by a dark colored curtain to protect *The Spiritual Ship's* valuable secrets. The sinister doorknob still sneered at me as I turned its malevolent face. Upon entering my somber character was instantly soothed by the melodic chimes as they echoed in the room announcing my arrival. I walked tenderly throughout the room as I admired the new additions that Gertie had acquired to entice her psychic seeking clients. The room echoed with my footsteps as the smell of patchouli still filled the air. My patience was waning as I waited for Gertie's sight; but fortunately my wait was brief as she appeared before me from the back room, her wispy figure gliding effortlessly to me as she embraced me with her arms.

"Jenny. I'm so glad to see you."

"I'm glad to see you too, Gertie. I've missed you."

"How are you? I've missed you so much."

"I'm fine... considering."

"I know. I'm so sorry, dear."

"Thank you. I guess it wasn't meant to be, Gertie."

"Please sit down," she said as she motioned to one of her velvet chairs. "Do you want to talk about it?"

"Not really. There's nothing to talk about. I'm actually here to talk about Johnny."

Gertie gave me a sobering smile as she placed her spindly fingers into mine. "You've heard, haven't you?"

"I just know he's in the hospital, is that right?"

"Yes. It's his heart, Jenny. It's failing him. He needs a new one or he will die." Gertie's head lowered as I noticed a tear trickle down her cheek. The first time I had ever seen her cry.

"I'm so sorry, Gertie. I had no idea."

"Johnny didn't want you to know. He made me swear that I would never tell you, that's why I haven't tried to reach out to you. I knew once I did, I wouldn't be able to keep this from you."

"Well, the doctors can help, can't they? I mean he's going to make it through this right?"

"I don't know. He possesses a rare blood type, AB negative, and they're having a hard time finding a heart."

"How much time does he have?"

"I don't know, Jenny, maybe a month, maybe a year. The doctors aren't telling us, but if I were to make a guess, I would say time doesn't seem to be on his side."

"I want to see him, Gertie."

"He would love that. He's been asking about you. He knows about you and Liam."

"Gertie, I'm leaving."

"I know, dear."

"You do?"

She nodded. "I knew this time in your life was coming. I just didn't know when."

"I have to, Gertie. I can't stay here, there are too many memories."

"Then you should go. It's time."

"I'm glad I saw you, Gertie. You have meant so much to me. I will never forget you."

"Nor I you, Jenny." Gertie stood up and hugged me tightly, the way you do when you know this is the last time you will see that person. "Take care of yourself, Jenny. I'm always here for you, even if it's only in spirit."

"I know, Gertie. Thank you." I left her standing in her ornately decorated room without looking back, the same way I left Liam's house. I didn't want to turn for one more glance. I had the memories I needed and that too was good enough.

The hospital room was dimly lit as I walked in. The sounds of a beeping monitor overshadowed my footsteps as I walked towards Johnny's bed. He was fast asleep. His face seemed withdrawn, and his skin was pale as the monitor informed me of his condition. Johnny was dying. I pulled a chair next to his bed as his eyes slowly opened.

"I must be dreaming, or dead. I see an angel before me," he said in a sweet but fragile tone.

"Johnny," I whispered. "Why didn't you tell me?"

"There's nothing to tell, Jenny. I'm going to be fine," he said smiling.

"I know you are," I said, returning his smile.

I was holding his hand as he squeezed it tightly. He looked at me earnestly and told me without speaking how sorry he was for what had happened between Liam and me.

"It's okay, Johnny. Just like you, I'm going to be fine."

I felt an obtruding object underneath his covers as my hand rested within his. "What's this?" I said as I pulled out a beautifully decorated silver pocket watch.

"My mom gave it to me. She wanted to give me time."

"Time?"

"Yeah, she said as long as I had this, time would be on my side, and in time my wounds would be healed." We both looked at each other, knowing what she really meant.

"Your mom's a very special lady, Johnny. I'm going to miss her but not half as much as I'm going to miss you."

"You're leaving then?"

"Yes, I can't stay here, Johnny. I love Liam, but he's in a different place, and for some reason he can't find his way back to me. I guess he needs time, just like you, and maybe just like me."

"He'll find his way back to you, Jenny. His love will help him find you."

"I hope so, Johnny."

I stood up and leaned down to Johnny, softly kissing him on his lips. "I'm always going to care for you. I'm sorry I couldn't give you more, Johnny. You deserve it, but I just couldn't help you."

"You've given me more than you'll ever realize, Jenny. I still love you and always will. Like I said, you'll always hold a place in my heart," he said as he took my hand and placed it over his beating chest. His heart pulsed through his skin.

"I still have this," I said as I pulled the crumpled paper heart from my pocket. "I will never forget you, Johnny."

"This is it, isn't it, Jenny?"

"Yes."

Johnny raised my hand to his lips as he gave me one final kiss. "Bye, Jenny."

I couldn't say goodbye to him. My eyes were filled with tears, and any movement from me would release them. I didn't want him to remember me like that. Instead, I squeezed his hand and walked away. He didn't say anything. Maybe he was just watching me. The only noise I heard were the machines as they kept their steady beat to my footsteps as I continued my walk away from Johnny, from Liam, and from the life I had hoped to have but never would, at least not yet.

Chapter Thirty
Time

They say time heals all wounds, and maybe that is the case for some. I hope it is for Johnny. I hope he is given the time to find a heart, a heart that will provide time for him to find true love and give him the life he deserves. I hope in time that Liam finds himself again and finds his way back to me. He is the love of my life, and like him, I am only half-alive when we are apart. He makes me whole. He is my only reason for being, and as I walk alone, I carry hope that our time apart will be brief and that in time, it will bring us together again.

I am crossing into new territory, forging forward as I walk on this journey, a journey I felt I was destined to be on with Liam, but until our time brings us back together I will hold him close to my heart and replay the times of our lives as my memories feed into my loneliness. Jessica told me that Liam and I were destined to be together, that our love was born long before we were, that it was kismet. But life has brought us many forks in the road to test this undying love we hold for one another, and only time will tell if we both pass the test. I know the demons Liam carries forbids him to be with me right now, and until he can rid himself of them, we can't be together. My body still feels his presence, and his touch is always on me, eternally embedded in my very fibers of being. Just as he wrote in his letter, I know he is with me in spirit, and I hope he can feel me surround him.

I don't know what the future holds for us. I do know that our souls were ordained to one another before our actual meeting. It was written in the stars, the same stars that Liam and I lovingly gazed upon during our time together, and the same ones that we gaze upon while we are apart. I will see Liam again, and we will be one once again. I am waiting for Liam, waiting for him to let go of his demons, waiting for him to find himself, and most importantly, waiting for him to find his way back home to me. Our dance will continue. The music has never stopped; we're just waiting for the next song. I am here for him. He knows that and knows where to find me. Whether we are physically together or only spiritually, our love will transcend to one another until our bodies can hold each other again. I carry this faith because that is all I have to hold on to and because I know that Liam and I are and forever will be kindred spirits.

****

Jamie Kincaid

    Jamie Kincaid grew up in Spencer, West Virginia. She has been a lover of words and a storyteller since she was a little girl. And although she carries two degrees, one in Marketing from Glenville State College in Glenville, West Virginia and the other in Education from Buffalo State College, in Buffalo, New York, her affair with writing always remained. She has traveled and lived in many areas but if you were to ask her where her home is, she would tell you in a heartbeat that it is and always will be Spencer.

    In her spare time, when she is not writing and taking care of her family, you can find her running miles and miles. She lives in Ohio with her husband and their three beautiful children and her golden retriever who remains faithfully by her side while she continues to write her next tale.

She would like to thank her family and friends for their love, support and belief in her. And for those wonderful friends who always came to her rescue to help her out of computer situations, (you know who you are!) And for Him, who lifted me up and made me realize this is who I am and that it was only a matter of time before the world would know that too, seeing her stories in print can only be described as epic for her, a dream come true.

Liam and Jenny... they are in each and every one of us, believe in fate, true love, kismet... pickles, wild horses, silly jokes, sweet tea, endless talks, endless nights, drives to nowhere, heart and soul, you 'n me, always here, always and forever, destiny 831.

The Kismet Series
by Jamie Kincaid

Book One: Kismet
Now Available

Book Two: Karma
Now Available

Book Three: Kindred Spirits
Expected Release: Spring 2016

Book Four: Keep
Expected Release: Autumn 2016

Made in the USA
Charleston, SC
10 May 2016